SERPENT'S RETURN

TRISH HEINRICH

FIRST EDITION
ISBN: 978-1-7331880-1-2

Edited by Maria D'Marco and Dan Heinrich
Cover art & design by Todd Downing

WWW.TRISHHEINRICH.COM
Published by Beautiful Fire
706 Hull Ave, Port Orchard WA 98366 USA

For Dan, The love of my life,
And for Rosalind and Cara,
The Lights of my heart

SUMMER-1947

CHAPTER ONE

Her short, shaking legs made the leap off the back porch a clumsy affair. Narrowly saving herself from landing face-first in the dry earth, Alice pushed off with her hands and ran toward the giant tree in her back yard. Tall dry grass and dandelions scratched her bare calves, but she barely noticed. Sweat itched her scalp and tears blinded her as she reached for the lowest branch and pulled herself up. Just getting into the tree wasn't enough though.

No, not nearly.

She climbed up and onto a branch at the back of the tree that had grown into a wide curved seat, perfect for her little body. In her haste to reach her hiding spot, the worn copy of 'Peter Pan' hidden in a part of the trunk fell to the ground and her heart sank. If he saw it, he'd know. He'd find her. She curled into a ball on the smooth branch, hoping he'd be too drunk to notice the book.

In that moment, the wind stopped shaking the fat green leaves and they fell silent around her, like a gentle curtain. The smell of summer roses and just-cut grass drifted to her through the twilight. Even the bird song seemed muted and distant.

"Please, let me be in fairyland!" she whispered.

The calm shattered like spun sugar when his clomping steps were heard just before he appeared on the porch, slamming the old screen door behind him.

"Alice! Get in here!"

She clapped her hands to her ears and squeezed shut her cobalt eyes. Fearful images assaulted her brain. Her father becoming a great naked eye, scanning through every leaf until he found her, dragging her down from her special place and into the house.

The slap of the thick belt against his leg, as he stumbled back and forth across the porch, kept time with the pounding of her heart.

"You better not be at that wop's house, you little bitch!"

A jolt of embarrassment and anger shot through her. He meant her best friend. The fact that he was only half Italian didn't matter to her father. Her friend was a wop through and through, only worthy of disdain.

An insane temptation to jump down and punch her father in his round, flushed face took hold. She sat up, small hands curling into shaking fists, but the sound of the screen door creaking open and slamming shut kept her in the tree. Soon, her father's harsh voice was punctuated by the sharp snap of his belt landing on her mother's flesh.

Anger drained from her, replaced by a terrible guilt.

Maybe she should've been brave and taken the beating. If she had, would it have prevented what her mother now endured? Or only whet her father's appetite?

A gentle breeze dried the tears on her flushed cheeks and made the tree leaves sing a rustling song of comfort. She wished the tree would close its arms around her, hold her tight, and carry her off to a tea party, where the outrageous antics of the others at the party would distract her mind. But, the tree was just a tree and the only tea parties she'd ever been to were those her mother played with her during the war, when it was just the two of them and their books.

A crash from inside the house made Alice jump, a whimper escaping her thin lips.

"Why's a raven like a writing desk?" came a whispered voice from below.

Alice looked down. An awkwardly thin boy with a large nose, wearing dirty cut-off shorts and a shirt buttoned the wrong way, stood looking up at her. He was too tall for his eleven years and his dark hair stood on end in the back. The grin on his face always reminded Alice of a silly elf, though she'd never tell Marco that.

Casting a cautious look at the back door, Alice jumped down, picking up 'Peter Pan' before taking Marco's sticky hand.

She wondered if he'd heard her father's slur, but his tanned face betrayed nothing but joy at seeing her. Alice squeezed his hand in gratitude for such a friend.

Marco held up a loose board in the fence that separated her back yard from his, so she could slip through.

The memory of the first time she'd done that shot through her mind, and she smiled. It had been a year since she'd come upon Marco sitting in his yard, reading a gloriously thick book. Before she could sneak back to her side, he spotted her and offered to share the book and his ginger cookies. Ever since, they'd been thick as thieves, never telling a soul about their secret way of getting to each other.

"Mama made way too much lasagna tonight...want some?"

Alice's stomach flipped. "Lasagna? That must mean Lionel is here, too."

Marco nodded. "I think he can smell it three blocks away."

As they stepped into the warm kitchen, the smell of garlic and cheese made Alice's stomach gurgle with anticipation. There was always a hint of some kind of cleaner under the delicious smell of Mrs. Mayer's cooking and every surface gleamed.

The walls were papered with a green and white checked pattern, with matching curtains that fluttered with the summer breeze.

"Bella Alice, you been up your tree again!" said Marco's mother, picking a leaf out of Alice's hair.

"Yes, Mrs. Mayer," Alice said.

Mrs. Mayer was an appealingly round woman with large brown eyes, like her son, and dark hair that was always perfectly styled. Her English was better than a year ago, but her accent was still heavy, and when she was tired or upset, she would cut loose with a rapid stream of Italian.

Mr. Mayer loved to tell the tale of how he, a shy bookish man, had swept the most beautiful Italian girl in all of Metro City off her feet, and had convinced her to move across the country with him.

Mrs. Mayer gave Alice a welcoming embrace, then shooed her and Marco to the sink to wash their hands.

"Lionel is already at table," she said.

Alice might've missed a good amount of dirt in her rush to claim a seat next to Lionel. She made sure to pause just outside the door to the dining room and smooth her shirt and frizzy dark braids, just like she'd seen an actress do in a movie once. Her heartbeat quickened, but this time it wasn't out of fear.

"You gonna stand there or go in?" Marco asked, starting to push past her.

Her pale skin flushed. "I'm just...I didn't want to be sloppy-looking at the table."

"I think you look just fine." He took her hand as they walked in.

Mr. Mayer, who was exceptionally tall, stood near the doorway, but Alice only saw the light-haired boy sitting at the table, his tanned cheeks stuffed with bread, full lips greasy with butter. He grinned as best as he could when he saw her and patted the chair next to him.

Alice practically skipped the short distance and beamed up at him before taking her seat.

"Did you get your new bicycle?" she asked.

"Sure did. Maybe tomorrow you can try it," he said, around another bite of bread.

"I'm probably too short."

"Okay, then you can ride on the handle bars."

"Isn't that a little dangerous?" Marco asked.

"Not with me in control," Lionel said, giving Marco a friendly punch on the shoulder.

Marco winced and rubbed the spot.

"That wasn't too hard, was it?"

Marco looked down and shook his head.

Lionel narrowed his navy-blue eyes. "Was it the Dorn brothers again?"

"Don't worry about it," Marco said, accepting a huge helping of lasagna from his mother.

Mr. Mayer took his seat next to Alice and smiled down at her through horn-rimmed glasses. "Are you enjoying your summer vacation?"

"Yes, sir."

"I understand you and Marco have made your way through our new books already."

She flushed.

"Don't be embarrassed." His voice was gentle, proud. "Knowledge is priceless."

"They're just stories," she said.

Mr. Mayer looked stricken. "My dear girl, there is no such thing."

"Ach, Steven, let the girl eat!" Mrs. Mayer chided.

He nodded. "You borrow any book you want. Okay?"

Alice nodded as he ruffled her hair. She looked up at

Mr. Mayer, her chest aching, as she thought how different Marco's father was from her own. After the first week of knowing him, Alice stopped flinching at his hugs, and after that, she sometimes found herself craving the gentle strength in this man's arms.

"Is it good, Alice?" Mrs. Mayer asked. "You want more bread?"

In answer, Alice shoveled a large bite of cheesy lasagna in her mouth, grinning as sauce leaked from the corners of her mouth.

Alice stayed as long as possible.

Dinner turned into dessert, and then games in the library, where she handily beat Lionel at checkers. Once the small mantle clock sang out nine o'clock, she knew it was time to face whatever waited for her at home.

Mrs. Mayer hugged her tight and made her promise to come see them tomorrow. "I make cookies, chocolate chip, yeah?"

Marco and Lionel walked out with her, though Marco couldn't take the chance of her father seeing him.

"Tomorrow," Marco said, his long face stern.

Alice nodded.

He hugged her tight, his shoulder blades sharp under her small hands.

It took only a few steps to get to her front door, but Alice tried to go as slowly as possible. Lionel glanced at the front window. It was dark, as Alice knew it would be. Once her father had passed out or gotten bored with abusing her mother, he usually fell asleep. But sometimes, when his anger was too hot to be sated...

Her palms became slick with sweat, and the lasagna and cookies in her tummy turned to a roiling mass.

"Hey..." Lionel said, forcing her to look at him. His square face took on a fierce look that made Alice wonder if she'd somehow made him angry. "If you're too afraid to go in, I'll sit with you for a little while."

"Won't your mom wonder where you are?"

Lionel looked at his old converse shoes, scuffing them on the sidewalk. "She's out with her latest boyfriend. Hasn't been home in two days."

"Sorry, shouldn't have asked."

"It's ok. I can handle it."

She smiled. "I know."

The door behind them gave a small squeak. Just when Alice felt as if her dinner might come back up, she heard her mother's voice.

"Alice? Lionel? You can't be out here. It's late."

Alice heard the unspoken worry: what if her father woke up?

"Sorry, Mrs. Seymour," Lionel said, giving her mother a lop-sided smile.

Mrs. Seymour smiled back, careful to stay in the shadow of the overhang. "It's alright, but maybe you two could talk more tomorrow?"

Lionel nodded. "See ya."

Alice smiled and watched him run back to Marco's to get his bike.

"C'mon sweetheart," her mother whispered, reaching out a thin hand. "I have something for you."

The dark of the living room felt thick and terrifying when Alice stepped in, her hand tightening on her mothers. It wasn't until they were in the kitchen, with its warm light and comforting smells, that Alice felt her shoulders relax. The cupboards had never been new, but they had been kept in good condition while her father had been away at the war. Now, a few doors were missing, as well as some of the knobs, but her mother had put on a fresh coat of paint to brighten them up. The ice box creaked if opened too quickly and half the space inside was taken up with beer. Sometimes, if her mother was feeling good enough, she would bake cookies or a pie, and the smell would over-shadow the pungent hops that seemed to permeate the house most days.

Turning to the round scratched table, Alice saw a small white pastry box. She looked up at her mom, about to ask what it was, when she was able to finally see her mother's face. Forgetting that any reaction would upset her mother, Alice started to cry.

Her mother's beautiful face had a new bruise on one high cheekbone, along with a cut above one eye, and a swollen, split lip. Usually, her father kept to her mother's body, unless he was especially drunk and angry.

"Don't cry sweetheart," Mrs. Seymour said, holding Alice. "It's not as bad as it looks."

"Stop defending him! He's a monster!" Alice hissed the words, fear of waking her father stronger than her desire to yell.

"He's not, Alice."

"Look what he's done to you!"

"Stop, sweetheart, please. Look here...look what I brought home for you." She lifted the lid of the pastry box and nestled inside was a small cake with pink frosting topped with small blue roses.

"I know your birthday was last week," she said, lifting the cake out, "but Will found out you hadn't had a cake and gave this to me today."

Alice wiped her nose and stared down at the beautiful little cake. Will was the owner of the diner where her mother worked. He was always sending left overs home for them or giving her mother the easy shifts, if he saw she was hurt especially bad. Many a day Alice had wished that Mr. Mayer or Will was her real father.

"Do you like it?"

"Yes, it's very pretty. Please, tell him I said thank you."

Mrs. Seymour hugged Alice, running her hand up and down her back and humming a lullaby. Alice had just turned nine and was really too old for lullabies, but if it made her mom feel better...

"I am so thankful you were born," Mrs. Seymour whispered. "You make me so happy."

Alice hugged her mother a little tighter and when her mother didn't wince in pain, she hugged tighter still.

"Should we cut the cake?"

"Yes."

Mrs. Seymour took two of the good plates out of their hiding place and poured two small glasses of milk. The cake was so small that she placed a half each on their plates. They ate in silence.

Alice somehow found room in her belly, even after stuffing herself on Mrs. Mayer's lasagna. She looked at her mother's thin hands and the unbruised cheek that had begun to look sunken and wondered if her mother had been able to eat any dinner.

After they'd quietly washed up and Alice was tucked into her small bed, Mrs. Seymour took out a faded green book and opened it to where they'd left off the night before. As the words floated down from her mother's lips, Alice sighed with pleasure, transported to a beautiful garden where there was nothing to fear.

Before she drifted off, Alice's mother kissed the tip of her nose and whispered, "Till next we meet, sweet."

CHAPTER TWO

The wind blew Alice's dark braids out behind her, drying the sweat on her face and neck as she careened down the street. Her bottom bounced on the handle bars of Lionel's bike as they hit a crack in the sidewalk. Sweat-slick hands slipped and for a brief moment Alice thought she might fall, but Lionel grabbed her arm just in time.

"Faster?" Lionel shouted.

"Yes!"

She screeched in fear and elation as Lionel let out a primal shout of pleasure. The shiny red and blue bike barreled past old wood fences and sagging porches.

Alice didn't have to hide her face, wondering if the people who lived there knew what her father was like. At this speed, she was invisible — free.

Their neighborhood of Park Side made up most of the southern tip of Jet City. At one time, it had been full of neat, well-kept homes. Small businesses had begun to flourish, and families had felt safe and proud to say they lived there. But, just before the war, Park Side had begun a steep decline. No one knew why, or if they did, they didn't bother to explain it. Now, many of the houses had overgrown yards and paint peeling off their fronts. The families that lived there were either too poor or too tired from scraping a living together to give much attention to what their home looked like. The few that were well-kept stuck out in strange contrast to the sad decay around them.

Though small businesses still existed, no one would say they flourished, and no one envied the owners, who had to pay protection money to the latest in an ever-lengthening list of petty crime bosses.

Alice, like most children who lived in Park Side, knew all of this and, like most of the children, chose to ignore it for the pleasure of an afternoon of play with friends.

Lionel slowed just a little to go around a corner, and then put on more speed, past the small grocer, around the bright bins of fruits and vegetables; people shouting at them as they dodged out of the way. Soon they arrived at what all the children of Park Side called The Warehouse.

It had once been part of the paper plant that had gone out of business during the depression. Several people had bought the old plant, but nothing ever came of it. The latest owner had constructed a huge brick wall between the Warehouse and the old plant, trying to keep the teens out. It only succeeded in antagonizing the bored ruffians, and so, just last week, the new owner had installed barbed wire over the top of the wall.

But The Warehouse was left untouched by any of this, as if someone had taken the ugly, old building out of time to preserve it. When she was with Lionel and Marco out here in their own world, or in the pages of a book, the restless ache in Alice's soul would quiet and she felt like she belonged.

Lionel skidded to a stop before the abandoned brick building, whose windows had been busted out by baseballs and rocks. Scraggly grass and weeds shot up through the cracks in the cement floors. There were places in the wall where the brick had crumbled, exposing old pipes.

The heat was a little less oppressive inside and the wide-open space was perfect for baseball or clandestine meetings. It had rained that morning and the brick was a dark red that reminded Alice of dried blood. She shivered as she jumped down, remembering her mother's face that morning and how her split lip had cracked open when she tried to smile.

It was empty inside and Alice hoped they would be the only ones to show up this morning. Since her father had started beating her mother, the neighbor children hadn't been kind.

"About time," Lionel said, watching Marco pedal toward them like crazy.

When he got close enough, Marco swerved and nearly fell off his bike trying stop without slowing down.

"The Dorn brothers!" he shouted, pointing behind him.

Alice could hear them now. Hoots and shouts as they neared The Warehouse. There were six Dorn brothers, all huge and mean. The oldest was sixteen and would've kept the others in line, but he wasn't around much these days. For as long as Alice had known Marco, the Dorn brothers had hated him, taking every opportunity to let him know it. From the way the five of them were yelling and laughing, Alice knew that they had seen Marco and were relishing another opportunity to torture him.

Lionel grabbed Alice's hand and pulled her toward his bike. She'd barely settled on the handlebars before Lionel was peddling for his life, whipping around the corner and down the opposite side of the street from the brothers. Marco was trying to keep up with them, but he was falling behind fast.

"They'll catch him!" she yelled.

Lionel glanced back and swore. The brothers were in

pursuit, the younger ones on bikes, while the older ones ran. Lionel slowed down enough to grab a lid off a garbage can, then he sped toward the brothers, and tossed the lid at the brother closest to the front. It hit him square in the face, knocking him violently off his bike. The rest screamed in rage and put on more speed.

Alice gaped at the accuracy and strength of the blow. "How did you do that?"

Lionel didn't seem to hear her, coming up behind Marco to protect him as best he could. "Hurry up!"

"I'm...trying..."

A rock flew by Alice's head, and then another. The third one hit Marco square in the back, and then another stung Alice's upper arm. If they could just make it to the end of the street and around the corner they'd be in the relative safety of a group of adults shopping.

They were nearly there when Marco's bike hit a garbage can, launching him over the top of the handle bars. Alice jumped off as soon as Lionel slowed down and ran to him. Marco lay in a pile of garbage, a gash just above his eye was oozing blood. Lionel rushed to him and picked up the baseball lying near Marco's bike.

"You think that's funny!" Lionel shouted, throwing the baseball with more force and speed than Alice had ever seen. It connected with the face of one of the boys rushing toward them, and Alice saw a rush of scarlet cascade from the boy's nose.

"You gonna pay for that!" the largest of the Dorn brothers yelled.

Lionel tensed, bringing his fists up.

"Lionel, no," Marco mumbled, trying to get up.

"Look out!" Alice screamed, jumping to her feet.

A younger brother ran up to Lionel and swung a bat down toward Lionel's head. Lionel caught it and pulled on the bat so hard the boy was lifted off the ground and tossed to the side in one swift motion. The oldest swung a meaty fist to Lionel's face. He dodged and punched the boy in the face. The oldest brother fell to the ground, and the other two still standing stopped dead, as if realizing this wasn't the easy pickings they thought.

Alice stared in shock. Lionel was more muscled than Marco, but he was still lanky for his age. And he was definitely not stronger than the Dorn brothers, who were built like bulls.

"What's wrong with you guys?" asked the Dorn boy, who tried to hit Lionel with the bat. "C'mon!"

He stood up and punched Lionel in the face, then another brother ran up and kicked Lionel in the stomach. A third grabbed the abandoned bat and brought it down hard on Lionel's back.

Without thinking, Alice ran into the fight. She'd never thrown a punch in her life, but in the past year she'd seen plenty of them. Balling up her small hand and letting all the pent-up fury in her little soul loose, she punched the smallest brother in the stomach. He fell to the ground in shock and Alice swung her foot viciously into his gut. The boy yelped, and Alice didn't see another brother come to his aid, or hear Marco's warning yell in enough time. The boy grabbed Alice and threw her to the cement. She tried to put out her hand to break the fall, but she landed awkwardly. The sound of the bone snapping reached her ears seconds before the pain registered and once it did her head swam with it.

Lionel took one look at her and roared with anger, grabbing one boy and tossing him to the ground, then punching another so hard he was lifted up before falling hard to the cement. He advanced on the Dorn boy that had punched Alice and pulled him up by his shirt. Lionel's face reminded Alice of her father's last year, when she thought he was going to kill her mother.

Marco scrambled over and grabbed Lionel's ankle, a look of deep concentration on his bloodied face. For just a moment, Alice thought she saw Marco's eyes become dark, almost black. She blinked hard and when she looked again, Marco's eyes were normal.

Slowly, Lionel put the boy down. "If you ever lay a hand on Alice or Marco again…"

The boy nodded, all bravado gone.

Before Lionel had let go of the brother's shirt, the other four had started running away as best they could with bloodied faces and at least one broken arm.

Alice tried to stand up and succeeded only in vomiting all over her shoes, the pain in her arm making her dizzy.

"Oh my gosh," Lionel said, grabbing her before she fell to the sidewalk.

"My arm..."

Alice looked up at Lionel and frowned. His lip was split and he was favoring his right side a little.

She opened her mouth to ask if he was alright, but only managed to vomit again, this time on Lionel's shoes.

"She needs a doctor," Marco said.

"I'll go to the grocer and see if someone can take us to the hospital," Lionel said, running around the block.

Marco sat down on the curb with Alice, letting her rest her head on his shoulder. It helped to not be moving, though the pain still made her feel nauseous.

"Are you ok?" she whispered.

He shrugged a little.

"Lionel...he was..."

Marco let out his breath in a huff. "Yeah."

Alice bent forward and threw up what little was left in her stomach, heaving at the end. Marco's cool hand gently rubbed her neck as she sat there, still too sick to move. After a moment, the pain lessened just enough to let her stomach relax. She leaned on Marco again, who put his thin arm around her and squeezed. He could always make her feel better. No matter how sad or angry or scared she was. One hug from him and the bad feelings seemed to melt.

"I'm sorry you got hurt because of me," Marco said.

She managed a shaky smile. "I'm not."

CHAPTER THREE

The cast was heavy and made it hard to hold the large book Marco had loaned her. Alice slammed it shut and grabbed a pencil, shoving it into the cast to extinguish the burning itch on her skin.

Her mother had been angry when she'd arrived at the hospital, especially when she'd heard how it happened. Lionel tried to defend Alice, but her mother wouldn't hear it.

"After all you've seen these past years, you go out and harm someone and get hurt in the process!"

Alice had started to cry, and after a few minutes, her mother hugged her close.

"Hush, sweetheart," she said. "I'm sorry I yelled. You can't do this though. Fighting doesn't solve anything — never has, never will." She'd wiped Alice's tears away and kissed her on the nose.

It had been a fairly clean break, according to the doctor. Once the cast had been applied, Mrs. Seymour drove the three of them back to Marco's house, where Mrs. Mayer had a similar reaction as Mrs. Seymour.

That was a week ago, and since then, they'd been careful to avoid The Warehouse, just in case the Dorn brothers were looking for payback. Staying near Marco's house, the three of them had desperately looked for new adventures, only finding that there was even less to do close to home.

This afternoon the rain had kept them indoors. After looking through the boxes of old clothes and pictures in the attic, they settled into the front room, which served as a library and office for Mr. Mayer. It was Alice and Marco's favorite room.

Huge bay windows showed the carefully manicured lawn and hydrangea bushes, red and white curtains were pulled back to let in the hazy summer sunshine. The wooden floors were covered in thread-bare rugs, their designs faded long ago. The chairs had been patched and re-stuffed several times, but Alice felt that made them all the more cozy. A small roll top desk sat in a far corner, papers and photographs in neat piles on its scratched surface. The walls were mostly taken up with towering, mismatched shelves that overflowed with books from every genre imaginable. Any remaining wall space was covered with photographs. Some were obviously family, their stern faces staring out at Alice as she read. Others were from Mr. Mayer's work as a war photographer, though nothing disturbing. Mainly buildings and people he'd met. A few famous faces, such as Patton and Churchill, held little interest for Alice. Who had time for photographs when there were so many books to read?

Unless your arm itches something awful! I hate this cast!

She redoubled her efforts with the pencil when Lionel threw himself on the rug in the Mayers' study.

"I hate it when it rains!"

"You live in the wrong place," Marco said, not even

looking up from his book. "Jet City is known for its wet climate."

"Thanks, Mr. Science," Lionel snapped.

It was rare that they got summer storms, but when they did, the rain came down in sheets. A bright flash nearby was followed by a rumble of thunder. Alice looked up at Marco, who smiled at her over the top of his book.

Lionel huffed again and tapped his fist on the floor, looking for all the world like a twelve-year-old about to have a tantrum.

Alice carefully took down the checker board. "C'mon, let's play."

"No, you always win," Lionel said.

"Not today, I won't."

"Letting me win is no fun!"

"Then, what do you want to do?"

Lionel huffed once again and sat up. "Checkers is fine."

Alice tried very hard to lose, but she ended up winning two out of three games and Lionel stomped out of the room.

Marco shook his head. "At least Ma left some cookies for him. That should cheer him up."

Alice knelt in the chair by the window, squinting outside through the wet glass. "I think it stopped raining finally. Why don't we go to the diner? I bet my mom will give us pie!"

"Pie?" Lionel said from the kitchen.

Marco laughed. "Let's do it."

They ran to the bikes on the front porch. Alice settled herself on Lionel's handlebars, careful not to lean too much on her broken arm.

With the rain gone, the air felt thick and clingy as they rode down to the small diner. The sidewalks were slick, so they didn't go too fast, but still, Alice could feel the tires skid around the corners in Lionel's haste.

As they pulled up at the diner, Alice had the same thought she always had: this was the oddest shaped building she'd ever seen.

Round in the front like an oval, the middle of the building suddenly became square-shaped, as if the builders could never decide exactly what they'd wanted out of it. When they entered, the three huge ceiling fans provided a little relief from the sticky heat. The blinds that usually covered the huge front windows in the summer were half open. The smell of hamburgers and pie made the three of them forget the sweat on their little bodies and the way their clothes stuck to them. They each sat on worn, red leather seats at the counter, waiting for Mrs. Seymour to notice them.

When she came around the corner from the kitchen and saw the three of them, she grinned. The bruises had started to fade just enough for her to hide them with a little extra makeup and her split lip was nearly gone. But Alice noticed the careful way she walked this morning and wondered if her father had taken a belt to her over the burnt dinner last night, after all.

"Hi, sweetheart," she said, planting a kiss on the tip of Alice's nose. "You boys want apple pie? Just took one out of the oven."

"Yes, ma'am," Lionel said, bouncing on the seat.

Her mom smiled, and Alice actually heard a low chuckle. It was so rare to hear her mother laugh!

In a moment, large slices of pie and glasses of milk appeared before them. The pie was still warm, the crust golden and the apples with just enough crunch as they nestled in the sweet syrup.

Alice gulped her milk, the cold fluid feeling so good as it traveled down her throat. Her belly full, her best friends around her, her mother's smile. She felt contentment so rare that she closed her eyes to hold onto it for just a moment longer.

"Now, Alice," her mother said, hugging her close, "you keep these boys out of trouble, alright?"

"Yes, Mama."

"Till next we meet, sweet," she said, planting one last kiss on Alice's nose before scooting them out the door.

Alice had just hopped on the handlebars of Lionel's bike when Marco bolted from his and ran to the door of the diner. He stared at the door, and then back at Lionel and Alice.

Once again, Alice could swear something strange happened with Marco's eyes, but it happened so quickly, she just couldn't be sure.

"What?" Lionel asked.

Marco opened his to mouth to say something as gunshots rang out, followed by screams. Alice fell off the handlebars, and Lionel pulled her to the wall of the diner under the window. Marco dove next to them. People walking on the street ran into nearby shops or ducked down in fear. They heard several more gunshots before Alice realized it was from inside the diner.

"Mama!" she said, squirming out of Lionel's grip.

Lionel pulled her back. "No, Alice!"

"My mama's in there!"

"The police will be here soon."

The silence was worse than the gun shots and the longer they sat there, the more Alice felt her stomach roil. Her heart beat so fast that she began to feel dizzy. Marco grabbed her hand and squeezed. Within a few minutes, her breathing evened out, but the fear that something awful had just happened remained.

An instant later, the door to the diner burst open and a man in a ragged jacket, clutching a dirty bag, ran out and disappeared down the street.

They crouched a few minutes more, as the sound of sirens became louder. People began standing and pointing across the street.

Someone inside the diner called for help.

Alice jumped up and ran in before Lionel or Marco could stop her. She looked around. Broken glass from the display cases glittered in the sun, plates lay in smashed heaps, and food was smeared on seats.

She saw Will and another waitress crouched down by someone lying on the floor.

Someone was calling for her, but Alice felt as if they were very far away. She ran to the spot where Will was kneeling.

"No, don't Alice!" Will said.

She jerked her broken arm out of someone's grasp and slid to a stop in something sticky.

Sprawled awkwardly on the floor, blood spreading out from her body like petals on a flower, was her mother. Alice was surprised to see how peaceful she looked, all the tension and worry gone. For a strange moment, Alice felt relieved for her, no more pain, no more shame.

But then, the knowledge that she was dead, gone forever, slammed into Alice's mind.

"Mama! Mama!"

Alice knelt, not caring about the blood on the floor or the hands trying to pull her away.

"No...no...no..."

She laid her head on her mother's breast, sobs shaking her small frame. A thin arm embraced her, and the blinding grief eased just a little.

People were talking all around her, some of them crying, some yelling, but none of it could penetrate the fog that Alice's mind had become. Before she was ready, someone with large, calloused hands was lifting her up and away from her mother.

"No, don't...!" she struggled, tried to hit whoever it was.

"Easy child," Will said, his apron grease stained and his breath smelling of cigars.

"I'm not gonna leave her!"

Will tried to hug her, but Alice wiggled out of the embrace and turned to where her mother lay.

In a short space of time, the police had surrounded her mother's body and there was no clear way through. Alice darted between them anyway, her cast catching on the pants of one of the officers, who scooped her up before she could get past.

"Let me go! She's my mama!"

The officer didn't say anything. He just carried her, kicking and screaming, out of the diner and to a waiting patrol car. She would've hit him with her cast, but it was caught under the man's arm. The officer plopped her in the back seat, where Lionel and Marco were waiting, and walked back to the diner without a word.

Alice's chest heaved uncontrollably, her body wet with sweat and tears. She gulped air, only to expel it with a grunting sob. Though she wanted desperately to stop crying so hard, her body wouldn't listen. Only when Marco hugged her tight was she able to start breathing a little easier.

"You got that book?" Marco asked Lionel.

Lionel frowned, and then nodded, taking a battered paperback out of his back pocket. There was an exaggerated drawing of a man in a white hat with two guns pointing out from the cover, his face set in a righteous frown. It was the kind of book Lionel loved to read, and Marco loved to make fun of, but today, none of that mattered.

As Marco started to read, Alice leaned her head on his bony shoulder. After a few minutes her tears began to dry up, until only a little hiccup and a flushed face remained.

The story wasn't good, and none of them, not even Lionel, seemed to enjoy it — but it distracted all of them just enough to be able to sit and wait. They didn't notice the daylight disappearing or the strange car that arrived to take a large black bag from the diner.

When Marco's voice started to get hoarse, the same policeman who had put Alice in the car peered in. "You boys her brothers?"

"No...friends," Lionel said.

"Should get you kids home."

"What about my mama?" Alice asked, her voice small and quiet.

The policeman scratched his head. "Honey, you want me to call your daddy?"

Alice started to cry again.

"You can take her to my house. We're neighbors," Marco said.

The policeman nodded, seeming relieved that someone, even a kid, was taking care of the grieving child.

Alice stared out the window at the houses of her neighborhood. She thought about all the mothers that were calling children to tables laden with warm food, or soothing scrapes and bruised hearts. She wondered how many of them knew how lucky they were. Had she?

Would there be stories and kisses tonight? Would she wake up soon and find her mother in the kitchen making toast and coffee, trying so hard to make sure all of it was perfect before her father came down?

When they got to Marco's front door, his father opened it in a panic and stared at the policeman. The kids walked past him in shocked silence as the officer told Mr. Mayer what had happened. Mrs. Mayer ran out of the kitchen, a steady stream of angry Italian coming from her bow-shaped mouth, but she was silenced by one look at Alice's tear streaked face.

"Bella Alice, what happened?" she asked.

"Ma—" Marco said.

Mr. Mayer closed the door and sighed. "Ah, Alice..."

And for the first time in her life, she knew what it was like to have a father hold her while she cried.

CHAPTER FOUR

The Mayers insisted that she sleep over, and since Alice couldn't bear the thought of going home without her mother's comforting presence, she readily agreed. The one thing she hadn't considered was how her father would feel about that.

Lionel had just gotten there, and the boys were trying to get Alice to eat some breakfast, when a hard knock shook the door.

"I'm here for my daughter," said a voice that was rough and harsh.

Alice felt her stomach drop, the small bite of toast turning sour in her mouth. Marco grabbed her hand and Lionel stood up, as if he would stop her father from taking her home.

Her father came into the kitchen, clutching a tattered hat. His eyes were redder than usual and Alice fleetingly thought that maybe he had been crying.

Why? He hated her.

"Alice," he said, his hands crumpling his hat convulsively "we need to go home. Your Aunt Diana is on her way. She'll be here tonight."

"Sir," Lionel said, standing up straighter, "could we come over and keep Alice company until then?"

Her father clenched his large stubbly jaw, fat lips pursing, and Alice felt her whole body tense with dread. She knew that look.

"It's okay," she said to Lionel, letting go of Marco's hand, "I'll see you later."

Lionel's tall body stiffened, and his square hands clenched as he stared at Mr. Seymour. Alice grabbed one of those hands and squeezed, trying to make him stop before her father lost all patience.

"We'll be here all day," Marco said, as they walked to the door, "if you need us."

"She'll be too busy to play with you," her father said, his voice harsher toward Marco than anyone else.

Once outside, her father grabbed her shoulder too tight and she winced.

"You too good to come home? Huh?"

"N-no, sir."

"I have to hear about your mother from some cop, and then I have to come home and make my own dinner, wondering where the hell you got to!"

He jerked the front door open and pushed her inside. The rant continued as he went to the fridge and opened a cheap beer. Alice felt her stomach begin to twist, realizing that now that her mother was gone, she was the only one left for him to lash out against. Tears burned her eyes again as she looked around. It felt as if all the color had been drained from the house and all that was left had been reduced to gray and brown. But, in that moment, a bright spot of color caught her eye and Alice looked up at her mother's old weekend hat, hanging up by the entry mirror. A smile tugged at her small mouth, and she reached up to touch the soft fabric, the brittleness of the flower.

"You listening to me, girl?"

She jumped. "Yes, sir."

His eyes caught sight of the hat, then the patched coat hanging next to it. It was like watching a balloon deflate, as the anger left him. He became so sad and pathetic that Alice was surprised to feel pity for the man. He reached out and caressed her mother's coat. He took it gently off the rack, and without another word, sat in his favorite chair. Alice stared at him, wondering if it was safe to leave or if he would scream at her for some reason that she couldn't think of. After many minutes passed, and he just sat there, hugging the coat, Alice crept upstairs.

"Alice!"

The voice was harsh and too loud. She bolted up, disoriented in the dark, feeling the gentle slap of fabric against her face.

Alice had wandered into her parents' bedroom after changing into some clean clothes. The emptiness of the room was somehow proof that her mother was never coming home and a hollow ache had taken root. Craving some kind of closeness with her mother, she'd crawled inside the closet and cried herself to sleep, surrounded by the faint smell of her mother's perfume on the clothes she would never wear again.

"Alice! Where are you, lazy girl?"

He sounded drunk and angry, she knew what that meant.

With shaking hands, Alice grabbed for the closet door to slowly close it, but she misjudged in her panic, pushing it open against the wall instead. Her father must've been just outside, because he came barreling in, his eyes wild.

"You hiding from me?"

"N-no sir," she said, trying not to scoot back.

"Get downstairs! I'm hungry."

Without thinking, Alice leaned on her broken arm to help herself up. The pain was unexpected and she whimpered.

"That's what you get for going anywhere with that wop! But we'll fix that, yes, we will. If I ever catch you over there again, I'll-"

"You can't do that!"

Alice clapped her hands to her mouth, blue eyes wide, as she saw her father's face change from anger to blind fury. His meaty hand swung toward her face with such force she was knocked back into the wall, a coppery taste bursting in her mouth. On instinct, Alice raised her arms to cover her head just as her father swung at her again, this time hitting her cast. She felt a sharp twinge of pain and cried out.

"Your mother never listened," he said, and Alice could hear the clink of his belt buckle as he loosened it. "Let you do whatever the hell you wanted. Poor little friendless girl!"

The belt fell across her small back. Alice pressed her hands to her mouth to try and stifle the scream. It would only encourage her father more.

"Thought you needed any kind of friends, as long as they were nice!"

The last word was punctuated with another lash, her back starting to feel aflame.

"Didn't think about the influence of those lazy—" another "—sons of bitches!" and another.

Alice couldn't hold back the cries of pain as her father's belt fell again and again.

"Shut it! I wouldn't have to do this if you'd just—"

"What?" said a voice. "What should a little girl do to make her father stop beating her?"

Alice dared to look between her fingers to see who

would be brave enough to interrupt her father in the midst of this, but the only other person in the room was her father. His red eyes darted around, body bent in anticipation of a fight.

"You won't find me in there," the voice laughed. "Afraid? You lazy son of a bitch?"

Her father let out a primal growl and ran down the stairs, shouting obscenities to the air.

At first, Alice couldn't make her body move. What if it was nobody, a trick, and her father caught her trying to spy on him? What if he defeated whoever it was, and saw her taking delight in someone trying to stop him?

But then she wondered if the person might be here to help. What if it was her Aunt Diana? What if it was the police? If they saw her, maybe they would take her away and she'd be safe.

She stumbled to the door and heard her father's clomping steps as he walked into the living room.

"What the hell are you doing here?"

The belt whipped through the air, but no one shouted.

In fact, it was her father who yelped.

"What are you...? No! Stop it!" Her father sounded terrified.

Alice wasn't at all sure she wanted to know who or what could make her father sound that scared, but, in the end, curiosity was stronger than fear.

She crept out onto the top step and peeked between the bars.

Her father fell onto his back as someone smaller than an adult, and thin, advanced on him. A second stranger stood to the side, hands clenched into fists. Their faces were hidden by stocking caps with eye holes cut out, but Alice could still swear she knew them.

"Leave her alone! Don't touch her again!" said the first

stranger, the voice unmistakably male, on the cusp of adulthood.

It was then that Alice saw black snake-like tendrils crawling on the ground, seeming to come from the masked person's outstretched hands. She squeaked in fear and tried to scoot back, but slipped in her haste and tumbled down the stairs. Her head hit the final step with a hard bang, bright spots piercing her vision.

When she opened her eyes, a face masked in a stocking cap leaned over her. She moaned, trying to raise her good hand to push them away, but her arms felt heavy.

"Is she alright?" the first boy asked the second.

"I think-"

The masked boy in front of her fell to his knees from a blow to the head by her father, who now loomed over her.

Alice wanted to run, but couldn't seem to make her limbs move. All she could manage was to curl onto her side.

"You little shits," her father hissed. "Who the hell—"

The air was rent by a scream of such terror that it pierced through the fog of Alice's brain and made her heart jump.

"No, stop! Please...please!" Now her father was crying, great screaming sobs. "Stop! God...please!"

The masked boy that her father had just hit stood up, hand to his head.

He ran toward the other masked boy. "That's enough!"

"Do you know what he was going to do to her?" said the first boy. "What he's like?"

"Yes, but you have to stop!"

"No! He deserves to suffer! I can make him...I can...I could save her, forever."

Alice slowly raised her head, feeling a sticky substance in her hair that oozed onto her ear. Her vision was cloudy, but she could just make out the two people. They were dressed in cut-off shorts and one wore a t-shirt and old converse shoes without socks. The other wore a button-up shirt with the bottom button in the wrong hole.

Alice blinked and noticed that the tendrils were now crawling all over her father, who screamed like the devils of hell were tormenting him.

In the back of her mind, Alice knew she should be horrified, but she just couldn't seem to care.

It was then that the taller of the two boys turned and Alice could see shocks of blond hair sticking out from the stocking cap that had been knocked askew when her father hit him.

"Lionel?" she whispered and shook her head.

No, that was crazy! What would Lionel and...?

"Mar..."

The tall one stopped and yanked on the other one. "I mean it...you have to stop!"

"...I can't..."

The tall one hesitated, then hit the shorter one, knocking him to the ground.

The tendrils disappeared, and her father's cries died down to whimpers as he curled into a ball.

The tallest one pulled her father up by his shirt front and hit him. "You come near her again and I'll let him finish you."

Her father sobbed something, then half-ran, half-crawled out the front door, not bothering to close it.

"Please, take me with you," she whispered, her mind starting to succumb to the fog. "Take me away, please, please, please..."

Her eyes closed and she could feel a gentle, feverishly warm hand caress her hair.

"It's okay," the voice of the shorter boy crooned. "You're safe. He won't hurt you anymore."

As much as she wanted to, Alice couldn't bring herself to believe him.

"We have to get out of here!" the second boy said.

"But, we can't leave her like this."

"I think a car just pulled up. C'mon! We can't get caught!"

"I'm sorry," the first boy said, his hand on her cheek. "You're safe now."

Alice tried to speak, but a strange fatigue began to overcome her. Just before she fell asleep, soft lips kissed her forehead and she sighed.

CHAPTER FIVE

Alice didn't know what happened when her aunt and uncle came into the house and saw her unconscious. She only knew she woke up in her bed, a doctor taking her pulse.

It felt strange to be tucked in, safe and warm, when she'd just been so terrified. Her Aunt Diana, a woman she had almost no memory of, was there with warm milk and a sandwich, in case she was hungry.

Alice wasn't. She wanted to ask if her aunt had seen two boys running from the house, but they had been so frightened of discovery that she had kept what happened to herself.

"You're safe now," Aunt Diana had said, a strange echo of what the boys had promised.

A shaky smile appeared on Alice's lips and she allowed herself to drift off to sleep, but it was by no means restful. Nightmares, so real that Alice forgot she was dreaming, made her cry and scream. She was certain that her father's hot smelly breath was on her face, his hands dragging her away.

A gentle voice roused her from the nightmares.

"Mama?" Alice asked.

But when her eyes focused, it was her aunt's face she saw and her strong arms that held Alice.

In the morning, her Uncle Logan, a scruffy-looking man with gentle brown eyes and an unruly mop of curly brown hair, was making pancakes in the kitchen.

"Good morning," he said, a grin on his wide mouth showing straight white teeth, "do you like jam or syrup on your pancakes?"

Alice felt herself flinch under his gaze and immediately regretted it. His square face softened, and he squatted down to her height.

"It's okay," he whispered, a sudden mischievous glint appearing in his eyes. "I won't tell if you want both."

A smile tried to tug her mouth up, but Alice bit her lower lip instead and nodded.

"Alright..." He turned back to the stove and flipped the two golden pancakes on her mother's ancient griddle.

Aunt Diana breezed in just then and kissed her husband. Alice stared at the love that shone in their eyes as the kiss ended, a sudden jealousy piercing her heart.

Why couldn't Mama be loved like that?

"Coffee is done," Uncle Logan said.

"Thank you." Aunt Diana kissed him again.

In a few moments, all three of them sat around the old scarred kitchen table, a feast of bacon, pancakes and juice set out.

"I see you have a climbing tree out back," Uncle Logan said.

Alice nodded as she shoved pancakes in her mouth.

"I used to have one when I was a boy. I'd hide treasures in it."

Alice nodded again, not looking him in the eye. She could feel her aunt and uncle exchange glances, and for a few minutes there was a thick uncomfortable silence around them.

"I was thinking," Aunt Diana said, "maybe we could go for a drive today? Would you like that?"

Alice shrugged, not sure what the point would be. What was there to see around Park Side?

"Or is there something you'd like to do?"

She was about to shrug again, when it hit her.

"I want to see my friends."

Aunt Diana smiled. "Of course, would you like me to drive you?"

Alice shook her head. "Marco is just next door, and Lionel...he's never too far away."

"Alright, stay as long as you like, sweetheart."

Alice shoveled the food in her mouth as quick as possible and was out the door before her aunt could ask any more questions.

Instead of sneaking through the back, which felt strange without Marco, Alice knocked on the front door.

After a few minutes, Mr. Mayer answered. He was haggard, with dark circles under his eyes, his tie askew.

"Oh, Alice," he said, "I'm afraid Marco is...he's not able to play today."

Alice felt as if someone had grabbed her heart and squeezed it.

"What's wrong? Is he alright?"

"He's...he will be fine. Just sick, a fever."

"Well...maybe I could read to him...or something?"

Mr. Mayer shook his head. "I'm sorry Alice, not right now. Maybe in a few days."

He closed the door and all Alice could do was stand there.

Tears stung her eyes as she walked down the steps, that hollow feeling that had settled into her heart when Mama died started to deepen.

Deciding that Lionel would likely be stopping by soon

and receive a similar rejection, Alice sat on her front steps to wait.

Hours passed, and it was clear Lionel wasn't coming.

More tears clouded her vision as she went inside and ran to her room. Not caring if she fell on her cast, Alice flung herself onto the bed and cried herself to sleep.

She woke to voices downstairs and bolted from her room, hopeful that Lionel might've come by after all.

But it became clear very quickly that it wasn't Lionel. It was a man's voice, deep and rumbling.

"If the father did indeed run out, well then, the girl must be put into a home."

Alice's stomach dropped.

The last thing she wanted was to live with her father, but a home would be just as bad.

"My sister wouldn't have wanted that," Aunt Diana said. "My husband and I have no children, and are in a position to take custody of my niece."

"Well, yes, I see how that might be better, if you're willing to do that."

"We are," Uncle Logan said.

"If the father doesn't return by the funeral, then he probably won't be returning at all. We can start the process after that."

"Thank you, officer," Aunt Diana said.

Alice sank to her knees in the hall.

Fear and relief flooded her in equal measure. She barely knew her aunt and uncle, yet from what she'd seen they were kind and good people.

Though Mama barely spoke of them. Why is that? Maybe it's false. Maybe after a little while they'll get tired of me or maybe...

"Do you think she'll want to go with us?" Uncle Logan asked.

"There's really no other option. Even if that man returns there's no way in hell I'll leave her with him."

"Agreed. When should we tell her?"

"Tonight, the sooner the better. That child needs to know that she's safe, first and foremost."

"There's nothing in the house to eat."

"I didn't have the chance to go to the market, what with the funeral arrangements.

"We'll go out then."

"There's a diner...but no, that wouldn't be a good idea."

"I'll look in the phone book. Why don't you go wake her up?"

Alice jumped to her feet and was almost to her room when she heard Aunt Diana's steps behind her.

"Alice?"

She turned around, afraid Aunt Diana would be mad at her for listening. Instead, her aunt smiled.

"Well? What do you think? Would you like to come live with us? We have a lovely home, and back yard. I own a bookstore, you'd have your pick of however many you want."

Alice licked her lips. "My friends..."

"Yes, I'm sure you'll miss them, but they can come visit as often as you want. And maybe in the summer months, you could stay with them?"

"Well...I-I don't...I don't want to stay with...*him*."

Aunt Diana nodded, a stormy look passing over her lovely features. "No, I wouldn't think you would."

"I...I guess so then."

"Wonderful. Why don't you wash your face and brush your hair. Uncle Logan is taking us out for dinner."

Alice nodded, a reluctant excitement taking root in her mind.

The next week passed in a flurry of packing and arranging

for the sale of the house. Alice often felt in the way as her aunt and uncle made phone calls, and ran errands, but they never seemed to treat her like it.

After two days, Alice went back to Marco's house, longing to spend the last few days with him and Lionel on the worn library rug. But once again, Mr. Mayer told her that Marco was too sick to see anyone. And no matter how many hours she waited on the front porch, Lionel never showed up either.

All too soon the day of the funeral arrived.

Rain pelted the windows and roof of the small church, as the minister read from a black Bible. Alice tried to be strong, to not cry, but tears fell from her eyes anyway.

Once the service was over and they pulled up to the house, Alice bolted from the car, not caring who wanted to talk to her. The cast made climbing her tree difficult, but soon she found herself safely ensconced in it's branches, the vibrant leaves shielding her from the curious eyes of mourners.

She found the book where she'd left it in the hollow part of the trunk and pulled it out. The pages felt brittle under Alice's fingers as she turned them. She didn't have to read the story, she'd memorized it long ago, but holding the book that her mother had read to her was a kind of comfort.

A soft summer breeze stirred the leaves in her tree, fat drops of water plopping onto her tightly braided hair and dark blue dress. The sounds of people talking drifted to her. She glared in their direction. So many people had come to her mother's funeral, but where had they been all this time? Where were her friends when her mother really needed them?

Where were *her* friends?

Hugging the book tight to her chest, Alice squeezed her eyes shut to keep the tears from falling. She didn't want to cry anymore. She wanted to scream and kick and punch someone.

Rage burst inside of her like a boil and she found her body trembling with it. She'd been mad before, of course, but this felt different. It burned through her, bright and hard, and she wondered if she'd burst into flames.

"Why's a raven like a—"

She snarled, jumping down in front of Marco, his brown eyes huge with shock.

"Where've you been?!"

"Alice—"

"The day I left your house my father beat me! Where were y-you? And then today, they-they buried my mama and-and, you weren't there!"

She kicked him hard in the leg, and then awkwardly slapped him across the face with her left hand as tears blinded her.

"Stop it!" Strong arms encircled her from behind.

"And you!" she said to Lionel. "Why-why didn't you...? Why did he do it?! I'll kill him someday, I will!"

Lionel held her tight against his chest as Alice screamed and cried. She wanted to hit the man who'd taken her mother's life, to beat him and make him feel as bad as she did. She wanted to take something away from him, make him know that hollow feeling inside that wakes you up at night, that no one can ever make go away.

Once her sobs had begun to quiet, Lionel let her go and Marco caught her in a tight embrace. She pressed her face into his slim chest, saying over and over what she'd do to the man who killed her mother.

"No, you won't," Marco said after a minute. "You won't, because you're better than him."

"Shut up," she said, wiping her nose with her fingers.

A violet hankie appeared next to her, and that's when Alice realized that half the house had emptied to watch her throwing a fit. Many of them shook their head, or gave her looks of pity mixed with curiosity. Heat rose to her cheeks, but this time it wasn't anger.

"Don't pay any attention to them," her aunt said, kneeling. "You go ahead and rage."

Alice looked into her aunt's large blue eyes. "Why didn't you take us away?"

Aunt Diana's face crumpled a little. "I tried. But your mom...she wanted to stay."

"Okay, everyone," said Uncle Logan, "show's over, back in the house, and give her some privacy."

"Do you want me to stay out here?" Aunt Diana asked.

Alice hesitated. "No. That's okay." Aunt Diana gave her a brief hug and walked back towards the house.

Lionel plopped down on the ground with a sigh. "I'm sorry I wasn't here this week."

Alice shrugged, sniffling.

"My mom, she...it's stupid. I think it is, but she went and got married."

"What?" Alice stared at him.

"Yeah, to that rich idiot she's been seeing, Jason James. Wanted me at the hurried-up wedding. So stupid."

"But, now you have—"

"Don't call him my dad." Lionel's face was stormy.

"Sorry."

"He hates me. Wants to send me away to some snooty school."

Alice looked at Marco, who was staring very hard at the grass. His small mouth was drawn into a severe frown and there were dark circles under his eyes, along with a purple bruise on his left cheek. Lionel had been protecting Marco at school for years. If he left for good...

"I'll be fine," he said, looking up at her.

"I'm not going!" Lionel said.

"Yeah, you are."

Lionel looked away, his square jaw clenched.

"Alice..." Marco said.

"I'm sorry I hit you," she said, touching his cheek where she'd left a red hand print under the bruise.

He smiled. "It's okay. I should've told you that I was...well, I was sick."

"Your dad said, but I...it just felt like you'd left. Are you alright now?"

"Yeah, just...didn't want to give it to you."

"I wouldn't have cared. I...I wanted you here. Both of you," she gasped, eyes widening. "Oh my gosh! I haven't told you about the two heroes."

"Who?" Lionel asked.

For the first time all week, she felt alive again as the story spilled out of her in an excited rush. Lionel and Marco listened, but they weren't as intrigued as she thought they'd be. In fact, Marco seemed more agitated than anything.

"Don't you think that's amazing?" she said.

Lionel shrugged. "Maybe."

"But they made him scared enough to leave." She stared at Lionel, a faint memory of blond hair under a stocking cap flashing through her mind.

He met her gaze. "What?"

She shook her head. *It's too crazy, there's no way...was there?*

"You hit your head," Marco said, tossing handfuls of plucked grass. "You don't know what happened, right? I mean do you remember anything?"

She bit her lip. "Well...it sounds crazy, but, one of them had these smoky snake-like things come out of him."

Marco's eyes became huge, but Lionel burst out laughing.

"Yeah, you definitely hit your head."

"I didn't imagine it!" She hit him on the shoulder. "It was real."

"Okay, sure. Smoky snake things!" Lionel shook his head.

"That's not the point! They helped me."

She chewed her bottom lip again. She'd tried to remember as much as possible from that afternoon, but a lot of it was hazy. And the parts that weren't...well, Lionel wasn't the only one that thought what she remembered was a little crazy. Alice couldn't believe it either sometimes. The last few days she'd started to wonder if they weren't just ordinary people who saw someone in need and helped. They had been so strong and brave. Two things she longed to be.

I want to be like them

The thought sent shock waves through her mind and soul, calming the little voice that nagged at her that life was supposed to be bigger, more than what she could see.

Straightening her little shoulders and looking them in the eye, she said, "And someday, I'm going to do the same."

Lionel laughed. "What?"

"I'm going to help people, too. People that can't help themselves."

"I don't think—" Marco said.

"Why not?"

"Because, you're a girl," Lionel said.

Alice felt that same flash of heat course through her body, her small hands clenching into fists.

"So what?"

"It's just that—" Marco said.

"You said it yourself, they were boys or men or what-ever. The point is you're a girl, and girls just don't—" The kick to Lionel's leg was swift, and hard enough to make him yelp. He scurried to his feet and stared at Alice. She closed the gap between them quickly, sending Lionel stumbling back and almost falling to the wet grass.

Marco ran between them and held Alice at bay. "No more fights."

"I can do it!" Alice said. "And when I do, no one will touch me again."

Lionel just stared at her, eyes wide.

"Okay," Marco said, "but, let's not fight. You're leaving tomorrow, right?"

Her aunt and uncle's home was in downtown Jet City and only twenty minutes away but it might as well be twenty hours. She hadn't let herself think about losing Marco and Lionel, but now...

Alice felt the fire within her smothered by all this.

"Then, let's just...I don't know. What do you wanna do?" Marco asked.

"Eat something?" Lionel said.

She laughed in spite of everything, and Lionel and Marco seemed to relax.

"My ma brought cannoli."

"Really?" Lionel grinned.

"Okay," Alice said.

They ate cannoli and chocolate chip cookies on the back porch. They climbed her tree, and Marco and Alice tossed out lines from books to see if the other could finish it, while Lionel stuffed a roast beef sandwich in his mouth. When the rain returned, they went up to her room and played games. When those were exhausted and the rain still hadn't let up, they lay on her bed, staring at the ceiling and talking about what they might want to be when they were older.

"A fireman, I think," Lionel said.

"Why?" Alice asked, stuffing a pencil down her cast to itch her arm.

"Dunno. I like the trucks, I guess."

"What about you, Marco?"

He stared at the ceiling, his long, thin face dark in thought. Lionel sat up and looked at him, a frown of worry on his tanned face.

"I used to want to be a photographer, like my dad."

"You could be."

Marco's expression darkened even further. "Maybe."

"I'm hungry," Lionel said after a moment.

Marco smiled. "You're always hungry."

"Do you think your aunt would mind if I...?"

"Nope."

Lionel scrambled off the bed and down the stairs.

The rain pelted the roof and her window like someone was throwing handfuls of pebbles. Somewhere in the distance, a rumble of thunder sounded. Alice laid her head on Marco's shoulder and closed her eyes. After a moment, his sticky hot hand grabbed hers and squeezed.

"I'll miss you," he whispered.

There was nothing she could say, she didn't know what word could possibly describe what she felt. So, she just nodded.

"We could write, I guess," Marco said.

"Yeah. I guess."

After a few minutes, they could hear Lionel clomping up the stairs. For some reason she couldn't understand, she knew that Lionel shouldn't see them so close. Reluctantly, she let go of Marco's hand and sat up, looking at the small collection of boxes that made up her young life so far.

"Your aunt says we gotta go," Lionel said. "You're leaving early tomorrow, I guess."

Her stomach dropped, tears stinging her eyes. It felt like all she did lately was cry. She wondered if this was her future, just a puddle of awful tears.

Marco grabbed Alice in a tight hug. She could hear his heart hammering behind his ribs, feel his thin body tremble a little. She looked up and saw him wipe away tears.

Despite that, he forced a smile and with one more quick hug, he bolted down stairs.

"I, uh...Maybe I'll come downtown and see you?" Lionel said.

"I'd like that."

He scuffed his old converse shoes on the wood floor, looking up at the ceiling, then down at his feet, then up again.

Since she didn't think Lionel was going to hug her, Alice threw her arms around him. Not right away, but eventually, his long, surprisingly strong, arms held her. She felt his cheek against the top of her head and wished he'd never let go.

But, of course, he did, and Alice saw that his cheeks were wet with tears he tried to pretend weren't there.

He gave her a crooked grin. "Well...good-bye, I guess."

Alice took a deep breath and made a decision. If she was going to leave, and maybe never see him again, she would do something that Lionel would never forget, something she'd wanted to try for months now.

"Til next we meet, sweet." And she leaned forward with closed eyes and puckered lips, planting a quick kiss on Lionel's full lips.

When she stepped back, Lionel's blue eyes were wide with surprise. Alice tried to say something, but instead of her lips, her feet moved. Without a backward glance, she ran down the stairs and into the bathroom. After a long hard cry, Aunt Diana coaxed her out and put her to bed.

"I don't want to leave," Alice whispered.

"I know," Aunt Diana said, "but, do you really want to stay?"

Alice was about to nod, but then realized that everything was different now. Her mother was gone, Lionel was leaving, and who knew what Marco would do without

Lionel's protection. Nothing that she loved about this place was here anymore.

"It doesn't seem like it now," Aunt Diana said with a gentle smile, "but there will be a lot of things to be happy about in the future. You just have to give all the new things a chance."

Uncle Logan knocked on the door, peeking his curly brown head around the corner. Alice felt her muscles tighten, her hands clutching the covers.

He noticed too, brown eyes sad behind his glasses. "I thought a little warm milk? Helps me sleep."

"You didn't put whiskey in that, did you?" Aunt Diana asked.

"Not in this one," he said, kissing her before setting the glass down.

"Thank you, sir," Alice said, trying hard not to flinch when he came near.

Uncle Logan hesitated, as if he wanted to say something, but thought better of it. He smiled at her instead and walked out.

Aunt Diana kissed her on the forehead. "Drink your milk and sleep. Lots to do tomorrow."

Alice lay awake, staring at her ceiling. What would her life be like now?

The more she thought about the possibilities, she felt an equal mix of terror and excitement. Maybe this was the way to become who she wanted to be. To learn how be a hero like those two that helped her. To be strong and invincible.

That night her dreams were filled with dark villains that were always vanquished by heroes that shone bright as day.

AUTUMN-1959

CHAPTER SIX

Warm fall sunlight tried its best to penetrate the foggy grime on the floor-to-ceiling windows of the dingy loft. It found small spots, where someone had tried to clean, and fell in gold trickles on the scarred wooden floors. The high ceiling made the cries of people practicing martial arts echo, even as the patched mats on the floor muffled the sounds of impact.

It was to one of these mats that Alice walked, bowing to her aunt, and then to the tall older black man before her.

This was her third spar of the morning, and though the air outside had succumbed to the chill of autumn, inside the loft it was muggy and sweat tickled down Alice's spine. She bounced just a little on the balls of her feet, her cobalt eyes taking in every move of her opponent. At last, the man rushed toward her. Alice blocked two quick punches and landed one of her own at his mid-section. Her roundhouse kick was then blocked and he threw her off balance, enough that she fell. Rolling to the side and jumping to her feet, Alice avoided his attempt at a pin. The man advanced on her again and Alice grinned. She saw the opportunity seconds before he did, but it was too late for him to change course. Tossing him over her hip, Alice spun with his body to pin him in one smooth motion.

"Very good," Aunt Diana said, fidgeting with the gold locket around her neck. "Switch."

Alice tried not to smile too much as she let Gerald off the mat. He might be her Uncle Logan's age, but Gerald was spry and strong, and had been training with Aunt Diana for many years.

This time, Gerald got the better of her, though she didn't make it easy. Again and again they sparred, Alice taking Gerald to the mat more often than not, though pinning him there was the real effort.

She had lived with her aunt and uncle barely a month, when Aunt Diana had taken her to the loft above their bookstore to watch a sparring practice. Alice had been awed by the power her aunt possessed and yearned to have the security such power could give. She'd begged her aunt to train her, but Aunt Diana had made her watch the practices for a month, to make absolutely sure Alice knew what she was getting into. One of the happiest days Alice could remember was when her aunt gave her that very first Gi, the traditional clothing for those that practice martial arts.

Gerald and Alice were both grateful when Aunt Diana called the end of practice. As they toweled sweat from their faces, Gerald spoke, his voice gentle, as usual. "Very impressive."

"You too, for an old guy."

He belted out a laugh and ruffled her dark wavy hair.

"I'd best be leaving. I've got patients waiting for me."

Gerald ran a health clinic in Park Side. He seemed to be able to tell just by looking at someone what was wrong with them and how to fix it. Due to the color of his skin, no hospital or clinic in downtown Jet City would hire him. It wasn't until Aunt Diana's philanthropic organization, The Charitable Ladies of Jet City, loaned him the money, that he had been able to open the small clinic in Park Side.

Alice waved good-bye and smiled up at her aunt, who gave her a warm embrace, saying, "You've done amazing."

Their six-inch height difference made Alice feel like a child next to her aunt, even though she had turned twenty-one several months ago. There were other differences between them as well. Where her aunt was lithe and grace-ful, with long, toned limbs, Alice was shorter and solid, with a curvy body and muscular limbs. If she should've been bothered by this, Alice didn't know it. She sometimes wished for smaller hips and breasts, but mostly she loved the strength her arms and legs possessed, and how her shorter stature gave her an unexpected advantage over many adversaries.

At least, Alice believed that it would, true adversaries being hard to come by.

"You really want to live here?" Aunt Diana asked, looking around the huge loft.

For decades, it had been used as storage and a make-shift practice room for Aunt Diana, Gerald, and a few others interested in martial arts, but Alice had coveted it for a place of her own since high school. And now, as a present for her college graduation, Aunt Diana and Uncle Logan had given it to her.

The brick walls had pipes running along them in several places, but were otherwise solid. The kitchen was laugh-able, with a fridge that no one dared open, a sink that shot out brown water, and no stove – not that Alice used one any way, as her cooking skills were abysmal. The space that would be her bedroom was just big enough for her bed and a tiny dresser, but nothing else.

The only bright spot was the bathroom, which her uncle had renovated the year before, using a beautiful, green tile.

Plus, there was a shower and sink that, somehow, had clean water.

"Now that the boxes are all gone, it's really not so bad," Alice said.

Aunt Diana arched an eyebrow. "You have your work cut out for you to make it livable, but then, you've always welcomed a challenge."

Alice beamed at the compliment. "I had a good example."

"Don't go buttering me up to get any help out of me. This is your endeavor."

"I know, which is why I convinced Uncle Logan to help me tear out the kitchen."

Aunt Diana shook her head. "That man would do anything for you."

"Since the day I moved in. Besides, wasn't there a promise of help picking out furniture attached to this gift?"

Aunt Diana tilted her head and frowned. "Was there? I can't recall."

"There better be, the only thing I'm worse at than cooking is decorating."

"We'll see. But now, down to present concerns. We have an afternoon tea to clean up for..."

Alice felt her stomach twist.

"You'll do fine," Aunt Diana said.

"Are you sure you want to do this? I just graduated. I don't know as much about all this as you do."

"Someday, it will all be yours, and you may be good at running the bookstore, but it's the Children's Home, and the clinic, and all the other endeavors that the organization will do that are most important. You need to understand how to keep them going when I'm gone."

"That's a long way off, right?"

Aunt Diana smiled. "Absolutely."

"Then, what's the rush? I mean, most of those ladies will

be gone by the time I take over for you, right? And besides, I think it would be better if I show my skills running a business before—"

"Alice, you will do fine. Just remember what we talked about. Smile, nod and no—"

"—politics or religion," Alice finished with a small eye roll. "I know...it's just...I never fit in with the daughters of those women at school, and I don't think their mothers are going to be any different. I still don't understand how you do it. You're not like them."

"I'll take that as a compliment."

"It is."

Aunt Diana sighed. "It's not easy. And there are times I'd like to punch some of them in the teeth. But, I just keep reminding myself why I'm there, of the people I am helping. I've learned that I can endure almost anything if it's for others, and I believe you are the same." She cupped Alice's cheek, running her slender thumb along Alice's cheekbone. "You have so much fire and strength. If you learn to channel it the right way, you will do amazing things."

Alice felt her heart swell with pride and she smiled. If her aunt believed in her that much, she had to give it shot.

"It will take time," Aunt Diana said, "but you will find your way of doing this, just like I did."

Alice gave her aunt a shaky smile and nodded. "I'll do my best."

"I know you will."

⸻

The tea room of the Grand Hotel was arguably the fanciest room Alice had ever been in. The ceiling was high and covered with frescoes of naked cupids flitting here and there, gilt trim around each. In the center hung a huge crystal chandelier. The quiet strains of a harp floated through the air from somewhere, though Alice couldn't see anyone playing an instrument.

A long table, covered with delicate white linen, sat in the center of the room, flanked on one side by French doors and on the other by an antique sideboard where teapots sat ready. Alice's eyes widened when she saw three tiered trays holding delicate sandwiches and exquisite cakes, the latter adorned with sugar flowers that looked as if they'd been plucked from someone's garden. There were also cookies in the shape of teapots, with frosted details to match the pots on the sideboard. Others had fresh scones with perfectly-browned tops. It all looked too beautiful to eat.

Each place setting had a teacup and saucer decorated with green and purple flowers, along with matching plates. Small teaspoons and delicate forks sat on top of white linen napkins.

As she followed her aunt into the room, Alice's blue heels sank into the thick light-brown carpet. She could feel her palms starting to sweat under her white kid gloves and rubbed them on the skirt of her tea-length blue and white floral dress.

"Stop fidgeting," her aunt whispered. "You'll be fine."

"Alright," Alice whispered back, hoping there wasn't any lipstick on her teeth.

The women turned to look at them as if Alice and Aunt Diana gave off the scent of unwashed masses. She watched Aunt Diana's smile widen and her posture straighten. Alice tried to follow suit, but only managed to feel tense all over.

A chubby woman with curly hair and a too-tight pink dress was the first to tear herself from the group and walk over. Just before she started speaking, Alice's nose wrinkled with the odor of rose water and gin that rolled off her.

As if sensing her distaste, Aunt Diana stepped just a little in front of Alice.

"Mrs. Barnes, how lovely to see you. How is your son enjoying marital bliss?"

"Well enough, I suppose. You know how it is with young people these days. All happiness and sunshine, and even if it wasn't, they wouldn't tell you anyway." Mrs. Barnes laughed, though there was no true mirth in it. "I was hoping that you'd had a chance to read my proposal for the introduction of a beautification program?"

Alice saw the corners of her aunt's mouth tighten.

"Yes, I did. I have a few suggestions for how to make it run a little smoother, if I might discuss them with you at a later date?"

Mrs. Barnes' smile widened. "Yes, of course. I'm so glad you're on board with this."

"And who is this?" asked a rail-thin woman with a pinched face behind Mrs. Barnes.

"Mrs. Grace," Aunt Diana said, "so wonderful to see you. May I introduce my niece, Alice Seymour."

Mrs. Barnes turned her small brown eyes on Alice and smiled a little wider, revealing yellow teeth, while Mrs. Grace looked Alice over with thinly veiled disdain.

Alice's smile felt tight. "Pleasure to meet you both."

"You're the one who just graduated from college?" Mrs. Grace asked.

"Yes, ma'am, tenth in my class."

"How...rare to see a woman finishing college."

"Didn't have much luck with romance, dear?" asked Mrs. Barnes, pity oozing from her lips.

Alice felt her cheeks flush. "It wasn't my focus, to be honest."

Mrs. Barnes frowned. "Really? You aren't interested in making your own family? Or maybe, you're just nursing a broken heart. You know, it took my Stella three tries to find her happily-ever-after. Don't give up, he could be just around the corner."

"Or, perhaps, it was difficult to find a man who was in your social circle," Mrs. Grace said. "College boys are looking for women who are from certain types of families, after all."

"I'm really more interested in running my aunt's book store. I didn't work so hard for four years just to—"

"Oh look, there's Mrs. Lucas." Aunt Diana gripped Alice's elbow hard. "I really must tell her about the beautification project before our tea gets under way. If you'll excuse us?"

"Of course – don't despair, dear," Mrs. Barnes said, giving Alice's arm a pat.

"Lovely to meet you, Miss Seymour," said Mrs. Grace, her voice saying anything but.

Her aunt guided her to a deserted corner of the room, nodding to a few other women on the way. Her smile never slipped, her gait never faltered, but Alice could feel her body vibrate with frustration.

"I'm sorry," Alice said, once they were out of ear shot, "but really! Not every woman goes to college just to hook a husband."

"Every woman here, besides us, did exactly that, as did their daughters. You are an anomaly, Alice. They don't like anomalies."

"Then why did you bring me here?"

"Because, for better or worse, you're going to have to learn how to navigate these waters."

Alice groaned. "So, put on a face, be someone I'm not? Is that what you do? I know for a fact that you hate that beautification project."

"Not that this is the time or place to discuss this at length, but yes, I do. You'll find that this is a game of sorts. You do your best to make their pet projects not have too much of an adverse effect on the city, and then, when you really need their backing, you call on them."

"Sounds awful."

"Yes, but necessary. Like many things in life." Aunt Diana's voice became just a touch annoyed. "You're going to find that out, Alice. Whether you like it or not."

Alice swallowed, shame welling up at the thought that she'd embarrassed her aunt. "I'm sorry. I just...I've heard all their comments so many times, from the younger versions of these women, and I don't care to hear it anymore."

"Then, perhaps, you should stick to the book store. It does take a certain kind of person to do this. You've always been a bit impulsive and straightforward, two qualities that might make forcing you to adapt to this an act of cruelty."

There was no spite in her tone, only a simple understanding and love that Alice had always found hard to resist. Her aunt had never manipulated her; she'd never had to. When it came time to choose a major for college, the choice was obvious. She wanted to be like her aunt; therefore, it had to be business.

It was a stroke of luck that Alice had a talent for it, at least the learning of it.

The execution might be a bit trickier.

Alice took a deep breath and shook her head. "No, you're right. Not every lesson is going to be easy, especially this one. But I must give it a try. I owe you that much."

"You don't owe me anything. Do this because it's what you want, not because of me."

"I want to do this, at least to try."

Aunt Diana nodded. "Alright, if you're sure?"

"Yes." Alice's voice was far more confident than she felt.

"Then, it's time to introduce you to someone." She nodded toward the door.

Alice turned to the doorway and gasped. Standing there, in a light green and white dress, her golden hair curled into a perfect bouffant, was the woman Alice most admired in Jet City, except Aunt Diana, of course.

"You didn't tell me Victoria Veran was a part of this!" Alice whispered.

"Unlike most of our members, Victoria wishes to remain anonymous."

"You're on a first name basis with her?"

Aunt Diana's full lips spread into an amused grin.

"Come on, before the others get to her first."

Alice's stomach dipped and turned. She had to ball her hand into a fist to keep from wiping it on her skirt.

I hope my hair isn't frizzed, and oh god, I really hope I don't have lipstick on my teeth, and what if she can tell that these damn heels are rubbing a blister on my heel? Why didn't I wear my old shoes?

She tried not to rehearse everything she knew about Victoria Veran, but it was no use.

Fleeing Nazi Germany at fourteen, Victoria joined the British secret service as a spy. In spite of opposition from her superiors, she became the most daring and successful of her peers. When it was discovered that she could interpret scientific calculations and formulas, she was assigned to the science division of the British army. It was there, at sixteen, that she met the love of her life, fellow spy and scientist, Tony Veran. Despite the twelve year age difference, and the fact that he was already engaged, they married as soon as the war was over. Though women weren't allowed to be a part of the Army's scientific division after the war, Victoria was known to have consulted with her husband as a civilian. She even became a silent partner in his business endeavors. When Tony was injured in a lab accident and became a recluse, it was Victoria who became the face of the company.

Alice admired how she faced down the sneers of the business men around her, expanding her husband's business into medical research, agriculture and genetics, as well as imports and exports and military contracts.

She was everything Alice longed to be: powerful, smart, respected. To her eyes, Victoria had risked everything and gained it all back and more.

"Mrs. Veran," Aunt Diana said.

When Victoria saw Aunt Diana, her small mouth spread into a smile of genuine affection.

"Diana..." She kissed Aunt Diana on each cheek. "I have told you a hundred times to call me Victoria."

"Won't the other ladies be a bit upset by that?"

Victoria's dove-gray eyes sparkled. "I should hope so."

Aunt Diana laughed and Alice took in the two women for a moment. They looked like they were the same age, even though Aunt Diana was eleven years Victoria's senior. Where her aunt was statuesque and athletic, Victoria was willowy and had the grace of a dancer. Her aunt's features were bold and beautiful, but Victoria's appeared fragile and rare.

"May I present my niece, Alice Seymour?"

Victoria's gaze rested on Alice, who tried very hard to think of something to say, but only managed a whispered, "Hello."

"I have so longed to meet you." Victoria pressed Alice's small hand in her long one. "Diana has kept me abreast of all your endeavors, including your education. I was impressed to hear that you graduated so near the top of your class."

Alice felt her stomach flutter. "Thank you, I...well, I was trying for valedictorian, but missed it by a few percentage points."

"Ah yes, something so small can have very large consequences. Even so, top ten is not so terrible," Victoria said, her voice betraying a hint of longing as she continued. "And you must remember, not every woman has the opportunity to go to college. You have been very fortunate."

"Yes, I think so."

Victoria smiled. "So, tell me. What are your plans?"

Alice stared at her for a moment. "My-my plans? Oh, yes, my plans."

Aunt Diana laughed. "You have to forgive Alice. She has admired you for years."

"Really? How so?"

Alice felt her face flush. "I...well, yes. I mean you are...your life is extraordinary and I...well, I just..." Alice took a deep breath. "If I may be honest?"

Victoria nodded.

"I admire your courage, for daring to be successful in business and life."

"You wish to be the same?"

"Yes, very much."

Victoria nodded again, her face becoming serious. "Then, you must have a spine of steel, and never let anyone take what you want in life. No one. Not even someone you love."

"You speak as though you are all steel." Aunt Diana's voice held a hint of discomfort. "But I've seen you act with great compassion and grace."

"Well, yes, but you've never seen me in a board room."

They laughed, but Alice noticed how Aunt Diana's wasn't quite genuine.

"By the way," Aunt Diana said, as the trio made their way to the table, "I heard the good news about the science complex breaking ground this month. It's been such a long time coming. Please, tell Mr. Veran congratulations from me and Logan."

Victoria smiled. "Thank you, I will. It's a shame that so many people are afraid of scientific exploration and discovery. Tony and I believe it's the gateway to a better, a more peaceful, tomorrow."

"I suppose their fear comes from the atomic bomb?" Alice asked.

Victoria nodded. "That is a very common argument, but to blame scientific discovery for how men use it isn't fair. Science can and should be used to protect us from dangerous men, but that's not its only possibility. There's so much good that can come from looking at discoveries with an eye toward building up civilization, not tearing it down. That is what my husband and I believe, at any rate."

"Your father would be so proud of both of you," Aunt Diana said.

The barest hint of a shadow passed over Victoria's bright features. "Perhaps. But I don't think he would've had the courage to see such a vision through to the end."

"In all I've read about you, I don't think I've heard much about him. He was a scientist, then?" Alice asked.

"Yes." Victoria's smile turned sad. "I'm sorry, I really don't like to talk about him. We did not part on good terms."

"I apologize for bringing him up," Aunt Diana said.

Victoria waved a long, elegant hand. "Don't trouble yourself."

In the span of a breath, the room fell silent, all eyes turning to the door, as it closed with a dull thud behind a short old woman.

She wore an old-fashioned black dress with a large brooch pinned to the high neck. Her hair was white and pulled in a tight knot at the back of her head. Most would only take in the sagging, wrinkled skin of her face, and the way her thin hand clutched the serpent-headed cane, but Alice noticed something else. The small blue eyes were sharp and alive beneath the hooded lids and her posture was erect, strong.

Though Victoria Veran was well known, Mrs. Frost was a legend.

She was already wealthy when she married the only son of a shipping magnate. Their whirlwind romance ended in tragedy five years into their marriage and, overnight, Mrs. Frost became one of the wealthiest women in the country. In the course of her lifetime, she expanded her late husband's holdings into oil, energy, precious metals, aviation, and government contracts. As of last year, Mrs. Frost had become one of the wealthiest people in the world.

And yet, with all that, Alice's admiration for her was muted, as other feelings took center stage.

More like fear and trepidation.

Glancing around at the women, who stood rooted to the spot, Alice couldn't help a little chuckle.

Looks like I'm not the only one.

"She does love to make an entrance," Victoria murmured.

"Oh yes," Aunt Diana said.

As if the comment was a magnet, pulling her gaze, Mrs. Frost's eyes latched onto Aunt Diana, and then slid to Alice, who expected her gaze to sweep the rest of the room. Instead, Mrs. Frost's thin lips twitched into a grin and, with determined, fast strides, she walked toward them.

Alice found herself wanting to flee.

"Diana." The woman's voice was gravely. "I see you have finally brought this niece of yours with you."

"Yes, Mrs. Frost, may I introduce—"

"Alice Seymour," Mrs. Frost finished.

The woman's eyes were so intense on her that Alice felt as if they could see straight through to her soul.

"Pleasure to meet you," Alice said, happy that her voice came out strong and not as a squeak.

Mrs. Frost cackled. "We shall see. Sit, everyone! I am hungry and it is time for tea."

Throughout the long, slow tea service, the ladies talked of whose child was at which university, who was engaged, who had become a grandmother, though she looked far too old. They included Aunt Diana as a mere nicety, their bored expressions showing how little they cared about what she had to say. No one spoke to Alice, choosing instead to give her sidelong glances at best, or at worst, bold stares of disdain.

It was just as well, Alice had very little to say to these women that they'd want to hear.

At last, Mrs. Frost rapped on the table, silencing the inane conversations.

"It is time to decide on our annual fundraiser for the Jet City Children's Home and the Park Side Clinic," Victoria said. "The renovation of the new space for the clinic is in need of finishing funds, is that right?"

"Yes," Aunt Diana said, "the new equipment is coming in at a higher cost than first estimated. The breakdown is explained in your folders."

No one besides Victoria opened their folders until Mrs. Frost did, and then the ladies only gave them a cursory glance. Alice looked around in disgust. She knew this was merely a way to make themselves look good to the society they so cherished, but if these women cared even a little for the people who greatly depended upon these places...

But, that would be asking too much.

Mrs. Frost's eyes shot up from the figures she had been studying, locking her gaze on Alice, who held it for a moment, as if daring the old woman to speak. But Mrs. Frost's gaze went back to the papers.

"A further delay would cause the residents to be without health services through the winter, is that right?" Mrs. Frost asked.

"Yes," Aunt Diana answered.

"Unacceptable. We must purchase the equipment as soon as possible."

The ladies around the table sipped their tea and

nodded, with the exception of Mrs. Grace, who said, "But if we just purchase the equipment without searching for less expensive options, well, it seems like a waste. Surely, these people can come into the city proper for their medical care for a few months while that's being done."

All eyes swung to Aunt Diana, who Alice had seen stiffen imperceptibly as Mrs. Grace talked. With a gracious smile, Aunt Diana said, "While I am a proponent of shopping around, the prices quoted here are the cheapest we could find to outfit the clinic as it must be. Besides, there is no way for the residents to make it into the city. Many do not have the extra money for taxi fare, and public transportation to that area has been cut in half by the current mayor."

"Well, something had to go if we were ever to restore our historical buildings," one of the ladies said.

Alice felt her shoulders tighten with the words, her smile disappearing.

"Of course," Aunt Diana nodded. "But it makes it more difficult for them to get into the city proper."

The words were out of Alice's mouth before she could stop herself. "Not to mention the fact that many can't afford the day off from work that going to the city might require."

All eyes landed on her, many of them hard with judgment. The only person that was smiling besides Victoria Veran, was Mrs. Frost, though Alice wasn't sure if it was friendly or not.

"Yes, Alice," Aunt Diana said, her voice holding a hint of caution. "That is also true."

"But that is not our concern," Mrs. Grace said. "We must think of what is best for all our charities, not just this one."

"And what other charities would you give this money to, Evelyn?" Mrs. Frost asked.

"There has been a desire among many of us to restore

our waterfront, which has been in a sorry state since the war."

Alice opened her mouth to speak and felt her aunt's hand on her knee give a squeeze of caution.

"The waterfront is in terrible disrepair," Victoria agreed. "But my husband, along with many of yours around this table, have been in talks for months to bring it to life once again. The formal agreements have yet to be signed, but it won't be long before they are, especially now that the science complex will be breaking ground so near to the waterfront. The city can't leave the rest of the buildings in such terrible disrepair while a beautiful new building goes up next to it. I think our money would be better spent elsewhere."

Some of the women nodded slowly, looking between Mrs. Grace and Mrs. Frost to see which way the wind would blow.

"I suppose that's true," Mrs. Grace said, her small mouth tight.

"Then, the new equipment will be purchased," Mrs. Frost said, her tone closing all further discussion. "Now to decide on the type of fundraiser we will have."

Alice endured another hour of talks about what kind of grand party these women wanted to throw. Her opinion of them plummeted further when they became more animated discussing a masked ball than they had when trying to help the poor of their city.

Finally, Mrs. Frost stood, calling the meeting to an end without a word.

"I would speak with you, Diana," Mrs. Frost said, giving Alice a quick, hard glance. "You can stay here."

Alice watched as her aunt's posture became ramrod straight and knew that the conversation wasn't going to be pleasant. She felt an illogical jolt of guilt, certain that any problem would have something to do with her. Squashing the temptation to march over to them and tell the old bat exactly what she thought of her, Alice decided instead to leave the room. Her new heels clicked on the shiny marble floors of the lobby as she made her way to the overstuffed, Italian leather chairs.

An older man, who had been seated nearby, got up and left his copy of the Jet City Chronicle on his chair. Alice waited a few minutes to see if he would return, and then snatched it up.

The front page held another story about the newest drug on the streets.

THREE MORE MURDERS IN WAREHOUSE DISTRICT
Police Baffled

She skimmed the first paragraph to get to the meat of the article, impatient to know what had been discovered.

Police are still trying to find the source of the newest lethal drug, which has caused a rash of violent murders across the city. Though no official name has been given to the hallucinogenic substance, most simply call it Fantasy. The recent increase of murders in the warehouse district has led some to believe that the main distribution center could be there. Though many of the instances of violence perpetrated by people while under the influence of the drug have been reported from every neighborhood in Jet City.

The police caution anyone who comes across someone who seems to be speaking to people that aren't there, or exhibiting violent behavior to get away from them immediately and contact the police. The users of this drug are unpredictable and have shown unusual strength and speed while under the influence of the substance.

Alice frowned and shook her head.

When she was living in Park Side, there was always someone trying to push the latest drug, and she saw plenty of people that didn't seem to be in their right minds. But this new drug was something altogether different. She knew that the newspapers weren't allowed to report the true scope of the drug's effects, the stories being too disturbing for the masses.

There'd been rumors that some became so lost in their visions that they bludgeoned their own families to death. In one case, the police found a man under the influence of the drug waving a lighted torch around and screaming about giant wasps. Others said the drug made you see your most cherished dreams fall apart around you, and that's why some killed themselves. Alice even heard someone at her college graduation say that his cousin had just been committed to a mental hospital from using the drug one time. His psyche was so destroyed that he was intermittently catatonic and violent.

From a purely business standpoint, it doesn't make any sense to have a drug that so effectively eliminates your repeat customers. Someone either has the wrong formula, and are using the general populace to test it, or they just don't care.

The thought that someone could be that uncaring chilled Alice. She decided it was time to divert her attention onto much more pleasant thoughts and scanned the paper until she found what she was looking for.

JET CITY VIGILANTES STRIKE AGAIN
By Logan Miller

• • •

Last night, the vigilantes known as American Steel and Shadow Master were seen saving a woman from a group of delinquents in the Carol Anne neighborhood.

The woman was walking home from her job at the local grocer, when three men approached her and attempted to steal her hand bag.

"I owe them my life!" the woman reports. "Who knows what those toughs would've done if they hadn't saved me!"

The delinquents were left unconscious when the police arrived, presumably by the brute force of American Steel. When they recovered consciousness, all three men reported stories of shadowy nightmares coming at them, a trademark of the Shadow Master.

"I don't know how he did it! Devils, demons I haven't seen since I was a kid, coming right out of the night!" says one of the men.

Though public opinion about the vigilantes is becoming more positive by the day, the Mayor and Police Commissioner have both issued statements condemning their actions and calling on all good citizens to report any sightings of the vigilantes.

When asked if there will be a reward offered for information leading to the capture of the vigilantes, the Mayor's office said it was under consideration.

"They should be giving them a medal," Alice said, flipping through the paper to see if there was any other news about them.

She had a passion for the vigilantes, and spent hours wondering who they were and how they did the things they did. Aunt Diana would sometimes speculate with her, and a light Alice had never seen before would shine from her large blue eyes. But then, Uncle Logan would change the subject, sometimes angrily, and Aunt Diana would leave the room.

Her aunt and uncle were equals in nearly everything, which had been a startling change when Alice first came to live with them. Uncle Logan never spoke ill of Aunt Diana's businesses or philanthropic endeavors. In fact, he was almost rabid in his support. Aunt Diana never complained about her uncle's sometimes bizarre schedule as an investigative reporter, even when he was gone for days at a time.

But, in this one thing, they were starkly divided and Alice wondered if it was the source of their recent fights.

A tall man with a nasal voice jolted her out of these thoughts. "Are you Miss Seymour?"

"Yes."

"There is a call for you at the front desk."

Alice frowned and went to the front desk, wondering who would be calling her here and why.

"Hello?"

"Alice? It's me, Rose."

Her frown quickly transformed into a smile. Rose was Gerald's daughter and had been her first friend in Jet City.

Being a bit on the shy side, and a genius when it came to anything scientific, Rose couldn't find a way to relate to the other kids on her block. In turn, Alice had felt too raw and unsure of everything to reach out to any of the kids on her street.

The first time they met, Rose had shown Alice a radio she had rebuilt that could get signals from another country. Instead of thinking her weird for not playing with dolls or tea sets, Alice had been hypnotized by her. After that, they practically lived at each other's houses after school and in the summer.

Even when Alice went to college and Rose was denied entry because of her skin color, the two of them found a way to see each other every week. Sometimes, Alice would sneak Science and Engineering textbooks off campus for Rose, who would devour them.

"How did you know I was here?" Alice asked, looking around.

"I looked through the door and saw you sitting there. I'm on a pay phone around the corner."

"Why are you calling me? Is everything all right?"

"Well, no. I'm supposed to meet with Mrs. Frost, but I'm nervous to walk in the front door. What if she didn't leave a note for me and they throw me out?"

"I could check."

"No, I'm gonna go around back, see if one of the maids will let me in. Could you tell her I'm coming? I'm late and I don't want her to think I'm not coming."

"Sure, but what are you meeting her for?"

There was a pause at the other end.

"Hello?"

"Yes, I'm here…" Rose's voice was quiet with hesitation. "It's a job, kind of a secret one."

Alice frowned. What on earth could Mrs. Frost need Rose for?

"Alright, I'll give her the message."

Rose sighed. "Thanks so much."

Really, the last thing Alice wanted to do was talk to Mrs. Frost, but she was terribly curious about what her aunt and the old bat were talking about, and now she was also curious about Mrs. Frost and Rose.

When she opened the door to the tea room, Aunt Diana was standing up from her chair.

"This conversation is over," Aunt Diana said, her face flushed and her tone hard. "My mind is set."

"Do you realize what you are doing?" Mrs. Frost's gravelly voice was cold with fury. "Denying the girl an opportunity like this?"

"It's not an opportunity, it's a burden!"

"They are often one and the same! And just because you could not shoulder it—"

Mrs. Frost's blue eyes suddenly caught sight of Alice and her jaw snapped shut.

Aunt Diana whipped around, her own eyes wide in surprise. She smoothed the front of her lavender tea dress and took several deep breaths.

"Thank you for your time, Mrs. Frost." Aunt Diana gathered up her and Alice's coat and walked quickly to Alice.

"Ready?" she asked.

Alice stared at her. "What was—"

"Put it out of your mind. Just a small disagreement."

She paused, and then looked sternly at Alice.

"Alice..." Aunt Diana's tone held a warning. "...put it out of your mind."

"Right. Yes. I will. It's just that Rose Allen has a message for Mrs. Frost."

"And what is that?" Mrs. Frost asked, walking toward them.

"She's coming from the back entrance and will arrive shortly."

Mrs. Frost huffed. "I left a note for her at the front desk."

"She was afraid of being turned away and embarrassed." Alice's blood rose and before she could stop herself she added, "And what made you think this hotel was the right place to meet with her? Why would you risk exposing her to people like this?"

"Alice—" Aunt Diana said.

"It is a good question." Mrs. Frost stepped closer to Alice, her gaze more appraising than angry. "And very boldly stated. If I cared to explain myself to you, I would."

"Mrs. Frost, good day," Aunt Diana said, practically shoving Alice ahead of her.

"Did I do something?" Alice asked, once they were in a taxi.

"No...Not really...it wasn't really...Alice, I truly do not want to talk about it."

"Alright, I'm sorry."

Aunt Diana sighed, pinching the bridge of her nose. It was what she did when a terrible headache was coming on.

"I can do inventory at the shop today, if you'd like," Alice said.

"Oh god! The inventory — I'd forgotten."

"It's alright, really. Why don't you go home and have a bath or a nap?"

Aunt Diana sighed again, a grateful smile on her lips.

"Thank you, Alice."

They were silent the short drive to Atlas Book Company. By the time they arrived, a light drizzle had started, driving any warmth from the autumn air.

"Please, don't be too late," Aunt Diana said.

"I won't."

"And remember, inventory doesn't mean reading."

Alice laughed. "I haven't done that since high school."

Aunt Diana gave her a tired, knowing smile as the taxi pulled away.

CHAPTER SEVEN

The heavy wooden door clicked shut behind her, shutting out the honking horns and busy lives of the people outside. From the first moment Alice stepped through the door of Atlas Book, twelve years ago, she'd felt transported to another world. The times her aunt and uncle couldn't find her in the house or with Rose, they had only to look in the book store. If she wasn't engrossed in a book, they'd find her curled up on the green and purple rug behind the counter, the scent of books and lemon furniture polish carrying her to dreamland.

Alice turned on the large yellow lamps hanging overhead and slipped out of the tortuous heels. She padded along on the shining wooden floors, slowly running her fingertips over the spines of the books stacked on the multiple floor-to-ceiling bookshelves. She took her time making her way to the small office in the back of the store, looking over every shelf to make sure nothing was out of place.

Finding a few children's books on the Science Fiction shelf, she snatched them up.

One was achingly familiar.

Opening the bright green cover with gold-embossed letters, Alice inhaled the smell of the last book her mother had read to her.

Not for the first time, since graduating college, Alice wondered what her mother would think of her life. Would she approve?

Her mother and Aunt Diana had parted badly, though Alice could never work out the particulars. And, although her mother had loved reading, she had never really approved of women having a life outside of the family — unless it was absolutely necessary, that is.

"Would you be proud of me?" she whispered.

A fat tear fell on the cover of the book. Alice shook herself and wiped it away. She'd be here very late if she didn't get busy.

———

Alice had trouble with her mind wandering to her aunt and Mrs. Frost, but still managed to get through most of the inventory. The rest she could do during shop hours tomorrow, since Mondays weren't very busy, as a rule.

As she turned off the lights, the wet plop of rain hitting the display window, punctuated by an occasional splash from a car driving through puddles, made Alice sigh. If she wore those new shoes, her feet would be soaked in minutes, but she hadn't thought to grab anything else.

She glanced at the small, dark back room next to the office and wondered if a pair of Aunt Diana's old galoshes might be in there.

More of an entryway to the loft, the back room was mostly taken up with a wide staircase, but also had a tiny broom closet, pegs and shelves for coats and shoes. There was a door just past the staircase that led to the alley.

She grinned when she found an old pair of galoshes, as

well as an wrinkled raincoat to protect her own coat, which was too nice to be subjected to the rain. The rain coat was too long, but Alice didn't mind, at least she'd be dry. Hoping she'd be able to get a taxi quickly, she dashed out the side door to the alley and fumbled with the keys.

"Damn it!" she said, as they clattered to the wet pavement.

The smell of garbage was pungent and the rain hammered the fire escape above her in a clatter of sound. It wasn't until she'd stood up from retrieving her keys, wiping strands of wet hair from her face, that she realized someone else was in the alley with her.

He was tall and broad-chested, and stepped slowly towards her. The lights from the street behind him kept his face in shadow, but Alice assumed from his posture that this wasn't going to be a friendly exchange.

Looking behind her, Alice saw two more men, both tall and lanky, closing in fast.

The raincoat would hinder her in a fight, so she shed it quickly, wishing the galoshes would come off as easily. The way the men were closing in forced her to have her back toward the building. Not the strongest position, but she would deal with it. She bent her legs, and brought her hands up, at the ready, her body humming with energy.

"How cute," the large man said. "You going to put up a fight?"

She couldn't help smiling.

The man lunged for her. Using his own momentum, Alice forced him into the wall behind her, head first. She kicked him in the face, and then turned to the other two men. They stared at her for a moment, which allowed her to move away from the wall, her back now to the street.

Dodging a punch, she sent one of her own into the second man's gut, while his partner circled around behind her and grabbed her from behind, his breath hot on her cheek. Stepping quickly to the side, Alice tossed him over her hip, then punched him in the nose. Blood splattered over her hand, the feel of bone meeting bone vibrating up her arm.

Ignoring the sticky blood between her fingers, Alice punched him again before his partner knocked her to the ground. She tasted blood in her mouth and spat it out. Jumping up, she raised her fists, ready to defend herself again.

But no attack came.

Instead there was a sound, like the whimpering of a child, followed by the scuffling of feet running.

"You should run, too," came a voice from the shadows.

She jumped and looked around.

"You won't see me," said the voice again.

"Why not?" She began backing toward the door to the shop. If she couldn't see this person, she couldn't fight him. And if she couldn't fight him, Alice needed to have a way to escape.

"Because, I don't want you to."

"Why not?"

"You know any other questions?" said a different voice behind her.

Alice yelped and collided into something solid and looked up to see a very tall man. Light from the street glinted off his blond hair and the silver gray of his shirt — and the gray mask that surrounded his eyes.

Suddenly, her entire world stood still. Was this...?

"American Steel?"

His full lips curved into a sideways grin. "Maybe."

"I-I just...I...um..."

"My friend is right. You should run."

"There's no one left, what's the rush?"

"There could be more coming," said the disembodied voice.

"Then, I'll stay and—"

"No...you won't," said Steel.

The excitement that made her heart pound was lessened considerably by his words and her cheeks flushed with anger.

"Who are you to tell me what to do?"

Steel stared at her, his smile widening. "No one."

She held his look a little longer and glanced around the darkness. There was nothing except garbage cans, the sound of cars on the wet streets, and the wet steps of the occasional passer-by.

Alice was shocked that no one had stopped to see what the commotion was about, but was also grateful.

Would the vigilantes have shown up if a civilian had tried to come to my aid?

"It does you no good to stand in the rain," said the disembodied voice.

"What about you, Shadow Master?" she asked.

Steel chuckled. "You did pretty well tonight. But maybe, in the future, try and stay out of trouble?"

He turned to leave and Alice felt her heart jump. Meeting them was what she'd been dreaming about for the past year. Was she just going to let him walk away?

"Why would I do that?" she asked, stepping toward him.

He stopped and looked over his shoulder.

"I took care of those guys before you arrived. I can handle myself. Just like you."

"Trust me, you're nothing like me," he said.

The desire she'd had as a child to be a hero had changed, eventually becoming a nagging disquiet in the back of her mind. Now, looking at someone, who was doing exactly what she'd dreamed of so long ago, was like having a light turn on and that long-buried desire burst from its confines.

She took a deep breath. "I could do this. What you do, I mean, or something like it. I'm smart, and I—"

"No."

"That's it? Just 'no'?"

"Goodbye."

With that, Steel jumped several feet into the air and grabbed a nearby fire escape. In seconds, he was on the roof and gone.

She stared in shock after him.

"Am I going crazy?" she looked around. "What?… How?"

Her mind tried to find an explanation, but there wasn't one; at least, not one that made any logical or scientific sense.

Rumors running through the streets about the vigilantes insisted that they had…powers. Alice had always rolled her eyes at such ideas, assuming criminals just didn't want others to think they were weak for being apprehended so easily.

But now…?

Alice shook her head.

"C'mon now. You're not a kid anymore. It's just…he's really…strong…"

———

Once the heat of the fight and her encounter with the vigilantes subsided, Alice felt chilled by her drenched clothes and hair. The cabbie took one look at her and offered to take her to the hospital free of charge.

"No, thanks, 1630 Summers Drive, please."

He stared at her a moment longer, then shrugged and pulled away from the curb.

Alice wondered just how bad she looked and rubbed the side of her face, wincing as she felt the beginning of a bruise where one of the men had hit her. Then she glanced at her knuckles, faint bruises already appearing, the remnants of blood drying on her skin. Suddenly, anywhere but home seemed like a good idea, but she also knew that her aunt and uncle would worry if she missed dinner. Besides, where could she go looking like this?

More importantly though: How did she explain all this?

She leaned back against the headrest and closed her eyes, trying to calm herself before facing her aunt and uncle. Questions whirled in her mind, refusing to be ignored.

Why was she attacked? They hadn't asked for money and didn't seem to want sex. It felt like they had wanted her, specifically — but why? Did it have something to do with the fights her uncle and aunt had been having? And if so, what could possibly be happening that would make someone do this?

Far too soon, the cabbie pulled up at the white and blue rambler. Her uncle's red '55 Ford Squire was sitting outside; his vintage motorcycle a ghostly lump in the yard under its protective tarp. The roses her aunt obsessively tended trembled as the rain hit them, and a shadow paced along the curtain in the study.

She hesitated, feeling as nervous as the day she had to tell her uncle that she'd broken his National Journalism award.

"You okay, Miss?" the cabbie asked.

She forced a smile. "Yep, thanks."

The galoshes slapped on the walk as she ran to the porch and eased the door open. Expecting someone to come running to her, Alice waited. When no one came, she thought maybe she'd be able to sneak to her room and tidy up before facing their barrage of questions, but the galoshes betrayed her, slipping out of her hands and landing with a thud on the hardwood floor. The door to the study flew open and her uncle stared at her, his curly gray hair wild around his head.

"What the hell happened to you?"

Alice opened her mouth to speak when Aunt Diana came rushing around the corner.

"Good God!" she said.

"I'm fine," Alice said, stepping away from their reaching hands.

"Fine!" Aunt Diana said, touching the bruise on Alice's cheek.

"Who did this?" Uncle Logan asked, his brown eyes flashing behind his glasses.

Alice took a deep, bracing breath. "Three men attacked me while I was locking up the shop."

"What?!" Aunt Diana exclaimed, blue eyes wide.

"Son of a—"

"I handled it! Believe me, they look worse."

"Do you think that's what matters here?" Aunt Diana said.

"I'm calling Detective Garrick," Uncle Logan said.

"No!" Alice said.

He stopped in his tracks. "Why not, you were attacked!"

"Yes..." She took another deep breath. "And I want to know why."

Uncle Logan held her gaze, and then folded his arms. "So do I."

Aunt Diana's look was pointed. "Logan—"

"Don't, Diana,"

"What is going on?" Alice said, her voice raised more than she'd intended. "And don't say 'nothing', because I'm guessing that's not true."

Uncle Logan removed his glasses and cleaned them with the hem of his untucked shirt.

"There *is* something, but it's nothing for you to be concerned with."

"For God's sake, Logan! She's not a child!"

"She's not you, either!" he snapped.

Alice felt an old, forgotten fear stir her in her belly and tried to push it away. Her aunt and uncle were nothing at all like her father and mother. Still, the sight of them yelling at each other wasn't easy for her.

"That's not what I'm saying. If this is putting her in danger, she deserves to know!" Aunt Diana's hands clenched into fists at her side.

"Not if I quit the story." Uncle Logan took a step toward Aunt Diana, his voice taking on a growl.

"You can't. The work you're doing—"

"Doesn't matter, if it puts people I love in danger!"

"What story?" Alice asked.

Their gazes swung to her, as if they'd forgotten she was there.

She quickly thought through what topics Uncle Logan had been especially fired up about in the last few months, and easily narrowed it down.

"The murders at the warehouse," she said, "they're more than they appear, aren't they?"

Uncle Logan sighed. "Sometimes, you're too damn smart."

Alice couldn't help smiling.

"To anger someone like this, we'd have to be talking about a crime syndicate, wouldn't we?"

"It doesn't matter, because I'm done."

"Aunt Diana's right, you can't quit. You must be getting close to something for them to do this."

"Someone else—" Uncle Logan began.

"Won't do as good of a job," Aunt Diana said.

"And besides," Alice said, squaring her shoulders, "I want in."

They stared at her.

"What?" Uncle Logan asked.

"I want to help."

Instead of the resounding 'no' that Alice was prepared for, Uncle Logan turned to Aunt Diana, fixing her with a sad stare. But Diana didn't look at him. Instead, she fidgeted with her locket and stared at the floor. It was as if he were blaming Aunt Diana for something, but Alice couldn't see what.

"It's time for dinner," Aunt Diana said at last, walking back to the kitchen.

"That's it?" Alice asked after Aunt Diana was out of sight.

"You should change out of those wet clothes before you catch a cold," Uncle Logan suggested, turning back to his study.

"Wait! You're just going to act like nothing happened now?"

"You heard your aunt, dinner is—"

"I'll do it anyway," she said, marching toward him. "I'll go out and investigate, and I'll find out who's behind this and you can't stop me. You know that."

He scrubbed a hand through his frizzy hair and sighed out a curse word. Alice waited for more, but when nothing came, she turned on her heel and ran to her room.

It wasn't until she'd changed out of her ruined dress that Alice realized she never got around to mentioning the vigilantes.

CHAPTER EIGHT

Frost glistened on the grass in the front yard and the sun was barely above the horizon when Alice left the next morning. By the time she reached the trolley, her fingers were red from the cold. She made a mental note to get her wool mittens out of the garage.

When she smiled at the person she took a seat beside her, her face ached, a not-so-gentle reminder of her skirmish last night. Some careful application of makeup had covered the impressive bruise on her jaw, which had given Alice an uncomfortable image of her own mother covering the evidence of assault. She comforted herself with the knowledge that this bruise wasn't the result of being anyone's victim. No, this was won in defense of herself, and she'd done much worse to the one who had dared lay a hand on her.

Or, she would have, if Shadow Master hadn't scared him away.

And then there was American Steel. She couldn't get the image of him jumping three stories onto a fire escape out of her head. Every possible explanation had been tossed aside at least twice. She was left with the feeling that something bigger was going on with the vigilantes. Something that defied logic.

As Rose often told her, she needed more data. That was why she'd left so early. Maybe, if she looked hard enough, she could kill two birds with one stone: find out more about the crime syndicate and see if anyone else had any theories about the vigilantes.

It would be at least three hours before Atlas Books should open and Alice needed every minute, if she was going to figure out how to help her uncle. Her pride still stung as she remembered the way she was dismissed. An argument would have at least shown something from them, but to be ignored! That was worse and only made Alice more determined to prove herself.

The loft above Atlas Books had once held six boxes stuffed with scrap books, filled to the brim with her uncle's articles, something her aunt had started doing when he'd won the Journalism award. Most of the boxes had been taken home, but Alice knew the most recent ones hadn't made it there yet and were in the back entryway.

Plopping down on the flowery rug in the children's reading area, with a thick note pad and pens, she began with the oldest articles in the box, about nine months back.

The articles on vigilantes she ignored for now, and focused on the others. The articles on the rise of crime in Jet City looked straight forward enough, but Uncle Logan had also written several editorials on the police force and District Attorney's focus on the vigilantes, instead of the real criminals. He never out right said, "crime syndicate", but the more Alice read, the more clear it was that he was talking about it in nearly every article.

Making a list of all the areas referenced, she put check marks next to each, depending on how often they were mentioned. Something tickled the back of her mind and she looked at the vigilante articles. They had begun with stopping small crimes, but as the months went on, they began tackling tougher criminals, even some who had eluded the police for years.

She then carefully re-read the editorials and articles Uncle Logan had written in the past three months and found that he had left subtle clues as to what he'd discovered about the crime syndicate. A few weeks after each article was published, the vigilantes would produce an impressive catch, usually related to one of Uncle Logan's articles.

Alice laughed.

He's working with them. Or at least giving them help. I wonder if he knows who they are? And if he does, how can I get him to tell me?

Another thought shot through her mind.

What if he'd asked them to watch me? Perhaps mentioned that he was a target of the syndicate? How weak does he think I am though, that I would need that?

But then, she thought of the opportunity having the vigilantes watch her afforded. If she could catch them when they were watching her, then maybe she could turn the tables and find a way to follow them. This would give her the chance to see if they did indeed have some sort of enhanced abilities. Plus, it would give her more information about the syndicate.

The morning paper smacked against the shop window, jarring her thoughts.

Or, maybe The Chronicle will tell me.

Flinging the doors open, she was startled to see a tall lanky man waiting outside the shop. After last night, her immediate response was to clench her fists, in case one of the men had come back for a second round.

But then, his thin lips smiled and he ducked his head shyly.

"We aren't open yet," Alice said, studying him.

"Oh, I can come back." His voice was hesitant and soft.

"Half an hour?" she offered.

He looked up, large brown eyes crinkling around the edges as his smile widened. "I'll do that."

She watched him walk away, his shoulders slumped a little in his trench coat. Something about him made her heart race, as if she should know him. But no matter how she tried, Alice couldn't place him.

He glanced back once, a look of tenderness on his long face. When he realized she saw him, he turned back so fast that he collided with a woman. He apologized, picking up the bag he'd knocked from her hands. The woman scowled at him, though Alice could tell the man was truly embarrassed and trying to help.

Something about the way he brushed the hair back from his face, the flustered smile...

He almost reminds me of—

"Are you open?" asked the woman he'd collided with.

"Uh, no, not yet. Half-hour."

The woman sighed. "Very well."

When Alice looked up, the man had disappeared. She frowned, hoping he would indeed be back.

He wasn't back in a half-hour, or an hour. The day passed in a slow trickle of customers, none of them the tall stranger. Alice tried to focus on the last of the inventory, but her mind kept wandering to that hauntingly familiar face.

Alice was in the back entryway, putting the box of articles away, when she heard the bell on the door chime. It was almost closing time and she was tempted to tell the customer to come back tomorrow, until she saw who it was.

His back was to her, as he looked at a book from the children's section.

When she'd seen him that morning, she hadn't noticed how broad his shoulders were, or the thickness of his dark hair. The hands slowly turning the pages of the book were a little bony, but elegant, with long fingers, looking as if they might belong to an artist or doctor.

She didn't want him to catch her spying on him, so she made sure her shoes clicked on the polished wood floors as she came around the corner.

He whipped around as though he'd been caught doing something wrong, and then smiled the same awkward smile as before, his brown eyes locking on hers.

Now, she was more sure than ever that she knew him.

"You've come back," she said.

"I'm sorry I was so late. I had a job interview."

"How'd it go?"

"Surprisingly good."

She laughed. "You can't be all that hopeless."

"Depends."

His long fingers played nervously with the pages of the book he was holding. She caught her breath as she saw the title: *Alice in Wonderland*. She looked at his face again, the high cheek bones and Greek nose that would've looked overly large on someone younger...

Taking a deep, shaking breath, she said, "Why's a raven—"

The door opened again, interrupting her.

Alice was ready to tell this latest intruder that they were closed, but the words froze on her lips.

Standing in the doorway was the single most beautiful man Alice had ever seen.

His head, topped with golden hair, seemed to tower over Alice. Deep set, navy-blue eyes took quick stock of her curvy figure before settling on her face. A crooked smile fixed on his full mouth. He moved toward her as Alice tried so very hard to make her lips form words, but it was impossible. If she looked like a fish caught in a net, this new stranger didn't seem to notice. He leaned on a nearby shelf, so close that Alice could feel the heat coming off his well-muscled body.

"Hi," he said.

Her smile felt too wide, but she couldn't stop herself.

"I was just looking for my friend here." He gestured to the first stranger. "And I guess I found something else."

A breathy laugh escaped her lips. "Uh...and what was that?"

He looked at the first stranger in confusion.

"She hasn't guessed it?"

The first one shook his head.

Any lust she may have felt evaporated like ice on a hot day. The events of the previous night were still alive and well in her memory. Alice wasn't going to wait for the attack this time.

The tall stranger was leaning toward her, so she drove the heel of her palm into his nose. Taking advantage of his shock, she swept his legs out from under him and forced her forearm on his throat.

"Don't move or I'll crush his throat!" she demanded of the first stranger.

The tall stranger's eyes were huge with shock, blood pouring from his nose.

"What the hell!"

"You think you can get the jump on me in my store! You should've learned from your friends last night that I'm not an easy catch!"

"Alice!" said the first stranger.

"You stay back!"

"It's not what you think," he said.

"We aren't here to hurt you," the other one croaked.

Suddenly, she realized the first stranger had used her name.

"How did you know my name?"

"Because...oh, hell!"

Surprisingly strong hands pulled her off the gorgeous stranger she had pinned to the floor. At first, she felt terror and anger warring inside of her, but after a moment, it became muted and her pulse slowed. Warm breath touched her cheek like a feather.

"It's Marco and Lionel," said the first stranger quietly.

It was like the first time someone had thrown her to the mat, that sensation of being slammed down to earth with such force all the air is forced out of your lungs, and the only thing you feel is mind-numbing shock.

Lionel jumped to his feet, holding his nose, which had stopped bleeding.

She backed up, eyes huge. All the times she had imagined what she would do if she ever saw them again. Her reaction now wasn't at all what she'd thought it would be.

At first, she started to cry, big heaving sobs that made as little sense to her as they seemed to make to them. Then she saw the confusion on their faces, the way they seemed to want to reach out to her, but didn't know if they should. She took in Lionel's bruised nose and Marco's look of pure confusion.

And suddenly, the whole thing seemed hilarious. Sobs became gut-wrenching bellows of laughter.

She took in great gulps of air, trying to stop her body from shaking, but all she did was laugh more.

"I-I thought you—you were—"

"Someone bad, obviously," Lionel said, his voice grumpy as he touched his nose.

"Oh! Oh, my God! I'm sorry," she said, walking to him.

Lionel flinched back and Marco gave a chuckle.

"It's not funny," Lionel said.

"A girl half your size breaks your nose. It's a little funny."

The bubbles of laughter were lessening, and Alice was at last able to catch her breath, small giggles escaping as she looked at the two of them.

"I can't believe it's you," she said, touching Marco's long face.

"I can't believe you broke his nose," Marcos grinned.

"Me, either," Lionel said.

"I'm so sorry." Alice touched Lionel on the shoulder. The hard, impressive muscles under her small hand made her stomach leap. A flush rose to her already red cheeks and she turned away before Lionel could see anything but embarrassment on her face.

"I feel sorry for whoever you thought we were," Lionel said. "Who was it, anyway?"

"Long story."

"You have dinner plans?" Marco asked. "You could tell us."

She looked at them, so many feelings careening through her body, but the strongest among them was the need to be with them. No matter what.

"Okay. Let me lock up."

Lionel nodded, and Alice could swear that his nose wasn't as swollen as it had been a minute before. But, she shrugged it off as a trick of the light.

Alice stared at the small sign above the door to Solomon's Lounge. She'd heard of it, of course. Everyone in Jet City knew of the famous speakeasy that had become a haven for jazz musicians and beat poets alike.

"You need a password to get into Solomon's," she said, eyeing her friends.

Lionel smiled. "So you do..."

"He loves this part," Marco whispered, walking down the stairs from the sidewalk to a red door.

"Is it just me, or is his nose not so bad?" Alice asked.

Marco just shrugged.

A burly, bald man glared through a window in the door at Lionel, who whispered something to him. The bouncer nodded and opened the door wide for them to enter.

"Down the rabbit hole we go," said Alice, a bounce in her step.

They walked down a narrow hall and through another door that had an eye of Horus painted on it.

The low thump of a bass was the first thing Alice heard, followed by the sultry strains of a saxophone. The lights were low with a strange bluish quality. They stepped onto thick, dark red carpet that spread out to walls and booths of cherry wood, old and scratched in places, but still lustrous. Blue velvet adorned the backs of the booths, which held the most bizarre mix of people Alice had ever seen.

In the first booth were two older men in suits, with women half their age draped over their arms as they sipped champagne. Next to them were six young people, around Alice's age, all dressed in tight black pants or skirts. One even sported a beret and sunglasses.

How does he see?

Cigarette smoke rose all around her like clouds from a genie's lamp, and indeed she felt transported into the pages of a book, as Lionel guided her around the circular room. They found a table with a side view of the stage, which was in the very center of the room.

As Alice took off her coat, a gorgeous Asian woman dressed in a clinging black and red dress stepped onto the stage. Her voice was soft, yet sure, as she sang an old love song.

She wanted to appear mature and cultured in front of Lionel, but Alice couldn't help an excited giggle.

"So? What do you think?" Lionel asked.

"It's amazing! How did you get a password for this place?"

"Well, you see...it's funny what having a man like Jason James for a stepfather can do for you — even if you do think he's a jerk."

"Not to mention that they like you." Marco nodded to a curvy blond, who was walking toward them.

"Long time, Lionel," her voice was low, like her décolletage.

Lionel leaned back in his chair as his navy-blue eyes raked up and down her body. "It has been, hasn't it, Doris?"

"You promised to call." A long finger pushed into Lionel's firm chest. "And you didn't."

"I'm sorry, baby, extenuating circumstances."

Doris' eyes flitted to Alice and turned cold. "I bet."

"How about a second chance?"

Her lips pursed for an instant, before spreading in wide grin. "Alright. Tomorrow? Eight o'clock?"

"I'll be here."

"You better. 'Night, Marco." And without a glance at either Alice or Marco, Doris sauntered away.

A sour taste coated Alice's tongue when she saw the lusty glint in Lionel's eyes.

"You hungry?" Marco asked her, a hint of sympathy in his voice.

Alice smiled. "Famished. I don't think they serve much food here though."

"They do for me," said Lionel, and waving down a short man, he began ordering half-a-dozen plates of food.

"I'm not that hungry."

"Don't worry, he'll eat what you don't," Marco said.

Alice laughed. "I remember how he'd eat half a pan of

your mother's lasagna, and then pie and milk. How is your mother? I think of her sometimes."

Marco shifted in the booth, eyes on his folded hands. "Oh, uh...she died about a year after you moved."

"Marco...I'm so sorry."

He nodded. "It was sudden."

Alice squeezed Marco's hand, a bone-deep sadness settling in her heart. "She was such a sweet woman. I'm so sorry I wasn't there."

"Thank you."

"What about your father? Is he still living in the house or..."

"Dad never really got over it. We went to Metro City to see mom's family after she died, and we were going to live there, but...I don't know, he changed his mind, and we moved to a small town in the Midwest, for some reason. But he was never the same. And...well, about a year after I graduated high school, he died, too."

Alice thought of several things to say, but all of them felt so empty. In the end, she put her arm around Marco's broad shoulders and hugged him. When she looked up, his olive skin was flushed and he ducked his head to keep from meeting her eyes. She wondered if she'd embarrassed him, though Marco had never minded physical affection before.

But then, his thin lips twitched with the hint of a smile, and Alice knew it was alright.

"What are you drinking?" Lionel asked.

"Gin and tonic," Marco said.

"Just club soda," Alice said.

Lionel scoffed. "What? No, it's on me. How about champagne?"

Alice shook her head. "No, really, I...I don't really like it."

Lionel stared at her for a moment, then nodded and said, "Okay, sure."

He ordered the drinks and an uncomfortable silence settled around them, for which Alice felt responsible. In the span of a few minutes, she'd opened a terrible memory for Marco and made Lionel uncomfortable, because she didn't drink.

When she looked up at Lionel to apologize, she noticed that his nose definitely looked better. There was virtually no swelling now, and the bruised skin had lightened to a yellow-green. She was about to ask about it when the drinks arrived.

"So," Lionel said, "you don't drink?"

Alice sighed. "No, I don't. I tried it, I don't like it." She hoped her tone would indicate that she really didn't want to talk about it, but Lionel wouldn't be put off.

"Not ever? I mean, not even to celebrate meeting long lost friends?"

She shook her head.

"Maybe you haven't tried the right drink."

"Lionel..." Marco's voice held a hint of warning.

"I don't want to," Alice felt her body tensing.

"Why not? I mean it's just strange. Everyone drinks."

"Well, not me." She was trying to sound firm, but it came out snappish.

"Maybe we should drop it, it's not that important," Marco said.

"I'm sorry, I just think it's a little weird."

"Do you remember my dad, Lionel? The one who'd drink, and then beat my mother? Well, it's strange, but I just don't care to be like him, okay?"

Lionel looked down at his drink and Marco stared up at the ceiling.

"Excuse me," she said, practically shoving Marco out in her haste to leave the table. "I need to...go."

"Wait," Lionel grabbed her arm as she passed him. "I'm sorry, I didn't think."

"No, you didn't. Are you always this self-involved?"

A look of shock crossed his beautiful features.

Alice sighed. "I'm sorry. You're pushy, and I speak before I think. We'd make quite a pair...of friends, pair of friends I mean."

Lionel chuckled. "Yeah, we will."

"I just...I didn't like the kind of drunk I was, the few times I tried it. And I just decided it was best to stay away from it, in case...well, in case I'm anything like him."

Lionel's eyes held hers and Alice felt like she was the only one in the smoke-filled room.

"I know I haven't seen you in twelve years, but I doubt you're anything like him."

She smiled, her body relaxing into a pleasant warmth as Lionel's thumb slowly rubbed her arm.

"Please, sit down?" he asked.

"Alright..."

"Should we toast?" Marco asked, once Alice was once again seated between them.

"To old friends," Lionel said.

The love song ended and their glasses clinked. As the quick beat of a new song began, Alice felt her spirits rise. She had never thought she would see Lionel and Marco again. Despite her best intentions, she'd lost track of them soon after moving to Jet City. But now, here they were, the three of them, sitting in Solomon's Lounge, laughing and talking as if no time had passed.

"How did you two find me?" she asked, once the food arrived.

Lionel tucked in immediately, his cheeks bulging with spaghetti.

"I saw you earlier, remember?" Marco said.

"Yeah, but was that an accident, I mean did you know my aunt owned that shop?"

"I was just walking around before my interview and

there you were." Marco's eyes settled on her, warm with happiness.

Alice shook her head. "That seems..." *A little too convenient.*

"I know," Lionel said, around the pasta in his mouth, "what are the chances?"

"But then, how did *you* know? You showed up there, too."

Lionel washed his food down with a generous swallow of whiskey. "I had lunch with Marco and he told me."

She looked at Marco, who seemed too focused on his plate of food.

"But, why didn't you tell me who you were when you saw me this morning?"

"I just...well, I didn't know if it would be strange seeing me there after all this time."

Alice frowned as she took a bite of steak and potatoes. It had been a long time since she'd talked with Marco, but she could still tell when something was wrong. And though he may not be lying to her completely, he was definitely leaving something out.

What is he keeping from me? And why?

"What job was the interview for?" she asked.

Marco smiled. "The Jet City Chronicle was looking for a photographer."

"And you got the job?"

He nodded. "I'm at the bottom of the list, and it's practically no pay, but I'm a photographer."

"I don't get the appeal," Lionel mumbled through a mouthful of bread.

"Earning a living, or taking pictures?" Marco asked.

"Both."

"Not everyone can afford to lay around all day and date socialites."

Lionel shrugged. "Only the fortunate ones, I guess."

Marco shook his head and laughed.

"So, you don't have a job?" Alice asked Lionel.

"I have an agreement with my stepfather. He pays me to stay away from him and my mother. What I'm more interested in is why you have a degree in business."

Alice opened her mouth to answer and closed it. "I never told you I had a degree in business."

The corners of his mouth froze in a tight smile.

"You mentioned college in the cab before we got here," Marco said.

"Yeah, and I just figured, you know, with the book store and everything."

Alice studied them both as they ate. Something itched at the back of her mind, like a puzzle piece you swear you just saw, but now can't find.

"How long have you two been in Jet City?" she asked.

Lionel shrugged, and was about to answer, when Marco cut him off. "Awhile, few months."

"Just a few months?"

"Yep," Lionel said.

"How many is a few?"

"What does it matter?" Lionel asked.

"Why won't you say?"

"Is something wrong?" Marco asked.

Alice focused on her plate, trying to figure out what it was that made her feel as if they were talking around something very important. But nothing came to mind.

"No..." She smiled. "Sorry, I just...after last night, I'm a little jumpy."

"That's right," Lionel said, accepting another whiskey on the rocks from the waiter. "You were going to tell us why you broke my nose."

"Except," she reached out to touch Lionel's nose, "I don't think I did. It barely looks hurt at all."

Lionel leaned back and gave a nervous chuckle. "I've

always been a fast healer. Now, this fight. What happened?"

"I was just closing up when these men came at me."

"And what did you do?" Marco asked.

Alice smiled and launched into her tale, not leaving a moment of the fight out, except the part where the vigilantes showed up. Something told her to let that go. Who would believe her anyway?

Telling the story was almost as exhilarating as the actual fight. By the time she was done, Alice was practically bouncing up and down in the booth from excitement.

"That sounds incredibly dangerous." Lionel frowned.

"You could've gotten really hurt," Marco said.

"But, I didn't. I'm not a weak little girl anymore. I've worked very hard to make sure that I won't ever be that way again. The first time someone tried to make me vulnerable, I was the one who was left standing, not them."

"Not without help though," Lionel said.

Alice stared at him. "How do you know that?"

"What?"

"That I had help? I didn't say—"

"Yeah, you did."

Her stomach dropped. "No...I didn't."

She really studied Lionel then. Ignoring the devastating good looks, she imagined him with a mask, the yellow light of street lamp shining behind him.

American Steel was very tall and broad-shouldered, and his voice may have been only a little lower than Lionel's.

"Are you...?"

"Alice—" Marco's voice was low with apology.

"Marco..." Lionel's voice held threat and fear.

"She's too smart to not know. And it's not like you were doing very good at keeping it from her," Marco countered.

"Now you're just confirming it!"

"And if you'd just let me answer some of her questions, maybe she wouldn't have figured it out," added Marco.

"So, it's my fault?" Lionel dropped his chunk of garlic bread on his plate.

"Yes, actually."

Alice felt her world tilt and contract all at once. The whole night made sense now. Why they showed up the day after she was attacked, the things they shouldn't know, but did. And as her mind recalled the articles she'd combed through, just that morning, she realized something that made her jaw clench with anger.

"You haven't been here a few months, you've been here almost a year. A year and you never bothered to find me. But you found my uncle, and — let me out — now!"

"Alice, wait." Lionel grabbed her arm, but she jerked it free.

"Don't! Just don't. I thought you'd come to me because you wanted to pick up our friendship, but you're just keeping an eye on me for Uncle Logan."

"No, well, yes, but that's—"

Marco cut in. "What Lionel's trying to say is that we wanted to find you before now, but we couldn't."

"Why not?"

"Because we promised your uncle we wouldn't," Marco said.

"And now he's going to kill us." Lionel drained his whiskey.

"He told you to stay away from me?"

Marco nodded.

The low flame of anger in her belly burst to life. "Let me out."

"Look, we're sorry," Lionel said.

"Marco move!"

"What are you going to do?" Marco asked.

"I'm going to find my uncle and give him a piece of my mind."

She shoved Marco's side, but he didn't move.

"Maybe you should calm down first."

"Get. Out. Now."

Alice held Marco's gaze without flinching. She'd have slammed him into the table if that wouldn't have gotten them all into trouble.

Finally, he moved.

"We're coming with you," he said, putting his coat on.

"No."

"Yes, or you don't go at all," Lionel said.

She stared at them, seeing that they were as determined as she was.

"Fine."

Her legs were short, but she kept a fast pace as they sped through the red door, up the steps, and out onto the sidewalk.

It had rained while they were inside, leaving the streets with a slippery wet sheen. A brisk wind toyed with the curls of her dark, bobbed hair and her heels beat out a harsh staccato as she marched along.

"Should we get a taxi?" Lionel asked.

"No, I need to walk."

It was no trouble for them to keep up with her, and Alice felt annoyed with herself that she was glad they were there. Even in the midst of her anger and hurt, she didn't want the evening to end just yet.

They were only a few blocks from the restaurant when Marco stopped, his head cocked like a dog that had caught a peculiar sound.

"What is it?" Lionel asked.

The street light behind Marco cast his face in a strange shadow. Though she was still angry, Alice felt as if someone had raked a cold finger down the length of her spine.

Did Marco's eyes go black for a moment? Like that fight with the Dorn brothers when we were kids...I thought I'd imagined that.

Alice stepped toward him, but Lionel darted between them, blocking her view of Marco.

"I thought...I heard something," Marco said, his voice distant, as if he were deep in thought.

"Where?"

Marco pointed a little way up the street. "Down that alley."

Lionel's face became tense. He glanced from Alice to where Marco had pointed.

"I can take care of myself," she said.

"Stay here." Lionel's voice was firm.

"No. You saw what I did to those men last night."

"And you've got the bruises to prove it."

"I'm still standing."

Lionel swore under his breath and took a domino mask out of his coat pocket. "Fine. But if I tell you to run, you damn well better run."

Alice nodded and slipped out of her heels, a small shiver going up her legs at the contact with the cold wet cement. As she followed them to the alley, she realized her knee-length skirt wouldn't allow her to kick.

"Lionel, rip this for me."

He looked confused, until she pointed at her skirt. Despite the fact that they were about to enter a potentially dangerous situation, Lionel smirked at her.

"I so rarely hear a woman say that to me."

She rolled her eyes. "Just a little above the knee."

He knelt and easily ripped the fabric. She expected him to stand up right away, but he paused.

"You know who I am, don't you? Not just an idea, but, you know."

Alice nodded.

Lionel sighed and stood up. "Your uncle is really going to kill us."

They were still a few feet away from the alley when Alice heard the wet slapping sounds and muffled gasps of a fight. Her heart sped up and despite the cold, her body felt on fire. She shed her coat, dropping it next to the alley wall Lionel and Marco were pressed against.

Marco closed his eyes, wrinkles appearing over his nose, as he concentrated.

"What are you doing?" Alice whispered. "Are you nervous?"

His eyes flew open and he stared at her.

It was eerie, the familiarity of it. Another day flashed through her mind, another place where someone was in trouble, and Marco had seemed to know it.

"What is it?" she asked.

"Alice—"

Moving easily around Lionel's out-stretched hand, Alice ran into the alley.

There were five men of various sizes, all fighting one person.

Aunt Diana's oval face shone with blood and sweat. Alice had seen her spar in class hundreds of times, but what she saw now made Alice realize that she had only glimpsed a pale imitation of what Aunt Diana could actually do. Her body moved so quickly, yet gracefully, as if she were dancing with her opponents, instead of inflicting bodily harm on them. Two collapsed against the dingy brick walls on either side of the alley. A third landed a brutal kick to Aunt Diana's abdomen, while the fourth easily spun around her back and—

"No!" Alice screamed, seeing the flash of a blade too late.

CHAPTER NINE

Aunt Diana's blue eyes widened in shock, her body arching up as the blade was thrust into her back. The man's arm came around Aunt Diana's neck and held her in place as he stabbed her once again, in the chest this time. Even in the low light, Alice could see the dark red pour out over her aunt's white blouse, just before she crumpled to the wet dirty cement.

All this happened in a few breaths. But to Alice, it had taken a long while to unfold, her mind stunned into uselessness.

She felt Lionel and Marco run past, the first sounds of their assault a distant thing.

The nearest attacker, a man with a pock-marked face and greasy hair, turned his attention to her and sneered.

"Hello, lovely."

The words shattered the haze on her mind and everything became alive. The feel of the grime under her feet, the sour smell of the man as he sauntered to her. The blood pumping to every muscle — and something Alice had never felt before — pure, white-hot fury burning in her belly, bringing the fight before her into sharp detail.

He dove for her and she grabbed his arm, easily dislocating it at the elbow, then driving her knee up into his nose, hot blood splattering on her knee. His other hand began clawing for her leg. Alice twisted his dislocated arm, and he screamed again. Driving her foot down onto his knee, she punched him in the face as he collapsed to the ground.

Never, in all the years she'd trained, had she possessed such simple, clean focus. It was as if the fire that had kindled in her belly was giving her a kind of power. She could hear a few men begging, fear in their voices and, once again, the past tried to intrude, the memory of her father's voice holding the same terror the last day she saw him.

In the back of her mind, a truth simmered and tried to come out, but she didn't have time for it now.

She had to destroy these men, make them pay for what they'd done.

At least, this time, I get the chance.

That's when the man with the knife came at her. He was taller than the others, with a barrel chest and meaty hands.

At any other time, Alice would have had a moment of doubt, since she was small, compared to this man, and he could easily overpower her. But, she looked into his cold eyes, and then down at the large knife, still wet with Aunt Diana's blood.

His fat lips spread in a gleeful smile and the burning in her belly spread like fire on dry brush through her whole body. She knew with a certainty that he would not be smiling for long.

He jabbed the knife at her and Alice jumped back, then somersaulted under his next attack. She swept his legs out and kicked him in the groin. His eyes bulged.

He rolled over, trying to get up. "I'll...kill you!"

Alice kicked him in the stomach, and then the face.

Grabbing the knife where it lay nearby, she pinned him to the ground and pressed the blade to his throat.

"Alice! Don't!" Marco yelled.

"We don't kill, not ever," Lionel said, standing beside her.

Alice barely sliced the man's skin, producing a trickle of warm blood. It would've been an easy thing to drag it across his neck, open his arteries, and spill all that red warmth onto the filthy alley. He deserved it, and much worse.

But, despite how much she hated this human bag of filth, she couldn't do it.

Hot tears coursed down her cheeks and she screamed at the man before tossing the knife away.

That's when he laughed. "Worse is coming for you. Much worse."

Lionel kicked the man across the face and he fell unconscious.

"Al-Alice," Aunt Diana moaned.

Alice crawled across the slimy cement, the stench of garbage stinging her nose.

Her aunt's eye was swollen and her lip split. A cut somewhere on her forehead caused blood to seep down one side of her face. But the worst was the blood on her chest. It soaked her blouse and her gold locket was quickly becoming a garish red.

Alice swallowed the bile in her throat and tried to smile. "I'm here. We're going to get you some help. Just hang on, please."

Aunt Diana's long fingers held Alice's hand with surprising strength. She pulled Alice down to her.

"I...didn't...want...this...for you..."

"Want what?"

"I was wrong..."

"I don't understand."

Aunt Diana coughed, pink foam on her lips.

"You shouldn't talk," Alice said, wiping her aunt's mouth. "Just rest, you have to rest...you can tell me later."

"No...no later..." Tears fell from Aunt Diana's large, blue eyes. "I...love you..."

"Don't do that. Don't say goodbye, this isn't goodbye!"

"Be...brave for...Logan...for the city..."

"The city? What are you talking about? You can be brave for Uncle Logan. You're not going anywhere!"

Her aunt's grip loosened and her eyes began to grow glassy.

"Stay with me!" Tears soaked Alice's cheeks. "You can't leave me...you can't...I won't let you!"

Aunt Diana's lips spread in a weak smile. "So...strong..."

Then her head fell to the side, lifeless eyes staring at nothing.

"No," Alice whispered, the shock numbing. "You...you can't die...you can't..."

Alice bent down to hug her, but stopped. Her hands ran over Aunt Diana's face and arms, the warmth still there, but no breath stirred her chest.

A large hand fell on her shoulder. "I'm sorry," Lionel said.

For a moment, Alice just stared her aunt's body. Then she cradled her aunt's head against her chest and sobbed, the wail of sirens in the distance.

By the time Alice, Lionel, and Marco walked into the hospital, her crying had slowed. She stared at the cracked linoleum, unaware when someone covered her shoulders with a thick blanket that smelled of disinfectant. Her feet were cold inside her shoes, which someone had recovered for her, but Alice barely noticed.

Police officers questioned Lionel and Marco right next to her, but their voices seemed very far away. Someone tried to offer Alice coffee, but she just stared up at them, their lips moving, but the words made no sense.

Her mind replayed those last moments, no matter how much she didn't want it to. She relived how bright Aunt Diana's eyes had been one moment, and then the next, so very dull.

Her aunt's blood had dried stiff and itchy on the knees of Alice's stockings and the bottom of her skirt. She realized she was staring at the dark red blotches and her mind settled on her aunt's last moments of life, and the words she'd said that didn't make any sense.

Then a voice cut through her thoughts.

"Where is she?! Let me see her! Now!"

It was like being underwater for a long while, and then breaking the surface. All the sounds that had been muffled and strange suddenly came into startling clarity.

"Uncle Logan," she whispered.

"I don't give a good goddamn what your policy is, he's coming with me! He's a friend and a doctor," Uncle Logan said.

Alice threw the blanket off and ran around the corner to the glass entrance doors.

Two security guards were restraining Gerald, even though it didn't look like he was struggling at all. Her uncle stood toe-to-toe with another security guard who was at least six inches taller than him. His salt-and-pepper curls were wild around his head and the usually gentle brown eyes were red and ferocious behind his spectacles.

Alice opened her mouth to say his name, but a broken sob escaped instead.

Before she could sink down to the cold floor, her uncle's arms were around her. She buried her face in his chest, the smell of peppermint and cigars a familiar comfort.

After a few minutes, Uncle Logan wiped her cheeks with calloused fingertips. His own face was red and wet, but Alice could also see a stubborn glint in his eyes.

Whoever had done this was in for a world of hurt, if Uncle Logan ever found them.

"I want to see her," he said to a doctor who'd just arrived. "Now."

"Mr. Miller, your wife's body—"

"I know, it's going to be awful, but I want to see her. And I want him to come with me," he pointed at Gerald, who had been forced outside.

"I'm sorry—" the doctor began.

Uncle Logan put his face inches from the doctor's. "What do you think he's gonna do? Infect people? I'm allowed a family friend in attendance if I need it, and I do. There's nothing that says that friend has to be white."

The doctor swallowed. "I...alright...but the security guards must accompany you."

"Not into the room."

"No, of course not."

The security guards glared at Gerald as he walked to Uncle Logan. Gerald never gave them the satisfaction of acting like he noticed.

"I'm coming, too," Alice said.

Uncle Logan shook his head. "You've already seen enough."

She crossed her arms and held his gaze.

He sighed. "Fine."

"Want us to come, too?" Marco asked from behind her.

Alice was about to say no, but looking up into his warm brown eyes, she realized that she desperately wanted him there.

Lionel and Marco fell into step on either side of her, their hands swallowing hers in warmth and comfort.

It felt like a long walk down to the morgue, but really it

was just down a hallway. When they stepped through the door, Alice was struck by how different the lighting was, a bluish white that cast a strange tint on everything. A simple metal desk with half a dozen file cabinets lined the walls of the wide room. To the far right were double doors where the dead bodies were processed and stored. The thought made Alice shiver. A harsh chemical smell permeated the air, sharp and pungent.

The two security guards started to come into the room behind Alice, when Lionel stepped in their way.

She didn't hear what he said to them, but apparently, it was enough to get them not only to stay out of the room, but walk away altogether.

The morgue attendant at the desk stared at Gerald, mouth hanging open like a caught fish.

"I'm sorry, you'll have—"

"We got permission," Uncle Logan's voice had an impatient edge to it.

"Oh...I...sure...name?"

The attendant looked through the same list three times before finding Aunt Diana.

"We haven't had the time to clean her up or perform an autopsy," he said.

"I don't care," Uncle Logan said.

The attendant paused before leading them through the double doors, where several bodies lay in shiny black bags waiting to be processed.

After checking four different tags, the attendant led them to the fifth one and unzipped it.

Alice gasped as the bag fell away, her aunt's bloody and bruised face surfacing as if by magic.

"I'll leave you, if you need anything—"

"Go," Uncle Logan said.

Tears fell from his eyes as he reached out and smoothed matted, dark hair from her pale face.

"Oh, God...Diana!"

Gerald stepped beside him, hand on his shoulder.

"You can do something, right?" Uncle Logan said to Gerald.

Alice frowned. What could he possibly do about this?

"Logan," Gerald's voice was low and heavy with sorrow, "you know that I can't."

"But if it hasn't been that long—"

"It doesn't work like that."

What are they talking about?

"Please, try, please!"

"My friend," Gerald said, tears falling down his dark, weathered cheeks, "if I could, you wouldn't even have to ask."

It was as if someone had taken away whatever strength Uncle Logan had been holding onto. He fell to his knees, sobs shaking his body.

Gerald knelt beside him, whispering something in his ear as he held Uncle Logan tight.

"I wish I could help him," Alice whispered, her confusion tempered for the moment by her uncle's grief.

She felt Marco shift beside her, that same cold feeling as before traveling down her spine.

"I can help him," Marco whispered.

"Are you sure you want to do that in front of..." asked Lionel, motioning to Alice.

"She knows most of who we are, and if it helps him, then how can I not?"

"Is this the time for riddles from everyone?" Alice's voice was sharp. "First them, and now you two. What could you possibly do for him, Marco?"

"Alice," he hesitated, "I have...abilities...special—"

"Powers?" she whispered.

He nodded. "It's hard to understand or believe, and

later, I'll tell you all about them. But for now, believe that I can help his grief lessen."

Alice licked her lips, tasting salt. "Alright."

Marco closed his eyes in concentration. When he opened them, Alice stumbled back. If Lionel hadn't been there to catch her, she would have careened into the nearest cadaver.

Marco's eyes were completely black. He then reached toward Uncle Logan, black wisps of smoke floating from his hands.

Alice stepped forward to protect Uncle Logan from the smoke, but Lionel stopped her.

"It's okay," he said.

The smoke twined itself around Uncle Logan, and after a few minutes, his sobs lessened, until he knelt quiet and still in Gerald's arms.

Marco sagged against the wall. When Alice saw his eyes again, they were normal, but bright with unshed tears. He looked so unsure, as if he wanted to hear Alice say what she thought. But she couldn't get any words past her dry throat.

"I have to...I need..." She bolted from the room.

When the attendant saw her, he jumped up from his chair, but she didn't stay to answer his questions. She needed air and movement.

Just outside the morgue was a door that led to the back side of the hospital, where a small parking lot was, along with all the trash bins.

She ran past the garbage bins to the sparse trees and grass that grew just on the other side of the parking lot. Here the air was crisp, cooling her flushed cheeks. Pacing through the rough brown grass, heedless of the snags ruining her stockings, Alice's mind wouldn't stop replaying everything.

The broken nose that has healed so quickly. Her childhood friends being the mysterious vigilantes. Aunt Diana dying. Uncle Logan's pleas to Gerald. Marco's powers.

I need to hit something! I need to run!

But she was far from the loft, where the punching bag hung, and there was no way she'd get far running in heels.

So, she paced. After the third time stumbling in her shoes, Alice tore them off. She could almost jog without them and the increased speed helped her mind slow down just a little.

She noticed Lionel striding toward her. "Alice!"

"Don't! Just...no more lies, no more surprises."

"I can promise no more lies, but the other..."

She continued to pace, as quick as she could, without breaking into a run. "You jumped three stories into the air the other night."

Lionel looked around. "Keep your voice down."

"I can't! Do you have any idea what tonight has been like for me?"

"Hard."

She laughed, bitter edges in it. "That's putting it mildly."

"Okay," Lionel said. "Yes, I did that."

"And your nose?"

"Healed."

"How?" The word felt like it was choking her.

Lionel looked down and sighed. "Do you remember that summer that I was in bed for a week? I had that strange fever?"

Alice nodded.

"The day I woke up and the fever had broken, I felt... different. I felt good first of all, really good, like I hadn't been sick at all. And then...I got out of bed, and went to get something to eat and ended up breaking almost everything I touched."

She stared at him. "I don't-"

"Somehow I had developed strength, a lot of it. I could bend metal with my bare hands, I could punch through a wall without breaking a bone. And when I did get hurt I healed, really fast. It took months to learn how to control it. Do you remember how stand offish I was after that fever? Well, that was why. I was terrified I'd hurt you or Marco or, if you did know that…that you would be afraid of me."

"A fever gave you powers?"

"Not exactly, at least, I don't think so. I don't know how I got them, honestly I don't."

"You didn't tell me?"

"I didn't know how you'd respond or if you'd even believe me."

"I would have, you know I would have. You were just scared."

"Yes, I was. I was ten years old and suddenly had super powers. Of course, I was scared!"

Alice stopped pacing and looked down at the wet grass and dirt.

"I'm sorry, that was unfair."

"I wanted to tell you before you left, but…it just didn't seem important, since I thought I was never going to see you again. And then, we saw you last night. It was like…well, we realized how much we missed you, and decided to take a chance on coming back into your life. We thought we'd be able to just pick up where we left off and keep everything separate…but, you're too smart for that."

"Is that a compliment or a frustration?"

He grinned. "Both."

"And Marco?"

"I can't tell you much, we have an agreement that each man's story is his own."

"But did he have…oh my God, are we really talking about super powers?"

"Yes, we are. Is that…frightening?"

She started pacing again, trying to sift through all the emotions rocketing through her body. It was a little frightening, more than a little, actually. Everything she'd known about reality, about what was real, and what was only possible between the pages of a good book, had suddenly blurred. If special abilities were real, what else was real? What else was hiding just under the surface of the world she thought she knew?

As she thought more about that, a tiny glimmer of excitement began to grow in her mind.

"Alice..." Lionel stepped close to her, stopping her pacing. "I don't want you to be afraid of me, or Marco. We keep all this a secret, because we know most people would, at best, turn away from us, and at worst, treat us like monsters. I never wanted you to look at me as anything, except...well, me."

The desperate fear in his voice softened Alice. Slowly, she reached out and took Lionel's warm, huge hand in her small one. His shoulders relaxed, a long exhale escaping his lips.

"It...It's going to take me a little bit to get used to this," she said.

"I expect that."

"Is that...for Marco, is that how his powers always are?"

Lionel nodded. "Promise you'll hear him out? I think he's pretty scared right now."

"I didn't mean to run, it was just so intense."

"I understand — and he does, too — it's just...well, his powers make him feel a lot stranger than mine do. And if you're too scared to have him in your life, I think it would hurt — a lot."

Alice shook her head. "I don't want that. I just..."

"I know. They're pretty freaky, especially the first few times you see them."

"How did I never know this? A year, and I never saw them?"

"Well..." Lionel turned back toward the hospital, pulling her along with him.

"Wait...did I?"

"Remember those two boys, who saved you from your dad?"

Alice's mouth gaped. "Oh my God. You two made me feel like I was seeing things, and the whole time, it was you?"

"Hey, we were pretty scared. That was the first time Marco had really let his powers loose — and we almost got caught by your aunt."

Alice hit him on the shoulder. It was lot like hitting a brick wall.

"So, is it...I mean, you really don't know how this happened? None of your relatives ever acted strange? You never came into contact with anything that might do this, a chemical or…?"

"You mean did I get a bath in radioactive water at some point? Not that I'm aware of."

Alice chuckled. It did sound ludicrous, but her mind was still trying to grab something logical among everything she'd just heard and seen.

"I don't know how this happened," Lionel continued. "Or if there's anyone else like me out there. Besides Marco, I've never run into anyone with powers. Well...actually, that's complicated. Let's just say no one else who has super strength."

"That you know about. Have you ever…? I mean, has anyone ever been-"

"Hurt by me?"

She nodded and watched a complex train of emotions cross his face. Lionel swallowed and looked down at his hands.

"Once," he finally said, his voice raw. "And since then, I've been careful, controlled, so it will *never* happen again.*

Alice put her hand in his and squeezed. She didn't know the whole story, but she could see how much it cost him to admit that much.

The back door opened just as Lionel was reaching for the handle and Marco's now-disheveled head peeked out.

"They're ready to leave."

Lionel nodded.

Marco fixed Alice with a brief pleading look before turning away. His shoulders slumped as he walked ahead of them.

She wished she could say something to him, anything. But, every time she opened her mouth, the memory of that snake-like smoke, Marco's black eyes, and the chill running down her spine, stopped the words cold.

Her uncle and Gerald were waiting by the car. Uncle Logan's eyes were red and his face had the haggard look of someone whose heart had been ripped out.

"I'll drive you both home," Gerald said.

Alice buried her face in Lionel's broad chest and held him tight. He smelled of leather and expensive cologne. It took Lionel a minute to hug her back, and when he did, his huge arms were like a curtain that someone drew over the pain of this night.

"Good night, Alice," he whispered.

CHAPTER TEN

The bag teetered with each punch and kick, the dull slaps echoing through the mostly-empty loft. Sweat dripped down Alice's back and between her breasts. She was tired and thirsty, but she couldn't stop because every time she did the anger and loss was unbearable. So, she kept at it until she could no longer lift her arms and legs.

Collapsing to the mat, tears mingled with sweat, her sobs were hidden in the remnants of breathless exertion.

"You need to drink," Rose said, tapping Alice's shoulder with a canteen.

"Who's watching the store?"

"If you haven't noticed." Rose eased down next to Alice. "We don't have many customers on the days I work."

Alice shook her head. "I shouldn't have snapped."

"I understand. You have every right to be angry."

Alice took a long swallow from the canteen. It had been three days and so far, no one was coming up with any leads about who had killed Aunt Diana. Not that Alice needed them to — she could guess who was behind this.

"You should take a break," Rose said. "Go see Logan."

"He's at his boxing gym."

"I thought he quit."

"He did. I guess we both need to hit something right now."

"Because you can't hit the people that killed her."

"Maybe not right now," she said, her legs shaking as she got up, "but I'll find them. You can bet on that."

Rose stared at the floor, a deep frown on her round face.

"What?" Alice asked.

"Nothing. I should go back to the shop."

"You said it wasn't busy."

"It's not, but I'm reading that physics book you borrowed for me."

"I envy how much you seem to get out of that subject. I could never quite grasp it."

Rose began to explain the theory she was reading about, her hands moving as fast as her mouth in her excitement. Alice forced herself to listen, the complexity of it a welcoming distraction from how she'd been feeling.

After several minutes, Alice shook her head. "I wish you'd had the chance to go to college. It's criminal that they wouldn't let you in."

"Mrs. Frost offered to pull some strings for me."

Alice stared at her. "Why didn't she?"

"Because, my dad wouldn't allow it."

"That doesn't make any sense."

Rose got to her feet and slapped her fist against the punching bag, the punch half hearted. "It does if…well, it does to him I guess."

"Is that what Mrs. Frost wanted to talk to you about at the hotel? Trying to change your father's mind?"

"No, not change his mind about that. It's complicated. I can't go into details, but she offered me a job."

Alice frowned, and then her eyes became huge.

"Not as a maid!"

"What? No! Mrs. Frost isn't like that. No, this is more in

line with my gifts, or talents, or...whatever you want to call them."

Rose was shifting from foot to foot, tapping her fist against the punching bag. Though she'd never advertised her intellectual gifts, Rose had never been ashamed of them either. If given a chance to shine, she usually jumped at the chance. So, why was she being so cagey about it all now? What exactly was Mrs. Frost asking her to do?

"What's the job?" Alice asked.

Rose looked up, her full lips pressed together as if she were bursting to tell Alice the truth. A few more minutes of the right questions and Alice knew she could get the answers out of Rose.

But then, Marco walked in, knocking on the open door, a deep frown furrowing his brow. When he met Alice's eyes, his body visibly tensed.

"Oh, um, are you here to...?" Rose asked.

"I'm an old friend of Alice's." Marco introduced himself and stretched out his hand.

Rose smiled as she shook it.

"Nice to meet you finally. I grew up hearing about you and Lionel."

Marco grinned. "Not much to tell."

"That's not how Alice made it sound."

Marco turned and gave Alice a panicked look.

"You know," Alice waved her hand. "Just all the stories about our exploits. Climbing trees, beating up bullies."

He nodded, a subtle relief relaxing his features.

"Well, it was nice to meet you," he said.

"You too," Rose said, glancing from Marco to Alice. "I should really be getting back downstairs."

Rose gave a little wave as she went down the stairs, the hollow thump of her footsteps the only sound in the loft.

Alice glanced at Marco, and then started unwrapping the tape from her hands. The heat of his gaze could still be felt though, even if she wasn't looking at him, and a heavy silence fell between them.

She'd been avoiding him, her feelings bouncing from glad he was there to frightened. How often had he manipulated her feelings and she hadn't known? If he had, was it because he believed it would help her, or because of a whim?

The memory of what his powers looked like still made her mouth dry, but she knew that he hadn't asked for this, any more than Lionel had. Marco had no control over how his powers manifested, did he?

There were so many questions and every time Alice thought she was ready to ask them, something happened; her uncle would need her, or her own grief would cloud any thought about anyone else. There were times when she'd look at Marco and all she could see was the tendrils of smoke coming out of his hands.

"Can we talk?" His voice was low, unsure.

She shrugged. "I suppose."

At the start of her sparring, Alice had opened one of the huge windows, letting in a pleasant autumn breeze. When she'd been punching and kicking, it had felt like heaven. But now it was making her damp body feel chilled.

She took her time closing it before turning back to Marco, who hadn't moved from where he leaned against the door jam, shoulders hunched, long hands shoved into the pockets of his pants.

There wasn't much to do while Marco stared at the floor, and the silence was starting to get to her. She finished off the canteen and toweled off every part of herself she could reach without stripping.

She was about to ask if he was going to say anything, when Marco looked up at her with such intensity Alice wanted to look away, but something wouldn't let her. In the back of her mind she wondered if it was him.

"You're afraid of me," he said.

"Yes," she whispered.

"You think I'd use my powers on you without your knowledge."

Alice nodded.

"You're wrong. I'd never do that, I promise you."

"Did you when we were kids?"

He looked away. "Yes. I was just learning about them. I-I didn't think about the breach of trust it was. I wanted to help you."

"When?"

"The times when you were afraid to go home. When you broke your arm. But mostly, when your mom died."

Alice thought about that. The innocent kindness that Marco had when they were children, coupled with that kind of power. How could he not use it for good? But that was then, and now, as a man with different desires, who fights criminals every night...

What has he become?

"I don't remember seeing..." What did she call those things that came out of him? "Those...the..."

"Shadows?"

Alice nodded, relieved that he had a name for them and knew what she was talking about.

"When I first got my powers, I would have to touch someone to manipulate their feelings. The shadows came later."

"Have you...have you ever hurt someone...or...lost control?"

"Lionel told you about us and your dad?"

She nodded.

"I felt this pure, righteous fury and it unlocked the full scope of my powers. That's the first time the shadows came, the first time I didn't have to touch someone to use my powers. But, I didn't understand it, and I couldn't rein it in. Lionel stopped me. After that, it happened at school. My parents had to send me somewhere else. I just...I had felt so powerless as a kid, and now I could make the Dorn brothers, and every other bully, see their worst fears. It was...it can be...intoxicating."

"Is it still hard to stop yourself?"

"Sometimes. It's hard when I can see into someone's mind, see their desires, all of them. Some people are so dark, it seems like it would be a good thing to make sure they would never be able to hurt anyone again."

"But, you can't...I mean, can you kill them with your mind?"

Marco shook his head. "No. But...the human mind can only handle so much. It's very delicate, actually, and if I wanted to, I could break it."

Alice felt a sour taste in her mouth. Thinking about gentle Marco doing something so horrible to someone was just about the worst thing she could imagine.

"Have you ever..."

He closed his eyes, shoulders slumping further, as if under a heavy burden.

"Once...It...I was still learning how to control it. I...It haunts me. And every time I feel that maybe I'm going too far, the memory of that stops me. I'm better at it now."

"What...I don't know if I can ask this—"

His eyes opened, a sincere hope shining in them.

"You can ask me anything, if it helps."

"What is it like? I mean you said you can see people's desires and fears. Can you make them feel anything you want?"

"No. I can amplify or decrease someone's negative emotions. To do that, I have to see what they love or fear, depending on what I want them to feel."

"But sometimes, it has seemed like you can, I don't know, sense other people's emotions. That's what happened when my mom died, isn't it? And then, the other night?"

"I can sense intense emotions. But again, only negative ones. It's how I knew you were in trouble after your mom died, I could feel your fear. It was...it was so strong."

"Does it ever hurt you?"

"Not really. If it's very intense, sometimes it lingers, like the taste of something on your tongue. But for me, it's in my mind."

"How awful, to carry that around."

He nodded. "I can clear it away much better now than I used to be able to, but sometimes..."

Alice wanted to wrap her arms around him, to tell him it would be alright. She took a few steps toward him and stopped. There were still questions that needed answers.

"So, the other night, you took away some of Uncle Logan's grief? How did you do that, did you, um, absorb it?"

"No, nothing like that. I just decrease it, almost like turning the burner down on a stove. It's the only good thing about these powers. I can help someone like that, but most of the time, it's really about...hurting them."

His face twisted in disgust and sorrow, and Alice knew that if he could choose to do so, Marco would get rid of these powers.

Because he doesn't want to hurt anyone. He never has.

"You save people all the time," Alice said, walking slowly toward him. "Anyone else might use them for evil, but you're trying to help others. That makes your powers a good thing."

"I try to believe that. It's easy for Lionel to know he's good."

"But, it's all a choice, isn't it? A choice to use them for good or bad, and both of you have chosen good."

Marco smiled.

"You'll have me thinking I'm a knight in shining armor next."

"If it helps. That's how I thought of you both, that night with my father. You saved my life. I'm sure lots of other people see you that way now, too."

"That would be nice."

"So..." Alice leaned on the wall next to him. "After you used your powers on my father, were you really sick?"

"Oh, yes. For some reason, tapping into my powers like that gave me a fever for three days. My mom called a doctor — and a priest."

"A priest?"

"Yeah, my eyes...I don't know if you noticed, but—"

"They get black."

"Lionel said he'd gotten a fever before his powers came on him," Alice said. "Did you have two fevers then or...?"

"No, just the one."

"So you woke up one day and you could feel what people were feeling?"

"Sort of...It came on gradually. By the time I could touch someone and manipulate their feelings, I had figured out that Lionel had abilities too and he helped me through it."

"That must've been so frightening."

Marco nodded. "I thought I was going crazy. If not for Lionel, I don't know what I would've done."

They stood inches apart, their heads down. Alice wasn't sure what to do now. Her fear of him had dulled to a low murmur.

Maybe, one day, it won't be there at all.

This was the Marco she'd known, and yet not. She looked up at him. The awkwardness of childhood had melted away and he'd become a handsome man, if not conventionally so. His body had broadened and developed enough muscle to give him an appealingly lanky body.

Marco must've felt her eyes on him, because he looked sideways, an unsure grin on his lips. A broad swath of dark brown hair flopped onto his forehead, almost in his eyes.

Alice hesitated, then reached up and brushed it back, her fingertips touching his forehead.

"You need a haircut," she said.

"No time."

His brown eyes held hers for a moment, an intensity that Alice couldn't define shining in them. Then he smiled, and it was gone.

She took a deep breath. "I'm sorry I ran."

"I don't blame you. Half the time I want to run away from me, too."

"Stop that, I mean it. I'm not going to let you talk about yourself that way. And after a while, it will get very annoying, so...just stop."

His grin widened. "Yes, ma'am."

She stepped closer and put her hand on his arm. "I mean it Marco. You define these powers, they don't define you."

The smile faded and he swallowed. "You really believe that?"

"I do."

Footsteps echoed up the stairs and after a moment, Rose peeked her head in.

"Call for you downstairs. It's Logan."

"Thanks, I'll be right there."

Rose nodded at Marco as she backed away, a questioning look on her face. Alice gave her a tiny shake of her head and Rose shrugged.

"What was that about?" Marco asked, having caught the last of it.

"Nothing. Just, well, Rose is constantly trying to get me to date someone."

"You don't date a lot?"

"Oh, I do, sometimes. Not lately." She walked toward the stairs. "Actually, not since graduation."

"You're just too intimidating."

"What a terrible thought. An educated woman is too intimidating."

"Well..." Marco grinned at her. "Not to everyone."

Uncle Logan had gotten edgier about her whereabouts in the last few days, but that wasn't the only reason he wanted her home. Something had come to light, something he didn't want to tell her, but knew he had to.

Running through the front door, she collided with Detective Garrick as he was coming out of her uncle's office. His bulldog face scowled at her and his breath smelled of cigars and whiskey.

"What the hell have you been doing?" he asked, looking her up and down.

"Working out my anger," she snapped back.

Garrick snorted. "Well, there's news, but maybe you should shower first."

She crossed her arms and stared into Garrick's small, bright green eyes.

"Alice," Uncle Logan said, coming down the stairs, "go on, we'll tell you after you've cleaned up."

With one last glare at the Detective, Alice ran up the stairs.

"You should really get that girl under control," she heard Garrick say.

"None of your business," her uncle replied, making Alice smile as she closed the bathroom door.

It was the shortest shower of her life. Slipping into some black, slim-fitting pants and a gray, fitted sweater, she ran a brush quickly through her hair and grimaced at the way the curls had frizzed. Taming her bobbed hair as best she could, Alice bolted down the stairs and was in the kitchen before Garrick had finished his glass of whiskey, an achievement indeed.

Marco was at the counter making a sandwich. When he turned to ask her something, his brown eyes widened at the sight of her, olive skin darkening. She looked down at herself, wondering if she'd put her sweater on inside out, but everything was as it should be.

He cleared his throat and turned back to what he was doing. "Hungry?"

"Starved."

"Can we begin, or do we need snacks first?" Garrick asked.

"Just talk, don't antagonize, for God sake," Uncle Logan said.

"We identified one of the men who attacked Diana. He's been arrested half-a-dozen times for assault, and once on suspected murder. Each time, his very expensive lawyers get him out on some technicality."

"And this time?" Alice asked, her small hands clenching into fists.

"He's out on bail," Garrick said.

"How did he get bail with a murder charge?" Marco asked.

"How do you think?" Uncle Logan said. "The syndicate has influence in the justice system."

"Not much of a surprise, I'm afraid," Garrick said, draining his glass. "The last District Attorney resigned under suspicious circumstances and the election of Jamison was...unconventional."

"I don't remember that," Alice said.

"You were studying for finals," Uncle Logan said. "There was a solid candidate, Joe Walsh. He'd worked his way up through small firms, a bulldog, but a fair one."

"What happened?" Marco asked.

"He went missing right before the election," Garrick said, the frustration in his voice coming out in a growl. "It affected the faith of the voters, and Peter Jamison was elected."

"I don't know much about Jamison," Alice admitted, with no small amount of embarrassment.

"You're not the only one," Uncle Logan said. "He's a mystery, though a rich one."

"And Walsh?" Marco asked, placing a sandwich in front of Alice.

"Was found two weeks after the election, in his summer cabin. No memory of how he got there or why he stayed for so long."

"You're thinking then, that because this man is out on bail that it means the syndicate killed Aunt Diana?" Alice asked.

Garrick nodded, his bald head shining in the kitchen light.

"But, with their history of protecting this guy, and now Jamison as District Attorney, I don't know how to make any of it stick," he looked at Uncle Logan. "I'm wondering if your informant might be able to help us out?"

Uncle Logan scrubbed a hand through his bushy hair.

"My source is drying up. He's given us one more lead that I think it may lead us to someone high up in the Syndicate, but I'm not sure."

"Can we get our mutual friends to investigate?" Garrick asked, nodding toward Marco.

Alice stared at him. "You know that he's—"

"Wouldn't be much of a detective if I didn't, now would I?"

"I'm working on it," Uncle Logan said.

Garrick leaned forward in his chair. "Logan, I know you

don't want to hear this, but this could be just the beginning, if you don't lay off this story."

"I'm not quitting!"

"Don't be a—"

"No! If they wanted me off the story, they went about it the wrong way! I'm getting the bastards, all of them! And to hell with the consequences."

"What about her?" Garrick asked, nodding at Alice.

"Alice can take care of herself," Uncle Logan said, though Alice could hear a measure of hesitation in his voice. "Besides, the sooner they're out of the way, the safer everyone in this city will be."

Garrick stood up so fast his chair nearly tipped over.

"Fine. You're gonna be stubborn—"

"I am."

"Just hope I don't have to fish your body out of the Sound, Logan. Let me know when the freaks go to work, so I can keep the cops out of their way."

"He just called you..." Alice said, once Garrick had left.

Marco shrugged and took a bite of his sandwich.

"We're not exactly normal."

Alice shook her head. "I don't like it."

"You should know better than to take Garrick's insults too seriously by now," Uncle Logan said, sitting beside her. "He admires the vigilantes."

"What happened to your source?" Alice asked.

Marco and Uncle Logan looked down at the same time. It was almost comical, except it meant they were trying to hide something from her.

"What now?"

"Don't worry about it," Uncle Logan said, giving her a sad smile. "It's not—"

"You just told Garrick that I can take care of myself, and whether you like it or not, I'm in this, too. I'm going to help you get whoever did this, so you better start treating me like a part of the team."

"It's not that easy."

"Why not?"

Marco looked at Uncle Logan, who said, "Absolutely not!"

"She'll find out, eventually."

"That's your reason for everything lately."

"How about the fact that she's not a kid anymore," Marco said, his voice edgy.

"This isn't about that."

"Enough!" Alice said. "Just tell me."

Uncle Logan turned away, his frown deepening, but Marco took a deep breath.

"Our source has been your father."

Shock forced her to laugh, a high-pitched giggle that made Marco and Uncle Logan exchange worried glances. It wasn't long before she felt her heart hammering in her chest and her breathing became difficult.

"He's...He's alive," she whispered.

"Yes," Uncle Logan said. "He was high enough up in the syndicate to have valuable information and has been feeding it to me for almost a year now."

Alice put her face in her hands as the world began to spin around her.

"And he stopped...talking?"

"Yes," Uncle Logan said.

"Why?" she asked, taking deep, even breaths.

Silence. Alice wanted to look up, but she didn't trust herself not to get dizzy again.

"Answer, please."

"He's refusing to talk to Logan anymore," Marco said, his voice thick with what he wasn't saying.

Alice laughed again, but this time it was filled with disgust.

"Because he wants to see me."

"Yes," Marco said.

"He's…" Uncle Logan hesitated.

"What?" she whispered.

"He's dying, Alice."

A moment ago, she would've walked into hell itself to get the men responsible for Aunt Diana's death, but facing the Devil wasn't something she had considered.

He's using his illness to try and guilt me into seeing him after all this time. Using my love for Aunt Diana to make me do it.

Tears fell hot and angry down her flushed cheeks. "Son of a bitch."

"You don't have to see him just because he's dying," Uncle Logan said. "And, we have one last lead, that might be enough."

"If it isn't?"

"Then, we can find another way," Marco said. "I have a few snitches that might help."

"And there's a few people that owe me favors in the less savory parts of Jet City," Uncle Logan said. "We don't need him."

She looked up slowly, wiping her eyes.

"Not yet."

They looked away from her and she laughed bitterly.

"If this doesn't work-."

Marco took her hand and held it, his thumb running over her knuckles.

"It will. And if it doesn't, we *will* find a different way."

"But not until after the funeral," Uncle Logan said, "give them the impression they've beaten us. Maybe make them careless enough to give us an edge.

The front door slammed and Alice could hear Lionel's heavy tread down the hallway. Coming into the room, he took one look at her and the grim faces of Marco and Uncle Logan, and asked, "What happened now?"

"Your source," Alice said, unable to keep the contempt from her voice. "My...father."

Lionel frowned and looked between Marco and Uncle Logan.

"Who told her?"

Uncle Logan held up his hand. "Too late for that, Lionel."

"Where've you been?" Alice asked, anxious to change the subject.

Lionel's face changed in a moment, a devastating grin appearing on his full lips, blue eyes sparkling.

"It's a surprise. You'll find out in about a month."

"A month? What kind of surprise takes that long?"

"The good kind. You going to finish that?" he asked, pointing to her barely touched sandwich.

She pushed it to him as the phone rang. From Uncle Logan's deepening frown, she could guess who it was.

"Mrs. Frost?" she asked, after he hung up.

"That woman," he said. "It's not enough she insisted on having the wake at her mansion. Now, she's taken over the damn guest list."

"I didn't think she and Aunt Diana were that close."

Uncle Logan paused. "There's a lot you didn't know about Diana. But..." he held up his hand when she started to ask. "Now's not the time."

Normally, Alice would've pushed, but there had been enough surprises today.

CHAPTER ELEVEN

The Frost mansion was one of the oldest and largest homes in all of Jet City. Resting on one of the city's two hills, it overlooked the downtown corridor to the south and the docks and water to the west.

The view from the front deck where Alice stood, showed the grand scope of Jet City, with its towering buildings, never-ending lines of traffic, and sluggish ships moving in and out of the small harbor. On a clear day, Alice knew that the mountains to the south would be clearly visible, their ever white caps standing in stark contrast against the rich blue sky. However, today the sky was shrouded in stale gray clouds that threatened rain, but didn't seem inclined to deliver.

A gentle breeze played with the leaves of the plants and flowers in the huge pots placed at even intervals along the railing of the deck. Alice touched a bright orange blossom and let the delicate petals fall through her fingers. She could see the beginning of the end on the other blooms, as if they were just barely hanging on before the first frosts would drive them into hibernation.

Green and white striped deck chairs and white tables

were scattered among the foliage. Abandoned drinks sat on a few of the tables, along with small plates of half eaten food.

Behind Alice, a string quartet played softly and waiters in black jackets circulated with food and drinks on shining silver trays. Socialites made uncomfortable small talk with select members of the middle class. There were few guests that Alice recognized, and of those, most gave her empty condolences and sidelong glances. She knew everyone wondered if she'd take over Aunt Diana's business and philanthropic endeavors, and most of them hoped the answer was 'no'.

The question had been circulating in Alice's head all week, and though she knew her aunt had believed she could do it, Alice wasn't sure she was the right person for the job. All her thoughts were occupied with getting the man who'd ordered her aunt's death, not on how to fund a new roof for the children's home or an expansion for Jet City's paltry homeless shelter.

"Maybe after I get the bastards..." she whispered.

But, was there going to be an *after*?

In the back of her mind, Alice wondered if there was more to it than just bringing her aunt's killers to justice. Wasn't what Lionel and Marco did against criminals what she had dreamed of since that night in her bedroom in Park Side?

Could I be a hero?

The thought thrilled her and made her guilty all at once.

Taking a generous gulp of the club soda in her hand, Alice heard shuffling steps behind her and hoped it wasn't another of those fake debutantes.

"I see you've found a refuge from the hypocrisy," Gerald said, coming to stand next to her.

"For the moment," Alice said, smiling at him.

Dark circles made his brown eyes look sunken, as if he

hadn't slept in years. He slowly raised his hand to light the cigarette between his lips, and then blew out a pungent white cloud of smoke.

"Rose here?" Alice asked.

Gerald nodded. "Surprised she came. You know how she feels about funerals and such. But she said Mrs. Frost needed her."

"I think that woman could get snow to stay cold in the summer."

Gerald snorted. "You don't know the half of it."

"Though, she couldn't get you to let Rose go to college."

Alice studied Gerald out of the corner of her eye, hoping she'd taken him by surprise.

He took a slow drag from his cigarette, eyes on the horizon. Most would only see a stoic man in a shabby suit, thrice-repaired dress shoes, newly shined. But years of training with Gerald had taught Alice to see the tiny clues he gave. His right eye squinted against the dull sunshine a little more than the other, his mouth was just a tad tighter on his cigarette.

"Nope," he finally said.

"She's brilliant."

Gerald nodded.

"Could be a pioneer in her field. Maybe even pave the way for other women and Negroes."

Gerald nodded again.

Alice sighed. He wasn't going to give up anything about it. So, perhaps, she should try a different tack?

"I've been thinking about that night, in the morgue, with my uncle."

There was the barest hint of a sigh as Gerald exhaled more smoke. "I expect there's a lot of things you've been thinking about from that night, besides your aunt."

"Oh, yes. Things that have turned a lot of my world upside down."

Gerald stubbed out his cigarette with the toe of his shoe.

"Be careful what you do with that knowledge, Alice."

She looked at him fully now. The tense muscles in his shoulders, the fact that he'd just lit another cigarette, when she'd never seen Gerald smoke more than one in an hour. The way he had always dodged any questions about his past. How he never wanted Rose to stand out in school, and now didn't want her going to college. His reputation among Park Side residence for being a miracle worker of sorts.

And, finally, what her Uncle had begged him to do that night.

It all fell into place and Alice gaped at him.

"You're one, too, aren't you? And you're afraid that Rose might be, and you don't want her to be found out."

Gerald took a drag off the new cigarette and exhaled.

"It's not exactly that simple. One day, maybe, I'll tell you about it, but let's just say that if the wrong people ever found out about Rose, she'd be in danger."

Alice swallowed the questions she wanted to ask. She would never want anything to happen to Rose. If it meant never knowing the real story, then Alice would live with that.

"What about you then?" she said.

"What about me?" he looked at her, a playful glint in his eyes.

He wants me to figure it out. Okay then.

Alice took a deep breath, a part of her was unnerved that she was having a conversation about super powers with someone she'd known most of her life.

"You heal people, don't you?"

He nodded. "Very good."

"When did you discover this about yourself?"

Gerald took another drag of his cigarette.

"I'm not like...you know who. I didn't wake up with this."

"Was it an accident or did someone do something to you?"

Gerald took a long time thinking and finishing his cigarette. So long that Alice thought he was choosing not to answer the question. She wondered if she'd over-stepped some boundary.

But when Gerald did speak, his voice had an edge of steel to it Alice had never heard before.

"Let's just say that I didn't know what I was getting into, and leave it at that."

Alice nodded. "Alright, sure."

They stood in silence for a while, a question itching inside Alice's mind. She wanted so badly to ask it, but felt like she'd pried quite a bit already. Once her drink was done, she chewed on the inside of her cheek, shifting from foot to foot.

Gerald chuckled. "Spit it out."

Alice's head snapped up.

"It's easy to tell when you've got something on your mind."

"I do, but...I don't know if you want me asking it."

"You want to know if I could've saved Diana."

Alice nodded.

Gerald sighed, a deep, sad sound.

"I don't know. It's a delicate thing to heal a body. Too much can be just as traumatic as the wounds a person has, more so even. Looking at Diana's body...I don't know."

She squeezed his hand, wanting to erase the haunted look in his eyes, but what could she possibly say?

A harsh staccato echoed on the deck as someone in heels approached. Alice forced her lips into the fake smile she'd worn all afternoon, and turned to see who was walking toward her. It was Veronica Veran, looking simply elegant, as always, in a black dress that showed off her willowy frame and long swan-like neck. A small black hat was perched on her perfect blond bouffant.

"Miss Seymour," she said, taking Alice's hand. "I am more sorry than I can say."

For the first time that afternoon, Alice believed someone who'd said that.

"Your aunt was such a dear woman and a good friend, she will be missed."

"Thank you, Mrs. Veran. Have you met Dr. Allen? This is Mrs. Veran, she's on the Improvement and Philanthropic council."

"Among other accomplishments, as well," Gerald said, smiling at her.

Alice was relieved to see that Victoria did not hesitate to shake Gerald's hand.

"And you run the clinic in Park Side," she said.

"Yes, ma'am."

"I will make sure Diana's death does not derail plans for finishing the expansion of the clinic. It's too important for Park Side."

"That's very kind of you."

"Well, I know you must be sick to death of all this smiling and handshaking. I just wanted to let you know that if you ever are in need of anything, please don't hesitate to ask me."

"Thank you, Mrs. Veran, that's a very kind offer."

Victoria dipped her head and walked with the grace of a dancer into the crowd.

"Nice lady," Gerald said.

"One of the few," Alice said, cringing as she saw Mrs. Frosts thin, sour butler coming towards her.

"Miss Seymour?" he said.

"Yes?"

"Mrs. Frost would like a word. I am to show you to her private rooms."

Alice sighed, wanting to tell the snooty man where to stick Mrs. Frost's summons.

"Good luck," Gerald said, grinning.

"Thanks."

If Alice had known how quickly the society matrons scurried away from a butler, she'd have hired one to escort her throughout the afternoon. He led her up the winding staircase, down an absurdly long hallway, and finally to a door half hidden in a dark corner. He knocked once and Alice could hear the scratchy, commanding tone from within. He opened the door and stepped aside.

For a foolish moment, Alice felt like crying. She was afraid and wished her aunt was here to guard against the formidable presence of this woman. Taking a deep, slow breath and focusing on the rising and falling of her chest, Alice stepped over the threshold.

The room was downright plain, compared to the ornate decor of the rest of the house. Large windows let in light through gauzy white curtains, illuminating overstuffed green chairs and a matching couch. A sidebar glistened with elegant crystal decanters and glasses, which had a simple coiled serpent etched on them, head dipping just below the body, as if in deference to the person holding the glass. The dark green carpet was thick under Alice's heels and she longed to take off her shoes and feel the soft fibers under her sore feet.

Instead of huge expensive paintings, the walls were covered in simply-framed black and white photographs. From the formality and obvious age of some, they seemed to be chronologically placed, a fact that made Alice roll her eyes. At the beginning were severe formal family pictures, the children aging as the photographs progressed. One portrait in the middle caught her eye, because the smallest member of the family, a tiny child in the knee-length dress and braids of the day, was actually smiling in glee, as if relishing her rebellion.

"I like her," Alice murmured, walking to the next group of pictures.

The family photographs were soon replaced with the soft focus of a glamorous age gone by. There was nothing about the dark-haired woman in them that would stand out in a crowd, she'd be quite plain actually, if not for the glint in her eyes that spoke of fire and wit. This was clearly the adult version of the child in the earlier pictures. There was one wedding photo, and Alice could tell that the formality of it was unnatural to the bride. She could now clearly see that the woman was Mrs. Frost, and her curiosity grew.

Scattered among more pictures of Mrs. Frost and her husband were pictures of three women, ranging from young debutantes to a bit older, at various places.

One of the women was Mrs. Frost, but Alice didn't know who the other two were. One of them reminded her of Aunt Diana, same statuesque body, same dark hair and bright eyes. The other was tiny, with a long face and light hair.

In one picture, the three of them wore large hats and suffragette sashes, an air of strength and expectations of greatness about them.

In another, the three women sat on what Alice recognized as the old Jet City pier, each held a slice of pizza and were dressed in only their swimsuits. Alice thought it an odd thing to memorialize, but perhaps it had been the first time they'd had pizza.

The last picture on the wall was of the three women, the statuesque one holding a baby. Their faces had aged a bit, and the smaller woman seemed to have gotten thin to the point of gaunt. They all smiled, but there was a sadness to it, and Alice wondered what happened to Mrs. Frost's two friends, especially the small one.

"I was a catch in my youth," said a gravelly voice behind her.

Alice jumped. Mrs. Frost's usual old-fashioned dress was simple today, an odd serpent brooch clasped just above her right breast. Her green eyes were rimmed in red as if she'd been crying. But what really shocked Alice was her bare stocking feet, and the fact that her white hair was hanging in thick curls to her shoulders.

"Do you recognize the woman in the middle?" Mrs. Frost asked, tapping the statuesque woman in the suffragette sash.

"No."

"It's your grandmother. We were quite good friends in our youth."

"My grandmother?"

Mrs. Frost laughed. "So many things you've not been told. That mother of yours—"

"You didn't know my mother," Alice said, a fire starting to kindle in her belly.

"Oh, yes, I did. She...well, did you never wonder why your aunt did not come get you earlier?"

Alice looked down at her hands.

"Because your mother did not approve of my influence. She blamed me for what your aunt became."

"My aunt was a business woman. And though my mother didn't think all that highly of women doing such things, I never heard her say a bad thing about Aunt Diana."

Mrs. Frost's cane thumped on the dense carpet as she walked to a nearby chair.

"Make us some drinks, and I will tell you the truth. It is past time you knew it."

Alice stared at her a moment, but when those piercing eyes narrowed on Alice, she hurried to the sidebar.

"Bourbon, neat."

One bourbon in hand, and a churning in her belly, Alice handed the drink to the old woman, and then sat across from her. Mrs. Frost held the glass in her gnarled hands and stared at Alice's empty ones. After a moment, she snorted and took a long drink from the glass.

"This is not the first time vigilantes have been in Jet City," Mrs. Frost began. "Although, it *is* the first time their work has caught so much attention. There is a tradition, I suppose you could call it, that began fifty years ago. A woman saw the misery of the poor around her and the callousness of the wealthy. She tried to make a difference from within this community at first, tried to change the minds of the rich. But that failed — spectacularly. Then one night, she saw an old man being assaulted by some thugs. She stopped them, and in payment for her kindness, the old man offered to help the woman in any way he could, with whatever she wanted. Feeling that this was a strange, but important, opportunity, she asked him what he had to offer. Among his extraordinary talents, was martial arts. Intrigued, the woman asked for lessons. It was not long before she discovered her talent for it and realized what she could do for the poor and helpless of this city."

Mrs. Frost sipped her bourbon as Alice stared at her.

"This...this can't be real!"

"I will not bore you with all the details of her transformation. But, suffice to say, she became something new to help the people of the city she loved. And when she..." Mrs. Frost grinned at her. "...when I — was too injured, too old to do it anymore, I trained another to take my place."

Alice felt her mouth go dry, the memory of something

her aunt had said a few days before her death, how something wasn't a gift, it was a burden.

"Aunt Diana?"

"Yes. She was..." Mrs. Frost's hand shook as she brought the glass to her lips. "She was special. But I neglected to prepare her for how hard it can be to tread the line. Diana was not ready for the damage such work could do to a person in here." She pointed to her heart.

"What do you mean?"

"It is hard to look at the evil in people's souls, night after night, and not start to think that perhaps the world would be better off if they simply did not exist. And to know that you have the power to make that happen, that you could do something the police cannot and will not. You could play God."

"My aunt would never—"

"What? Get rid of a killer, who twice had been released on a technicality?"

"She...did she?"

"Essentially. Put him into a coma that he never woke up from. After that...she was more afraid of herself than the criminals that she fought. It was over then, I could see it. She refused to quit, at first. Almost got herself killed and that is when your uncle and I made her hang it up." Mrs. Frost chuckled. "First and only time your uncle and I agreed on anything."

Alice shook her head. "I can't believe it. She never told me any of this, not a hint. And you...you, a vigilante!"

"I was not born this old, you know."

"There's never been a word about this in the press."

"Do you really think the press would care about or believe the stories of a female vigilante? And the few times anyone, your uncle, for instance, brought a story to their editor, no one was interested."

"But, my aunt would never have kept something like this from me."

"Even if she did not want you doing it?"

Alice stared at her.

"She was afraid for you. Afraid you would fall prey to her mistakes. But," Mrs. Frost leaned forward, pinning Alice with her hard gaze, "I think you are made of different stuff than Diana. And if you are willing, you could become the right woman at the right time, as I was."

Alice shot up from the couch and turned from Mrs. Frost. Her pulse was so fast she felt her body shake with each beat.

All her life, Alice had felt a deep restlessness, a painful conviction that she was meant for more. When she'd gone to college and began taking over Aunt Diana's businesses, Alice thought for sure she'd feel peace at last.

But in the midst of every accomplishment, there was something missing, something more just beyond the scope of her vision that called to her. Frustration had dogged her life because she didn't know what it was or where to discover it.

With Mrs. Frosts words, Alice knew, at last, the answer to those questions. Tears fell from her long lashes as she stared destiny in the face, afraid and also longing to grab a hold of it.

This is what I've looked for. This is who I'm meant to be! All this time...all the paths of my life have led me here. Aunt Diana, why couldn't it have been you to show me this?

She shook those thoughts away.

It doesn't matter. I'm here now...What does someone say before they take the sword out of the stone?

The thought made her giggle and she wiped the tears off her cheeks.

Taking a deep, steadying breath, Alice said, "What do I have to do?"

Downing the rest of her bourbon, Mrs. Frost got up and walked to what appeared to be a closet door on the far side of the room. She tapped on it once, softly.

Alice could've been knocked over with a feather when she saw Rose open the door.

"Can we come in?" Mrs. Frost asked.

Rose nodded, disappearing back into whatever space the door led to, as Mrs. Frost followed her.

"Come along, Alice."

The room was brightly lit and far bigger than Alice would have expected. Tools of various shapes, sizes, and functions took up two walls, while three long tables formed a U-shape around the room, leaving just enough room between them for Rose to squeeze between each table.

A soldering iron sat next to something that looked half-finished, tiny bolts and screws scattered around it. Two large sketch pads sat on one table, next to what looked like blueprints of some kind of body armor. Alice unrolled the blueprint edges a little to get a better look. There was drawings of full body armor, from head-to-foot, made up of small, over-lapping plates. Alice scanned the room, looking for any signs of the armor, but not finding it.

"Do you want to see what I made for you?" Rose asked, bouncing on the balls of her feet in excitement.

"Absolutely!"

Rose motioned to a sheet that was covering something in the far corner of the room. She jerked the sheet down dramatically, a huge smile on her face.

"Ta-Da!"

Alice stared at the dress form, which was draped in a set of odd looking clothes.

"Well?" Rose asked.

"Perhaps you should explain it to her, dear," Mrs. Frost said, her raspy voice tinged with dry humor.

Rose took the top piece off the dress form. It looked to Alice like a thick, stiff, long sleeved shirt with a hood attached at the back. Rose handed it to her, and it was heavier than regular clothing, but not so much that it would be cumbersome. That's when Alice noticed that the shirt was actually two pieces: an under shirt and then a vest that fit snugly over the top.

"The vest," Rose said, unzipping it. "is a bit of added protection, not impervious to bullets, but it should help with knives. And it will also help keep you safe from brass knuckles and such. The under shirt is the same material as the vest, which is reinforced leather that's specially treated. The result is that it's exceptionally strong, but light enough that you can still move."

Alice ran her fingers over the leather, feeling a hard plate of some kind inside the fabric of the vest.

"What's inside the vest?" she asked.

"Some extra plating," Rose said, her eyes sparkling. "Something I came up with myself. Like I said, not bullet proof, but incredibly flexible and strong."

Alice felt her pulse quicken, her hand shake as she lifted what she had thought was a hood.

"That will fit over your head, to hide your identity," Rose said.

Alice stared at the cowl, the eye holes, the delicate pattern of a snake head that appeared between her eyes. That was when she noticed that the color of the leather for the vest, shirt and cowl was a purple so dark it looked black. The snake pattern was in green, and it curved sensually from her head, over her right shoulder and down across her chest, as if the snake was wound around her body.

The thought made Alice feel a strange sense of power.

But she didn't get to think about it too long, because Rose had moved to the dress from once again.

"No way are those fitting me!" Alice said when Rose handed her a pair of matching pants.

"Yes, they will."

"But…they're…I mean-"

"You have to wear something fitted so that it does not get in the way," Mrs. Frost explained from where she sat. "And besides, do you really believe Rose would make you something ill fitting or unflattering?"

Alice looked at Rose. "No, of course not, I'm just not used to…well, these look so…skin tight."

"They are," Rose said. "But, so is the shirt and vest. Well, the vest will add a little bulk, but not enough to make you look bad."

The pants were the same dark purple, reinforced leather. A continuation of the snake pattern ran down where her right hip would be, across her right thigh and to the left thigh, then down her shin and her ankle.

Alice handed the pants, shirt and vest back to Rose. "Alright, so what shoes do I wear?"

Rose grinned, motioning to a pair of knee high black boots on a nearby work table.

"I had quite a time finding boots small enough for you," Rose said, handing them to Alice. "But I eventually did."

"They feel weird."

"That's the shin guards I installed inside the boot. Shouldn't hinder your mobility, but if it does, let me know. I can make adjustments."

Alice nodded. She felt overwhelmed with all this. Suddenly she was being given everything she'd ever wanted, including a suit of special clothes that would help her become-

A hero. I'm going to be a hero.

Alice grinned. "This is so amazing, Rose. Thank you so much!"

"She is not finished yet," Mrs. Frost said.

Rose took the boots from Alice's hands and gave her an odd looking, fingerless glove. It was made from the same reinforced leather, but just past the wrist, it had that extra bit of armor that the vest had. It went up her forearm and stopped just below her elbow. Along the top of the fore arm piece was what looked like a chamber from a gun.

Alice gave Rose a questioning look.

"It's for these." Rose handed her a clip of small needles. "Each has enough anesthesia to knock out a full-grown man. If you use it on someone smaller, you must remove it right after it's injected, so they don't overdose."

"Why would I—?"

"You're small," Rose went on, "and you may need to quickly subdue assailants, if you can't defeat them in hand-to-hand combat."

Alice didn't know what to say to that.

"The trigger is here." Rose pointed to a small button on the underside of Alice's wrist. "It's a little stiff to keep you from accidentally shooting it."

Alice slipped it on and tried it a few different ways, shooting blanks into a mound of fabric in a corner. At last, she figured out that triggering it with her other hand was easiest.

"We can make adjustments, if needed," Mrs. Frost said.

"There's these, too." Rose handed her two dark purple batons in what looked like a hip holster. Winding along the length of each was a purple snake.

"I've never used batons."

"Good idea to learn, then," Mrs. Frost said. "I have someone in mind to teach you."

"Who?"

"Dr. Allen."

Alice shook her head. "I shouldn't be surprised by anything anymore. Wha...what do I call myself?"

Mrs. Frosts thin lips spread in a wide grin. "What those before you were called: The Serpent."

Goosebumps lifted the hair on Alice's arms.

None of it made sense, not really. It was like finding herself suddenly living in a fairy tale. Alice kept expecting herself to wake up and be in her room, in the same old world, with the same old role to play.

But, as her fingertips ran down the suit and her mind turned over the name she'd be taking on, Alice felt something fall into place. This was real, maybe the most real thing she'd ever felt.

She smiled at Mrs. Frost.

"When do you go after the Syndicate?" Mrs. Frost asked.

"Shadow and Steel, and I suppose, now me, are going in two days. One of the heads is supposed to be at the warehouse district to take possession of something."

"One of...?"

"According to Uncle Logan's source, there are three."

"Like Cerebos of old," Mrs. Frost said. "Your gear will be at your uncle's house tonight."

"In a cardboard box?" Alice asked, handing the glove back to Rose.

"Of course not. In a special foot locker that will only be able to be opened by you."

"Here's the combination," Rose said. "It's a special lock that will require the code to be changed every month. When it's time, a small light will blink on the keypad."

"You should spar in the suit, to make sure you're used to it, before going into a fight," Mrs. Frost said.

"So, I suppose this was what your meeting was about the other day?" Alice asked Rose.

"Yes. I wanted to tell you so badly! But Mrs. Frost swore me to secrecy."

"So instead of going to college, you're stuck in a room making stuff?"

"You make it sound like a prison. Do you have any idea how long it would take just to get interviewed for a job at a lab, much less how slim a chance I'd have of actually doing anything interesting? They might let me be someone's secretary, but more likely, they'd show me the door. I have the chance to make discoveries and experiment here in a way I'd never have otherwise. Not to mention, using my gifts for something I believe in."

Alice smiled. "Sounds like we both get to live our dreams."

Rose giggled. "Just wait 'til you see what I have in mind, if I can get it to work. You might not be the only one out in the field."

"Alright," Mrs. Frost said. "Let's leave Rose to the work for which I am paying her."

Rose waved good-bye and turned back to the table with the tiny screws and bolts.

"How did you know she could do all this?" Alice asked.

"I have known that child all her life and have been privileged to see her gifts long before most. One day, women like Rose will be given the fair chance they deserve."

Back in the other room, Mrs. Frost poured herself another bourbon and said, "Now, I want a report after the mission. You will come here on the pretext of learning how to properly take over Diana's legacy at least once a week, more often, if I deem it necessary."

"What will I really be learning?"

"I will share my wisdom with you, if you will deign to listen. And, in a few years, you will indeed take over Diana's interests."

Alice's shoulders slumped.

"The world sees in one dimension," Mrs. Frost said, walking with determined steps until she was so close Alice could feel the woman's breath on her face. "When people look at me, they see a rich old woman who is to be humored and respected...and feared, just a little. That is all. Those few who have had the unfortunate experience of my deeper qualities rarely forget them. But, for most, that still does not keep them from underestimating me, simply because of my age. Now, let us talk about you. Young, brash, no time for the rich women of Jet City, except to turn your nose up at them. How long do you think it will be before someone, somehow, knows you are The Serpent? Before Diana's legacy is neatly divided and destroyed?"

It felt worse than Alice had imagined, to be dressed down so well.

"To be The Serpent, you must have a public self that is so different from your true self, that no one would suspect who you really are. I will teach you how to have that *and* how to be The Serpent. If your alter ego can be satisfying in some small way, so much the better."

Alice nodded. As much as she hated to admit it, the old woman's logic was sound.

"Good. Now, I am tired and you are likely already missed. Off you go."

Mrs. Frost slumped onto a chair, as if her body was too heavy to hold up any longer.

An hour ago, Alice had thought Mrs. Frost was a moody old bag, who harangued her aunt for no reason. Now, she was ashamed of such thoughts. Here sat a woman who had lived an extraordinary life, who had given that life to Aunt Diana, and who was now offering it to her.

Glancing at the old woman again, Alice felt tears sting her eyes.

"I don't know what to say," Alice whispered. "What you've given me..."

"I have given you nothing," Mrs. Frost said, her voice weary. "You earned it every day, as you grew and learned from Diana, to stand here as the woman you are now."

Alice turned to leave when she heard her name, strangely gentle on Mrs. Frost's lips.

"Do not give in to vengeance. It is a dark and terrible path. Diana would not want that."

It was the one promise Alice wasn't sure she could make, but she felt like she owed Mrs. Frost something, after all this.

"I promise to try."

"Good."

Once out of the room, Alice walked as slowly as possible, until she reached the end of the hall. She could hear the string quartet still playing, the tinkling of glasses and plates, the low murmur of conversation.

Everything was the same, except her.

CHAPTER TWELVE

For the next two days, Lionel, Marco, and Alice went through their plan for attacking the warehouse until she felt numb with boredom. At last, the night they'd been waiting for arrived and Alice couldn't sit still. Every book she picked up was discarded a few minutes later. She walked around the block three times before realizing it wasn't helping and was just making her more nervous.

Taking her gear out of the foot locker, Alice checked it all for fifth time that day. Her eyes fell on the layer of dust that was coating the furniture in her room and wondered if cleaning might calm her a little.

When she was done, she felt satisfaction in seeing the room spotless, but her nerves were still prickling around her insides.

But, at least the sun has set, finally. I wonder where Uncle Logan is?

Alice was surprised to see how dark the house was downstairs, and the only light seemed to be coming from her uncle's study. She realized that her aunt had always been the one to insist on lights, even in empty rooms.

She didn't like a dark house, for some reason.

Grief suddenly gripped her, and she tried to tamp down the tears in her eyes. It wouldn't do to be thinking of this tonight; she had to be focused.

"Alice?" Uncle Logan asked, standing in the now-open doorway of his study.

She scrubbed tears away and forced a smile.

Uncle Logan gestured for her to come in and sit down, and then he poured himself a glass of whiskey. He'd never been much of a drinker and Alice had always been grateful for that. But in the last week, he'd gone through two bottles and was working his way through a third.

He must've seen her eyes on the glass in his hand, because he patted her shoulder and said, "It's my first tonight. I'm cutting back, you don't have to worry."

He flopped down in his worn, patched chair that smelled of old cigars and ink. Taking his glasses off, Uncle Logan rubbed his eyes.

"They promised me, Lionel and Marco. Promised that they wouldn't drag you into all this. And now here you are, hours away from..."

Taking his hand, she squeezed.

"Why are you so frightened of this?"

A clock ticking in the silent house was the only sound for a while before he answered.

"Because...after all you went through as a child, I just wanted a normal life for you."

Alice tried to picture a husband and children, a house to be cleaned, meals to be cooked. A million days of the same stretching out until she couldn't see the horizon. No matter what joys she knew could be had in being a mother, or being a wife to loving man, her soul recoiled from it all.She wondered if it was because of what she'd seen with her own father and mother, despite all the loving relationships that came after them. But no, Alice knew it wasn't that simple. Her heart had always lived in other places, in adventures no respectable girl was supposed to have.

"I don't think," she said, her voice gentle, "that I was ever going to have that."

Uncle Logan let out a tired, resigned sigh. "No, I guess not. There's an awful lot of Diana in you, you know."

Alice felt the tears burn her eyes again and nodded. Not for the first time, she wondered if her mother's calm, kind nature was inside of her somewhere. But she was starting to doubt it.

"Alright," Uncle Logan said, putting his glasses back on. "You hungry?"

"For what we can scrounge up?"

"Mrs. Muir from across the street brought a casserole."

Alice shrugged and followed him into the kitchen. She was the furthest thing from hungry, but knew her uncle wouldn't eat if she didn't.

Two hours later, Alice found herself standing in front of her bedroom mirror, wondering if she'd made a mistake.

"Rose wasn't kidding," Alice said.

The suit fit alright. It clung like a second skin to every inch of her, except the vest which, like Rose had predicted, did indeed add a little bulk. Alice was grateful for more than the protection the vest offered, as it covered her torso in such a way that the suit wouldn't showcase the dips and curves of her upper body. But that didn't help with her hips, butt and upper legs, which she'd never cared about until now, when they felt on display in the skin-tight suit.

She turned to look behind her. "Hmm...not as bad as I thought."

But then she thought of Lionel, and her pale skin flushed with heat.

"Oh, God. I can't do this."

"Alice?" Uncle Logan asked outside the door.

"Uh...yeah?"

"Everything okay?"

"Uh..."

"Can I come in?"

"Um-m...okay..."

Every muscle in her body tensed to keep her from grabbing the fluffy robe on her bed.

Uncle Logan didn't smile, which Alice was simultaneously glad and embarrassed about. His brown eyes looked troubled as they slowly looked her over.

"I...remember your aunt...wearing something like that," tears glided silently from behind his glasses.

Alice felt her throat tighten as tears began to burn her own eyes.

"She'd be proud, you know? But she'd also tell you to be careful."

"I will, I promise."

Uncle Logan wiped his tears away and smiled.

"I'm not sure I can comment on your appearance in this without sounding inappropriate."

Alice felt a fresh wave of heat inflame her skin.

"But," he said, "you have nothing to be ashamed of. If that's your only hesitation, then take a deep breath and get over it."

A nervous laugh shot out of her lips.

After a moment, she took a deep breath and with eyes closed, pulled the cowl up over her head. Opening her eyes a moment later, she saw that the person staring back at her was neither weak nor ridiculous.

There was a freedom in the cowl and suit that Alice had never imagined. Wearing this face, she could let the deepest parts of herself out, let the strength she had restrained for so long, in the name of propriety, be on full display.

"You're sure you're ready?" Uncle Logan asked after a moment.

"Yes."

"You didn't spar in the full suit yesterday, the cowl—"

"Is perfect. I can see fine, and the suit doesn't feel strange anymore."

He nodded. "C'mon, I have something for you."

When he opened the back door onto the alley behind the house, Alice gasped in shock at what she saw.

Gleaming black and silver in the moonlight, kickstand out and ready for her, was her uncle's Vincent Black Lightning motorcycle.

Her mouth dangled open and she wanted to say something, but nothing except a squeak came out.

He laughed. "I thought you'd need some way to get to the missions."

"But-But, this is...I mean you never...and it's so..."

"If you don't like it—"

She snatched the key from his outstretched hand before he could finish and straddled the bike. She caressed the chrome of the handle bars, down to the sides, her fingers sliding along the ridges of the engine.

When other girls dreamt of ponies and diamond rings, Alice imagined speeding down the street on this bike, smiling at the envious stares of the boys and girls walking on the sidewalk.

The motor purred to life, smooth and low. She smiled, a warm thrill starting in her seat and spreading throughout her body.

"It's been a year since you were on a motorcycle, and that was out in the middle of nowhere. Remember to be careful of cars, they might not see you, and take the turns easy. The Lightning is a smoother ride than the dirt bikes you're used to," Uncle Logan said. "And please, please, just be careful."

"I'd tell you not to wait up, but..."

"Just...get the bastard and come home."

Snapping the kickstand back, she revved the engine a little before leaning forward and speeding down the alley.

The barest hint of sea salt was always in the air in the warehouse district, though you had to sift through the tanker exhaust and factory smoke to smell it. Jet City had been a port town at its birth and the warehouses had spread out before the development of the downtown areas. As the wealth of the city blossomed, changes had to be made to the warehouses nearest the city.

It wasn't enough to merely house goods; no, these buildings had been converted to elegant showrooms where the rich could view the newest furniture, jewelry, art, or whatever had just come off the ships. Waiters wandered the huge spaces giving endless glasses of champagne to bored socialites as they spent their husband's fortunes.

But the further south one went, the brick facades became faded, the windows murkier, the alleys dark and smelly. It was a lucky night if one in four of the streetlights hadn't been busted out. If you drove too fast, the pot holes, common in the southern neighborhoods, would quickly make you slow down. The invisible dregs of Jet City made this part of the city their home.

In between the posh warehouse showrooms to the north of the warehouse district and the dank, dreary warehouses of the south, sat an odd assortment of buildings. Not classy but not run down, these warehouses took on a split personality of being kept up, yet housing nothing and no one very glamorous. Where the north and south had distinct personalities, this middle ground was plain and respectable. It's streets were well lit, but not bright. The businessmen easily ignored, because they didn't deal in anything remotely interesting to either the rich or the corrupt.

What better place to hide something illegal?

Alice rode down an alley that ran behind the warehouse she was meeting Lionel and Marco at. It was across from a smaller warehouse that the Syndicate controlled, and would provide a good place to wait and see if their target showed. They had agreed that caution was important on this mission. If they blew this, who knew if they'd get another shot?

Parking the Lightning by some trash bins and hoping it was hidden well enough, Alice stepped out and was surprised to see Marco and Lionel standing a few feet away. The light was dim in this alley, and at first, she couldn't see their faces.

"It's me," she said, smiling.

"I can see that," Lionel said, his voice halting.

"It's an amazing suit," Marco said. "Makes us look like amateurs."

The light glinted off the brass knuckles he wore on each hand as he tugged at his dark blue dress shirt and matching pants, which were tucked into brown combat boots.

Alice reached up to adjust Marco's mask.

"Maybe Rose could...Lionel, is something wrong?"

He was staring at her, his eyes glinting behind his domino mask. When he didn't respond, Marco smacked him on the shoulder and Lionel snapped out of whatever he was thinking about.

"Uh...I just...That's...interesting."

Alice had a moment of wanting to crawl behind the trash bins and not come out. But, why should she? It wasn't as if she was naked. Yes, the suit was tight and showed more of her shape than anything she'd ever worn, but what was wrong with that? Her body was strong and powerful.

And I'll be damned if I'm going to be ashamed of it.

"It's a suit," Alice said, squaring her shoulders and looking up into Lionel's eyes.

"A tight one."

Alice reached up and grabbed the front of his dark gray turtleneck, forcing him to meet her gaze.

"I'm a part of this team, not one of your debutantes to be ogled. I didn't put this on for you, I did it for me. If it's going to be a distraction, then maybe you should leave this to Marco and me until you can get your head in the game."

Lionel stared at her, his mouth open in shock, only a few inches from her face. If she moved a little closer...but, she looked away and let him go. Even if he did want to kiss her, which Alice doubted, this wasn't the time or place.

"I'm sorry," he said, straightening his shirt. "It was a shock to see it. You look...amazing, in a vigilante kind of way."

Alice couldn't help smiling. "Thanks. Now, can we do this?"

Marco walked to the end of the alley and looked around the corner. He held his hand up behind him, signaling them to hold. Alice felt her very bones hum with energy and had to tense her muscles to keep from bouncing on the balls of her feet to get it out.

"Car," Marco whispered at them. "A driver, and someone...oh my God! It's District Attorney Jamison!

"You're sure?" Lionel asked.

"Absolutely, I just took the guys' picture this morning. There's another man, but his face is hidden by a hat. He's tall and slim."

"If we get Jamison here and if there's proof in the office above the warehouse...," Lionel's voice dripped excitement. "Well, that's a big hit to the Syndicate."

"If he's one of the heads of all this, why is he in such a high-profile job?" Alice asked.

"Maybe because it's the last place anyone would look," Marco said.

"They'll probably go to the office straight off," Lionel said.

"The other guy with Jamison must be one of the other heads. We could get two in one night!" Alice said.

"Slow down," Marco said. "We focus on Jamison, he's the one we're here for. The other would be a bonus, but not the focus. Agreed?"

They nodded.

"Marco, you go in first," Lionel said. "Alice and I will follow."

"What's your code name?" Marco asked her.

She took a deep breath that sent tingles down her spine and whispered, "Serpent."

Marco stepped out and walked the short distance across the street. Lionel and Alice stayed several feet behind Marco, keeping to the sparse shadows. Whether because Marco was all in dark colors or because of his gift, he was so well hidden that no one saw him until it was too late.

"C'mon," Lionel said after a moment.

They slipped inside the warehouse door, careful not to trip over the two men who were passed out beside it. Alice glanced at Marco, his eyes black, an ephemeral cloak of shadow twining itself around him like a living thing. A moment of fear closed around her throat, and then she reminded herself who this was. Under all the shadows and power, it was still Marco. That would never change.

The ground floor was full of the dark outlines of huge machines, making Alice feel like a bug in a strange forest. The chill of autumn had settled into the space, cooling the sweat that trickled down her back and legs.

They rounded a corner and saw the stairs that led up to a glass-enclosed office with the shades drawn. Alice and Lionel crouched low to stay hidden, while Marco reached out, dark tendrils flowing toward two men. One of them started to weep like a child, while the other one fell on all fours, cowering from something none of the them could see.

Lionel ran for the stairs, Alice right behind him. Without a word, he picked her up and jumped straight up, landing outside the office with a heavy thump.

He'd just set her down when the door was jerked open and three men came running out. The first two went straight for Lionel, who punched one hard enough to lift him off the floor. The third grinned down at Alice.

"What are you supposed to be?"

She smiled, grabbing his arm as he tried to punch her. Pivoting, she knelt and threw him over her shoulder, and then pulled his arm until his elbow gave a loud pop. His scream echoed through the landing outside the office.

Not trusting that to keep him out of the fight, she kicked him across the face.

Behind her, Lionel gave a grunting shout. She turned and saw two men hitting him with pipes. The nearest one had his back to her, so she ran up and brought her foot down hard onto the back of the man's knee, throwing him off balance. A swift kick to the face and he was down.

For just a moment she felt a thrill of victory, and dropped her guard. They could really do this!

Then someone tackled her from behind and her face hit the floor hard. She felt warm blood on her cheek and her ears rang.

"Darts!" Marco yelled.

She hesitated. She could do this without Rose's cheats.

Driving her elbow up and into the face of her attacker, she rolled over as he jerked away from her, and within moments had him on his back. The shock of the blow to the head made her a little slower than usual, still it wasn't something the man had anticipated. Taking advantage of his surprise, Alice drove her fist down into his face, blood spurting from between the man's lips. Reaching back to hit him again, Alice's arm was jerked back as someone lifted her up.

This new assailant dragged her by her arms away from the door as a mysterious man in a wide brimmed hat and a beefy man with a square face bolted for the stairs. She knew the beefy one had to be Jamison. Hate boiled in her belly as she saw him running away.

"No!" she screamed.

She used the dart then, firing blindly into the man holding her. It must've been a decent shot because he released his grip, and fell to the ground. She could see Lionel fighting off a very large man, and Marco was nowhere in sight. Jamison had just gotten to the bottom of the stairs. She couldn't let him get away!

Running halfway down the stairs, she climbed onto the hand rail and launched herself at Jamison, barely hearing Lionel's scream of warning.

She fell into him and they tumbled to the ground. It was easy to pin him, though he was a large man. Somewhere in the back of her mind, she knew that she should dart him and drag him out, but the fury of Aunt Diana's death came crashing in on her. Her fists barreled down again and again, a scream of rage flying from her lips.

Then, the hard barrel of a gun pressed against her back and stopped her cold.

"Get up," hissed a voice.

Slowly, her legs shaking, Alice got to her feet.

Jamison stumbled up, backhanding her as soon as he was upright. A second blow followed the first, opening the cut on her cheek further.

"Your friends leave you?" he sneered.

She spat at him, getting a punch across the face in return. The coppery taste of blood filled her mouth.

He grabbed the gun from the other man, pointed it at her head and cocked it. A cold fear burst inside of her, but she wouldn't let him see it. Keeping her eyes on his, Alice tried to unleash all the hate and anger inside of her through that stare.

Jamison's green eyes became huge, and he choked with fear. The man behind Alice gave a cry of panic and crawled away. Alice didn't hesitate. She grabbed Jamison, intending to throw him to the ground. But, she hadn't counted on the gun, which suddenly went off, and the fear on his face vanished instantly.

The shot had hit Marco, wherever he'd been hiding.

Realizing her mistake, Alice tried to shoot a dart at Jamison, but Lionel got there first. He punched Jamison, the impact throwing him to the ground. Loud shouts and the heavy tramp of feet echoed throughout the warehouse behind them. And sirens whined in the distance, closing fast.

Lionel grabbed her and ran for the door.

"Jamison," she said, pulling away.

"We can't! No time!"

"I can dart him!"

But it was too late. Lionel burst out of the door, pulling Alice with him.

"Shadow!"

"He's going to meet us in the alley."

Three sets of headlights screamed around a corner.

"Shit!" Lionel said, running.

She had no choice but to follow him, doing her best to keep up with his long stride. They could hear angry shouts behind them and Alice hoped no one was following them.

Marco was sitting near the Lightning when they bolted around the corner, his right arm hanging at his side, blue sleeve wet with blood.

The shouts were getting closer. They'd been followed.

"Get him on the bike," Alice ordered, straddling it and starting the engine. "It'll be faster and safer than you jumping over the rooftops."

Marco settled behind her, gasping with pain. Lionel gave them one worried stare before jumping up onto the third floor fire escape and onto the roof.

"Hold on," she ordered, tearing out of the alley, the ping of ricocheting bullets behind them.

Alice hid the Lightning once again down an alley, this time behind Gerald's clinic in Park Side. One light was on, and after Marco knocked four times on the back door, it opened. The back room, which Alice had always thought was a store room, had a table and instruments at the ready. Gerald's dark eyes were serious as he ordered Marco to take his shirt off. Alice slid her cowl off, the cool air welcome on her sweaty head. In spite of the seriousness of it all, she was surprised to feel a moment of admiration for Marco's well-muscled torso. He'd been skinny to the point of frailty when they were kids. But now...she blushed and asked Gerald how it looked.

"The bullet went through, missed any bones," Gerald prodded gently and Marco sucked in a sharp breath.

For a small wound, it was bleeding quite a lot.

Another knock sounded, and Alice opened it to let Lionel in. The moment he was in the clinic, he ripped his mask off and glared at her.

"What the hell was that?" he demanded. "You should've used your darts! Or waited for me! I would've been right behind you and we could've had him. But you tore off by yourself."

"You were a little busy," she said, not sure if she was angrier at him or herself.

"Why didn't you use your darts?" Marco asked through clenched teeth.

"Because...I don't know. I'm not used to them, I guess. What does it matter? I almost brought him down without them!"

"But you didn't," Lionel said. "And because of you—"

"No, Lionel," Marco said, laying back against the table.

"Marco got shot!"

"Not her fault."

"Take this argument somewhere else!" Gerald said, eyes blazing. "He's not clotting fast enough and I need to concentrate."

Lionel marched into the adjoining room and slammed the door, but Alice didn't want to leave Marco. She went to his other side, and noticed how pale he was.

Marco tried to grin at her, but it came out as a grimace.

"I'll be...fine. No...worry."

"Go," Gerald said, closing his eyes in deep concentration as he used his gift.

Guilt made her want to stay, but Gerald was in charge.

She went into the next room and found Lionel sitting in a chair, his face in his hands. When he looked up at her, his blue eyes smoldered with worry.

"This could've been you," he said. "That gun to your head...he almost killed you."

"But, he didn't, because of Marco."

Lionel nodded, and then laughed.

"Why do I still feel so responsible for him? He can reduce anyone to a sobbing mess in seconds, but I still feel like I need to take care of him. And now there's you...I can't watch out for both of you."

"Who says you have to?" She knelt in front of him. "We both know the risks and we accept them. We're not kids anymore."

A hint of a smile graced his lips, and his eyes looked

almost tender as they scanned her face. But then he frowned and shook his head.

"Why didn't you use your darts?"

She sighed, anger blossoming once more. How many more times was he going to ask that?

"I know I made a mistake—"

"And it cost us."

"I know!" She jumped up, pacing the room in short strides. "You don't think I'm furious with myself right now? I know I screwed up! Let it go!"

"Let it go?" He got up, anger darkening his face.

"Yes! Do you think you're helping by driving the guilt in deeper?"

Lionel opened his mouth to speak when the door opened and out came Gerald. His frown was annoyed to say the least.

"He'll be fine. Stitched him up, and with what I was able to do, he should be completely healed in a few days. But in the meantime, he should rest. He needs time to replace the blood he lost."

"Thank you, Gerald," Alice said.

He glanced at her, and then walked up to Lionel. Toe to toe, Lionel was at least seven inches taller than Gerald, but the older man still somehow managed to make Lionel look like a scolded child, as he drove his finger into Lionel's chest and fixed him with a firm stare.

"A good leader gives people the chance to learn from their mistakes, gives people time to become a team. You can't do that...well then, maybe you shouldn't have this job."

"Yes, sir," Lionel whispered.

Gerald turned his dark eyes on Alice and she looked down at her boots.

"And you, when someone gives you a weapon, you use

it. You've got good instincts, Alice, use them. Or next time this could be worse. Understand?"

She nodded.

"Right then. Let's get a look at you."

Alice had forgotten about her face until Gerald's gentle fingers prodded the cut. She winced at the sharp pain, knowing she'd also have a fine set of bruises to go with it in the morning.

A tingling, cold jolt went through her, the pain dulled, and a strong impulse to close her eyes overwhelmed her. Suddenly, she found herself being eased onto a couch by Lionel's huge hands.

"Is that...normal?" she asked.

"The first time or two, yeah," Gerald said. "I don't do something this strong for most people. You might feel a little sore the next few days, but nothing too bad."

She patted her cheek and was amazed to feel a scab where the gash had been.

"Give Marco a few hours to sleep, then get him home. Hopefully I won't see you back here for a while."

And with that, Gerald slipped into his worn coat and was out the door.

Lionel sat next to Alice on the couch, an uncomfortable silence between them. When she dared sneak a glance at him, he was staring at the floor, his beautiful face etched with worry.

Slowly, not sure he'd welcome any comfort from her, Alice took his hand in hers. It was square and warm, the fingers so long they made hers look like a child's. He twitched a little at the contact, giving her a quick squeeze and a boyish smile before jumping up from the couch.

"I think Gerald has a coffeemaker around here — want a cup?"

She nodded, trying very hard to push away the feeling of rejection that welled up in her throat.

CHAPTER THIRTEEN

The coffee was cold, and so was Alice, but she didn't want to go back inside. Frost sparkled on the front lawn of Uncle Logan's house and Alice wondered if anyone had bothered to cut back Aunt Diana's rose bushes.

I should've thought of that before now.

She snuggled deeper into the thick blanket and picked at the peeling paint on the porch swing.

It had been almost a week since they failed to catch Jamison, and though the warehouse had contained over a thousand dollars worth of Fantasy, and everyone was calling it a blow to the mysterious drug syndicate, Alice felt keenly unsatisfied.

Especially when the police told her that they had no evidence, except the word of three vigilantes, that District Attorney Jamison was anywhere near the warehouse. Two days later, it came out that Jamison had an air tight alibi.

Alice, Lionel, and Marco had spent every night trying to get proof that Jamison was involved, but besides some low-level drug pushers, their search yielded nothing of real use.

"Don't blame yourself," Uncle Logan had said. "You came home safe, that...that should be enough."

But it wasn't. Not for her, and though he would never say it, not for him. The person that ordered Aunt Diana to be killed still walked the earth, breathed air.

Mrs. Frost had demanded a full account and sniffed out what Alice wasn't telling her almost immediately. She'd expected a tirade, a lecture, something. But what she got instead was far worse. Mrs. Frost's wrinkled face frowned at her, back straight as she sat in her chair, hands folded over the head of her cane, like a dowager Queen looking on the new, lesser Monarch.

"You've learned a lesson, I think," was all she'd said.

"Yeah: don't be stupid," Alice murmured.

She knew what she should do next, but every time she thought about it, Alice felt sick. Last night, she had a dream about her father for the first time in years. He was beating her with hist belt, her screams echoing through the cavernous house. And no one came to help her.

Now, sitting in the cold on her Uncle's front porch, Alice could still feel phantom lashes stinging her skin. She closed her eyes tight against them, trying so hard to remind herself that she wasn't helpless anymore.

———

A little while later, the screen door creaked open and Alice could tell by the light tread that Marco had ventured out. The smell of pancakes and bacon drifted toward her, making her stomach growl.

"I thought you'd be hungry by now," he said, smiling down at her.

The gentleness of his look banished the dark memories and she took the offered plate.

"Join me?" she asked, scooting over.

The swing was just barely big enough for the two of them. Before he could protest, Alice threw some of the blanket over Marco and leaned against his side, his body radiating a welcome heat.

"Is this okay?" she asked, when he shifted.

"Yeah, the arm doesn't hurt anymore."

"I still don't know why he couldn't just heal it completely."

"Says it's better if my body works with his powers. I don't know, I'm not the doctor."

He grinned down at her, his brown eyes dancing, and then opened a small paperback and began reading as she shoveled the hot food in her mouth. Alice snuggled a little closer, and without a word, Marco raised his long arm for her to settle beneath. She turned so that her back was against his side, his arm draped over the back of the swing. It was tempting to grab that long, calloused hand and hold it, or bring his arm around her shoulders, making him hug her tight, but instead, Alice took a large bite of syrup-drenched pancakes.

"Did you make these?" she asked, her voice muffled from the amount of food in her mouth.

"Yeah."

"I bet Uncle Logan is grateful. I can barely boil an egg."

Marco laughed. "I'm sure that's not true."

"Don't ask me to prove it, you might not survive the experience." She leaned back and smiled up at him.

There was a moment, when their chuckles had faded and Alice was still looking up at him, that it seemed as if Marco began to lean down, his brown eyes resting on her lips. But then he blinked, and looked back at his book.

Alice sat up. "How did you learn to cook?"

He shrugged. "I was always curious about it and Mom started teaching me just after you moved. Then, after Mom died, I had to do the cooking for Dad and me. What she taught me stuck and I just kind of filled in whatever I didn't know."

"I still can't believe she died so soon after I left."

Marco nodded. "Sometimes...I still want to call her and tell her something, hear her voice."

Alice did touch his hand then, wrapping her small fingers around his and squeezing.

"Didn't mean to bring us down even more than we already are," she said.

"You still pouting about that?"

Her eyes snapped wide as she turned to look at him.

"What?"

"Let it go," he said, meeting her stare. "You keep beating yourself up about it when you should be learning from it and moving on."

"You're not the one who cost us Jamison."

"No, I'm not. Doesn't mean I haven't screwed up a mission before."

"Lionel blames me."

Marco shrugged. "He'll get over it."

The screen door creaked open again and Uncle Logan stuck his head out. His eyes were even more bloodshot, the circles underneath more like trenches, and Alice wondered if his hair would ever stay close to his scalp again, considering how much he was running his hands through the gray curls.

"I just wanted to know," Uncle Logan said, his voice halting, "if you've thought about what you'd like to do?"

Alice took a deep breath, the pancakes and bacon churning in her stomach.

Before she could speak, Lionel walked through the front gate, his frown deep.

"Lionel, what's wrong?" Marco asked.

"I know this is your decision Alice, but I think as part of the team I should get a say in it," the words falling out in a rush as if he'd rehearsed them.

"A say about what?" she asked.

"You going to see your dad."

"Oh really? And what's your opinion?"

He grit his teeth, his cheek twitching a little with the stress of it.

"I think we can do this without him," Lionel finally said.

"Thank god!" Uncle Logan muttered, slumping against the door frame.

"You too?" Alice asked. "Don't any of you think I can handle Douglas?"

"It's not a matter of handling anything," Lionel said, coming up onto the porch. "It's the fact that you shouldn't have to invite that man back into your life, in any capacity. I know that between us all we can find Jamison without his help. You just have to trust us. Can you?"

Alice looked from Lionel's beautiful face, to Marco's darkly mysterious eyes and then to Uncle Logan, whose haggard expression said it all.

I hate to admit how relieved I am but...stubbornness doesn't seem a good enough reason to go see that bastard again.

"Alright," she said, a weight lifting off her shoulders, "let's do this our way."

CHAPTER FOURTEEN

Vigilantes Help Police!
  New age of cooperation dawning?
  *The mysterious crime fighters known only as 'the Vigilantes'
have aided police once again in apprehending members of the
drug syndicate responsible for selling the drug Fantasy. The
arrests occurred at the Jet City docks early this morning.*

  *There has been no official word on whether or not the Police
Commissioner will be revoking his call for the Vigilantes to be
arrested on sight. Unofficial reports from inside the Jet City
precinct have indicated that ire toward the crime fighters is
waning.*

  *Could this be a new era in cooperation between police and
masked Vigilantes? Or is it only a temporary reprieve for the
city's unknown guardians? While public opinion would suggest
the former, word coming out of the Commissioner's office leans
toward the later.*

"You going to stare at that thing all day?" Uncle Logan
asked, parking the car in front of Atlas Books.

  Alice shook her head."I just can't believe it! In the span

175

of three weeks we've managed to take down three different locations and helped arrest more than a dozen men, yet every time there's nothing to connect Jamison."

"You'll catch him. It's only a matter of time."

She stared at the paper a few seconds more and a grin began to spread on her face, in spite of her frustration.

"It's a nice write up."

Uncle Logan shrugged. "I do try. C'mon, put that down and let's get inside."

"Alright, alright."

Alice looked at the darkened book store with skepticism as they stepped out of the car.

"There's no one in there."

"Not in there," he said, walking down the alley to the back door.

When they stepped inside, a very excited Lionel clapped his hands and laughed.

"Finally! I was starting to think you'd never get here!"

"I didn't think you liked bookstores that much," Alice said.

Lionel's smile made her legs weak and she couldn't help the silly giggle that bubbled up.

He ran up the stairs, which had been repaired and newly stained. "Hurry up!"

When she turned the corner toward her loft, Lionel was holding the door open for her. She stepped through, hands flying to her mouth as she saw the transformation.

The floors had been refinished to a rich, reddish brown and now shone as if new. Her small kitchen had new, light wood cabinets and off-white counter tops that gleamed. A matching orange fridge and stove were nestled into their spaces. Alice laughed at how little she'd probably use them. The wall of windows had been cleaned and filmy white and brown drapes hung dramatically to the side.

"Where did all this come from?" she asked, her voice breathy with surprise.

Floor-to-ceiling book shelves were on the wall between her newly-finished bedroom and the small bathroom, a rolling ladder leaning against it. Her old punching bag and sparing dummy had been replaced with new ones, and a small set of weights were resting in a corner. In the center of the huge living area was a dark brown leather couch, with three matching chairs. A low, expensive-looking coffee table sat in the middle of them. Against one wall was the most beautiful stereo Alice had ever seen, records neatly organized beside it. In front of one window was a simple, but extremely well-stocked bar, with glasses that had...

"A serpent!" she squealed, snatching up one of the glasses.

"A house warming gift," said a raspy voice behind her. "For the club soda you love so much."

Mrs. Frost's small eyes glittered as she leaned on her cane.

"And a reward for a job well done."

"Thank you, this is very...I'm amazed."

"I only gave you the glasses," Mrs. Frost said, gesturing to Lionel, who was talking with Uncle Logan. "He did the rest, or he paid for the rest, anyway."

Alice walked over to Lionel, her mouth hanging open. She wanted to kiss him, and resisting that temptation was extremely difficult.

"I'm going to make use of your bar," Uncle Logan said.

"So, you like?" Lionel asked, his grin making her resolve melt.

She put a hand on his solid arm and kissed him on the cheek. He went stone still for a moment, his navy eyes intense on hers. She didn't let go of his arm, didn't move away, and neither did he.

"I love it," she said, her mouth suddenly very dry.

Lionel smiled and stepped way.

"I'm glad. You want a drink? No, you don't, that's right. Um...club soda?"

Before she'd had a chance to answer, he was halfway to the bar and Alice felt heat rise to her pale cheeks. It was like being abandoned on the dance floor at junior prom all over again.

To her great relief, Marco and Gerald stepped through the door at that very moment. Gerald handed her a large, brightly wrapped box.

"Rose wanted to be here," he said, "but she's engrossed in an experiment."

Alice nodded. "I understand."

Gerald gave Uncle Logan a nod and walked over to get a drink.

"Excuse me?" said a pimply delivery boy, who had just shown up at the door with a simple flower arrangement. "Miss Seymour?"

"That's me."

He handed her a clipboard, and then the flowers, once she'd signed for them. The simplicity of the roses with sprigs of jasmine was exactly what Alice would've chosen for herself. She glanced at Lionel as she placed them on the coffee table, wondering how he had known so much of what she'd love.

However, when Alice opened the card, she found they weren't from him.

"I am sorry that I am unable to attend your house warming but hope these flowers will brighten your new home,
Victoria Veran"

Alice felt genuinely humbled that a busy woman like Victoria, who had been Aunt Diana's friend far more than hers, would take the time to send a personal card with the flowers.

The sound of the crisper in her new fridge opening and closing made her turn in confusion, but when she saw Marco, the frown quickly turned into a smile.

"Those will spoil," she said, peeking playfully over the top of the door. "Or I'll mutilate them in attempting to cook them."

Marco closed the door and put his hands in pants pockets, a playful glint in his brown eyes.

"What if I came over and cooked them?"

"Every day?" she asked. "Because, that's a lot of food."

"If you want."

She giggled, then realized he was being serious.

"I could teach you." He stepped a little closer to her. "Or I could just do it myself."

"You're serious?"

He nodded.

"I wouldn't mind seeing you every day," she said, not realizing, until it was too late, what that might sound like. "I mean, I do have to eat, and it would be better for me than coffee and toast, which is all I can cook."

A shy grin lit up Marco's long face, and it looked like he was about to say something else when Lionel stepped up and handed them both a drink.

"To maybe thawing the icy hate of the Jet City Police Department," Lionel said.

"And catching criminals," Marco added.

"And a shiny new apartment," Alice chimed in.

Jerry Lee Lewis's electric voice exploded from the stereo and Lionel held out his hand, eyebrows cocked in a silent question.

Without a second thought for how he'd made her feel

only a few minutes before, Alice let him lead her into the open space between her couch and the sparring area.

"And this is when I take my leave," Mrs. Frost said, stopping Alice. "Tomorrow morning, my house, you have a baton lesson with Dr. Allen."

Giving Lionel a grim stare, she walked with her best speed out of the loft.

"I don't think she likes me," he said, spinning Alice into his arms.

She laughed. "I don't think she likes many people."

"I'll win her over. I have a way with women."

"Good luck with that one."

He winked, and Alice had no doubt if, given the chance, he could indeed charm the old woman.

Many hours and club sodas later, when Gerald and Uncle Logan had gone home, Alice found herself nestled on the couch between Lionel's broad body and Marco's lean one, her head resting on Marco's shoulder. Billie Holiday was on the record player now, with a velvety night sky draped over the city.

"I'm hungry," Lionel said.

Marco chuckled. "You're always hungry."

"Can't help it."

Alice stifled a yawn.

"You want us to leave, get some sleep?" Marco asked.

"No," she said, a kind of panic in her chest.

Despite all the times she'd dreamed of her own place, now that it was a reality, Alice felt scared of the solitude. It was the last thing she'd admit though, especially after all that Lionel had done to get the loft livable.

"I have an idea," Lionel said, his fingers tapping on the arm of the couch. "What if we got some cots for me and Marco, and we used them after missions or whatever. Make this our kind of...headquarters."

"Do they make cots big enough for you?" Marco asked.

"If I paid enough, yeah."

Alice felt a sudden, profound relief.

"That's a great idea. I love it!"

"We wouldn't be stepping on your toes?" Lionel asked.

She shook her head, not caring that she was staring at him so openly. If he noticed, Lionel didn't show it. Just ruffled her hair a little and proceeded to raid her fridge.

"He's the other reason I bought so much food," Marco said, his grin wide as he got up to help Lionel.

Alice closed her eyes and leaned back into the soft leather of the couch. Lionel and Marco's conversation about deli meats faded into the background, as contentment wrapped itself around her like a warm blanket. This is how it would be, this was her future. The three of them, together again, and forever.

She didn't feel Marco take the glass from her hand, or Lionel lift her up and place her gently on the new bed.

When she woke in the morning, it would be to Marco's freshly baked cinnamon rolls and Lionel singing Elvis off-key at the top of his voice.

Mrs Frost would have her training from morning to noon, with breaks for fancy teas and debutante balls, much to Alice's dislike.

But for now, she slept and dreamed of the three of them, invincible to whatever came.

SUMMER-1960

CHAPTER FIFTEEN

The hypocrisy Alice felt, pretending to sip champagne to celebrate the long overdue opening of Aunt Diana's children's home, was nothing compared to the sensation that her brain was slowly becoming over-cooked oatmeal while she listened to the inane conversations around her.

"I mean, really," a newly-married young woman said. "How was I supposed to set up house with place settings for only eight? It's impossible. So, I told my mother..."

Smile plastered to her full lips, Alice searched the crowd for anyone that she could convincingly extricate herself to go talk to.

Her efforts were soon rewarded at the sight of a tall, familiar, blond man. His navy-blue eyes were also scanning the crowd, and when they met hers, Lionel's crooked smile deepened and he raised a glass of champagne to her. The tailored, dark blue suit fit him so well that Alice wondered why any other man would bother trying to wear a three-piece suit, as it wouldn't look half as good.

She could see Lionel surrounded by three of Jet City's most eligible debutantes. They laughed and flushed, their eyelashes fluttering at alarming speeds. They all had the full breasts and small waists that made them treasured specimens of female beauty, their pedigrees were impeccable, and their ambitions perfectly bland in comparison to any man they would marry.

As she continued watching him, she could see that he barely spoke, though he nodded a lot. His smile, which was usually so lively, looked as stiff as her own, and it struck Alice that he was even more bored than she was.

"That sounds so awful," Alice said, realizing too late that she had interrupted the newlywed's story. "I'm sorry, but I see someone that I simply must speak to before he leaves."

With the woman's dainty mouth hanging open, Alice took off toward Lionel.

When she'd left the loft two hours earlier, her dark curls were perfectly tamed in the bob she'd become accustomed to and Alice prayed it still looked half as good, as she felt the tell-tale tickle of frizzing hair. Her dark green heels gave her a bit more height than usual and the sleeveless emerald-green cocktail dress hugged the curves of her breasts and hips, in a way that made her feel proud of her figure, almost sensual in comparison to the tiny-waisted women in the room. Still though, she wished the ceiling fans were doing a better job at keeping the room cool, as a trickle of sweat fell from her underarm down the side of her body. As she navigated the press of bodies to the center of the room, where Lionel was, the oppressive June humidity seemed to get worse. Alice briefly wondered if her mascara was running down her cheeks and how the hell the rest of the women didn't seem to have a trace of perspiration.

Whoever thought it had been a good idea to have a cocktail party in the afternoon, in the middle of summer, should be shot.

Lionel's eyes danced as she came near, causing the two women with their backs to Alice to turn. They just barely managed to conceal their jealousy.

"Miss Seymour," said Mary Ansel, the niece of Mrs. Grace. "This is quite a party."

Alice smiled, trying her best to make it look gracious.

"Thank you. We wanted to reward the hard work of so many who helped my aunt's dream finally come true."

"Your aunt was Mrs. Diana Miller, then?" said a round-faced blond with a feline look in her green eyes.

"Yes, she was."

"And did you always want to take her place doing...this?" asked another, a redhead, who wasn't trying to hide her contempt in the least.

"No, actually, but I had little choice."

"Didn't I hear that you have a degree in some-thing...what was it?"

Alice felt her smile tighten. "Business."

"Yes," Mary said, her smile dripping condescension, "it is lucky that you had the prescience to have something to fall back on so early in life."

Alice glanced up at Lionel, whose grip on the cham-pagne flute seemed a little too tight, even as he expertly held his fake smile. She'd get no help from him, not that she needed it. Wading through the thorny sea of society judg-ment was something she and Mrs. Frost had gone over quite a lot lately.

She forced her smile wider, showing her straight white teeth. "Fall back on?"

"You know," said the redhead, "because you're not married." And what was unsaid was louder than ever: and you're not likely to be.

"Yes, I see. Well, what can I say? I believe that a woman who uses her intellect, rather than exchanging it for a matched kitchen set and twelve place settings of silver, is someone who will one day look back on her life and be satisfied."

"As opposed to what?" asked Mary, her eyes blazing.

Alice shrugged. "I don't know, you'll have to tell me in a few years."

"I suppose we will," the blond said, leaning closer to Lionel.

"Ladies," Lionel said, three pairs of adoring eyes turned to him at once, "I am sad to have to leave you, but I must speak with Miss Seymour for a moment."

The blond was downright hostile in her look, while Mary and the redhead gave Alice a chilly smile. Each made their farewells to Lionel as enticing as possible, before being swallowed in the crowd of cocktail dresses and three-piece suits.

Lionel blew out his lips and drained his champagne.

"Thank you. I think my step-father must know how much I hate these events, and that's why he keeps sending me in his place."

"It's strange he donated so much to the renovation project when he doesn't even live in Jet City."

"He donates to a lot of charities, good for taxes and press releases."

Alice nodded. "You don't have to stay."

He smiled down at her again and offered his arm. She felt like the winner of some unspecified prize as she took it.

"I can't abandon you to the sea of boredom just yet."

"How chivalrous."

"I try. Now, when do you leave?"

"Why? Did you have something more fun we could do in mind?" she said, looking up at him with a playful grin.

He really did look amazing in a suit, especially when he blushed.

"No," he said, his voice losing a bit of its cockiness, "your uncle said you were going to the warehouse early to scout the location, for the tenth time, and I wanted to know why."

She smiled at a fat matron and her horse faced daughter whose full attention was on Lionel, all the while anger was starting to simmer in her gut.

"Because this is the first solid intelligence about Jamison's whereabouts we've had in months and I don't want to mess it up."

By now they'd made it to the other side of the room by the stage where Alice would be forced to give a speech in a few minutes. It was a fraction of a degree cooler here, beyond the press of bodies and Alice dropped the syrupy smile she'd worn all afternoon.

"I'm tired of losing," she whispered to him, her fists clenched.

"Losing? We've helped the police severely curtail the Fantasy drug trade these last few months, and earned their respect."

"But we haven't gotten him! And until we do-"

"You can't make it about revenge, Alice," Lionel said, his eyebrows knitting together over stormy eyes. "It never ends well."

"I know but…every time I come back empty handed all I can think is that I let Aunt Diana down."

"Hey," Lionel said, his hands on her upper arms.

She could tell that he wanted to hug her, but they both knew the folly of such an action in a room full of society gossips.

We are already giving enough grist to the rumor mill by talking privately like this.

"We're close," he continued. "That tip from our snitch looks solid. If everything goes well…"

Alice nodded.

They'd been close three times, and come up short.

Fourth times the charm?

"There you are," said a raspy voice behind Lionel.

Mrs. Frost was leaning on her serpent-headed cane, her mouth twisted in a sour expression.

"Mrs. Frost," Lionel said, turning up the charm as he bent over her hand. "You look ravishing this afternoon."

Her expression didn't change, though Alice swore she saw a twinkle in the old womans' eye.

"You are monopolizing the most important woman in the room, young man," she said.

"You're right, how terrible of me," he turned to Alice and gave her a conspiratorial smile. "Until later?"

Alice returned the grin and watched as he crossed the room, seemingly oblivious to every heart that broke as he passed.

"That one is trouble," Mrs. Frost muttered.

"Yes, the good kind," Alice said before she could think better of it.

Mrs. Frost tapped her cane on the floor and grunted, a sound that Alice knew was disapproval but she didn't care in the least.

When she turned back around, Alice thought she saw a look of intense pain cross Mrs. Frost's wrinkled visage before she turned away, her shoulders hunching. As Alice was about to reach out to her, Mrs. Frost's shoulders straightened and she turned back around, a deep frown etched on her face.

"It is horribly hot in here," Mrs. Frost growled

"This gathering is ridiculous, you know," Alice said, not even trying to hide her contempt toward Mrs. Grace as the woman walked by.

"Yes, I do. But if you want to keep improving the city, you need to humor the peacocks with the purse strings."

"You have purse strings, why can't I just humor you?"

"Because your charms do not work on me. I see you managed to offend some of the younger peacocks."

"It wasn't hard. My very existence offends them."

Mrs. Frost sighed, pressing her lips together. "If you would at least attempt to be civil, then we could begin work on some significant projects. Your aunt knew how to get what was needed."

"Well, she's not here. You have to make do with me."

"I am trying to do just that, but you resist every lesson!"

"Because this," Alice waved a hand at the afternoon party, "isn't what I want. I want...well, you know what I want. This is your idea."

"A public persona is important."

"And being a bookstore owner wasn't good enough!"

"Not by half!"

Alice turned away, her face flushing with anger. She hated this woman half the time and the other half wanted to hate her, but couldn't, for some reason.

Maybe because Aunt Diana trusted her. But I'm not my aunt, and no matter how much she tries to make me be her, I just can't!

Guilt laced with more anger suffused her and Alice had to step away for a moment to calm down.

"I will never be what you want me to be," Alice said when she came back.

Mrs. Frost tapped her cane on the hardwood floor.

"We want the same things. But, not unlike someone else I know, you are too stubborn to see that right now. One day, and I hope it is soon, you will."

Not likely, you old bat!

"Now..." She handed Alice a piece of paper with a simple speech on it. "Smile, and speak clearly, just as we practiced."

"This better be the last one of these for a while," Alice muttered to herself.

At that moment, Mrs. Grace ascended the dais and took command of the room. Her pinched face was doing its best to seem happy at having to introduce Alice, but it was obvious she'd rather be working at a soup kitchen just then.

Taking a deep steadying breath, Alice climbed the stairs to dais and began.

"Thank you, everyone, for coming to celebrate the opening of the Diana Miller Home for Children."

Alice, Lionel, and Marco perched on the roof of an empty warehouse, the lack of a moon, and a few deliberately broken street lights, hiding them nicely. The night was clear, the faint scent of salt on the warm air.

"Criminals don't have a lot of imagination when it comes to locations, do they?" Lionel said, as they stared at a darkened warehouse.

It was only a few blocks away from their first mission together, though to Alice's eyes it looked identical.

"You'd think, after a few times of getting busted, they'd find some variety," Lionel continued.

"Never gave it much thought," Marco said.

"You're grumpy tonight," Lionel said.

"No, I'm focused."

Lionel shrugged.

"There," Alice said, pointing at the thin man that had just exited the warehouse.

He walked three paces, lit a cigarette, and adjusted his hat.

"That's the signal," Marco said.

The particular warehouse their snitch had led them to was supposed to have a safe with specific shipping schedules and proof of money laundering . It was also supposed to have Jamison himself coming to pick up the information.

Lionel jumped down into an alley with Alice in his

arms. Marco soon followed, his grappler making it possible for him to swing down the fire escape.

"I really need to thank Rose for this," he said, putting the grappling gun in his shoulder holster.

"Not to mention the body armor," Alice said, with a playful smile.

"Yeah," Marco said, with much less enthusiasm.

After several close calls with chest wounds, Rose had made a chest piece for Marco from the same material she'd constructed Alice's. He grumbled about it at every opportunity.

The new suit, however, Marco didn't mind so much. Instead of a plain dress shirt, Rose had made him a collarless black shirt out of a ballistic nylon that wasn't overly stiff. Over that, he had a dark gray vest made of the same specially-treated leather as Alice's suit. It zipped up to his collarbone, and with the under-armor, helped protect his torso. His new shoulder holsters held two grappler guns. And instead of having to worry about losing his brass knuckles, Rose had made gloves with the weapons inside of them, along with forearm guards. His pants were the same ballistic nylon as his shirt and were tucked into armor-reinforced boots that laced up to his knees. He'd flat out refused to wear a cowl, so Rose made a custom-fit mask and put a harmless, light adhesive on it to keep it from being easily ripped off.

Rose surprised all of them when she produced a smoky gray leather duster to top off the suit.

"How am I supposed to fight in this?" Marco had asked.

"It adds an air of mystery. Figure it out," Rose had answered, before turning back to her work bench.

She'd been right and Marco had indeed figured it out.

Once Lionel had gotten a look at Marco's new costume, he pouted for a full ten minutes until Rose brought out his new one.

Instead of a simple mask, Rose had made Lionel a blue leather cowl that concealed his light hair as well as his identity. The rest of his suit was ballistic nylon that somehow managed to cling to his muscled body. The suit was actually quite simple, with just a blue shirt, to which the cowl was attached, and a pair of dark red pants, but on Lionel it was heroic. Rose somehow found reinforced, off-white, knee-high boots that fit Lionel's huge feet, and after pestering her for two weeks, Rose also made him a pair of off-white fingerless gloves that, as Lionel put it, completed the suit quite nicely.

They ran across the street and to a small door on the dark side of the warehouse. Alice hoped their snitch had remembered to lock all the others to keep anyone from getting away. Once inside, they found themselves in a small entryway filled with empty boxes. The labels said the boxes were supposed to contain canned meat, but when Alice saw the tiny symbol at the left corner of the box her heart stopped.

"Look," she whispered.

It was a leafless tree with three stars above it. Most would see that and think it was a harmless little drawing, but Alice had learned in the last few months that the symbol she was looking at was a code for the drug, Fantasy.

"Jackpot," Lionel said.

"We should've brought back up," Marco said, his eyes turning black.

"Why?"

"There's ten men, and a couple of them...it's strange, there's something not right."

"Like they've been sampling the product?" Alice asked.

Marco shook his head. "I don't know, they're definitely erratic though."

Lionel moved into the lead position. "Can you take them out from here?"

Marco's shadows appeared and began weaving themselves in and out of his legs and arms. After nine months, Alice had gotten more used to Marco's powers, but sometimes they still made her skin crawl.

"Not the drug users. But, I may be able to take care of three of the others."

"Do it. Let me handle the users. Alice, you..."

"Take out whoever comes at me?"

Lionel smiled. "Yeah."

Alice double-checked her darts, which she had started to call serpent bites. They'd come in handy often, and Alice had begun to count on them in a fight. Tonight, she wasn't going to make the same mistake she had before. This time, she'd use whatever was at hand to bring Jamison to justice.

She crept into the warehouse, keeping to the shadows of the stacked crates and machinery around her. When she was in the middle of the warehouse, whispers of conversation started to become clearer.

"Please, I just...I need more!"

"I'm sorry, we discussed this," said a man with a deep baritone voice. "Phantasm decides who gets what, and when. You're not on the list."

Who is Phantasm?

The muffled sounds of someone grabbing another, then a brief struggle reached Alice where she was crawling along behind the crates. If she could get closer maybe she could see what was going on.

And if Jamison is here yet.

"You need to calm down," said the baritone. "You remember what we do with rabids?"

"I remember!" The man's voice was getting hysterical. "But, I've still got enough in me to make this interesting. We both do!"

194

Alice was close enough now to see the men. They were standing at the bottom of a wide set of metal stairs. The man with the baritone voice had his back to her, his black suit straining at the enormity of his body. He was facing four other men. Two of them were sweating far more than the humid night warranted, their eyes blood shot and wild. They were each being held back by men who appeared to have nearly as much muscle as Baritone. What Alice found surprising was that the two sweaty men were relatively small, compared to the others, yet the muscled men were having a hard time restraining them.

What are they on? I've never heard of Fantasy giving people enhanced strength.

She squatted down behind some of the crates to watch and listen. If she could learn something new about the Syndicate and what they were doing before all hell broke loose, she had to try.

On the other side of the warehouse came a set of terrified screams.

Baritone sighed. "I told you not to bring the new guys. Phantasm scares the shit out of them every time."

"Phantasm's here?" asked one of the sweaty men. "Let me go! I need to see him!"

Alice gasped as one of the sweaty men broke free and snapped the neck of the muscle man behind him. It looked no harder for him than breaking a twig.

Baritone drew a gun and unloaded it into the other sweaty man, who was just barely being restrained.

Baritone started to reload. "Get the other one and—"

The sharp report of a gunshot rang out, breaking one of the few lights. Muffled sounds of fighting echoed in the warehouse.

"Damn it!" Baritone said. "Go find out what the hell is going on!"

I have to get to the office on the second floor! If Jamison hears the gunfire he might escape. But how am I going to get past this guy?

Baritone turned and walked a few steps in her direction. She saw that one of his eyes was hidden under a patch, a deep scar running under it from his hairline to his square chin. He scanned the area above her and Alice held her breath, looking for a good moment. She had to get a jump on him. Fighting head-on with a guy this size was something she could do, but would rather not.

Baritone turned around at the sound of someone falling into crates, followed by more gunfire and screams. Seeing her chance, Alice shot a serpent bite and hit his cheek. The man swatted his face as if killing an insect. For good measure, she swept his legs out and landed a swift kick with her reinforced boot to his face, but the man was still lucid enough to catch her foot and push back. Alice fell, and as the man crawled toward her, she rolled to the side, and balancing on her hands and one knee, she kicked him in the face.

Blood streamed from his nose, and from the glassy look in his eye, Alice expected Baritone to simply fall over.

He didn't.

Staggering to his feet, he towered over her, meaty hand snapping out and seizing her arm.

She pivoted, ramming her elbow in his solar plexus and hearing the satisfying groan of air from his mouth.

But, still he didn't let go.

"You're not supposed to be here, Serpent," Baritone said in her ear.

"Never could resist a dark warehouse." She feinted a hit to his groin and hooked her foot onto his ankle instead, sending Baritone to the floor.

He laid there for a moment and Alice thought she'd finally done it.

Then he rolled over. His movements were sluggish, but there was a feral glint in his eye.

"He'll have your head for this," Baritone's words were slow.

"Who? Jamison?"

Baritone laughed. "He's a pawn. You...have no...idea."

He collapsed face first. Alice waited to make sure he was out, and then heard the soft thud of a body behind her.

She turned to see someone lying unconscious a few feet away. Lionel was on the stairs, fighting off one of the muscle men. Alice was surprised to see blood on Lionel's face. It wasn't unheard of for him to be wounded, but it was rare.

If he's blocking the stairs...

She looked around, trying to see if Jamison was running through the chaos around her but she couldn't see him. Lionel gave a cry from the stairs where he was locked in a fight with a large, muscled man.

Alice jumped onto a nearby crate and launched herself at the muscle man, landing on his back. She pressed her gauntlet into the man's neck and shot a bite. She jumped off just before he fell back, tumbling down the stairs.

"Where's Marco?" Alice asked.

Lionel's eyes grew huge behind his cowl and he pushed her down. "Look out!"

The glint of a knife flashed above her head. Before she could stop it, the knife was lodged in Lionel's chest.

He stared at it and staggered back.

Alice looked up and saw that it was the other sweaty man, the one who'd broken one of the muscle men's neck.

He laughed, a high-pitched sound that chilled her blood.

"Not so special are you, Steel? A dose here, and one there, and I can," he pulled the knife free, "be even better than you."

Lionel fell onto the stair behind him, blood flowing freely from the wound.

Alice had a moment of true fear. What if the knife had pierced Lionel's heart? Was that something he could come back from?

The sweaty man raised the knife again to finish Lionel off. Alice snapped out of her shock and punched the man in the stomach. He took the hit and laughed at her. Then he back-handed her, almost sending Alice over the railing.

"Stupid bitch!"

He was thin, shirt and pants hanging on his frame. How he'd managed to land a blow that was even stronger than Baritone, Alice had no idea.

And it didn't matter.

Sweaty man raised the knife again.

Lionel kicked the man's knee cap, and Alice heard a sharp crack.

The man barely reacted.

Alice raised her gauntlet and shot him with two serpent bites, just for good measure. Then, she kicked his legs out from under him. Sweaty man fell down the stairs.

Alice expected him to get back up.

She didn't expect the knife to be lodged in the man's gut.

He pulled it out, blood on his teeth as he grimaced.

"You'll both be sorry! There's more of me coming and you'll wish I'd killed you tonight!"

He staggered toward the stairs, and then fell, like a puppet with cut strings.

Alice stared at the man in shock. But then, the smell of smoke stung her nostrils and she knew things had gone from bad to worse.

"Steel?" she said.

He staggered to his feet. One huge hand was pressed to his chest, and Alice could see his labored breathing.

A man came running behind Lionel swinging a bat down towards his head. He stopped cold as if someone had frozen him place. His eyes became huge and he screeched in terror as shadows wound around him. Marco appeared behind the man, duster swirling around him as he punched the man and threw him over the railing.

"It should...heal," Lionel took a step and stumbled.

The blood was staining his shirt, spreading out.

"We have to go," Marco ducked under Lionel's arm and pulled him up. "One of the men started a fire. It's burning up the crates."

"No," Lionel said, grabbing the railing. "We need the evidence… or it's all a bust!"

Without a word, Marco ran up the stairs.

"C'mon," Alice said, "we have to get you out of here."

The smoke was so thick now that it burned Alice's eyes and was making it hard to breath. When they got to the side door it didn't budge.

"That little—" Alice said, throwing herself against it.

"He was playing us," Lionel growled. "Move."

Lionel took a deep breath and threw himself against it. The metal door bent, but didn't open. He did it again, this time clutching his chest wound and wincing. The hinges groaned and gave way a little.

Alice coughed from the smoke.

Lionel pressed against the door and, after another minute, it gave way.

He pulled Alice through and into the clear air. She coughed as they ran across the street.

The flames spread fast and Alice wondered if there had been an accelerant in the warehouse, maybe a chemical used in the creation of the drug.

Bottom windows began breaking, flames seeping out from them, and Alice looked around in a panic, realizing Marco wasn't there.

"Shadow?" Lionel yelled.

"Shadow!" Alice echoed, running to the alley.

He wasn't there.

She scanned the roof tops, but there was no sign of him.

"Shadow!" she yelled again.

"Here!" he answered, running down a side street.

Alice threw her arms around him.

"You got it?" Lionel asked.

Marco nodded, coughing.

"There was something weird in the office. Like a lab of some kind. I don't think this was just about Fantasy."

Lionel winced and leaned against the wall of a nearby warehouse.

"Let's talk about that later. Right now, we need to get him to Gerald's," Alice said.

Usually, Lionel leaped across rooftops as Alice and Marco rode on the Lightning to and from missions. But tonight, Alice knew that wasn't an option. She patted the seat behind her and stared at him until he sat. Alice had never driven the motorcycle with someone Lionel's size behind her.

"This will be interesting," she said as the Lightning purred to life.

"I'll meet you there," Marco said, shooting his grappler onto a fire escape and zooming to the top.

The wail of sirens began to echo as they sped away from the burning warehouse and Alice knew that Detective Garrick would have some choice words for them tomorrow. As would Mrs. Frost.

But all that paled in comparison to the lead weight in her gut as she began to grapple with the logical next step in catching Jamison. For months she'd avoided thinking about it or, if she did, Alice made excuse after excuse about why they didn't need Douglas' help. Tonight had been their last shred of intelligence, the last chance to catch Jamison.

Marco and Lionel would try to come up with alternate plans, they'd try and tell her that it was just a matter of time, to be patient. But she knew that wasn't true. They'd used every contact, called in every favor and still, Jamison eluded them.

We don't have a choice anymore. It's time.

CHAPTER SIXTEEN

VIGILANTES TORCH WAREHOUSE

Police are currently looking for the vigilantes known as American Steel, Shadow Master, and Serpent in connection to a warehouse fire that occurred late last night.

The warehouse was connected to the crime syndicate that has been distributing the drug known as Fantasy. Detective Garrick told the Chronicle that the warehouse could have contained thousands of dollars' worth of the drug.

The police have been looking for information regarding the identity of the person behind the dangerous hallucinogen, known as Fantasy, for nearly a year. With scant leads and no arrests, this warehouse could have contained information as to the identity and whereabouts of the distributer of this drug.

Detectives are now attempting to sift through what is left of the warehouse in hopes of uncovering anything that may lead to some success in this case.

When asked to comment, the Mayor's office released this statement:

"Although many in Jet City owe a debt to the vigilantes for their service, this careless act raises some serious questions as to whether the vigilantes should be allowed to continue. We will

hold a special city council meeting to discuss this issue and decide what is best for the people of Jet City. The Police Commissioner will advise his men on how best to handle the vigilantes until such time as more permanent laws are in place. In the meantime, we ask all citizens to neither detain nor encourage the vigilantes."

Despite such statements, citizens who have been helped by the vigilantes took to the streets and have been seen protesting outside City Hall. A representative of the citizens has stated that they will break into the city council meeting to have their voices heard, if need be.

This, coupled with the recent violent protests on behalf of negro college students, has police on edge, with some voicing concerns that perhaps it isn't worth keeping the vigilantes in Jet City, after all.

Alice sighed as she set the paper down on her coffee table. Even the loud thump of Mrs. Frost's cane as she paced up and down the loft couldn't distract her from the way her stomach twisted.

Mrs. Frost grunted out an annoyed sigh and Alice clenched her jaw. The woman had shown up early, waking Alice up and demanding to know if she'd seen the morning paper.

Alice jumped off the couch and began spooning coffee grounds into the percolator. There was no way she was going to let Mrs. Frost berate her without a little caffeine in her body.

"Well?" Mrs. Frost asked, small eyes boring into Alice. "What have you to say for yourself? All the goodwill you have spent months building up with the police and city council is gone in one night!"

"We made a mistake."

"Yes, that is obvious."

Alice spun around, eyes blazing. "You never made a

mistake? A mission never went sideways for you? We did our best. None of us expected someone crazy on Fantasy to torch the place!"

"If you had brought the police with you for a mission like this, perhaps it would not have happened. You would not only have preserved your reputation, but garnered even more respect. Now," Mrs. Frost shook her gray head, "you will be lucky if they allow you to start over."

Alice threw the spoon into the sink and watched as the percolator warmed up. It was nothing she hadn't said to herself a dozen times, but to hear Mrs. Frost say it just made Alice angrier.

"This was all about catching Jamison. You have been so focused on that, you didn't think the mission through. You are far too impulsive," Mrs. Frost continued. "And so is Lionel. Sometimes, I think Marco is the only one with a brain between the three of you, but he lacks the spine required to make both of you stop and listen."

"Enough! I know we made a huge mistake! I don't need you rubbing my face in it. And I certainly don't need you insulting my teammates."

"Oh no, heaven forbid I do that!"

"What do you want from me? A blood oath to run every decision past you in the future?"

"If I thought it would make any difference, I would accept your sarcastic offer in an instant." Mrs. Frost sighed, easing herself down onto a chair. "What I want, Alice, is for you to see the larger picture. To plan and decide things, based not on one mission, but instead to look down the road, to see a year or two from now. How do you want the city to see you? What do you want to have accomplished for them? Your actions in everything you do will determine the answers to those questions, will determine your ability to protect the city, which is what ultimately matters. Not your thrill when you punch a man or see your name in the paper."

Heat rose to Alice's cheeks as she poured the coffee. What was so wrong with getting a kick out of those things? And how was she supposed to make sure that every mission added up to some future legacy?

She asks the impossible! No wonder Aunt Diana quit!

"Are you going to at least offer me a cup of that?" Mrs. Frost asked.

Alice poured her one, but didn't join Mrs. Frost at the table. The two sipped their coffee in silence, listening to the distant thunder of a summer storm. Soon, the patter of rain against the windows filled the silence and Alice closed her eyes, enjoying natures symphony.

"Alice," Mrs. Frost's voice was low, almost gentle.

It made her eyes snap open in surprise. There had been a handful of times Alice could remember hearing that tone from Mrs. Frost.

The woman met her eyes, a strained look on her face, bordering on pain.

"Are you—"

"Fine." She waved her hand and took a deep breath. "I am well, thank you, just a little indigestion. Coffee on an empty stomach."

"What did you want to say?"

Mrs. Frost frowned, looking into her cup. After a moment, she shook her head, spine straightening. "Nothing, it can wait. Don't forget, later today, you have the Ladies Auxiliary tea at two o'clock."

Alice sighed and set her cup down. "I think there's far more important things to be doing than that, don't you?"

"No, I do not. I doubt punching a criminal will provide food for a poor family's table, or shelter for them. This part," Mrs. Frost pressed a wrinkled finger to the table, "of your life, is just as important as what you do at night. The sooner you see that, the better."

Alice took a large swallow of coffee, knowing that she had to tell Mrs. Frost what she'd decided, and knowing she had to do it today before she lost her nerve. Mrs. Frosts eyes bore into her as silence dragged on.

"What is wrong?" Mrs. Frost asked at last. "You never just accept what I say in these matters without at least a snort or roll of the eyes."

Alice kept her gaze on her coffee, the words stuck in her throat.

"You've decided to see him, haven't you?" the old woman asked.

Alice nodded, tears itching her eyes.

"My dear that's…very brave. You can skip the tea, just this once. I have a feeling this will be taking all your energies today."

"Thank you."

Mrs. Frost walked toward her and patted Alice's hand.

"He can't hurt you anymore, but you already knew that. These fears, they are normal. Just remind yourself that you have the power now, not him."

"I'll try."

Jet City's prison was a mammoth pair of rectangular buildings overlooking the newly-expanded freeway on one side and the blue water of the Sound on the other.

After being searched and signing in, a guard escorted her and Uncle Logan down a hallway painted a robin's egg blue, which was strangely cheerful. One turn to the left, however, and they were in a new wing with ash gray, bare walls.

They stopped at a glass door that looked several inches

thick and was steel-reinforced. Beyond it, were the prisoners who were dying or injured.

My...father.

"You don't have to do this," Uncle Logan said, holding her hand. "We can try-"

"No," she shook her head. "There is nothing else to try."

"I wish...Alice, we never wanted him to be in your life again."

"I know, and he's not. He's a means to an end."

Uncle Logan squeezed her hand.

"I'll be right out here."

She nodded, and walked through the door before her courage failed.

Only three patients lay in the daffodil yellow room with it's paintings of seascapes and wheat fields. Large windows to her right over looked the water, which must've been quite nice on a clear day instead of the overcast one they were having now.

The beep of a machine at the far end of the room drew her attention to where a frail man lay under white sheets and a thin blue blanket. He was propped up with three pillows behind him, a pair of glasses perched on his large nose to aid him in reading the battered paperback he held.

Even at the distance of so many years, with the ravages of time and illness written all over his features, Alice knew it was Douglas.

Her stomach churned as she walked toward the man who had made her childhood a nightmare.

Once she was close enough, Alice recognized the cover of the book with a distant jolt of shock.

Asimov...he reads the same books I do.

"It's not time for my-" he said, looking up over his glasses.

The moment his watery eyes met hers, Alice felt a jumble of emotions burn through her.

Sadness.

Anger.

Fear.

Confusion.

They swirled in a terrible cocktail of fire in her veins until she felt her heart pounding in her chest, sweat breaking out on her cold hands.

She wanted him to speak, to laugh, to do something. Anything rather than just stare at her.

But in the end she had to break the thick silence around their little corner of the room.

"Hello," she said, her voice rough, small. "I'm-"

"Alice," he said, his voice flat but his eyes moist. "I… You have your mother's eyes."

At the mention of her, anger rose up to win the battle for dominant emotion, and Alice clenched her hands at her sides.

"You should know, you blackened them often enough," she said before she could stop herself.

He looked down, closed the book slowly and nodded.

"Yes, I did. I assume you're not here for pleasantries."

"No."

"Well? Ask then."

Anger turned to hate in the span of seconds, burning through her as if her blood had been changed to lava.

There was something she wanted to ask, needed to, that was true. But it wasn't about Jamison. In that moment there was only one question that occupied her brain, the one she'd asked hundreds of times as a child: Why?

Why had he beaten her mother?

Why had he been so cruel?

Why couldn't he love her?

Tears welled up, hot and terrible in her eyes and she looked away.

No. I won't give him the satisfaction of knowing the wounds he gave me still hurt.

"Jamison," she said instead, her voice surprisingly steady. "I want to know how to prove that he's involved with the Syndicate, beyond doubt."

Douglas crossed his horribly thin arms, lips pressed together as he studied her. She hated the scrutiny, but refused to look away.

"I see. And what do I get in return?"

A bitter laugh escaped her lips.

"I don't owe you anything."

"I want you to keep visiting me," he continued, as if she hadn't spoke. "Once a week, for thirty minutes."

The thin scrap of control Alice had been clinging to evaporated and she advanced on the old man in his sick bed.

"You made my life hell, and now you want me to-"

"Visit your dying father."

"You're not my father. The man that raised me is waiting just beyond those doors. You're just…You're just biological product."

"Well, this 'biological product' has the dying wish of seeing you once a week. Or there's no deal."

Swearing under her breath, Alice turned and paced a few feet away from him, taking deep breaths in an effort to get back some control.

I could walk away and Uncle Logan wouldn't blame me…But I'd blame me. I need to find Jamison.

She glanced over her shoulder to see Douglas had gone back to his book and realized, with maddening frustration, that he had nothing to lose in this. But she did.

The desire to hit him was overwhelming and she was just barely able to contain it. He'd played this perfectly, knowing how important his information was and what she'd do to get it. She'd thought her escape from him was permanent and he'd barged into her world again.

Only this time, she wasn't helpless. Yes, he had a lot of power over her with the information he was hoarding. But she had power, too. The power not to be affected by him, to not let him make her his victim ever again.

"Fine," she said, walking back, her spine straight, "I'll come see you once a week for thirty minutes."

He looked up at her over the top of his glasses, his expression bland.

"But?" he asked after a moment.

"But I decide what we talk or not talk about. If we sit here for thirty minutes reading without saying a word, then that's what we do."

"Done. Now, you want to know about Jamison, right?"

"Yes."

He folded his glasses up and closed the book.

"The first thing you need to know is Jamison is one of three."

"I know that, three heads of the Syndicate."

"Well good for you doing your homework and everything, may I continue?"

She rolled her eyes and waved him on.

"The…what does the newspapers call it? Oh yeah, the Fantasy drug syndicate has three leaders. I only ever worked for Jamison, so I can't tell you who the other two are. All I can tell you is they aren't to be messed with."

"Oh really, and why is that?"

The wrinkles on his forehead deepened, eye brows knitting together.

"You believe in evil, girl?"

She raised an eyebrow at him.

"After a childhood with you? Of course I do."

Alice had to give Douglas credit. He only flinched a little at that.

"I only ever saw the other two once, but it was enough for me. They're pure evil, and won't be intimidated by you and your friends in masks."

Her stomach dropped.

"Oh yeah, I know all about what you do with your nights," he said, grinning. "I guess your aunt's influence outweighed your mothers at the end."

"You shut up about them, you're not worthy to even think about them."

"Alright, alright, enough with the theatrics. All I'm saying is that Jamison is a good target, stick with him and leave the other two alone."

"Besides the bone quaking evil," Alice said, crossing her arms, "why should I?"

"Word in the organization was that those two had some kind of…mutually assured destruction. If one turned up dead, the other would exercise their plan. From what I heard, it was bad enough to start a war in the city. And I'm guessing you don't want that."

"No, I don't."

"Well, then, stick with Jamison, and we'll all be happy."

"Where is he?"

"You're in luck actually. Tonight he'll be having dinner at a little Chinese restaurant in the Dregs, the Red Dragon."

"How do you know that?"

"Because he has dinner there every third Monday of the month. They close the place down for him and everything."

"Alright, but how is that going to help convict him? He's just having dinner there."

"No, he's meeting one of the others there. No idea which one, it changes all the time. But they'll have a very creative accountant there with some very cooked books."

Alice's eyes widened.

We could get two out of three of them!

"No, don't even think it," Douglas said, pointing a

finger at her. "Remember. Mutually assured destruction. You want to get Jamison before the other two arrive, he's always early to this thing."

I don't take orders from you old man.

"Fine," she said instead, "what time is this clandestine meeting?"

CHAPTER SEVENTEEN

Marco's brow was wrinkled with thought as he asked, "You're sure about this?"

Alice nodded. "If you'd seen him, you'd know he was telling me the truth."

"It's really that easy?" Lionel's voice was bright with shock and excitement. "We just show up at the Red Dragon?"

"When have you *ever* known a mission to be easy?" Marco said. "Just because he's going to be at this restaurant doesn't mean this will be straightforward. Douglas didn't say more about what kind of war would be sparked if we got the other two?"

"Or who they were?" Lionel asked.

"No, he just said it would be bad. But, I've been giving it some thought."

Marco's eyebrows raised.

"I've learned not to like that look."

"What if we're just a little late?" she asked, not able to contain her grin. "Then we could at least see who these others are."

"But if they bring their own men, we could be seriously outnumbered."

"Not if we alert Detective Garrick," Lionel said, his face lighting up. "They could be our back up. Just think of it! We could nab all three of them and then no one could say anything about us. I bet the mayor would even give us a medal."

"Before you go writing your acceptance speech," Marco said, "are we sure we want to tackle this? I mean, calling in the police is a good call either way I think, but…we have no idea what we could be stirring up."

"C'mon! This is what we started all this for. To defeat these kind of men who think they're above the law. Think of how many people have died because of Fantasy, think of the people we could save by seriously crippling the syndicate."

"I'm surprised you didn't mention the women we could date," Marco said.

"Well, that goes without saying."

Alice rolled her eyes.

"Glory aside," she said, "it's worthwhile to at least try. This is going to be hard even with backup. Douglas said that everyone in that place will be heavily armed, including the employees. And he also said that Jamison might have super strong goons."

"Like the ones we saw at the warehouse?" Marco asked.

"The same."

"Okay, so I hit a little harder than usual. We can do this!"

Alice couldn't help being affected by Lionel's excitement, not that she needed much encouragement to indulge her own feelings. She'd dreamed for months about avenging Aunt Diana's murder, and now she could not only do that, but dismantle a large part of the syndicate.

"Alright," Marco sighed. "What's the plan?"

Alice's body hummed with energy, a now-familiar sensation that preceded every mission. She crouched on the rooftop of an apartment building that sat a few buildings down and across the street from the small restaurant. Alice took a deep breath, the smell of Chinese food drifting on the warm night air, a hint of something sour behind it.

She'd loved coming to the International Quarter or the Dregs, as some called it, when she was a girl. Crammed into the far northwest corner of Jet City, the Dregs was a place where cultures clashed in a brilliance of businesses, homes, and traditions. Bright red-and-gold paper lanterns danced in a breeze perfumed with barbeque chicken. Small kosher delis sat across from dry cleaners and bakeries selling Mexican sweet breads and Gallinas.

Aunt Diana and Uncle Logan had frequented the delis and restaurants, knowing most of the owners by name. Alice had always been entranced by the riot of sights and sounds. One Lunar New Year, her aunt and uncle had brought her to the Dregs for the celebration. Never had she seen so much color, or eaten so much food. She remembered how everyone, no matter their background, had celebrated.

As she scanned the buildings around the Red Dragon, Alice became distracted by the fact that not much had changed. The same signs, repainted every year, graced the windows of the businesses. The sidewalks were as swept and neat as they had been when she was a girl. Flower boxes filled to bursting with bright blooms dotted the apartments and outside of some of the businesses. Even the smells were the same. A part of her wished that the Syndicate had just left this part of the city alone.

Focus! No time for trips down memory lane.

Most of the buildings had small alleys behind them, but

the Chinese restaurant also had a small passageway to the left of it where Alice could see trash bins and boxes from food deliveries. The garbage bins created a barrier between the passageway and the alley, and with everything stacked into it, it was very narrow.

Not a great place for a fight.

A door opened on the passageway side of the restaurant, and a man in an ill fitting suit stepped out and lit a cigarette. He walked to the end of the passageway and looked up and down the street, then up at the buildings. Alice ducked down, even though she knew that he wouldn't be able to see her where she squatted in the shadows on the roof.

After a moment, Alice heard a car pull up. She peeked over the edge of the roof and saw Jamison step out of his black Cadillac, anger warming her blood.

Patience. This is almost over.

Two bulky men stepped out with him and the car drove away. She watched them walk into the restaurant and disappear.

"One down," Lionel said where he was hiding a few feet away.

Alice knew that this would be the hardest part: waiting.

As the minutes ticked by, the more Alice's instincts screamed at her that she was losing her one chance. She closed her eyes and breathed, trying to calm her nerves.

"There," Marco breathed.

Alice didn't recognize the short, delicate man that got out of the car, but he held himself with a lethal grace she found unnerving. Just by watching the way Jamison stepped out and shook his hand, the way the huge men around him stood straighter, responded to his words with such speed, Alice could believe he was a dangerous man.

Once Jamison and the mystery man had gone inside,

two of the guards gave orders to the others and followed their masters. The others tried to look nonchalant, as if they stood outside restaurants smoking all the time.

"Garrick just pulled up down the block," Lionel said, nodding to the left.

Alice looked over and just caught a glimpse of headlights before they were extinguished.

"And the others are down there," Marco said, nodding to the right.

Alice couldn't help a smile. "Then it's time."

The clang from Marco's grappler as it connected with the fire escape on the apartment building seemed far too loud and Alice hoped no one had heard it. Lionel jumped to the ground with Alice in his arms. She hated the momentary feeling of weightlessness, but it was better than swinging from the grappler.

Lionel and Alice crouched in the shadows cast by the apartment building. Marco moved across the street to the guard in the passageway, his duster flaring, and shadows writhing around his body.

A moment later, Lionel and Alice followed towards the passage.

Marco began manipulating one of the guards, who ran to the edge of the passageway in a panic. Lionel hit him, lifting the man off his feet, and then down onto his back. As Lionel straightened from checking that the guard was alive, a man came out of the front of the restaurant, and rounded the corner to the passageway.

He saw Alice first, and one drew a huge dagger. He lunged for her and she kicked the dagger out of his hand, then grabbed his lapel and shoulder. When she pulled, he tried to grab her shoulder and take back control. He was stronger and Alice was about to lose her balance, so she drove her foot onto his thigh, using the momentum to bring them both to the ground. Wrapping her leg under his head and around his arm, she pulled, feeling the elbow pop. The man screamed and Alice shifted her leg, and smashing his face into the dirty sidewalk.

Someone came up behind Alice, pulling her off the now unconscious man and out of the passage. An arm snaked around her neck and tightened. She fought to find any purchase at all to stop this man from suffocating her. Unable to gain any traction, she shot a dart into his meaty thigh.

Usually, the victims of a serpent bite were down fast or easily subdued, but this man was still holding onto her neck. Panic burned on the edges of her thinking, but she shoved it aside and fired another dart into the man's leg. Finally, he let go of her, falling to his knees. She crawled away, gulping air, her lungs burning and throat raw.

A huge hand appeared in her field of vision. The moment before she shot it, she realized it was Lionel's. As he pulled her to her feet, he scanned her body for injury. Alice looked around, the bodies of about half a dozen guards lay in the passageway or at the mouth of it. She was amazed that no one else had come out of the restaurant.

"When those guys don't come back, they'll know. We gotta get into the back of the restaurant. Are you okay?" Lionel asked.

She nodded, trying to ignore the pain in her throat.

As they ran into the passage, a man opened the side door and looked around. Upon seeing the three heroes, he raised his gun and Lionel jumped in front of Marco and Alice. When the bullets hit him, Lionel gave a grunt of pain, but leapt forward and punched the man, knocking him out.

After nine months, Alice still wasn't used to seeing Lionel get shot, even if he could walk it off.

The shots warned the others inside and Alice could hear

glass breaking, as the restaurant's front door was being broken down. Garrick and his men were in play now, and Alice knew they had to get Percy's personal guards, who were a different breed of soldier, according to Douglas.

The trio burst into a small kitchen, crowded with two stoves, a huge sink, and a long table in the center for food prep. Two men grabbed cleavers and butcher knives and ran for them. Alice dodged two swipes of a gleaming butcher knife, stepped back, and then dropped down under a third swipe, kicking the legs out from under the man wielding it. He fell hard onto the cold linoleum, the butcher knife still in his hand. She aimed a serpent bite, but the man batted it away with the flat side of the blade. Then, jumping up, he took a slash to her middle, the blade scraping against the leather of her vest. He screamed in frustration as Alice punched his face, and then landed a kick to his gut. She was going in for another kick when he brought the blade up, aiming for the soft underside of her jaw.

Suddenly, the man's eyes bugged and he began beating the air with the knife in his hand. Alice glanced up and saw Marco walking toward them, his shadows twisting in the air. Just over Marco's shoulder, Alice saw more men running into the kitchen. One aimed their gun at Marco's head.

Alice rushed forward, falling to her knees and skidding to Marco's side while shooting a serpent bite at the gunman, whose aim went wide, hitting Marco in the shoulder. The shadows began to dissipate, like mist in the sun, though they didn't dispel completely. Marco had learned to maintain his concentration while wounded, and the man with the butcher knife ran out of the kitchen as if chased by hounds from hell.

The man with the gun turned his weapon on Alice, who pivoted on her hands, lashing her leg around to kick the man's legs out from under him. The gun went off, the bullet taking out a light in the ceiling. She shot him with another dart, and when he still attempted to raise his gun, she jumped on him and hit him in the face.

They pushed the kitchen door open, and Alice's heart beat out a wild rhythm as her senses adjusted to the chaos of so many people fighting in a small space. Her eyes started scanning for Jamison but she couldn't find him.

"Focus Serpent," Lionel said.

She nodded, gritting her teeth just before running into the fray.

She shot the nearest goon with two serpent bites as he lunged for her and hoped it was enough to at least slow him down, as she ducked under the punch of a second assailant.

Lionel grunted nearby, doubling over as a man hit him. Alice thought he must have a pipe or bat or something, but when she saw his empty hands Alice started to wonder just how many enhanced goons were here.

With great trepidation, she drew her batons. Her lessons had proceeded well, but she'd never drawn them in a fight until now.

"Down!" she shouted as another hit made Lionel double up.

He dropped to a knee and Alice launched herself off his back, bringing her baton down on the man's head before landing behind him. He was dazed enough for Lionel to finish him off, which was good, because another man dove right for her. She brought the baton across the man's face, but he blocked her, grabbing her wrist. She was close enough to kick him in the groin. When he doubled over she brought her other baton straight at his face, blood splattering from the impact.

Despite this, the man only stumbled back, dazed for a moment, before launching himself at her. She fell with him to the floor, landing hard on her back, something wet beneath her.

He brought his hand up to punch her and she jerked away at the last second, his hand connecting to the floor with a crunching sound. She shifted, bringing her legs up and over. With one quick motion, she flipped him to his side, his arm in her grip. She pulled up hard. The elbow popped, but in that instant a boot flew towards Alice's face, knocking her back. She felt blood in her mouth and bright spots blew up in her vision as her grip went limp. She felt herself being lifted by the front of her vest, and then a hard blow crashed into her stomach, pushing all the air out of her. She couldn't breathe.

"You're a real pain the ass," said a voice she'd only heard once but knew very well.

Jamison.

The inner strength that had held all her pent up fury for nine months was gone when her vision cleared enough for her to see him. One thought blazed in her mind: He's responsible for Aunt Diana's death.

She found air once again and let out a scream of rage as she swung her batons in quick succession at Jamison's face. He dodged all three times, and on the fourth swing managed to intercept Alice's wrist. He twisted it savagely. The gauntlet didn't let him break her wrist, but it still strained something. She felt a pop and screamed in pain.

"Oh yeah," he grinned, "I've had some improvements made to myself since we last fought. This might hurt a lot."

She could hear her name being called, distantly it sounded as if the fight could be winding down. But the only thing that mattered was this moment, this man.

Breathing through the pain in her wrist, Alice kicked Jamison in the groin and he released her hand. Then she delivered two quick right hooks to his face, cradling her injured wrist at her side. He laughed at her and stood up, wiping a trickle of blood from his lips.

"Cute, but pointless," he said.

She was about to shoot her last serpent bite into him when his fist careened toward her face, followed by an explosion of pain from her jaw.

The impact of the blow and that blinding pain sent Alice to her knees.

"You just had to stick your nose in!"

Jamison kicked her hard and Alice didn't just lose her breath, she could feel a sharp, terrible pain in her chest.

He's enhanced…he's going to kill me.

He yanked her up by one arm, dangling her like a prize. Her jaw and chest screamed in agony, pain clouding her mind.

"Now you find out what happens to-"

A gunshot rang out and she was dropped to the floor, landing hard on her injured wrist. When she tried to cry out, the pain from moving her jaw was like nails being driven into her skull.

All around her was chaos, as more gunfire erupted. Someone shouted her name again and Alice wanted desperately to get to them, but couldn't see who it was.

Surrounded by the last of the fighting, and in no position to be able to defend herself, Alice felt panic rise in her throat. With grunts of pain, she drug herself toward the far end of the restaurant. Her vision began to get dark around edges, as each movement brought fresh waves of pain from her wrist, jaw and chest, but she pressed on.

A hand landed on her shoulder and Alice tried to wrench herself away.

"It's me," Lionel said, slipping his arm under her.

She moaned as he picked her up, her mind starting to go fuzzy.

He gasped. "Oh God, hang on, I'm going to get help."

A distant kind of consciousness began to overtake her as Lionel carried her outside to a waiting squad car. In tremendous pain, tears fell down her rapidly swelling face.

Two people got in the car with her, one of them kept saying something to her and the other hissed in pain. As the car pulled away with a squeal of sirens and tires, Alice felt more and more like a spectator to her injuries.

At some point in the pain-induced haze, the car stopped and someone picked her up. Alice wanted to fall asleep. She tried to ask if she could, but excruciating pain shot through her head and she cried out.

"It's okay," a voice said. "It's going to be okay."

"Put her down there. Tie this around Marco's shoulder and make it tight."

Marco...What happened to Marco?

Alice's mind cleared for a moment and she tried to sit up, but someone was holding her down. She looked in panic at Gerald's weathered face and tried to speak.

"Hold still," he snapped, and she felt the tiny sting of an injection.

The fogginess returned, and Alice couldn't remember why she'd been so afraid. Who was it for? Why did her face hurt?

Before she could ask, a blessed sleep overcame her.

———

The first thing Alice was aware of was the smell of burnt coffee.

The second was nauseating pain.

"Alice?" Marco asked.

She tried to open her eyes, but only one obeyed her. After a few moments of forced blinking, Marco finally came into focus, his thin lips smiling, cuts and bruises on his long face.

It took another minute or two for Alice to realize he was shirtless. Her eyes strayed from the bandage on his shoulder to a huge purple bruise on his chest. She reached out slowly, as if her hand was reluctant to obey, and brushed her fingertips over the bruise.

He caught her fingers in his warm hand.

"It looks worse than it feels."

Alice wanted to call him a liar, but her mouth was too dry and her jaw hurt when she tried to move it.

"Awake are we?" Gerald said, his dark face showing the falsehood of the nonchalance in his voice.

"What...?" she croaked, wincing with the effort.

"Don't try to talk," Gerald said, fingers checking her pulse. "I've fixed your broken jaw, but it'll be sore for a few days, and the concussion was mild, all things considered. There were some torn tendons in your wrist, which I've also repaired, but you still shouldn't use it for a few days, so I splinted it. The most serious were the broken ribs. I had to do the most healing on those but they will still ache. You've got some bad bruising on your face and your eye is swollen shut. I did what I could to help it all heal quickly, but you're just going to have to deal with it for a few days."

She tried to nod, but the effort brought a fresh wave of pain. Her gaze swung to Marco and the bruise on his chest. It looked like an impact wound.

And then it hit her.

He was shot! Without the under-armor he'd be dead.

Tears welled as she looked into his brown eyes, realizing how easily she could lose him. The thought made her throat close up and her chest constrict.

"Hey," Marco said, smiling down at her. "I'm okay, honest. Gerald took care of the shoulder and this hurts a little, but it's going to be fine."

Her fingers tightened on his hand, a desperate need to hold onto him making her cry even more. She wanted to tell him how impossible it would be to recover from losing him. But the pain in her jaw wouldn't let her, and in the end, she drew his hand toward her, pulling him in close. He knelt, and pressed a light kiss to her forehead.

"You took quite a beating," Marco whispered.

"She's going to need to go back to her loft and rest," Gerald said, loading up a needle with what Alice could only assume was a painkiller.

"Logan should be here soon," Marco said, his fingers caressing her forehead absently, "but we can stay with her until then, you don't have to."

Gerald nodded. "She'll need someone to be there in the morning, just to make sure she doesn't do too much. Rest is what she needs."

"We can do that, too," Lionel said from the doorway.

Marco jumped up, a look of guilt flashing across his face. And was Lionel looking jealous? No, he couldn't be, could he? It all confused Alice, but she couldn't latch onto any thoughts as the painkiller started making her mind fuzzy.

Sleep was closing in on her, but before she succumbed, Alice had to know something. She looked up at Marco, opening her mouth just a little.

"We got Jamison and the other one," he said, as if reading her thoughts. "But...he's not...they're-"

"Garrick shot Jamison," Lionel said, still keeping his distance. "It was the only way to get him off you. And the other one was caught in the cross fire. The accountant, however, was unharmed."

"Whether he lives to testify is another matter."

Dead...they're both dead.

Douglas' words rang in her mind, and Alice was coherent enough for a few moments to fear the consequences of what they'd done tonight

"Get some rest," Lionel said. "We'll take care of everything."

Her mind fought to stay awake, to take all this in, but the painkiller Gerald had given her was too strong. Before she could react much at all, sleep covered her mind in a warm blanket.

CHAPTER EIGHTEEN

It was almost comical, the sight of three grown men jumping every time she moved or sighed. No need was too small for their notice, no desire unattainable. If she wanted ice cream, Marco was out the door before she could tell him what flavor. If she wanted a book, Uncle Logan ran down to the shop and insisted on reading to her. And if her room began to annoy her with its lack of anything interesting to look at, Lionel was there to lift her up and carry her to the couch.

All of it was nice for the first half of the first day, and then Alice began to be annoyed. She was injured, but healing at an incredible speed. There wasn't a need to be waited on hand and foot!

By the afternoon of the third day, she'd had more than enough of being coddled.

"Where are you going?" Uncle Logan asked, rushing toward her.

"To the bathroom," Alice said.

"Here I'll—" Lionel said, reaching for her.

"I can walk to the toilet!"

Lionel and Uncle Logan looked at her like anxious

parents seeing their toddler walk for the first time. It felt so good to be back on her own two feet that she started to walk a little faster, and immediately regretted it. Her head started to throb and feel cloudy. She grasped her sparring dummy until it passed, refusing to look behind her at the men who were just waiting for any sign that they should swoop in and help.

Once she was finally in the bathroom, with the door closed, she sat down on the toilet with a sigh of relief. The world took a while to right itself and once it did, she was more frustrated than ever.

"I better be past this tomorrow," she murmured.

Apparently, she'd taken more time in the bathroom than she thought, because when Alice opened the door, Lionel and Uncle Logan sprang at her. Her body ached and her head began to pound like someone was beating it with a hammer, but she forced a smile and shuffled to the couch. Uncle Logan was there to fluff the pillows and Lionel handed her a bowl of re-heated beef stew that Marco had made.

"Where is Marco?" she asked, realizing she hadn't seen him since yesterday.

"Got called in on assignment," Uncle Logan smiled. "Said to tell you he'd make cinnamon rolls tomorrow, if you wanted."

A hard knock on the door cut off Alice's retort that what she wanted was to be left alone.

"Where is she?" said a harsh voice Alice instantly recognized.

"Come in," Lionel said, as Mrs. Frost pushed her way past him.

Her piercing blue eyes looked Alice over, the wrinkles on her face deepening with her frown. She turned a steely gaze on Uncle Logan. "You did not inform me that she was this bad."

"Well, she is," he said.

Alice looked from one to the other as they stood on either side of her.

"I see." Mrs. Frost placed both hands on the head of her cane. "You blame me, do you?"

"I just don't think you need to know everything."

"I will inform Gerald that he needs to attend to his patient and get her fit."

"You will not! She needs time to heal, she's not a machine!"

Mrs. Frost opened her mouth to respond, but Alice had reached her limit.

"Enough! I'm not fragile, and you should've told her. And Gerald has done all he can do, so don't bother him."

Uncle Logan's stubbled jaw tightened and he glared at Mrs. Frost for a moment longer before going to make himself a drink.

Mrs. Frost turned her gaze on Alice and sat down.

"I assume they have not been keeping you informed."

"About what?"

"She doesn't need to know this right now," Uncle Logan said. "What can she do about it?"

Alice stared at him.

"What is it? Why are you keeping things from me?"

"It wasn't just him," Lionel said.

"Unbelievable!"

"Yes, quite," Mrs. Frost said, giving both men a cold stare. "She deserves to be treated with respect by the two of you, not as some wilting violet."

What's happened in the world to make Mrs. Frost and me in agreement for a change?

"Fine," Uncle Logan said. "The past twenty-four hours, three different places have been shot up by unknown men. Garrick told me that the places were traced to the second boss at The Golden Dragon."

"Douglas warned me about this," Alice said. "It sounds like the remaining boss has started trying to consolidate."

"Yes, and that's not all," Mrs. Frost turned her attention to Alice. "This will not be easy for you to hear, but you need to know. Last night, Victoria Veran returned home after a fundraiser to discover her two children and her husband murdered in their home."

Alice's stomach fell.

"Oh god...Oh my god...is Victoria alright? I mean, was she-?"

"She is alive," Mrs. Frost said. "But we need to know if this is a random crime or somehow tied into the Syndicate. If perhaps Diana and Victoria were working on something that threatened their interests."

"Why would Victoria be a part of all this?"

"She likely isn't," Uncle Logan said.

"Even you can't deny that the timing is rather suspicious!" Mrs. Frost said.

"Even me? What the hell does that mean?"

"Stop," Alice said, her head really starting to hurt now.

Mrs. Frost and Uncle Logan looked away, their faces furrowed with frown lines.

"Mrs. Frost," Alice said. "Why would Victoria be connected to any of this?"

"I don't know, but, as I said before, the timing is too strange for her not to be."

Alice chewed on her lip, trying to remember if any of Mr. Veran's business dealings could be connected to Fantasy in any way.

There is one person who might know…but I'm not due to see him until next week.

Sirens wailed in the distance and Alice glanced out the window to see smoke rising from somewhere on the waterfront.

A moment later, Alice jumped as the phone let out a

shrill ring. Uncle Logan's face was grim as he listened to whoever was on the other end. He made some assurances to them and hung up, running his hand over his face. After a minute, he drained his glass of whiskey.

"That was Detective Garrick, he says that smoke is the work site of the Veran Foundation's Science and Research Institute. Someone has burned all the supplies there and all the preliminary work."

"So first Victoria's family and now this," Lionel said. "That can't be a coincidence."

Alice clenched her jaw against the pain her head and set her feet on the floor.

Looks like dear old dad will be getting next week's visit today.

"I need to get dressed."

"And do what?" Lionel asked, putting a large hand on her shoulder to stop her.

"I have to talk to Douglas, find out what is going on."

"Wait if you do that then-" Lionel said.

"He already knows about me."

"What?!" both Mrs. Frost and Uncle Logan said.

"And I don't think he's going to tell anyone that will believe him," Alice continued. "He's dying and not likely to be getting any visitors."

"This can wait until—"

"What? Until Phantasm blows something up or kills someone else? We can't sit around here and wait for him to strike!"

"She is right," Mrs. Frost said. "This could be nothing but rival business leaders looking to discredit and ruin investor faith. Or, it could mean something far worse. Either way, you need to find out what you can."

"I'll take you to the prison," Lionel said.

Alice nodded. She wanted to believe that Victoria's family being murdered was just a tragic event and had nothing to do with taking out Jamison and the other. Guilt nagged at her as she slipped on a pair of capri's and a soft, sleeveless blouse. A question rose up in her mind and refused to go away.

If Tony Veran was involved and he was the one that was supposed to be punished by the syndicate, why was Victoria left alive? Could she be in league with the one leader left?

Warm summer air bathed her face as she sped through the city with Lionel, Elvis crooning on the radio. The car stopped far too soon, and Lionel helped her out. She stood for a moment, eyes closed, letting the bright sun warm her skin.

Lionel's hand touched her elbow, snapping Alice back to reality, the prison looming in front of them.

"Here." He handed her a pair of large sunglasses to hide the still-healing bruises around her eyes.

"Not your style," she said, slipping them on. "Who do they belong to?"

He shrugged. "I don't remember."

"One day, you'll have to settle down, you know."

Lionel grinned. "Maybe you could help me with that."

Her stomach flipped. "If you ask very nicely."

He laughed and offered her his arm. She tried not to lean too heavily on him, but couldn't help it. If she moved too fast her head began to swim. Falling on her rear wouldn't help right now.

It was just like last time. Same hallway with the robin's egg blue, down the same gray hall and then to the hospital wing.

"I'll be right here if you need me," Lionel said.

When she stepped through the doors, she noticed that the room was missing one of its patients, his bed stripped and waiting for the next man.

She glanced over at Douglas who sat up in bed, face drawn in a stern frown.

"I can guess why you're here," Douglas said. "Just couldn't help it, could you?"

Alice slid the sunglasses off and sat on a nearby chair, her back giving a twinge of pain.

"Someone worked you over good," he said, eyeing her remaining bruises.

"Jamison packed more of a punch than I anticipated."

"So, you're seeing the consequences of your actions today? Is that why my weekly visit is early?"

"Yes."

Douglas shook his head, loose skin swaying under his chin. His eyes looked a little more bloodshot today, and his skin had a gray pallor to it that Alice hadn't noticed before.

I wonder if he's close to the end, which means I won't have to visit all that much.

She winced with sudden guilt and tried to move past such thoughts.

"Shouldn't you be in bed?" Douglas asked.

"I'm fine. I need to know why the leader of the syndicate might be targeting the Veran family, specifically Victoria Veran."

Douglas shrugged. "No clue. As far as I knew, no one had dealings with that family. Unless they had something to do with the person that cooked up the drugs."

Alice's ears pricked up at that.

"Do you know who that is?"

"The same one that's now leader of the whole damn thing thanks to you. Don't know their real name, and never saw their face, they always wore an old gas mask and suit. Boys called him Phantasm."

Alice sat up straight.

"You know it?" he asked.

"I've heard the name before. Thought…well, thought it was just another goon. But he's the leader?"

"Yeah, was some big shot scientist before the government shut him down. That's all I know and all I ever wanted to know. The guy's something else, a different breed of criminal. His men aren't natural."

"What do you mean?"

"He does something to them. Makes them strong but takes away their personality. My buddy used to call them Phantasm's Automatons. They were just like that, too, robots every one of 'em."

"And no one ever said who they were or-"

"No. And I'm stopping you right there. Don't even think about going after Phantasm."

Alice glared at him.

"You don't get to tell me what to do or try and protect me. You lost that chance a long time ago."

"I know that," he said, looking down at his hands. "I know you hate me, and…with good reason. But you're still my daughter-"

Anger sent Alice jumping up, ready to bolt from the room. She instantly regretted it as nausea hit her and the room spun. Alice plopped back into the chair and leaned over, taking deep breaths to calm herself. She couldn't show him any more weakness, she wouldn't!

"You shouldn't be here, go and rest."

"I'm fine I just…need a minute."

"Alice-"

"Don't ever call me that again," she said, looking up at him through the dark curls that had fallen into her face. "I'm not your daughter or your responsibility."

Douglas exhaled through his nose.

"Fair enough."

"I need to know because if I'm responsible for Victoria's family dying, then I need to make it right."

"Is that what happened then? Huh…"

"What?"

"Well…I mean….Mutually assured destruction."

Alice stared at him and then laughed.

"So what, Victoria Veran is Phantasm?"

Douglas chuckled. "It does sound insane when you put it that way. A woman being that ruthless! No, but I'd bet Tony Veran was connected somehow."

Alice only half listened as Douglas talked more about who Phantasm could be. Pieces of this puzzle were starting to come to her and Alice didn't like what she was seeing.

He's right. No one would suspect that a woman could be a crime boss with a reputation like Phantasm's and that would make it a very good cover. But Victoria? No, absolutely not. She's…she's my friend. I know her. She couldn't be so cruel.

Shoving those thoughts to the back of her mind, Alice concentrated on spending the last ten minutes of her visit quietly reading a book, pretending not to feel Douglas' gaze on her every so often.

Though the book was good and she was more than ready to stop thinking about all this for a few hours and sleep, Alice still felt that nagging suspicion in the back of her mind and made a reluctant mental note to look into it.

CHAPTER NINETEEN

It was a shock the first time Alice stepped foot in the huge underground gym that Mrs. Frost had built in her home. Even though she knew Mrs. Frost had to have trained during her time as Serpent, she somehow never thought the woman would keep such a place next to her wine cellar. The equipment was somewhat antiquated and the place smelled like it hadn't been used all that much in the last two decades, but it was good enough for Alice's baton lessons. New mats had been purchased, as well as a punching bag.

Alice had used it sparingly at first. But when Mrs. Frost kept insisting that she needed better training, both as Serpent and Aunt Diana's heir, Alice began to train there almost every day.

Gerald had cleared her a few days ago for physical activity, so Alice had been using every moment she wasn't in the book store to train. If things were about to get ugly, she wanted to be ready.

Alice threw up her crossed batons to stop Gerald's downward attack. Sweat poured down her body and itched her scalp.

"So, Douglas believes that the only reason the Verans would be targeted is because they were somehow involved with this…Phantasm?" Mrs. Frost asked from where she sat observing them.

"Yes," Alice hissed as Gerald put pressure on his attack.

"But you do not believe that it's Victoria specifically?"

She twisted to the side, just as Gerald's baton broke through hers, letting his forward momentum propel him down. Alice swung her baton down on his back, a light tap only, of course.

"No, I don't."

Mrs. Frost paused, hands clenched on the head of her cane, there was no doubt that Mrs. Frost heard the hint of uncertainty in Alice's voice.

"The manner of the attack on Victoria's family matches those of others who have fallen afoul of the Syndicate. Coupled with the attack on the construction site of Victoria's Science Foundation and-"

Gerald attacked Alice in a flurry of baton thrusts and swipes, sending her stumbling back.

"Come now, concentrate!" Mrs. Frost exclaimed.

"On what? You or him?"

"Both!"

Never had Alice wanted to swear at an old woman as much as she did in that moment.

"If…" she said, dipping into a roll to avoid the baton connecting with her head, "…we knew what—" she brought her batons up again and swiped Gerald's legs, "—Tony was working on…maybe something against the Syndicate?"

"Or on behalf of Phantasm."

Alice grunted as Gerald's thrown baton hit her in the stomach.

"Gerald, that will do for today."

Gerald nodded and wiped his face with a nearby towel.

"Are you alright?" he asked Alice.

"Yes, but I have to wonder. If you can fight like this, why aren't you out there? Or were you, and I just don't know about it?"

"I never was, not really. And I'm not out there now, because I'd rather be healing than hurting. This...well, I learned this because I had to."

Alice wanted to ask why, but Gerald turned away to get a drink of water and she knew that was the end of it.

Mrs. Frost began walking to the door. "Alice, come with me."

The only thing Alice wanted to do was shower and eat something, but when Mrs. Frost commanded Alice had learned the hard way that you obeyed.

She followed Mrs. Frost up the stairs and into the private hallway that led to her rooms. You had to admire the old woman, she was sneaky. The private halls had several different entry points. One from the underground gym, one from the kitchen, using a seemingly in-operative dumb waiter, and one from what looked like an abandoned storm cellar out behind the house. Mrs. Frost had insisted that Alice know every inch of the halls, to the point where she could navigate them blindfolded.

Though a little annoyed at the exercises at first, Alice was starting to see the benefit. In her last few fights, her senses were better, and her focus sharper than before.

When they entered the private upstairs study, Alice was glad to see a light lunch, two towels, and her change of clothes. She guzzled the water and dried her face with one of the towels as Mrs. Frost walked to her desk. Beside it were three large, ordinary-looking, document boxes.

"I requested these a few days ago and expect you to find some very interesting information in them." Mrs. Frost grinned.

"What are they?"

"See for yourself."

Alice threw back the lid and pulled out the first file. The minute her eyes saw the first page, Alice gasped.

"Are they all..."

"Yes."

She flipped the lid off the second box and pulled out another file. Though the work that the Veran Corporation had done since Tony Veran's tragic accident was public knowledge, what he was doing for the government after the war wasn't. In fact, no one had ever been able to find out anything, other than he was badly burned and his back injured at the government facility where he worked. Even the address of the facility hadn't been public knowledge, nor were the names of the people who worked with him. But what Alice now stared at, nestled in each box, was all that information, and more, about the secret project.

With shaking hands, Alice lifted a few pages out of the file. She felt like she was discovering some hidden treasure.

"How did you get these?"

"It does not matter. What does matter is what Tony was working on, and possibly still had been, before his death."

"It's public knowledge that the Veran Corporation has government contracts, including what the contract is for. This," she pulled out another file, "is top secret."

Mrs. Frost sat down with a sigh that sounded more painful than tired.

"Buried in the quarterly reports for the corporation is a small consideration for medical research and development. It is so small that, by all appearances, it could be charitable."

"But you don't think it is?"

"I am not sure. That is where you come in. I do not have the patience to sift through all this. But, I have a feeling you would be delighted."

"Not that I'm complaining, but wouldn't Rose be better

suited for looking through scientific research?"

"If you need her expertise, she is, of course, at your disposal. But what this needs is someone who can see all the disparate pieces and fit them together." Mrs. Frost smiled. "Have I thought wrong?"

Alice laughed. "No, you haven't. This is...well..."

"This is not an opportunity to find out more about your favorite business woman." Mrs. Frost's voice was sharp. "I need you to be detached. To accept whatever may come up, to not be blinded by your admiration of the woman. Is that clear?"

"Do you think," Alice swallowed. "I mean, the idea of a woman vigilante is still laughable would it be...I mean-?

"Do I think a woman is capable of being the villain as well as the hero?"

Alice wasn't sure she wanted Mrs. Frost's honest answer, but she nodded anyway.

Mrs. Frost paused. "We all, man and woman, have the capacity for great good, or great evil. Just because someone is taught to be gracious and soft, doesn't mean they can't also develop a spine of steel when needed. I suppose...Yes, I do think a woman can."

"I was afraid you'd say that," Alice said with sigh.

"My dear, if she isn't what you thought she was, you must accept it, do your duty because no one else will. This is your burden, no matter your feelings about the person."

"Did you ever have to fight someone you cared about?"

Mrs. Frost looked down at her cane and Alice swore she saw a grimace. When the old woman met her gaze again it was bright with tears.

"Once. I don't wish it on you my dear. But we don't always get to choose who our adversaries are. Now," she cleared her throat, straightening her spine. "The memorial for Victoria's family starts in two hours. I assume your uncle is picking you up?"

Alice nodded.

"I will leave you to it then."

Once the door was closed, Alice nibbled on the sandwiches waiting on the coffee table and did her best to push away the suspicions her mind had been wrestling with.

I need to look at these without bias, if that's even possible. I wonder…who was the last person to even see these?

Glancing at the clock on the wall, she smiled.

"Two hours…let's see how much I can find out."

Soon she was lost in the files. Most of the math and chemistry was beyond her understanding, so she focused instead on the notes and the names of the people. There were five lab assistants at the beginning of the experiments. And three months later, a sixth was added. At first, Alice didn't recognize the name, but the more prevalent it became, the more she felt as if she should know it.

"V.G. Muller...Muller...I've read that somewhere..."

She began pacing up and down the room, when it finally hit her.

"Muller was Victoria's maiden name. V.G...Gertta...is that her middle name? Could that be her? And why would she use that name?"

She wrote it down with several question marks around it.

Though Victoria had been a partner in her husband's scientific endeavors after the war, the common assumption was that she acted as a civilian consultant. But, if Alice was correct, Victoria had been more than that. She'd been Tony's most trusted lab assistant.

But, why keep it hidden?

"Maybe married women weren't allowed to have a job like this? I could believe that, even now," she muttered, a spark of anger rising in her.

She had a hard time discerning what the two experiments were at first. They weren't referred to outright, each having code names. One was called Sea Breeze and the other Hercules.

"Hercules? That's...oh my God!"

She scanned the files with that name and leaned against the wall, mind reeling.

"Physical enhancement, just like Percy's men, and the ones at the warehouse. But why kill Tony if he's the one giving you the goods?"

Pressing her fingers to her eyes, Alice felt a headache beginning. The clock above her chimed and she bolted to her feet.

"No! No, no, no!"

She ran into the private bath and did her best to cleanse the dried sweat off her body.

Just as she was slipping into plain black heels, someone knocked on the door.

"Miss Seymour?" the butler said. "Your uncle is here."

"Thanks! I'll be right down."

Racing down the stairs and through the front door, the bright sunlight momentarily blinded her. Slapping on the pair of wide sunglasses Lionel had loaned her, she slid into her uncle's red '55 Ford Squire.

"Sorry, I was just—"

"I know what you were doing," he said, charcoal eyes hooded by a deep frown.

"Why are you so angry? I thought-"

"You almost died taking out two of them. And now you're going after the third. Did you even stop to think that…God, I can't believe I'm saying this! That Douglas might be right? That this is something you should just walk away from, leave alone? If a career criminal like him is afraid of this Phantasm, then that should tell you something."

"It does."

"And?"

"That I might be the only one to stop them."

Uncle Logan's mouth tightened into a thin line.

"Alice, you might be a damn good fighter but you don't have powers, not like Lionel and Marco. You could get killed."

His voice broke a little on the last word and Alice's growing anger was mitigated. She took a deep breath and tried, with every shred of self control she possessed, not to yell at him.

"I don't expect you to understand this, but I know that I'm supposed to do this. Powers or not."

"A calling, huh?"

"Yes, actually."

He shook his head.

"You sound just like Diana at the beginning."

"Is that so bad? Is it so terrible to know who I am and what my place is in this world?"

"No, of course not! It's bad that you can't see the danger until it's beating the crap out of you."

"I learn from every mistake, you should know that about me by now. I won't be caught off guard again, not like that."

"So stubborn," he muttered.

"Just like you."

They didn't speak the rest of the ride.

Victoria's mansion was on the the outskirts of the city, nestled in a gated community with other opulent dwellings. The drive along the winding, shady road would've been nice under other circumstances, but today Alice just wanted to be far away from her uncle's angry silence. After passing four other mansions with ornate gates and security systems, they finally arrived at the Veran Mansion. The heavy, wrought iron gates were open, and the tires of her uncle's car crunched on the gravel drive as they waited behind three other cars. Alice admired the simple, finely-manicured gardens extending along the gravel drive, the faintest scent of jasmine and lavender on the hot air.

At last it was their turn to get out of the car. Uncle Logan opened the door for her, and took her hand gently in his.

"I know you feel a responsibility," he said. "And a part of me couldn't be prouder of your courage, but I don't think you really know what you're getting into."

"I'm not doing it alone," she squeezed his hand. "Lionel and Marco are with me. It might be hard, but I know we can do this. We got Jamison and the other guy, didn't we?"

"And look what happened to you."

Alice clenched her jaw, which still ached a bit. Would nothing but total surrender be good enough for him?

"I just want you to know when to walk away," Uncle Logan said.

A sweating young man in a valet's uniform asked for Uncle Logan's keys.

Alice took a deep breath, accepting Uncle Logan's arm as they got in line to wait with other black-clad guests to go inside.

"I'll try. I promise," she said.

"I guess that will have to be good enough."

Inside the tastefully decorated great room the air was surprisingly cool. Great piles of ice twinkled in the lights under trays of chilled food. Two long bars, with attendants busily mixing drinks, were on either side of the room. The soft sounds of Debussy underscored the subdued conversation. If not for the sea of black dresses and suits, Alice wouldn't have known this was a memorial for Victoria's family.

At the far end of the room, a small podium had been set up with three portraits in front of it. One was of a handsome man with dark hair that receded from his high forehead, bright green eyes framed by dark glasses, and a gentle smile on his wide mouth. Tony Veran had been a war hero, a scientific genius and philanthropist, not to mention, the love of Victoria's life until the Syndicate cut him down.

Two smaller portraits sat next to Tony's, showing toe-headed children on the cusp of adolescence. Pale skinned, with the delicate features of their mother, the boy was older than his sister, and had wanted to follow his parents into the scientific field. Like their father, they were innocent. But unlike him, they weren't given a chance to see what their lives might hold, what great things they might accomplish.

Alice wanted to meet the person who could do such a thing to a child, so she could...what? Kill him?

The thought was disturbing, not least of which because it felt like the right thing to do. She shook her head, trying to dislodge the picture in her mind of Serpent taking a life. It was the one line that Aunt Diana and Mrs. Frost never crossed, the one she couldn't contemplate. Not when she had to be clear-headed and find Phantasm before anyone else lost someone they loved.

Alice jumped when a door behind the podium opened. At first, the doorway was blocked by a huge man in a black suit. His height and hair reminded Alice of Baritone from the warehouse, but she shook it off. He was likely dead or in custody. And why would he be here, anyway?

The man stepped aside and Victoria walked through. Her pale hair was swept back in a simple knot at the base of her neck. Her black dress hit just below her knee and moved like ink in water as she walked with a dancer's grace to the podium. Her large, dove-gray eyes were red-rimmed and bright, as if she'd been crying for days, and her usually perfect red lips were pale. She scanned the quieting crowd, and her gaze lingered on Alice. The stare sent ice through Alice's veins, dredging up those suspicions.

"My friends..." Her voice was soft and yet hard at the

same time. "It means so much to see all of you here today. I will not pretend to understand why these things happen. I saw much during the war to make me doubt in the innate goodness of humanity. But...when I met my husband, he helped me believe again. Having him gone..." She looked down, long hands gripping the sides of the podium. When she looked up again, her eyes, usually so full of warmth, had become hard and cold.

"I want to make it clear that I will be taking over my husband's business and philanthropic interests, effective immediately. Seeing his dreams come to fruition will be my total purpose, for as long as it takes. Starting with the Science Research and Fellowship Institute on the water-front. He believed in what science could give humanity, in the hands of the right people. And I do, too. Thank you, all of you, for being here and for your compassion, your support."

She left the podium as abruptly as she'd arrived, the guests looking around, unsure whether to applaud or simply walk away. In the end, it was a little bit of both.

Victoria took a few moments to shake hands with several women and their husbands as she moved toward the balcony. She looked back once at Alice, who felt that same rush of ice as before.

"You should go to her." Uncle Logan's hand was gentle on her arm. "Your aunt meant a lot to Victoria and it might help to speak to you."

Alice took a deep breath and walked outside. Humidity hit her like a blow, bringing sweat to her skin in moments. The scent of jasmine was heavy in the air, it's sweetness like a thick syrup in her nose. The balcony ran along the side of the home, looking down on a large back yard with a badminton net, a swing set, and lounge chairs. Alice swallowed, thinking of the children that wouldn't be playing there anymore.

The heat had kept everyone in the house, which Alice now realized was probably why Victoria had chosen to come out here. Alice saw her, standing with her hands clasped behind her, the angle of her elbows perfectly elegant, her feet positioned as if ready to dance. Tears dripped off her pointed chin, though her head was high and her body didn't shake with even the hint of a sob.

The slow staccato of Alice's heels sounded harsh and unpleasant as she slowly walked toward Victoria. Stopping a few inches away, Alice leaned on the railing next to her, not daring to look at the grieving woman.

"It's strange," Victoria said, her voice so quiet Alice had to strain to hear her, "I had forgotten about when Tony had proposed to me, until the newspaper said it was VE day. Perhaps...so many other things get in the way, and we forget the little moments...little hands...little voices..."

"I'm so sorry, Victoria," Alice whispered.

Victoria didn't say anything at first and Alice wondered if she'd heard her. But then, Victoria turned to look at her and Alice could swear that, for a mere second, there was a fiery coldness of pure contempt in Victoria's eyes. And then, it was gone, and all Alice could see was a woman who wanted to scream and sob, but couldn't, because everyone was watching.

"Did I ever tell you about my father?" Victoria asked.

Alice shook her head and frowned at the odd change of subject.

"He was a brilliant scientist, quiet and gentle. Many of his colleagues before the war were Jewish, or of some other ancestry the Nazis hated. I used to sit and listen to them while they smoked and talked of science, dreaming of how it could make the world better."

Her gaze became distant, and the gentle smile on her lips faded.

"But then, the war came, and those men...I was fourteen

when I fled my home and volunteered with the SIS. I thought…I don't know what I thought. That I could save some of them by becoming a spy, I suppose. I had six successful missions before my first failure."

"What happened?"

"We were compromised and captured. When the Nazis discovered who I was, they took me to a lab where my father was working for them." Her voice took on a hard edge. "He told them that I was smart, that I would make a good lab assistant. I assume he thought he was saving me, that I would stay with him. But the Nazis weren't that considerate."

She swallowed, her hands tightening until the knuckles turned white.

"Victoria?" Alice said.

"The concentration camp they took me to was infamous for its experiments. I wasn't given quarters with the other prisoners, or given a number, but everything else…I was to assist one of their doctors. When I refused, he made me watch as he tortured a woman. For hours that was all I could do, just sit and watch. Until he handed me a gun and told me that if I didn't shoot her, he would keep going. I believed him when he said he could make it last for days. So I took the gun, pressed it to her temple and pulled the trigger."

"Oh my God," Alice whispered.

"After that I did everything he asked and I waited and watched for a chance to escape. The doctor had taken a liking to more than my intellect by this point, and I made use of it. One night, after he'd finished with me, I drugged him, slit his throat and escaped. I didn't want to be in the field after that, so I applied to the Science Division of the SIS instead and I met Tony."

Alice could almost picture it. The delicate young woman, who'd gone through hell and the dashing, gentle stranger. Had he helped her heal? Was he the reason she was able to move past those horrors?

As if reading her mind, Victoria looked at Alice through the tears in her eyes.

"He helped me see that there was still good in the world. That my gifts could help protect it, maybe even bring it out in greater ways. After the war, I made myself a promise that I would never shirk from doing what needed to be done to protect the innocent of this world." She looked away as if she'd said too much. "But, in all the endeavors I encouraged Tony to do for the betterment of mankind, I failed to protect my own family."

Alice felt her heart squeeze with sympathy. She reached out a hesitant hand and gently touched Victoria's shoulder. Her head snapped up, and Alice immediately pulled away.

"I'm sorry, I just—"

"It's alright," Victoria said, a tight smile on her lips. "I know you only meant to help."

There was a hardness to those words that stung and Alice took a step back.

"If I could," Alice said, trying so very hard not to reveal too much. "I would—"

"Bring the person responsible to justice?"

Alice nodded.

"That's very sweet of you," Victoria said. "But people like this meet justice, eventually. It's only a matter of time. Now...I'm sorry, but I really want to..."

"Of course, yes," Alice said, turning away.

As she walked, Alice could feel Victoria's eyes on her back, but when she turned at the doorway and looked back, Victoria was standing with her back to Alice, hands clasped behind, head high.

CHAPTER TWENTY

Early evening sunlight streamed into Mrs. Frost's private office. Fans circulated stale air, and a tray of iced tea sat on the low table, but neither Alice nor Rose was paying attention to the refreshments.

Rose looked at Alice, and then back at the boxes of information Mrs. Frost had produced about Tony Veran's Army experiments. She clapped her hands like a child at Christmas and flung the lid off the first box.

"I thought you'd be interested." Alice smiled.

"Interested? Are you kidding? To be able to read scientific notes in Tony Veran's own handwriting, to see his process, his thoughts...it's amazing! I can't believe you're letting me do this!"

"Well, besides the fact that I knew you'd love it, I can't make heads or tails out of the notes. I need an expert."

Rose had already opened the very first file in the box and was scanning the notes.

Alice handed her a glass of tea, but Rose waved it away.

"How long do you think it will take to decipher all this?"

Rose didn't look up. After a minute, Alice waved her hand in front of Rose's eyes.

"Hm-m-m?"

"How long?"

Rose tore her gaze from the page before answering.

"Oh, well, it depends. Maybe a few days."

Alice nodded and plopped onto the couch. Her thoughts spun and twirled in the silent room. She'd been trying to figure out why Tony Veran would've allowed his strength serum to be used by the Syndicate, if indeed it was. By all accounts, he'd been a good man, who had used his wealth and intelligence to make the world better.

Maybe he threatened to expose the Syndicate? But then, why didn't Victoria die? Was it just luck that she wasn't in the house?…Or by design because she's…No, I'm not going to think about that! We don't have enough proof.

Rose sat down next to her.

"You seem preoccupied."

"I'm surprised you noticed."

"Well, your silent scowling is very loud."

Alice nudged her playfully and was about to say something when Rose winced, grabbing her side.

"What happened?"

Rose sighed. "You remember that protest at Jet City College?"

Alice stared at Rose. "You were there?"

"I couldn't let my friends protest something like that and not show up. I've been on the sidelines of all this for so long and I wanted to be a part of it, to change all this."

"How did you get hurt?"

"When the violence started, a couple of the women I was with grabbed me and we ran. I fell and hit my ribs on the curb, broke one of them."

"Your dad—"

"I've never seen him so angry. He healed me, and then tried to restrict me to this house, like I'm still thirteen!"

"He is strangely protective when it comes to you," Alice said.

"He says it's because of my mom, but what does that have to do with protesting discrimination and racism? He should be proud of what I'm doing, not trying to hide me away like some fragile princess!"

Alice had seen Rose truly angry only a handful of times and each time was always shocked at the passion that burned under her friend's peaceful exterior.

"What are you going to do?" Alice asked.

Rose shrugged.

"I don't know. But I'm done hiding away. If he wants me to stay in my lab, he'll have to lock me in."

"I wouldn't put it past him."

Rose grinned. "Yes, but I'm very good at solving problems."

The butler knocked on the door, his voice stiff. "Miss Seymour, a Mr. Mayer is here."

"I'll be right down," Alice said.

Rose's grin widened and her eyebrows waggled.

"What's that for?" Alice asked.

"Marco's here, huh?"

Alice felt her stomach drop, as laughter burst from her lips.

"Yes, as a friend. One of the theaters is playing Casablanca for this weekend only, and he's taking me to see it."

"Uh-huh."

"Cut it out. It's not like that between us."

"Well..." Rose reached for an iced tea. "If you say so."

It's not.

A nagging feeling tickled the back of Alices mind.

Hot, humid air rushed at Alice as she stepped out of the movie theater. She could feel her wavy, bobbed hair begin to frizz and her palms become sticky with sweat. She self-consciously rubbed them against her teal-colored, sleeveless shift dress and sighed.

"I can buy two more tickets, if you want to go back inside," Marco said, his thin lips twitching into a grin.

"Don't tempt me," she said, nudging him in the side with her shoulder. "I'm glad you didn't have to work tonight. I'd have hated to miss seeing Casablanca again."

"I'm sorry I haven't been around much lately."

Alice shrugged. "I understand."

"Yeah, but I feel like I abandoned you."

"I had as much help as I could take, what with Uncle Logan and Lionel barely letting me bathe myself."

Heat rushed to her cheeks as she realized what she'd said.

"I don't mean that they...I just...they were very...um...attentive. Too much so, actually."

"You were pretty badly hurt, even after Gerald helped you. I can understand why they would be like that, but they also don't understand how strong you are. Give them time, they'll see it."

"So, you're saying you do?" Alice said, her smile teasing. "You were at my beck and call when you were there."

He looked down and laughed.

"Yes, well, I'm not saying I won't help you when you need it."

"Or get me Rocky Road when the craving strikes."

"That, too. Speaking of, you want to get some?" He pointed to the bright sign of the ice cream parlor a block away.

"Do you have to ask?"

"So, do you like Casablanca better now or when you saw it as a kid?"

Alice looked up in thought. "I don't know. I still love it, but..."

"What?"

"It's not as romantic as I remember it."

Marco looked at her as if she were insane and opened his mouth to comment, but Alice held up her hands to stop him.

"When I was a kid, I thought it was so romantic that Rick let her go. But now...I don't know."

"He sacrificed the woman he loved so she could be happy. Have a real life."

"If he really loved her, he should've fought for her."

"But you're missing the point. He loved her enough to know she'd never be truly happy with him."

"Why, because her husband was a politician and rich?"

"O-o-or, maybe because he believed Ilsa loved her husband more than him."

"Would you do that? Let the woman you love go on without you?"

"Absolutely." His voice held a note of seriousness that seemed deeper than their conversation warranted.

Alice look up at him with a confused frown, and then saw the sadness in the depths of his dark brown eyes.

Is he...Is Marco in love with someone?

The thought was oddly uncomfortable and Alice put on a playful smile to hide the fact.

"Who's the lucky lady?"

"What?" Marco said, his voice hesitant.

"It's obvious you're speaking from experience, and whoever she is...she'd be an idiot to let you push her away."

"I'm not...these powers, they make it...difficult."

"Why? You think the right woman wouldn't accept you?"

"No, that's not it, I just...it's hard to explain."

"If she really loved you—"

"It's not a matter of that. I mean...it's complicated, and besides that, there isn't anyone, not really."

"You don't want to talk about this, do you?"

"Nope, I'd rather get ice cream."

He smiled down at her, reaching out to tuck a stray curl behind her ear. His fingers brushed her jaw, leaving a cool fire in their wake. Alice shivered, and was surprised to feel desire warming her insides.

"Well, then," she said, grabbing his hand. "Let's go."

Though they'd held hands many times before, this time it felt intimate in a way Alice wasn't sure she was ready to understand.

They'd only gone a few feet when a loud, annoyed voice from behind stopped them.

"Well, well, well."

Marco dropped Alice's hand and turned in surprise.

"Didn't expect to see you two here," Lionel said, his face tight with a forced smile.

The round-faced blond with the feline stare, from the Children's Home dedication, was draped across Lionel's arm. Alice nodded at her, but the woman ignored her.

When Alice turned her attention to Lionel, she was surprised to see how truly annoyed he looked. Was he having a bad date, or did it have something to do with Marco taking her out?

Alice shook her head at that. Why in the world would Lionel mind that? But the feeling wouldn't go away, and in fact, grew a little as she saw the distinct light of jealousy in his eyes.

"Casablanca was playing," Marco said, waving a hand

at the theater. "And I had promised Alice we'd see it before it left."

Lionel nodded. "I see. Well, we were just going to get a drink at the Solomon Lounge. You want to join us?"

The blond rolled her eyes. "But, we only have reservations for two."

"That's alright, they can make an exception for me. What d'you say?"

Marco looked down, and then at Alice.

"Not for me, thanks, but if you want to go, that's fine."

Alice shook her head. "I'm not really dressed for—"

"Oh, come on! You two need a little excitement." Lionel's voice had taken on a hard edge and Alice noticed his face was getting flushed.

"I think we have enough, thanks," Alice said, turning away.

Lionel grabbed her arm, jerking her back around. She felt his fingers dig into her skin. An old, nearly forgotten, fear shot through her.

"Let her go," Marco said, stepping up to Lionel.

Alice stared in shock as they glared at each other. Lionel's body tensed as if he were ready for a fight, while Marco's face became stony, his fingers twitching like they did just before he used his powers.

She'd seen them argue before, even seen them come to blows once, but this was different. Marco usually had enough patience to diffuse Lionel's temper and impulsiveness. Maybe it was seeing Lionel grab her, maybe it was her fear. Alice could understand that, but what was Lionel's excuse? He'd never laid a hand on her that wasn't helpful or considerate.

It was then, caught in the middle of this, that Alice noticed a red, rather large, scratch along Lionel's cheek.

Pulling her arm out of his grasp, Alice reached for it, but Lionel jerked away.

"What happened?" Alice said.

Lionel blinked, shaking his head like someone who'd just woke up from a bad dream. "I-uh-It was just...something from..."

"That hobby of yours?" Marco asked.

"Right, yeah. My...hobby."

Alice's frown deepened. "You'll have to tell me about that sometime."

Lionel wouldn't meet her gaze and, for a moment, she thought he was about to apologize. But then, his crooked smile reappeared and he looked back at his date, who'd retreated a few steps, compact out and checking her makeup.

"Shall we?"

"Sure," she said, taking his arm without another look at Alice or Marco.

"I'll see you two later?" His tone was light, but underneath it was a desperate pleading.

"Definitely," Marco said.

Lionel smiled and walked on as if he had just been having a friendly conversation.

"What the hell was that?" Alice asked.

Marco sighed. "We went patrolling last night—"

"Without me? Again?"

"Lionel is scared you're going to get hurt again. He keeps telling me that you're busy doing research and rather than argue with him, I went. We were attacked, same kind of guys as at the restaurant. One of them had a large ring on one hand, and when he punched Lionel, he scratched him with it. Gerald said he thinks the reason it's not healing is because there was a foreign substance on the ring. He can't see anything wrong with Lionel, exactly, but that substance is in Lionel's bloodstream. He doesn't know how long it'll last or what it's going to do."

Alice felt her stomach twist. "It's not poison?"

"Gerald said he didn't think so."

"Didn't think so? Lionel could drop dead!"

"We've run into poison before, it has no effect on Lionel."

"Unless the Syndicate and this Phantasm have found one that will."

She sank onto a nearby bench and buried her face in her small hands.

The bench creaked as Marco joined her.

"This isn't your fault."

"I wish everyone would stop saying that!"

"Maybe when you start believing it, we will."

She looked up at him and sighed, desperate to change the subject. "Lionel wasn't his usual self tonight; do you think it has something to do with whatever was on that ring?"

Marco looked down at his hands.

"I'm not sure, there could be other reasons for tonight, not that it excuses grabbing you like that."

"I've never seen him like that. He was...aggressive, angry."

"Did he hurt you?"

Alice shrugged. "He scared me. It's funny...it's been twelve, almost thirteen years, since my dad beat me, and someone I know and trust grabs me like that...and it all comes rushing back."

"I'm sorry."

"You don't have anything to apologize for."

A square-bodied, newspaper delivery truck pulled up at the news stand across the street, dumping bundles of newspapers with a dull thud before speeding away.

"I'm gonna get a paper, want anything?" Marco asked.

She shook her head, trying not to feel panic at the thought that Lionel was infected with something lethal. How would the Syndicate even know how to create something lethal to Lionel? Did they have blood from one of the crime scenes Lionel had been at? Was there someone they knew who could get close enough to Lionel for that? Maybe Phantasm was using one of Lionel's dates?

Alice had to chuckle at that idea, the blond looked about as threatening as a box of crackers.

"Alice, look at this," Marco said, a deep frown hooding his eyes as he handed her the newspaper.

Underneath an article about two more deaths from the drug Fantasy was a headline that stopped Alice's heart cold.

RECLUSIVE MILLIONAIRE IDENTIFIED AS CRIME LORD

A source with the Jet City Police Department has confirmed that reclusive millionaire Percy Marsh has been identified as the crime lord behind the Fantasy drug syndicate, following a raid on a restaurant in North Jet City.

"Oh my god," Alice said, staring at the newspaper. "Percy Marsh?"

"Yeah, and," Marco flipped the paper to the business section and pointed at the front page headline.

"Veran Corp has just bought up the controlling share of Marsh Enterprises…" Alice said, a sinking feeling in her gut.

"Alice-" Marco began.

"I know. I just…I can't, not yet. I need more proof. This could be anything, including just a smart business deal. Marsh Enterprises is one of the top pharmaceutical firms in the country."

He sat down next to her and sighed.

"Okay, I won't push. But my instincts are saying something isn't right. Just... promise me that you'll let yourself see it, if it's true?"

"I'll try," she said, leaning her head on his shoulder. "Remember when all we had to worry about was out running the Dorn brothers?"

Marco chuckled. "Yeah, those were the days, huh?"

CHAPTER TWENTY-ONE

It was two weeks since Alice had first begun to suspect Victoria before she was finally ready to ask Douglas for help. Every lead they had on Phantasm or the syndicate had turned up either a small-time operation or an abandoned one. It had gotten to the point where Garrick was starting to accuse them of wasting police resources. Alice was desperate for something, anything that might give them a clue about Phantasm's real identity.

Alice thought she'd gotten used to seeing Douglas frail and gray, but she wasn't prepared for the moaning and thrashing she saw that morning when she arrived for her visit.

"Quit your whining, I'm only a few minutes late," said a nurse, hanging up a clear bag on an IV hook.

"It's...it hurts!" Douglas groaned.

Alice stood there, frozen as she watched him fight against the urge to cry out.

When the nurse had stepped aside at last, Douglas had tears running down his cheeks. He looked over and saw Alice, eyes wide with horror.

"You're early," he said, tone harsh and accusing.

"Sorry," she whispered.

"You should be grateful you've got any visitors at all, man like you," the nurse said.

"That will be quite enough," Alice said, glaring at her.

The woman's thin mouth gave a sour twist and she stomped out of the room.

Douglas was trying his best to breath evenly, but his thin body was tense on the bed for the first ten minutes or so of their visit. Alice didn't even attempt to speak, she just pulled her book out of her bag and began to read.

"I'm sorry you saw that," he said, his voice croaking like a frog.

Alice shrugged. "It's part of dying I guess."

"Yeah."

She handed him his book without him asking, and he gave her a tiny smile of thanks.

How the hell do I ask a favor after seeing that?

They settled into their usual, tense silence, the only sound was the occasional ruffle of pages turning. Alice gave a good impression of someone reading, but really her mind was running over clues and possible locations where they could go to next. She chewed on her bottom lip, unaware that Douglas was studying her.

"Out with it," Douglas said after another ten minutes.

"What?"

"You're taking too long to read that page, so something must be on your mind."

Alice sighed and snapped the book shut.

"Fine, yes, I wanted to ask you about Phantasm."

"You really are as stubborn as…never mind. You're just going to keep digging and digging until I help you so might as well. Go on, what do you want to know?"

"I need to know anything you can tell me about Phantasm's business holdings. Any place he might be vulnerable."

Douglas laid back against his pillows and frowned at the ceiling.

"He kept his personal holdings secret for the most part. But Jamison used to talk about a few places that all three of them had stakes in. If it's still running, he'd have taken over. A few were fronts for distribution and the like."

"Can you tell me any of them?"

"A small bakery in Park Side was the only one I knew of. Jamison used street kids as delivery mules."

Alice frowned in disgust.

"Children?"

Douglas shrugged.

"It's not the worst thing Jamison did to kids."

She felt sick at hearing that, but also a little proud that she'd helped get rid of a man like that.

"What bakery?"

"The Dough Boy."

Alice chuckled.

"Yeah," Douglas said smiling. "I remember that place, too."

"Best sweet rolls in the city."

"Your mom was always trying to figure out that recipe. Only thing she ended up doing was making lumps of half-cooked sugar dough."

"Or rock hard balls."

They sat for a moment, each with a smile on their faces for the precious few happy days before drunken tirades and beatings took over.

Alice was the first to realize what she was doing and shook herself out of it. He'd grieved for her mother, she believed that. But she wasn't about to reminisce with the man who'd made the last few years with her mother a living hell.

"Thanks," she said, jumping to her feet.

"Alice?" he said, just before she opened the door. "Be careful."

She wanted to turn around and smile at him, reassure him, or just see that look of true concern on his face. But instead, she simply nodded and bolted out of the room without a backwards glance.

Alice wished she could find more excuses than just missions to ride the Black Lightning, but people had started associating the bike with Serpent, and she couldn't risk someone making the connection. Still, when she could ride it, she took every opportunity to open it up, zipping between cars and whipping around corners at speeds that would inspire Uncle Logan to give her a very long talk.

The Dough Boy was at the end of a street in Park Side where small businesses had been attempting to thrive since before she was born. Some had managed to make it longer than five years, but most learned the hard way that to have a business in Park Side, you either had to know someone that would help you protect it, or deal with monthly break-ins.

She had just finished stashing the Black Lightning down an alley when footsteps, soft and shuffling, sounded behind her. Turning with her fists up, Alice came face to face with...two wide-eyed children.

The gangly, tow-headed boy shoved someone small behind him and put up his own skinny fists.

"You better leave us alone," the boy snarled.

Alice couldn't help smiling, and knelt to look the boy in the eye. "I'm not going to hurt you."

"Are you the Serpent?" said a small voice behind the boy.

"Yes, I am. What's your name?"

From behind the still defensive little boy came the most mesmerizing child Alice had ever seen. Everything about her was pale. Her delicate skin on her delicately pointed face. Eyes such a light blue they were almost white. Hair that, though it was dirty and limp, was still a beautiful flaxen color. Alice couldn't help staring at her as she stepped into the pale moonlight. And for the first time since she was a child, Alice thought that maybe she'd wandered into fairyland.

The boy frowned at the little girl.

"Emmeline! She could be lying."

"She's not, I told you the Serpent was real!"

"You kids shouldn't be around here, it's dangerous."

"Yeah? Where we supposed to go?" the boy asked, his bottom lip protruding a little in defiance.

"Wait a second," she said, running back to her bike.

It took a few minutes to find a business card for the Children's Home, though it was bent and had a smudge of something green on it.

"Here." She gave the card to the boy. "Take a cab and go here, the matron will pay the fare."

"There's no cabs around here," he said.

"Go to the end of the street and take a right, walk two blocks and you'll see some cabs, I promise."

The boy stared at the card, and then frowned up at her.

"If you're trying to trick me—"

"I'm not, I swear. This is a good place, a safe place."

Emmeline bounced on her tiny feet and giggled, a sound that reminded Alice of what she always thought Tinker Bell might sound like.

"Thank you, Serpent!"

The hug Emmeline gave her was a shock, mostly because Alice had never engendered trust and affection while in the guise of the Serpent. She hugged the little girl back, cringing when she felt Emmeline's ribs and sharp shoulder blades.

"If you're hungry, they'll open the kitchen for you," she said. "All you have to do is ask."

The boy grabbed his sister's hand and almost dragged her out of the alley, Emmeline beaming the whole way.

Alice stared at where they'd disappeared around the corner. All the hours Mrs. Frost had tried to get through to her about the importance of the charities she was a part of and Alice had never been able to grasp it, thinking how could it compare with being a hero?

Now, with one simple act, Alice was beginning to understand. What she'd just done had its own thrill, one that she suspected would last longer and do more for those children than every mission she'd been on in the last month.

With a smile on her face and bounce in her step, Alice climbed the fire escape to the roof where Lionel and Marco were waiting.

"Where've you been?' Lionel asked, his body tense.

Though Lionel had been trying to make up for his behavior on the street two weeks ago, there were moments when Alice would glimpse a feral temper in his eyes. It always made her feel a little afraid of him, no matter how much she told herself that Lionel would never hurt her.

She studied him for a moment, noticing how his hands kept clenching into fists, as if he couldn't wait to fight someone, anyone.

"I had to take care of something," she said, giving him a wide berth as she walked toward the edge of the roof.

"Thugs?" Marco asked.

She shook her head.

"I'll tell ya later."

"There've been groups of two kids leaving every ten minutes, packs on their backs," Marco said.

"When did the last pair leave?" she asked.

"About fifteen minutes ago. It's a good bet they're all out."

"And on the street with all those drugs," Lionel said, his voice an annoyed growl.

"We can't beat up kids," Marco said, his voice carrying an edge.

"I didn't say we do that! But—"

"Enough," Alice said. "We have a job here. If we shut this down then chances are those kids won't have to do this anymore. We can alert Garrick when we finish and he can bring them to the children's home."

Lionel looked away, his jaw tensed.

Taking a chance, Alice touched his arm.

"I don't know what's going on with you, but we need you. Are you up for this?"

After a moment his breathing slowed and he nodded.

As they crept down from the roof and looked at the bakery across the street, Alice felt a prickle of apprehension. There were no guards, and the quiet on the street felt artificial, as if someone had told everyone to clear out.

She looked over at Marco, his shadows twirling around the edges of his gray duster.

"Do you feel—?" she began.

"Something's strange," he said, eyes black.

"What?"

He cocked his head to one side, the shadows writhing faster around him before slowing to a crawl.

"Never mind it's...I don't know, someone in there was...excited."

"Like they know we're coming?" Lionel asked.

Marco shook his head.

"I don't know. The feeling is gone, it just disappeared."

"Maybe...Maybe we should abort," Alice said, the words sticking in her throat.

It was the last thing she wanted to do but walking into a trap wouldn't do any of them any good.

"No way!" Lionel said. "This could be a major part of Phantasm's business."

"But, if they're expecting us, then it could be a trap."

"What if I go in the front and you two go through the back, take them by surprise from two fronts," Alice said, trying to find a way to do the mission and be safe.

Lionel snorted. "Yes, because you're such a powerhouse."

Alice felt anger heat her face. "What is wrong with you tonight?"

Lionel opened his mouth to retort but Marco was there first.

"If you two want to fight we should go back to the loft. Otherwise, we have a job to do!"

"Fine!" Lionel threw his hands up. "I'll go around back and the two of you can handle the front."

Alice tried to tell him to wait, but Lionel was across the street before she had the chance.

"Has he been like this-?"

"All day," Marco finished for her. "He's angry, I can feel it coming off him in waves."

"Why?"

"I don't know, but right now we better get in there before he starts tearing up the place."

They ran across the street without incident, Lionel disappearing down the narrow side alley and around to the back of the bakery.

The shades on the front windows of the bakery were drawn and the door was a thick wood with three padlocks, not unusual for this neighborhood. Alice tried the door handle. To her surprise, the door gave a little. None of the deadbolts were engaged, not even the handle lock.

Her eyes met Marco's, which were once again completely black.

"Maybe-" she whispered.

Then the sounds of Lionel fighting at the back of the bakery met her ears, and she knew that there was no aborting the mission now.

Alice pushed the door open and stepped over the threshold, Marco waiting behind her. She paused a minute to make sure no one was waiting with a gun or anything to ambush them before Marco came in.

A small lamp behind the counter gave just enough light to see the outline of the tables, chairs stacked on top. A faint sweet smell hit her when she opened the door, and for a bizarre instant, she wondered if someone was baking sweet rolls. But then the scent became sickly, like flowers that had gone rotten in a vase.

She was about to turn and ask Marco if he felt anything when rough hands pulled her further into the room.

"Serpent!" Marco called out, just before the door was slammed in his face.

Alice drew her batons and turned in the direction where the hands had come from.

A man stood in the dim light. His face in shadow from the wide-brimmed fedora he wore, a suit of black hanging from his tall, thin frame.

Alice opened her mouth to say something when the sweet smell hit her even stronger and she gagged. That's when she saw a thin fog floating along the floor, the faint light casting a pale sheen on it.

Alice stepped back to try and get to the door, but the room spun and she landed on her bottom. The sounds of Marco banging on the door and Lionel fighting at the back of the bakery were starting to become distant echoes in her mind. She expected to go to sleep, but instead, she drifted in a half-awake state.

"Wha-What is...?"

"Oh no, don't try to fight it," said a deep strange voice from the fog.

Terror, stronger and more real than anything she'd ever experienced stabbed her mind. Waking nightmares lifted themselves from the fog, a shadowy figure with a belt ran toward her, raising his arm.

"No!" She raised her arms and felt the sting of the lash.

Again, it fell as she sobbed, trying so hard to crawl away.

"What are you seeing, little snake?" said that voice, and Alice felt fingers slither across her face. She batted them away with a screech, eliciting a snarling laugh from whoever it was.

"Look at me, little snake."

Like a child who believes that if she just keeps her eyes shut the scary thing will go away, Alice couldn't look. She shook her head, whimpering.

A swift kick to her abdomen made her double over, followed by a punch to her face. Her stomach burned with pain and she tasted blood in her mouth. A man as thin as Phantasm shouldn't have been able to hit so hard, and Alice was reminded of Percy's enhanced strength.

Against her will, Alice's eyes flew open as he reached down and pulled her up by the front of her suit. His face was lit just enough in the meager light for Alice to see it. What she saw made her scream in terror, her fingers desperately trying to pry the man's hand off of her.

"You love them, don't you? What would you do if they were broken? What would happen if they died, bloody?"

The man threw her down and when Alice looked up she saw it.

Marco's hand, slick with blood, fingers twitching.

"You can't help them, just like you made sure I couldn't help the ones I loved!"

The man, who had to be Phantasm, kicked her in the stomach again. Alice gasped with pain and terror. She tried to crawl to Marco, but no matter how hard she tried, she couldn't reach him.

"Alice...help...Alice..." His voice was garbled, as if he were speaking half under water.

"I-I'm t-trying...M-Marco! Marco...just...!"

"Worse than watching them die," said Phantasm, his distorted voice low, "is having them hate you, I think."

Someone loomed over her. At first, she saw her father. But then it became Lionel. His face cut, blood smeared on his suit, he opened his mouth and screamed at her.

"He's dead because of you! I'll never forgive you!"

"No, no..." she sobbed.

Lionel continued to scream, but this time it was in pain and grief. Alice barely managed to scramble away when she saw that same, looming figure running toward her, belt raised high. She half-crawled, half-ran the other way, tripping and falling face first into a pool of sticky blood. Screams and sobs were one and the same to her now. She tried to find a way out of the blood, but it was all around, seeping slowly through her suit and onto her skin, bathing her in its condemnation.

"Alice..." said Marco from somewhere. "Alice..."

She curled into a ball and screamed uncontrollably, all the voices rising in a cacophony of terrifying nonsense around her.

CHAPTER TWENTY-TWO

She was drowning in a dark sea of fear and ghosts. They grabbed at her, raising her up, only to push her down again. Arms and legs held down, no chance to break free.

Something sharp and hard pierced her skin.

A rush of heat tore through her.

Voices echoed through her head. Were they friendly? She couldn't tell.

Finally, she was too tired to fight anymore. She took a deep breath. It felt like she was inhaling cobwebs.

When the darkness came, she embraced it.

Out of the oblivion came a blinding light, sending jagged stabs of pain into her skull. Alice tried to raise her hand to shield her eyes, but her arm was so heavy. She wasn't sure where she was at first, but at least the voices had stopped and breathing didn't seem so difficult.

Her eyes finally adjusted to the bright sunlight, and she could've cried with relief to see her eyelet curtains fluttering in a warm breeze, the prism she'd hung by her window cast rainbows across the small dressing table in her room. A gorgeous smell wafted over her and Alice felt her stomach rumble and twist with hunger, her mouth filling with moisture.

Swallowing was strangely difficult, her throat raw and dry. She saw a glass of water on her bedside table. But when she tried to sit up to drink it, the pain in her head became unbearable. The glass slipped from her fingers onto the floor as she fell back onto her pillows. Dark spots appeared in her vision, that same swell of fear and darkness threatening on the edge of her mind. The only defense she could manage was a weak whimper.

She didn't hear footsteps or the door opening, so when a hand touched her wrist, Alice screamed, batting her hands at the person as she kept her eyes shut tight.

"Alice."

The voice was so familiar...

"Alice, stop."

Who?

"It's Lionel, stop!"

She did, and slowly opened her eyes, wincing at the bright light. Strong hands held her wrists in a gentle grasp. The face was square and beautiful, wide lips with a grim set to them. Deep set, navy-blue eyes, ringed with dark circles, straw-colored hair that stuck up in odd angles, as if someone had run their hands through it hundreds of times.

As it all came into focus, so did her memories of him screaming in grief. It was so vivid that she flinched and tried to raise her hands, but Lionel held her wrists fast.

"It's me," his voice cracked. "You're safe now."

When she didn't say anything, Lionel leaned a little toward her and smoothed stray curls away from the sweat on her forehead. Tears lit up his eyes.

"Don't you know me?"

She did, but those dreams or visions...they were all mixed in.

Slowly, Alice reached up and pressed her palm to his stubble covered cheek.

"You're...real?"

Her voice sounded like the croaking of a bull frog.

Lionel let out something between a laugh and a cry.

"Yeah, I'm real."

Relief hit her like a blow and she began to cry, huge gulping sobs that shook her whole body. Lionel lay down and cradled her against him, the occasional plop of moisture falling onto her head from his tears.

"I'm so sorry," he said. "If I had just stopped and listened to Marco this wouldn't have happened to you. Why didn't I listen?"

"It wasn't...your fault."

"I wish I could believe that."

Alice swallowed, her throat on fire. "My...throat?"

"I forgot, you shouldn't talk too much. You strained your vocal chords pretty badly. Gerald would've healed you, but at first you wouldn't let anyone near you, and then, once you'd calmed down, he didn't know what was in your system. He wanted to wait it out."

She pressed her cheek harder into his chest, winding one arm around his waist. He was so solid and safe, in spite of his strange behavior the last few days.

"I'm sorry," he whispered again.

"Stop it," she whispered into his chest. "Just...hold me."

His arms tightened around her, and after a few minutes his body relaxed against hers.

They lay like that until a knock sounded on the door. Lionel sat up and Alice could see Gerald coming in, face haggard.

"I need to examine Alice. Could you call Logan, let him know she's awake?"

Lionel nodded, looking back at her with a smile before leaving the room.

Gerald sat down gingerly and took her pulse. When that was finished, he closed his eyes and Alice could feel the cool tingling of his power moving through her. The headache lifted and her throat no longer felt on fire.

"What happened?" he asked.

Licking her lips, trying to find the courage to talk about it, Alice was at a loss for words. The effort of trying to remember brought the images and feelings back, not as strong, but it still made her tremble.

Gerald nodded, as if she'd said volumes.

"It's some kind of neuro-toxin. Not unlike what Lionel was dosed with. The effects on him...well, I'm not positive yet. But I do know that what you were dosed with acts as a hallucinogen. How did you come into contact with it?"

"It was...a gas...sweet smelling...and...there was—"

Her body flinched as Phantasm's face flashed through her mind. It couldn't have been real, could it?

"Alice, this is similar to the side effects of Fantasy, except, in most cases, there's an intense craving for the drug afterwards. Are you...Do you...?"

"No." Her voice was soft, but firm. "No way in hell."

Gerald's shoulders relaxed.

"Are you saying it was the drug?"

"I don't know, but it's a possibility. Did you see who did this?"

She nodded again.

"Was it the one you're after?"

"I-I think so. His...face..."

Gerald's frown deepened.

"Your mind was probably changing what you were seeing and hearing."

She licked her lips again.

"A-a gas mask, full face...but not. It kept changing, a-and I thought...it was..."

He patted her hand as tears fell down her face again.

"It's alright. You need rest. We can go over this later. It looks like the toxin has almost worked its way out of your system. It's been a longer duration than most people exposed to Fantasy, but there's no sign of permanent damage. You should be fine in a few days."

"What was Lionel dosed with?"

"I still don't know, but I'm working on it. Get some sleep," he said, getting up to leave.

"Where's Marco?"

"He was affected by the strength of your fear. He found it hard to control his powers around you, so he's kept his distance."

"But I smell—"

"Yeah." Gerald smiled for the first time since he walked in. "He's been cooking at your uncle's house to keep himself busy. Then Lionel brings the food over, what he hasn't already eaten, that is."

Now it was Alice's turn to smile.

"Can I see him?"

"He's not here right now. He and your uncle got called in to the paper."

"Why?"

"Nothing serious, not really. Nothing that can't wait until tomorrow. I mean it, sleep, or I'll dose you."

Once the door was shut, Alice tried to sleep. Her body ached with fatigue as if she'd been fighting for days, which she supposed, in some ways, she had been. But her mind wouldn't stop turning things over and over. Questions, images, words. Instinct told her that there was truth hidden somewhere in all she'd seen and heard, a clue that would help her know who this was.

And under all that was something darker — something Alice didn't want to face.

Phantasm had made her feel helpless. A long time ago, she'd promised herself she would never feel again. Her face flushed and her muscles tensed as she replayed it over and over in her mind. The way he had gotten in her mind, the agonizing terror and the inability to find a way out of it all.

Never again. I will never let that monster to that to me again!

The sun had begun to lose its potency and the air took on the delicious coolness of late afternoon by the time Alice's mind finally let her succumb to sleep.

The scream tore itself out of her throat, her hands peeling the sheets off her legs in a panic. She had to bury her face in her pillow, the light was so bright. Alice wondered if she'd really slept at all until she realized that it was morning sunlight streaming into the room.

The door opened, but Alice didn't look up to see who it was. Fear began to give way to a deep burning anger that she was just beginning to understand.

"Whoever you are, stop hovering and talk!" she said

"Are you...I mean, what's wrong?" Marco said.

Hearing the compassion and gentleness of his voice made Alice feel bad for snapping, but not enough to expel her anger completely.

"Bad dream. Why are you just standing there? Afraid I might hurt you?"

"Yes, actually."

That made her look up, hot tears running down her cheeks. A retort died on her lips as she took him in, the warm sunshine lighting up every gold undertone of his skin and brown hair. His hands were in his pockets, and there was a day or two's growth of beard on his long face. It added to the golden tint in his skin.

His clothes were rumpled, the first two buttons of his shirt undone and she could just see a little hair peeking out of the top, the outline of firm shoulder muscles visible.

He was staring at her and when she looked back into his eyes her thoughts burst out onto her tongue.

"I never noticed...you've got red in your eyes, like a...cinnamon color."

He smiled and looked down. "How poetic."

That made her laugh a little. "I'm sorry I yelled. I—"

"You don't have to apologize."

"It's not you, I'm actually very glad to see you. Very glad."

His smile was gentle and a little relieved.

"I'm sorry I couldn't be here, it was just too much."

"Gerald told me. I hear you've been busy though."

"When you woke up I thought you'd be hungry."

"Starved."

She tried to stand up, but the room spun and she fell back onto the bed. Marco rushed to her side and tried to help her, but she jerked her arm away, the anger flaring back to life.

"I just need a minute!"

He frowned, studying her.

"I'm sorry, I just — I don't need help."

"Alright." He backed up a few steps, but kept his gaze firmly on her.

As if he's waiting for me to fall on my butt again. I'm fine! I'm strong and...fine.

But Alice knew that wasn't true. The anger burned brighter, at the thought of anyone trying to help her walk or bring her food or even look at her with pity.

With clenched fists, she rose slowly, muscles tight as she put one foot in front of the other. It was slow, but she finally made it through her bedroom door and into the living room, where Uncle Logan, Lionel, and Gerald were all waiting for her.

Behind the worry in their eyes, Alice saw pity. She pressed her lips tight and focused on the couch, though she could feel their gazes watch every slow step.

"Why don't you sit down," Uncle Logan said, smiling at her.

"I don't want to," she said, turning towards the punching bag.

She'd show them. She'd walk all around the loft, show them she was strong, she was alright.

Even though the others might not have thought she was being smart to take laps around the loft, by the time she'd finished her third time around, Alice's legs had stopped shaking and her head had cleared.

"Can I get you some coffee?" Marco asked.

"That would be great."

When she reached out for it he walked past her and put in on the table instead, looking at her with a silent demand that she sit down.

For some reason, maybe because it came from Marco, and not Lionel or Uncle Logan, Alice obeyed. Soon after, Marco placed a plate of warm pancakes dripping with butter and syrup in front of her.

Lionel quickly joined her, as did Uncle Logan and Gerald. They sat in silence, everyone sneaking glances at her, but no one daring to ask anything. Finally, she got tired of it all and looked each one in the eye.

"Ask! Whatever it is you want to know. Or if you want to say something, just do it. This...whatever this is, it's driving me crazy."

"I need to give you one last examination," Gerald said, his voice firm, "just to be sure all the toxin is out of your system."

"After breakfast."

"And then, you rest," Uncle Logan said.

"No, I'm fine. I have things to do."

"Like?"

She glared at him. "I'm fine."

He glared right back, pointing his fork at her as he spoke.

"You just woke up screaming. Again. It took you fifteen minutes to be able just to walk normally, you've got dark circles under your eyes that rival mine, and who knows if this poison will pop up if you try to fight. You're not fine. You rest or so help me God-"

"What? You'll tie me down?"

"Don't tempt me."

They stared at each other, anger flushing their faces.

Lionel cleared his throat. "I have an idea."

She dared him with a look to treat her with kid gloves.

"How about if I take you out tonight? Someplace nice, maybe the Elliot? That way you could just spend the day relaxing, getting ready for something fun, instead of feeling like an invalid."

It should've diffused her completely.

Finally, after all this time, he wanted to take her out, treat her like...well, someone special. But the only thing it managed to do was surprise her enough to take the edge off her anger.

"The Elliot? That's...I don't think I've got anything to wear."

Lionel smiled his crooked smile.

"I'll buy you something, just write down your size and favorite color and I'll send it over today. Shoes, too."

Her mouth opened and closed, but no matter how much she tried, Alice couldn't think of an excuse. And why would she want to? She'd waited a long time for this.

Alice smiled.

"That's very generous, Lionel. I'd be happy to do that."

If he noticed that she wasn't exactly enthusiastic about the offer, Lionel didn't show it. She scribbled what he wanted to know on a piece of paper and he grabbed it with glee.

"I'll pick you up at eight."

When she looked back at the table, Marco's face was tense, his eyes just a little too focused on his barely-touched pancakes. Alice brushed his knuckles with her fingertips and his head jerked up. A profound sadness lit his brown eyes for just a moment, and then it was gone.

He smiled.

"I should start to clean up. Made quite a mess."

The rest of them finished their breakfast in a hurry. Uncle Logan left with barely a good-bye and Alice felt a small twinge of guilt that quickly gave way to her growing anger.

When Gerald declared her clean of toxins, Alice felt relieved, and then immediately worried. If she was, then why was she so angry?

"You don't have to go out if you don't want to," Gerald said, his voice low. "You've been through quite an ordeal."

"I'm not some delicate flower."

"That's not what I'm saying. But sometimes, being pampered doesn't heal some wounds. Maybe try something physical." He nodded at the punching bag. "Get it all out."

She swallowed, uncomfortable that he had read her so well.

Marco was the last one there, though he'd flown through the dishes. He was just putting away the last of them when Alice came out of her room in sparring gear.

"You sure—"

"Yes, I am," she snapped, almost running to the bag.

At first, she tried to hit it with the proper form, but her

body felt wild and too contained, like a river swollen with rain that was held back by a dam.

Images from the gas hit her mind and she flinched.

"Alice," Marco put his hand on her shoulder.

She grabbed his hand, stepped back, and elbowed him in the gut before she could stop herself. Marco's breath came out in a cough and he stumbled back.

When she turned to look at him, Alice expected anger, or at the very least indignation. His eyes were wide as they stared into hers, a glimmer of understanding shining in them. Marco caught his breath and took off his button-up shirt, a thin undershirt the only thing covering his chest and back. Stretching his arms and neck, he walked to the edge of the mat, bending his knees into a ready stance.

It took her a moment to respond. In her current frame of mind Alice was afraid of really hurting him. But he nodded at her, as if giving her permission to get out all the things that were bursting inside.

Phantasm's distorted face lanced through her mind again, his words ringing in her ears.

And fury rolled over Alice.

With a yell, she charged at Marco, attempting a round-house kick to his face. He dodged and punched her in the stomach. She grabbed his arm and pulled him down as she lost her balance. They rolled on the mat. Marco started to pin her when Alice slipped out of his grasp and scissored her legs to get to her feet.

They sparred again and again. Each time, Alice felt her anger and fear lessen, like puss being drawn from a wound.

She and Marco were grappling on the mat, looking for a chance to pin the other when something in Alice broke and she began to cry. Her arms went limp and the sudden change in resistance caused Marco to fall on top of her.

He propped himself up on his elbows and stared at her.

"Are you—"

Alice threw her arms around him and buried her face in his neck as she wept. After a moment, Marco's hand cradled the back of her head and his arm wound around her back, holding her lightly but with strength.

"Thank you," she whispered once the tears subsided.

"For what?"

"For knowing what I needed."

"Any time."

She leaned back and realized that he was laying half on top of her. "I...I'm sorry I hit you."

It was the only thing she could think to say because her mind had suddenly stopped working.

He swallowed, brown eyes flitting to her lips and back to her eyes. "It's alright I...I shouldn't have...interrupted."

"How long can you stay?" she whispered.

"As long as you want."

What she wanted was changing the longer they lay intertwined on the mat. Her hand ran slow and unsure over his bare shoulder and to his bicep. Marco's eyes held hers with an intensity she'd never seen, his breath picked up, chest brushing hers with each exhalation. She looked at his mouth, noticing for the first time a tiny scar on his upper lip.

"Where did that come from?" she asked, her finger touching the scar.

"Uh...I think...playground, actually."

Her laugh was breathy with nerves. "That all seems—"

"Very long ago."

"But not."

He shook his head. "No."

Alice moved her hand to his cheek and looked into his eyes once more. The connection pulled at her, like a gentle tug on a rope. She felt heat start to build in her body, leaving a growing desire in its wake. Before she could stop herself, she leaned forward, lips inches from Marco's.

The phone echoed shrilly through the loft. They both jumped, nearly hitting their heads together. It took Marco a moment to untangle himself from her and sprint to the phone.

Her face felt flushed and an aching sensation had begun to grow just below her belly.

I almost kissed Marco...

"Yeah, I'm still here...I'll ask her," Marco said.

He turned toward her, his face tense even though he was smiling. "Lionel wants to know if blue is alright instead of green."

Alice frowned in confusion until she remembered why Lionel might be asking a question like that.

"Yes, it's fine."

Marco nodded and relayed the message.

There was a very long minute after Marco hung up the phone where neither of them spoke. Alice wasn't sure what to think of what had just happened. Had Marco noticed what she was about to do? How could he miss it? And what did he think of it, of her? What would this do to them?

She chanced a look at him. He'd put his shirt back on and was staring out the window, hands in his pockets. While his back was to her, Alice took a good long look at her best friend.

Same lanky, broad shoulders, same thick dark brown hair. Same soul that had always known hers at a glance. But now, in a moment, everything was different.

But do I want it to be? Does he?

So much had happened in the last few weeks. The world had tilted and things that had felt solid were now shaky. Alice wasn't sure she wanted one more thing to change, especially if it would cost her Marco's friendship.

"Well," she said, "I should get cleaned up."

He turned around, the smile on his thin lips looked

forced."Yeah. Are you excited? The Elliot...it's a pretty big deal."

"I know he's trying to help, but to be honest, I wish he'd picked a different night. I'm not sure it's what I want."

"You could tell him that."

She shook her head and smiled. "He was so excited. And Lionel isn't the type to just sit with me and read, anyway."

Not like you would.

The thought brought a new rush of heat to her cheeks and she turned away to hide it.

"Anyway," Marco said, opening the door, "try to have a good time."

"I will. Whatever you're doing tonight, be safe, please?"

His smile this time was genuine.

"I promise."

Alice had just managed a quick shower when a knock sounded on her door.

"If that's Uncle Logan checking on me..."

She flung the door open to see Rose standing there, a bag full of notebooks hanging from her shoulder.

"I'm finished," she said, stepping inside, her brown skin dotted with sweat. "And I was going to wait, but I thought you'd want to know what I've found."

"Yes, please. Do you want something to drink?"

"Water?" Rose said, taking out the notebooks and setting them on the coffee table.

Alice filled a glass with ice water and handed it to her. When Rose barely met her eyes, Alice felt her stomach drop.

"What's wrong?"

"I just...I'm not sure you're going to like this."

"Okay...why don't you just, you know. Out with it?"

Rose nodded.

"Well, you may have already figured this out, but Hercules was a strength enhancement experiment, similar to the super soldier programs that were rampant during the second world war. Sea Breeze was an experiment which would allow an army to subdue an enemy target without a shot being fired, kind of like...well, taking away all the aggression from an enemy, making them a kitten instead of a tiger. But, in each instance, the test subjects became more violent and unpredictable."

Alice nodded.

"At first glance, it looks like Tony was in charge of all the experiments right up until the end, but...well, here."

Rose handed Alice one of the notebooks. She read the three pages twice, her stomach knotting up, hands shaking as she did.

"That's not possible," she said after a moment.

"It is, Alice."

"Are you sure?"

Rose nodded.

"I checked it three times. The first few equations in the file that Marco found at the warehouse and the equations in the last two files of the army experiments are identical. As are the behavioral notes."

Alice sank onto the couch, face in her hands. After a moment, she felt the couch shift as Rose sat next to her.

"I'm sorry," she whispered. "I didn't want it to be true either. But...I don't think the Syndicate would've killed Tony if he were supplying them with this enhancement drug. And..." Rose took a deep breath. "...and it sounded like this Phantasm was the one in charge of the experiments at the warehouse. If that's true—"

"Victoria is Phantasm."

"She could be."

"But she," Alice jumped up and began to pace. "I mean, how would she even know how to do this? If she was an assistant that doesn't mean she would know how to duplicate the experiments, would it?"

Rose looked through the pile of notebooks and pulled another one out.

"These later equations are far more elegant than Tony Veran's earlier work. And this one," Rose pointed to a complex string of numbers and letters, "is especially strange. What he's doing at the very beginning of the experiment doesn't feel like the natural progression of thought when looking at all his attempts together. And the last two, even the notes aren't in the same voice as the previous reports."

"And let me guess whose name is on those."

Rose nodded. "V.G. Muller."

Alice sighed and leaned back.

"So, Victoria, if that *is* her, was doing the work later on."

"Not just later on. V.G. Muller doesn't show up until after the first three months. During that time, six test subjects had died. But when Muller shows up, the experiments begin to change. The men don't die, though they do experience adverse effects. I think...I think Muller was really the lead, and the only reason to keep that secret would be if—"

"Muller was a woman and Tony's wife," Alice said. "Any indication that either experiment could be Fantasy?"

Rose shook her head.

"And, just for good measure, I had Mrs. Frost check out the other lab assistants. Apart from Muller, every other one is either dead or working in a different job, far away from Jet City. No one knows where Muller is. And," Rose opened two file folders, holding them side by side, "I know you can't read this, but the equations from the file that Marco found are definitely a continuation of the Hercules experiment. It looks like they're trying to make it last longer than the earlier experiments with the Army. Back then, the effects would wear off after a few hours, not to mention that psychosis would develop after more than six doses."

"What about addiction? The man I saw in the warehouse, if he was on this, was definitely addicted to it."

"It's possible. This is altering body chemistry in a significant way. But what's clear is that someone who knows what they're doing, someone who isn't just making this up from whole cloth, is behind what you saw at the warehouse and with Jamison."

Alice felt as if someone had kicked her in the gut. She'd wanted to get Phantasm and bring the Syndicate down, more than anything. But if it meant going against Victoria...

And what does that say about who killed Aunt Diana? If Victoria is involved with the Syndicate, if she is Phantasm, did she order it? And what about last night? She tortured me.

The thought made bile rise to Alice's throat. Her aunt and Victoria had been friends, colleagues. They'd also been the two people Alice had looked up to most in her life. She had trusted Victoria, and the woman had forced her to see brutal images, had weakened her.

Alice glanced at her punching bag, wishing she hadn't showered already. All the peace she'd found in sparring with Marco earlier was gone. Her muscles tensed, her hands clenched into fists and released.

I have to calm down. We still don't have a motive. I mean, why, with everything she has, would she do this?

"There's one more thing." Rose handed her a file folder. "Look at the date on this experiment."

Alice gasped.

"It's a week after the accident."

Rose nodded.

"Tony was in critical condition after that accident and

the lab was supposedly destroyed. Yet there's one last experiment dated a week later."

"It's for Hercules...and it says that the test was a success, but doesn't mention a test subject."

"And look whose name is on it."

Alice didn't have to, she could guess.

"Muller."

"I think that Victoria, if that's really her, injected herself with the Hercules serum."

That would explain why Phantasm was so strong last night...if she's really...

"Wouldn't the Army have seen this and done something?" Alice asked.

"That wasn't with the Army records. It was with the files from the warehouse."

Alice threw the file down and paced between the coffee table and the window.

"Why would she do this? Why?"

When Alice had finally stopped pacing, she stared out the huge windows. Everything looked so normal, so peaceful on the streets below. People walking to and from work, meeting friends, cars honking, impatiently waiting their turn in the ever-growing traffic. For a moment, Alice wished she was still just one of them, going about her life, her only worry what books to order for the shop or what to wear on a date.

And I'd be bored out of my mind.

Rose came up beside her and squeezed Alice's hand.

"I'm sorry. I know this has to be so hard for you."

"Thanks, it's not your fault. You found what I asked you to. It's just — I never thought being Serpent would be so complicated."

"You thought it would just be punching crooks and getting your name in the paper?"

"When you put it like that it makes me sound quite vain."

Rose laughed.

"You're the furthest thing. I admire what you do, night after night."

"I couldn't do it without you."

"I don't know about that."

"I do. You have an amazing gift. I wish you could use it more."

Rose shrugged.

"I'm happy, at least for now. Maybe someday...but who knows?"

CHAPTER TWENTY-THREE

Alice had to admire Lionel's taste. The dress was the perfect robin's egg blue to make her cobalt eyes shine and her pale skin glow. It was styled to be form-fitting, hugging every sensuous curve as the skirt fell in a straight line to just above her feet. A knee-high slit on the side exposed her calves when she walked. It had only one shoulder strap where a small, dark blue brooch clasped a silvery sheer fabric that trailed behind her. The shoes were silver, ankle-strap heels that didn't pinch her feet or make her feel as if she were walking on stilts.

She'd managed to have her hair reset earlier that day, the dark, bobbed curls shining perfectly, making Alice feel a little like Elizabeth Taylor. It had been a while since she'd had any reason to wear makeup more substantial than the basics, but she'd managed to remember how to highlight her eyes and make her lips look luscious.

Checking her reflection one last time, Alice was trying to calm her nerves when Lionel knocked at the door. He never knocked, even though it wasn't his house, and so she had to smile at the formality of it.

When she opened the door, he was in a dark gray suit with a blue tie, holding a bouquet of gorgeous white roses.

"They're beautiful," she said.

He laughed, his gaze moving up and down her body.

"I was going to say the same about you."

She could feel a deep flush in her cheeks and motioned him inside. His eyes followed her, a hungry glint in them that made Alice feel a little uncomfortable, as if she were the prey and he the hunter.

"Should we go?" she asked, once the flowers were in a vase.

He walked slowly over to her. For a moment, Alice wondered what Marco would look like in a suit like Lionel's. What would it be like to have him give her flowers and take her out?

I'm not here with Marco, I'm here with Lionel. He's the one I've wanted since we were children.

So then why did she still remember the shape of Marco's lips as she traced them with her finger, the way his arms felt around her.

"You alright?" Lionel asked.

"What…? Oh, yeah, sorry, just a little tired I guess."

"If you're not up for this-"

"No! Are you kidding? I've looked forward to it all day."

Lionel's lips set in a crooked grin.

"Me too."

She took his arm and pushed thoughts of Marco away.

Lionel's car was waiting for them, shining silver in the lamplight. As the engine purred to life, "Will You Still Love Me Tomorrow" by the Shirelles poured out of the radio.

Warm summer air drifted into the car through the open windows as Lionel took a slower than usual speed through the streets of Jet City. She could feel his eyes keep sliding over to her and couldn't help glancing at him in the same way.

Then, for no reason, a giggle escaped from the back of her throat.

"What?" he asked.

"I don't know," she said, "but for the first time I can remember, I think you're nervous around a girl. And that girl is me!"

A flush of red tinted Lionel's skin. "Well this is kind of new territory for us."

Alice's breath caught. She had wondered, hoped even, that this might signal more than just a kind gesture after what she'd been through.

But before she could explore it more with him, they were stopping in front of the brightly light restaurant.

The Elliot was in the newly-renovated part of the waterfront and sat halfway over the water, supported by great, sunken pillars, like a pier would be. The walls were almost entirely made of windows so every table had a view of the water. On sunny afternoons, the patio was stuffed with socialites sipping cocktails.

As they stepped through the door, a man took her shawl, while another led them through the restaurant. The floor was a shining, dark wood off-set beautifully by crisp white table cloths. The lighting was low and intimate, but enough for the crystal glasses to frost the room with a subtle glitter.

Lionel had timed their dinner for that perfect moment just before the sun dipped below the water, lighting the sky and water with a fiery glow. Their table was secluded, shielded from the other dinners by a screen. A bottle of wine chilled in a sweating bucket by the table, the china shining gold and orange.

A waiter in a tuxedo handed her a menu on thick cream-colored paper, beautifully bound in a crimson book. Lionel kept peeking at her from the top of his menu, making her laugh. Alice was trying her best to relax. After all, no matter the trappings, it was just Lionel.

"I can't decide, everything looks so good!" Alice finally said.

"May I?"

Alice nodded. "Sure. If you think you can get it right."

He whistled. "A dare! Alright, missy."

Lionel rattled off three courses of food that Alice had only ever read about in books. She hoped they tasted as good as they sounded.

As the waiter walked away, Lionel stared at her, admiration shining in his eyes.

"I know I said it at the loft, but...you look stunning."

"Part of that is the dress. You have a good eye."

"I've dressed enough women..." He paused, realizing what he had just said. "I mean—"

"It's okay. I'm not ignorant of your past."

He frowned.

"Even so, I don't want you to think you're just one of many. You're — Alice. You're unique."

"I'm just stunned at this place," she said, suddenly wanting to divert the conversation. "It's so beautiful; I never imagined."

"My stepfather knows the owners," Lionel said, his voice hardening a little. "But I've never actually been here before."

"Really? Why not?"

Lionel shrugged, his eyes holding hers.

"No one I wanted to bring here."

She took a deep, shaky breath.

If I don't say something, these nerves are going to keep intruding. I have to know what he's thinking.

"Lionel...I'm confused. What is this? What are we—"

"We're having dinner, and talking about something other than 'work'."

"Is that...*all?*"

"For now," he said, his voice low and a little unsure. "Is that okay?"

Alice smiled. "Yes, it's perfect."

He let out a breath of relief and smiled.

Dinner couldn't have been better and they laughed with an ease they hadn't experienced in a while. A few times Alice could swear that when Lionel looked at her, there was a vulnerability in his gaze that she'd always wanted to see.

"It's nice on this part of the waterfront, we could go for a walk," he said when they'd finished eating. "Unless you're too tired."

"No, I'm fine."

He smiled at her and she slipped her hand under his arm. If she hadn't been wearing such high heels she would've felt like a child next to him. But as it was, possibly for the first time ever, she felt appealingly small.

They walked in the opposite direction from the massive construction going on, where old rotting buildings had been torn down to make way for new arcades, curiosity shops, and other tourist traps.

The Elliot sat at the beginning of the finished part of the water front — not to mention, the richer part. With a luxury hotel, small boutiques, and, of course, the crown jewel: The Foundation for Scientific Discovery.

Lionel paused by the site where The Foundation was being built. The refuse from the fire had been cleared, a huge hole in the ground was now the only thing left of what had been started.

If Victoria has her way, some of the greatest scientific minds in the country will work here. But to what end?

"They just released sketches of this place. It's amazing," Lionel's words tumbled out, eyes shining and oblivious to the weight on Alice's mind. "Two towering buildings for science experiments, and then in the middle is supposed to be a building made out of four interconnected spheres representing — something — I can't remember."

"The four scientific disciplines."

He nodded. "Yeah."

"I didn't know you were interested in this."

"I like buildings, always have."

"Why didn't you become an architect?"

"Too much reading, you know how I am with that stuff. Anyway, it felt like I'd been...I don't know, called to something else."

"And if you hadn't?"

Lionel shrugged.

"I don't know. I never thought about it before my powers, not seriously, and after? Well, it seemed sealed in fate, so to speak."

"What about being a fireman?" Her smile was teasing.

He burst out laughing.

"Oh yeah! That's right, I liked the trucks. What did you want to be?"

"I don't know. I think most of my time was spent just trying to survive Douglas."

"And you did, beautifully."

Alice felt heat rush to her face.

"I wonder sometimes, what my mother might think of me now. She was smart, but so suspicious of women doing anything except being a wife and mother."

"But, she worked."

"Because she had to. Mrs. Frost once told me that my mother wouldn't let Uncle Logan and Aunt Diana come get us, because she didn't approve of my aunt. I used to wonder about that until I found out who my aunt really was."

"You think your mom knew?"

Alice nodded.

"And didn't want me around it."

"You're worried she's looking down on you and not happy with what you've become?"

"Something like that."

He tipped her chin up and stared into her eyes. Alice felt her heart stop, there was so much naked admiration in his gaze. His fingertips lingered on her round cheek, a smile turning up the edges of his lips.

"I know she'd be proud of you."

A jolt of desire lanced through her body, filling her mind with images of their naked bodies entwined on her bed.

"Alice," he whispered her name like a plea and she closed her eyes.

"Well, isn't this sweet?"

Alice jumped at the voice and turned to see half a dozen men with pipes and knives surrounding them. The one who'd spoken came out from behind Lionel, a smirk on his oily face. His beady eyes raked up and down Alice in a way that made her stomach turn and her fists clench.

"Maybe we'll have us some fun before turning you over to our boss."

"You can try," she said, throwing a punch at the goon nearest her.

He clutched his broken nose before she kicked him in the chest, shoving him into the man next to him. They both fell to the ground and Alice picked up the dropped pipe just in time to slam it into the next attacker's throat, crushing his windpipe.

She grabbed the slit in her dress and yanked, opening it several inches, giving her room to maneuver.

One of the men lunged for her, and caught a handful of the sheer fabric attached to her shoulder strap. It ripped and threw her off balance. She fell hard to the ground, landing on her back. The man was on top of her before she could stand, landing a jab to her face.

Her legs were tangled in the dress and she couldn't flip the man. She tried to throw instead, but her reach was too short and he pinned her arms down by her head. He took a knife out of a back pocket and ran the tip down her cheek, drawing a thin line of blood. Alice raked her fingernails down his face and he screamed, loosening his grip on her other wrist. She screamed as she punched him in the face..

As he swung his arm back for a blow, he was yanked off her.

She rolled over, quickly staggered to her feet, and took in the bodies lying around in various states of consciousness.

Lionel was holding the man who had been on top of her. He cocked back his arm and punched, without holding anything back.

"No!" she screamed, rushing toward him.

It was too late, the man's head snapped back, his nose caved in. Lionel threw another punch, and another. What had been a man's face quickly became a mashed pulp of muscle and bone.

She grabbed his arm to stop him.

"Enough!"

He roared as he threw another punch into the man's face.

"Lionel, stop!" She pulled harder.

He dropped the man onto the pavement, and with a snarl, turned in her direction. Blood coated his hand and was splattered on his suit.

Alice almost didn't recognize him. His eyes were wild, spittle flying from his mouth as his breath came in unnatural pants. His face was so red Alice was afraid he would collapse at any moment.

"It's Alice," she said, holding out her hands. "It's me. Lionel, please, calm down."

Sirens blared in the distance, getting closer.

"We have to go," she said, glancing at the man who lay in a bloody heap at Lionel's feet. "Come with me, please."

It was as if her words drained all the fury out of him. The tension was released in Lionel's muscles and he sagged like a marionette with its strings cut. His breath was still rapid and ragged, but the light of rage had faded from his eyes.

He stared at Alice with remorse and shame.

"Oh god, no...no! Alice! I—"

The sirens were getting louder.

"We have to go," she said again, pulling on his arm, this time to get him up and moving.

"I killed him."

"Yes...but—"

"You go, I have to stay."

"No, Lionel this isn't you, something is wrong. We have to get you to Gerald."

Lionel shook his head, never taking his eyes from the man.

Alice grabbed his face and turned it to her.

"I am not leaving without you. Now, get up and let's go!"

"Maybe I can help."

Alice's head jerked up at Marco's voice.

He was in his guise as Shadow Master, his eyes black and his powers already seeping toward Lionel. Within moments, Lionel was calm enough to stand up.

Alice stared at him. Shock and anger warring within her.

Was he following us?

Marco nodded toward a darkened alley across the way.

"Make for that alley and jump the roof tops until you're back at the loft. I'll get Gerald."

She wanted to demand an explanation, but the police were almost there.

"Let's go," she said as Lionel picked her up.

When she turned to look for Marco, he was already gone.

When they got to the loft, Lionel tore off his suit jacket and tie, and went to the bathroom, slamming the door behind him. Soon after, the shower started.

Alice stared at the door, body shaking.

Lionel killed someone.

Lionel lost control and killed someone.

The thoughts ran in a loop until she wished there was a way to open her skull and tear them out. Instead, she walked to the bar and grabbed the whiskey bottle. She held it in her hand, wondering if she could indulge just this once.

"No." She set it down with a loud clunk. "Lionel needs me to be lucid. I can't...God! If there was ever a time—"

She closed her eyes and stifled a sob with her hand. If there was any day that was made for crying, it seemed to be today. And that made her laugh, because she felt as if the day had stretched to encompass an entire week, with all she had experienced.

And that thought, in turn, made her cry again.

Her cheek stung with all the facial movements, and Alice remembered that one of the thugs had cut her face. A large first aid kit was under her bed, filled with supplies only found in hospitals. She pulled a piece of gauze out, dabbed some peroxide on it and pressed it to her cheek. It stung but her mind was too full of other things to mind it much.

Lionel had told her months ago that he'd worked hard to make sure he never killed anyone ever again, it had seemed the most important decision of his life when he'd told it to her. Alice knew there was a story attached to it, a painful one and that what she'd seen Lionel do tonight must be dredging it all up.

I wonder what it was…I wonder how in the world I can help him now?

By the time Lionel finally finished his shower, Alice had calmed her frayed nerves and was sitting on the couch. When he emerged, his blond hair stuck up all around and he'd left his shirt mostly unbuttoned, exposing his well-muscled chest.

He sat down next to her, once again tense, like a coiled spring, and Alice wondered if he'd pop. That thought should have been frightening, after what she had seen him do, but it wasn't.

"I never wanted you to see me like that…" His voice broke. "What you must think of me."

"No," she said, her hands gentle on his face as she turned him to look at her. "It's not your fault. I know it."

"Yeah, that's what everyone keeps telling me. But…" He raked his hands through his hair, turning away from her. When he spoke, his voice was soft. "It's a relief in some ways. I hold myself in such control all the time, so I don't hurt anyone. Even good things, hugging and holding, and…I can't ever forget my strength…that I could hurt the people I love just by touching them. But when the anger takes over, I don't worry, don't feel afraid. God, Alice! What does that say about me?"

She turned his face back to her.

"That you've paid a price for this gift and it's hard. That you're human."

"I feel like a monster."

"Marco and I know you better than anyone. You're not a monster to us."

"How can you say that? After what I've done? What if...what if this is it? What if I stay like this forever? I could never be with...you'd hate me one day, Alice."

"I could never hate you," she whispered. "I would do anything for you."

"If I ever hurt you-"

Maybe it was the left over adrenaline, or the date, or just the fact that they were sharing the same breath. Whatever the reason, Alice leaned in and kissed him.

He moaned, just a little in the back of his throat, as if he were, at last, right where he wanted to be.

She teased his lips open, and ran her fingers along his shoulders. Lionel's arm wound around her waist, pulling her to him. Alice started to straddle him when he pulled back.

"No, Alice we can't."

She stared into his eyes, bright with passion, knowing for the first time in her life that he really wanted her and why he wouldn't let himself.

"I trust you," she said.

"But I don't trust me. Not until this...thing is out of me. I could lose control and...If I ever hurt you I'd never forgive myself. Please, believe me. I want you," he cupped her face with hands, "God do I want you. But I can't until Gerald fixes whatever this is."

"Alright," she said, forcing a smile. "I've waited this long."

He smiled a sad, beautiful smile.

"Not much longer. And in the mean time, still friends?"

"As if that would ever change."

"Thank you. And I swear-"

"Yeah, yeah, you say that to all the girls."

She punched him playfully on the shoulder and forced herself not to look at him. If he so much as had an ounce of longing in his eyes, Alice knew that would be it for her.

His smile faded when touched her cheek where the man had cut her, a storm of emotions crossing his face.

"I'm fine," she stood up, putting some much needed distance between them just as a frantic knock broke through the apartment.

Lionel shot up, his eyes wide in fear.

"It's Gerald," said a muffled voice behind the door.

"Come in," Alice said, making sure her dress was adjusted properly

She was surprised to see Marco come in behind Gerald. He looked from Lionel's barely-buttoned shirt to her rumpled dress and hair, and walked to the kitchen to make coffee.

Alice had a sudden terrible need to tell Marco that nothing had happened, not really. And then she remembered that he'd been following them.

And that's it's none of his business really.

She opened her mouth to demand an answer to why Marco had been there in the first place, when Gerald interrupted, saying, "Why don't you change? This is going to take a minute and that dress looks like it's seen better days."

"I'll buy you a new one," Lionel said, attempting levity, but it didn't reach his eyes.

When she emerged a few minutes later in a soft bathrobe, Marco had poured coffee and laid out the sticky buns he'd baked a few days before. Even though he'd done things like this for months, there was a nervous energy about it tonight, as if he needed to keep busy more than ever before.

Alice was again about to ask Marco about following them when Lionel's frightened voice stopped her.

"Well?"

Gerald sighed. "The toxin, or whatever it is, has...it's hard to explain. I'm not even sure what I'm looking at, but it seems that it's altered you, somehow. From what I've been told about what has been happening—"

"*Been* happening?" Alice asked. "This has happened before?"

"Twice," Marco said, "though not as...brutal."

"Once, right after the scratch, and...the night you were gassed. I could feel it before we went in...I think that's why I was so reckless. I didn't want you to know," Lionel said. "At least not until we could fix it."

"And that's just it," Gerald said, "I'm not sure I can. This has possibly changed the aggression centers of the brain. You've spent a long time building control over your anger, because of your strength, and this is overriding that."

"Can't you just purge it?" Alice asked.

"I don't think so, not without killing him."

Alice paced, her mind reeling.

Whatever had been done to Lionel was from Phantasm, she was sure of that. But why do this to Lionel, why make him stronger, in a way?

"You love them, don't you? What would you do if they were broken? What would happen if they died bloody?"

She swore under her breath, and then louder as bone deep anger coursed through her.

"What is it?" Marco asked.

Alice told them what Phantasm had said to her.

I swear if this is Victoria...

"That almost sounds like he's punishing you," Marco said. "But for what?"

"Douglas said that Percy and Phantasm had something over each other," Alice said, pacing again. "We took Percy out and that must've set his retribution in motion."

"What was it though?" Lionel asked.

"Something personal, would be my guess," Gerald said.

"Why?" Alice asked.

"People like this, they don't tend to scare easily and they usually have at least one thing they'd die for, one weakness, however well hidden, that can be exploited. Usually, it's family or friends."

"We could look at reports from around the time we took Percy out," Marco said. "See if there were any murders that stick out."

Alice felt her stomach turn.

"There's one murder."

All three men looked at her with such sympathy, such care and all Alice wanted was something to punch.

Namely Victoria.

"We don't know-" Gerald said.

"No, but it's looking more and more like it's her," Alice said.

"Okay, her family was murdered," Marco said. "But whatever was done to Lionel, that doesn't have a connection to Victoria."

Her mind spun, thoughts fluttering around like leaves in a wind storm. Retribution, revenge. Innocent people killed. Lionel poisoned. His aggression centers altered...

"Yes it does," she whispered, a sick feeling settling in her gut.

"How do you know that?" Lionel asked.

"The research Rose and I have been doing, Tony Veran was working on something that was supposed to take out the aggression centers of the brain, or at least dull them for a time."

Gerald nodded. "There was lots of talk about that kind of weapon after the war."

"Only this didn't work, it made all the subjects more aggressive."

Three sets of eyes stared at her.

"I think..." She sank down onto the couch. "What if—"

"Tony Veran was working for the Syndicate?" Lionel asked.

"They wouldn't have killed Tony, if that was the case," Marco said.

"That just leaves Victoria," Gerald said.

Lionel laughed. "What? C'mon, she's a smart woman, I'll grant you, but this kind of thing?"

"She's a brilliant scientist in her own right," Alice said.

"Why would she give that to the Syndicate? What's the motive?" Marco asked.

That was the question that had been nagging Alice since her conversation with Rose earlier. What Alice knew of the passionate, brilliant philanthropist and scientist didn't line up with the monster that had drugged her.

There must be a way to either vindicate her or find out for certain.

"If we could break into the Veran Corporation," Lionel said. "Maybe we could find an antidote or something."

"Or the formula for what they dosed you with," Marco said.

"That's not going to be easy," Gerald said. "And I doubt Garrick would back you up on it."

"What choice to we have?" Lionel's voice took on a desperate tone. "We have to fix this!"

Alice smiled as an idea formed.

"We don't have to steal anything. We're going to ask her for it."

"We're going to what?" Marco asked.

"I can go to her and ask for her help. If she didn't give it to the Syndicate, then she'll be confused, but will help us. And if she did, maybe she's remorseful now, maybe she has no idea what they've done with it. Either way, it clears her."

"And we're back to square one," Marco said.

"Yes, but at least we know she's innocent."

"But, if she refuses?" Lionel asked.

Alice sighed. "Then..."

"How will you do this without revealing any of us?" Marco asked.

"I'll think of something. We have to try."

They nodded.

"It's better than breaking and entering," Gerald said as he gathered his bag. "And Lionel, you might want to limit your fights, especially alone. Maybe stick with Marco, since he might be able to siphon off some of your anger if the need arises."

Lionel tensed his jaw and nodded. Before Gerald had closed the door, Lionel was pouring himself a generous whiskey and for several minutes he stared out the window, taking large gulps.

"There's no use beating yourself up," Marco said to Lionel. "It won't happen again."

"How do you know?"

"We'll be there, helping you."

"Speaking of," Alice turned to Marco, her face flushing with anger, "why were you following us?"

Marco looked down, hands in his pockets.

"Well...I was worried."

"About me," Lionel whispered.

"Yes. If anything happened—"

"You thought I'd hurt her."

"I didn't say that."

"Then what?"

The two men stared at one another, Alice caught between them. She had the distinct feeling of being trapped between two angry animals.

"Stop it, this doesn't help anything," she said.

With one last glare, they turned away.

"You shouldn't have followed us, Marco, but," she took

a deep breath, "I'm glad, in a way, that you did. I don't think we could've gotten out of there without you."

"Still, it wasn't okay," Lionel growled.

"No, it wasn't." Alice touched Lionel's arm, "but neither was keeping this from me. You should know me better by now than to think I'd turn away from you."

Lionel swirled the whiskey in his glass, staring at it a moment. "I'm sorry."

"Me, too," Marco said.

Alice nodded. "Okay, now that we've got that taken care of, I need some sleep."

"I'll get the cots." Lionel downed the rest of his whiskey. "You get the sheets."

Before Alice turned to go into her room, she caught Marco's eye for just a moment. She remembered the way he'd looked at her when they'd almost kissed and swore she saw a glimpse of heat in his gaze before he turned away.

Barely an hour ago I was kissing Lionel, ready to sleep with him. And now I'm thinking of Marco?

She ran a frustrated hand through her tangled hair and closed the bedroom door.

"First cure Lionel, then decide which man you want in your bed. Simple, right?…Ugh!"

CHAPTER TWENTY-FOUR

Alice stumbled out of her room in the morning, stifling a yawn. She was surprised to see Marco already awake, until she noticed that his cot looked like it had hardly been slept in. He was still in the black shirt and pants that were part of his Shadow suit. The rest of his gear lay on his empty cot. He sat on the couch, a cup of coffee in front of him and a novel by a new author named Heinlein, open on his lap.

Lionel let out a sudden, rumbling snore and turned over, muttering something about clams.

They both stifled giggles, not wanting to wake him.

Marco's hair flopped down into his eyes and before he could brush it back, Alice reached to run her fingers through it. She'd done it hundreds of times before, but this time was different somehow. When she was done, Marco's dark eyes were intense on hers, the merest trace of longing in them.

"You need a haircut," Alice whispered.

"I don't have time."

"Do you like that book?" she asked, wanting to focus on something, anything, other than how tempting it was to run her hands through his hair again.

"It's alright. I think I like Asimov better."

Alice nodded and went to get a cup of coffee. Not wanting to just sit and stare at the wall, she plucked a book from one of her shelves and sat next to Marco.

Without a word, he raised his arm and she scooted next to him, her back pressed against his side, head resting on his shoulder. They'd sat like this a hundred times, finding comfort in the world of their books, and the warmth of their friendship. Alice had a moment of tension thinking about their last sparring session, but it faded in seconds as Marco's arm settled around her and they both sank into their books.

She had no idea how long they sat like that, but when Marco finally spoke, her coffee was gone and the sun had just fully risen above the horizon.

He set his book down on the coffee table by his cup.

"I know you may not want to talk about this, but...we have to."

Alice felt her stomach flip.

It's about yesterday, almost kissing him. I knew it! I've made him uncomfortable. But it was nothing...really.

"Wh-what do you want to talk about?" she whispered.

"Victoria."

A whoosh of air flew out of her mouth, but the relief was short lived. As much as she didn't want to hear that Marco was upset by what happened yesterday, talking about Victoria wasn't the alternative she'd wanted.

"I know this is hard for you, but we have to consider the facts."

"I am. There's just one missing piece of the puzzle: Why?"

"Fear..." He closed his eyes. "You wouldn't believe the things I've seen people want to do because of it."

"Afraid of what? The Third Reich fell, she married the

love of her life, and is one of the most powerful women in the country."

"No, she isn't. She was married to a powerful man — she was a wife. No one believed in her or treated her as the real power in that corporation. And if she had to hide her real identity, just to work with Tony's research after the war, what else has she had to do? You know better than most what the world sees when it looks at a woman who wants something more."

Alice closed her eyes, a deep sigh escaping her lips.

"Alright, but how is working with the Syndicate—"

"Or leading it."

"How is that getting her what she wants, whatever that might be?"

"I don't know. But, maybe, you could find out when you talk to her. As difficult as it will be, you have to be dispassionate about her to find out the truth."

Alice stared ahead, her mind spinning over dozens of different possibilities and connections that might answer her question, but in the middle of it all was a raw nerve of disappointment and anger.

This woman had been the person she remembered every time a man in her business class would pinch her rear or tell her she was lost. Every time a professor marked her paper more harshly than the other students or overlooked her in discussions. Every person that treated her as less intelligent and worthy of notice, simply because she was a woman. Rebelling against all these things was used by Alice to help spur her on.

And when it got to be too much, all she had to do was remember how her aunt and Victoria had carved out lives for themselves, despite all opposition. If Victoria could do it, she could, too.

Alice had felt a kinship with Victoria and despite everything that pointed to her being Phantasm, Alice still did.

What does that say about me?

"Do you think..." Alice paused, her small fingers winding through Marco's long ones. "Do you think Phantasm, whoever it is, had something to do with Aunt Diana's death?"

Marco sighed, his eyes hooded by furrowed brows. "Probably."

She turned away as a sick anger began welling up inside of her.

After a moment, she could feel warm strong arms pull her close. She rested her head on Marco's chest, and the curve of her body melded perfectly into his. The gentle sound of his heart calmed her mind, creating a peaceful island in the middle of so much uncertainty.

She trusted what Marco had promised, that he would never use his powers on her without her permission. But there were moments, like this one, when she had to wonder how it was possible to feel so at home in someone's arms.

Lionel's loud snore jolted her out of such thoughts and Marco's arms fell away. Lionel's head jerked up, blond hair spiked as though he'd been electrocuted. He squinted at them, lips pouting as if he were angry he'd awakened himself.

"What time?"

"Early," Marco said, standing up. "There's coffee and food in the fridge that even Alice can't mess up by reheating."

"I've gotten very good at reheating, thank you very much."

She smiled up at him as Marco laughed and walked to the door as if he couldn't wait to leave.

"You could stay for breakfast," Alice said, stopping him just before he closed the door.

He smiled. "No thanks. I should...well, your date was interrupted and I don't feel like being a third wheel."

"You're not."

"It's okay, really. I gotta get ready for work."

Alice was confused by the feeling of rejection that stabbed at her. Yet when she turned and saw a shirtless Lionel grinning at her with a mouthful of stale sticky bun, the feeling evaporated.

"So, gorgeous," he said around a second bite, "what should we do today?"

The next day, Alice stepped out of a cab in front of Victoria's beautiful home, her stomach roiling with nerves. Dressed in what she hoped was a respectably modest blue pencil skirt and sleeveless, boat-neck blouse, Alice took several deep breaths as she stared at the Veran's front door.

"Now or never," she said to herself and knocked.

A chubby man with a sour expression soon answered. When she told him who she was, he gestured for her to follow him.

Alice felt her pulse quicken as her black heels echoed in a quick rhythm on the white and gray marble floor. They walked past two different rooms, both with doors shut tight. As they approached the third room, the door opened, and a large man stepped out with his back to Alice.

When he turned to face her, the world slowed and became silent. The air left her lungs in a rush of shock, and her pulse sped up.

Standing there, single eye glaring at her, was Baritone.

Instinctively, her hands clenched and her feet widened into a defensive stance.

Baritone looked like he was about to walk past her, but then his one eye narrowed, the scar that ran under his patch puckering. He was close enough for her to smell the tang of his cologne.

"We must not keep Mrs. Veran waiting," the butler said. "She is a very busy woman."

The words brought her crashing back into the world around her.

"Yes, of course..."

She swallowed and tore her eyes from Baritone, who hadn't moved. She walked past him, sweat trickling down her now shaking body, feeling the man's gaze on her. She knew he wouldn't move until she was out of sight. Whatever doubts Alice had been clinging to disappeared. She had no choice now but to accept the truth.

Victoria was Phantasm.

Victoria had poisoned Lionel.

Victoria had tortured her.

The butler opened the door and stepped aside for her to enter.

It was the last thing Alice wanted to do, but she thought of Lionel and squared her shoulders.

She could do this — she had to.

It was a beautiful room. Any other time Alice would've loved sitting in one of the soft pink and gray chairs, sipping tea, and reading one of the hundreds of books that lined the white shelves. The faint smell of jasmine floated on the quickly warming air and Alice could feel the faintest breeze from the open French doors and ceiling fans.

"So good to see you," Victoria said, giving Alice a gentle embrace. "I must say, you look tired — not sleeping?"

Alice felt her skin crawl at Victoria's touch, but forced her smile to widen.

"Oh, yes. Bad dreams, nothing to worry about."

"Some believe that bad dreams are our conscience trying to expel guilt." Victoria's eyes took on a hard glint for a moment.

Have some experience with that, do we?

Just then, the butler arrived with a tray of cakes and iced tea. Once the butler had served each of them, he placed the tray on a side table and left, closing the door.

Victoria took a dainty sip of tea. "I hope you weren't too startled by the man who just left."

Alice was spared trying to make a response by nibbling on a cake.

"He's a ghastly-looking fellow," Victoria continued. "But after what happened with Tony and the children...well, I felt that I needed some security. He's the best body guard money can buy, apparently. Though I wonder how many decent people he may frighten away along with the dangerous ones."

Alice wanted to believe her, but just couldn't.

"Do you think you'll be attacked again?" she asked in the most sincere tone she could muster.

"Anything is possible. And in my experience, it's best to err on the side of caution. Oh, I almost forgot!I was going to call and ask if you'd like to help with the Park Side Clinic celebration. It's ten days away and I'm desperate for volunteers."

"Anything to help Gerald and the clinic. What are you planning?"

The question felt horribly loaded to Alice.

"There's this huge open field, of sorts, where an old warehouse used to be, right by the old paper processing plant."

Alice smiled. "I know it well, it used to be one of my favorite haunts."

"I had forgotten you grew up there." Something in Victoria's tone said that she hadn't forgotten at all. "Anyway, I'm going to host a sort of party for the neighborhood, to celebrate the opening of the new clinic."

"Are you going to make the rich of Jet City mingle with

the poor of Park Side? Won't that make some enemies for you on the board?" Alice asked.

Victoria shrugged.

"Perhaps. But I think they've been too separate from the people they are supposed to be helping. I expect some very good things to come out of this event. I've ordered huge tents and game booths. I want to make it a family event. Maybe bring in new clients for the clinic."

"What kind of help do you need?"

"Why don't you run one of the booths. Maybe put Miss Grace and her friends in their place by telling them what to do."

Alice choked on her tea.

"You've got some of the board and their families volunteering?"

Victoria laughed.

"Yes! And it took some doing, let me tell you. Can I count on you?"

"Absolutely."

"Good."

"How are your other interests doing?" Alice asked.

Victoria's smile tightened just a little.

"What other interests?"

"The Science Foundation. Who is spearheading the staffing, now that Dr. Veran is gone?"

"Me, of course," Victoria said.

"It is good of the board to not cause too much of a fuss over your involvement. I imagine it's been difficult for you, since Dr. Veran's death."

"Yes, it has, but I have been involved in the Science Foundation from the beginning, so they are quite used to me by now. But enough about that, I don't think you came over here this afternoon to talk about me. What can I do for you?"

"Well," Alice took a deep breath. "You see, a friend of mine was recently attacked. He was injected with a toxin that has made it difficult to control his anger. I have been reading about your husband's ground-breaking work in behavioral science and was wondering if he ever did any experiments with anything that might help?"

It was a thin story, but she hoped that by drawing on the persona of a somewhat helpless young woman, she could sell it. She watched as Victoria took a slow drink of her tea, then folded her hands in her lap.

"I think he did do some work in that area, but I don't see how I can help you."

"If he kept copies of his research here at home, perhaps a chemist you know might be able to engineer a cure?"

Victoria smiled at her, and then, pity oozing from her voice, said, "It must be hard to watch your friend suffer and not be able to help him. I know how that feels. But unfortunately, if my husband did do work for the Army, and I showed that work to a fellow scientist, Tony's reputation would be tarnished, people would think he was a traitor, and I can't have that."

Alice felt her pulse quicken. If seeing Baritone hadn't been proof enough, Victoria's careless slip was.

"I never said anything about the project being from his time with the Army," Alice said, hoping her voice wasn't as accusing as it sounded.

Victoria paused, then smiled at Alice.

"You didn't need to, I knew what project you meant. Tony was always very open with me about his work."

"Did he ever mention one of his research assistants with this project, a V.G. Muller? Maybe I could talk to him?"

Alice could swear she saw Victoria jerk a little, as if someone had poked her with a sharp object.

"He mentioned him, of course, but Dr. Muller died in

the accident that wounded Tony. I'm sorry, but I can't help you with this."

Then how is Muller's signature on the last experiment a week later?

A very familiar, very angry voice interrupted the awkward silence that had settled on them.

"I do not care if she is in a meeting! I will see her this instant!" Mrs. Frost said.

The butler ran into the room and opened his mouth to say something when Mrs. Frost charged into the room.

"Victoria, you have crossed a line and I will not have it!"

Victoria set her iced tea down and gave Mrs. Frost a benign smile.

"Whatever are you talking about?"

"You have enlisted the help of the Philanthropic Society to force the Mayor and City council—" Mrs. Frost began.

"Force is a strong word."

"—to legalize the use of police officers who have been altered by drugs!"

Alice could only stare. This had to be dream. How could she really be hearing and seeing all this?

"Come now, Mrs. Frost," Victoria said. "They aren't drugs. Really, you make me sound like a petty criminal."

Or a not so petty one.

"I am concerned by the increase in these...well, individuals with, shall we say, special abilities," Victoria said. "If the vigilantes are allowed to operate outside of the law, what will stop others? And those others may not try to stop crime, but cause it. Do you have any idea how potentially destructive these people are? The police aren't equipped to handle them."

Alice cleared her throat, feeling it tighten in panic.

"What special abilities are you referring to?"

In answer, Victoria held out a manila folder.

Alice opened it with some trepidation. Inside were clippings of newspaper articles with notes in what she assumed was Victoria's own hand. The notes were interviews she'd conducted with anyone who'd been saved by the Jet City vigilantes. Further down in the pile were clippings from Metro City, and a place Alice had never heard of, Desert Springs.

All of them had to do with strange goings on, people either saved by those with strange talents and abilities, or those who had been harmed by them. One particularly disturbing article talked about a group of boys and men that were found in an alley, their bodies completely drained of water. Another spoke of a young boy, who reportedly made a tree grab the school yard bully and squeeze him so hard his ribs broke.

Most of the articles were from papers that Alice had never heard of and were likely small presses. But the Jet City and Metro City articles were from respectable newspapers.

She bit the inside of her cheek as she tried to think of the right way to respond.

"Really Victoria!" Mrs. Frost said. "Half of these clippings are from newspapers that aren't worth the paper they were printed on! Are you giving in to hysteria based on gossip rags?"

"There were rumors," Victoria said, ignoring Mrs. Frost's comment, "of the Nazis conducting experiments on people to try to make super soldiers. Though the United States condemned such practices, they too tried to unlock what was believed to be the hidden potentials of the human body and mind."

"You believe these—?" Alice said, curious in spite of herself.

"Some, yes, but regarding others, the timeline of when

319

they'd have had to be exposed to enhancing chemicals doesn't match up."

Alice's ears perked up at the mention of 'enhancing chemicals'.

"What if," Victoria came from behind her desk, "these others were just born this way? What if this is random, and the person with the power was not examined for the possibility of nefarious actions. It would mean that super-human powers would be in the hands of someone who could use them for evil, to subjugate humanity or destroy them."

"You would attribute insidious motivations to anyone with powers?" Mrs. Frost asked. "That is perhaps too extreme, don't you think?"

"Especially since some, like the Jet City vigilantes, help people," Alice said.

"Yes, but what's to stop even them from seeing them-selves as above the law? To take matters into their own hands and stand in judgment, just because of their special abilities? What if they started to see themselves as better than us?"

Alice swallowed. She'd had similar concerns when she first found out about Lionel and Marco. And there were still moments when she wondered if they could ever feel their special powers might justify them stepping over the line.

And even if I believed they would never do that, what about these other people? Who are they and what do they believe?

She shook her head, disturbed at how quickly fear was taking root in her heart.

"It's not...I mean," Alice said. "we can't ever know what anyone will do with the abilities they've been given."

"My thoughts precisely," Mrs. Frost snapped. "You tread a very precarious line, Victoria."

"I accept that and believe it is worth it to protect this city, maybe even the entire nation."

"What are you proposing?" Alice said, trying to keep fear out of her voice.

Victoria's gray eyes gleamed.

"For many years, the Veran Corporation has had a small Scientific Research branch, which has engineered a serum that, when injected, can enhance a person's natural strength and stamina. Human trials have been very promising. So, I asked permission for select members of the police force to have access to the serum in order to combat this new threat. They would become a sort of special unit."

If Victoria's human trials were anything like the two men Alice had seen at the warehouse, she didn't think it was very promising at all.

"The government canceled the super soldier program, because it was too risky," Mrs. Frost said. "And you wish to re-invent it with a private police force? Do you not see the danger in this, Victoria?"

"No, I do not. I see a world still in need of protecting from a threat no one saw on the horizon."

Mrs. Frost shook her gray head.

"You see villains where there are none."

"I remember, quite well, what happened to my country when a man no one saw as a threat came to power. One man, Mrs. Frost, with no special abilities. What will dozens of men and women do if they possess god-like powers? We have the chance to make sure we are defended against them. But, we must do it now!"

Marco's words from yesterday morning rang in Alice's mind and she felt pity for Victoria. To live your life under the cruel taskmaster that fear could be, seeing potential threats everywhere, never being able to trust.

"It is too fraught with danger," Mrs. Frost said. "What is to stop the person in charge of these police officers from themselves becoming a villain?"

"That will not happen."

"How do you know?" Alice asked.

"Because, I would be in charge of it."

With sudden terrible clarity, Alice felt the pieces of the puzzle fall into place. She could see what Victoria, with all her fear and power, could do with a private army of enhanced people. A sick knot twisted in her stomach, and she was very glad she hadn't eaten much today.

"I see you are both against me in this," Victoria said.

In her voice, Alice could hear what she wasn't saying. *If we do not stand with her, we are her enemy.*

"I cannot agree with what you propose," Mrs. Frost said. "There are too many terrible possibilities."

"Worse than these... *people* running around unchecked, able to do anything they please?"

"Victoria, I don't think we have anything to fear from them," Alice said. "They simply want to live their lives."

She shook her head.

"My dear, I have seen what power unchecked can do. I do not wish that upon the world again. And if I can stop it, I will."

Alice followed Mrs. Frost out onto the front steps of the house where a dark green Cadillac was waiting, the driver moping his brow before opening the door for them.

"Get in," Mrs. Frost ordered as she walked down the steps.

Once Alice was sitting beside Mrs. Frost, the car rolled down the quiet drive.

Mrs. Frost tapped her cane on the floor of the car as if she were squashing a bug, her face set in a wrinkled scowl. After a few moments, it was clear that, for the first time since Alice had met her, the woman was speechless.

Alice took a deep breath, feeling a desperate need to break the silence that pressed around them so heavily.

"I was talking with Victoria before you arrived."

"So I noticed. What were you discussing?"

Alice told her quickly, leaving nothing out.

"And you are sure this man you saw was at the warehouse?"

"Positive. He has a very distinct appearance."

"So, then, what did you learn from everything this afternoon?"

"She's Phantasm. I didn't want to believe it, but...she is."

"I believe you are correct, and I am sorry, truly, my dear. I know what she has meant to you."

Alice felt tears burn her eyes and forced them away. She would cry later, if she still wanted to. Now was the time to think and act.

"A person like Victoria," Mrs. Frost said, slowly as if she were weighing each word, "who believes she is the only one to know what is wrong and right...a person like that is very dangerous."

"Even though the police haven't been our biggest supporters, there's no way they would agree to such a risky venture."

"Victoria will find a way to make them come around to what she wants."

Alice nodded. "Then, we have to stop her."

"And quickly, too. However, Victoria is not some two-faced District Attorney or legendary drug lord that everyone will believe you are justified in hunting down. She is a respected woman, a philanthropist, and a wealthy individual with a very long reach. Speaking as someone with similar gifts, I can tell you it will not be easy to convince anyone of what she is doing, until it is too late."

"So, no help then."

"Until you have proof, no."

They fell into silence, each lost in thought. Alice tried to be detached, to think like a hero and not let her feelings cloud her judgment, but each time she thought of a way to find proof or to harm one of Victoria's interests, a pang of guilt and anger would spring up in her. She had looked up to this woman, wanted to be like her. Now, she had to face the fact that Victoria had a deep dark side, one that was threatening the lives of hundreds, maybe thousands, of people.

And even if she didn't order Aunt Diana's death, she was a leader, she could've stopped it and she didn't. But why the Syndicate?

"What I still don't understand," Alice said, "is why she became a part of the Syndicate? How does that help her achieve her aims?"

Mrs. Frost paused, and when she spoke, her voice was quiet but firm.

"It is very hard to be constantly undervalued and thought less of for wanting something more than the world is willing to give you. After a while, you begin to think of other ways to earn the respect you feel you deserve. If Victoria could not find equality in a law-abiding part of the world, she obviously thought she could find it in the unlawful one. And, she did."

"But you must've felt the same as Victoria and you never did anything like that."

Mrs. Frost fixed Alice with a hard look. "I may not have turned to crime, but I certainly did something that would be perceived as just as awful. I grasped for the power to accomplish my goals just like Victoria has. The only difference is I never crossed the line into villainy."

"So what now?"

"Since we now know that Victoria is leading the Syndicate," Mrs. Frost said, her voice all business once again, "we must consider the criminal activities that the Syndicate is still engaged in. Perhaps we will discover clues about her ultimate plan."

"Well, we know that they're still manufacturing Fantasy."

"How?"

"Because it's still out there. It's profitable, probably one of the most profitable drugs on the market despite its side effects."

"And Victoria is a business woman. She would not harpoon her best product."

Alice nodded. "And Gerald believes that whatever I was gassed with is either a form of Fantasy or very close to it."

Mrs. Frost's head whipped around, eyes wide in her wrinkled face.

It took only a second for Alice to come to the same conclusion.

"She's turning it into a weapon! But, why? Why would you do that to a population you're trying to protect? If that's what she's trying to do."

"Think, Alice. How could she use it to turn Jet City against the heroes?"

Alice rubbed her sweaty palms on her pencil skirt.

"Chaos. If she can cause enough of it as Phantasm, the city might begin blaming the vigilantes for encouraging people to take matters into their own hands, whether they be hero or villain. Then, she can swoop in, as Victoria, save the day and get the recognition and power she's been craving. And, the Science Foundation is the perfect cover for making all the enhancements, or whatever she might see as necessary, to make her perfectly safe world."

Mrs. Frost nodded. "Once the Science Foundation has opened and Victoria has worked her influence on the mayor and city council, she will have no use for Phantasm."

Alice lay her head back and closed her eyes. How did

they stop someone who was so powerful and respected — and whose plan was well underway?

They rode the rest of the way in silence, the revelations laying heavy between them. The driver pulled up in front of Atlas Books and Alice felt a longing to sit on that worn rug in the children's section and curl up with a book and a cup of tea.

"Here." Mrs. Frost handed Alice a small box. "A gift from Rose."

Inside were three smaller, rectangular boxes. Alice saw a button on the side and pressed it. The sides of the box unfolded to reveal a strange oval mask with straps on either side.

"A gas mask," Mrs. Frost said. "In case you come into contact with that Fantasy gas again."

A fear Alice hadn't realized she was holding onto dissipated, and she smiled.

"Thank her for me, will you?"

"Of course."

As Alice stepped out of the car, Mrs. Frost leaned forward to give a final admonishment.

"Be careful, whatever you decide to do. Victoria has always been a formidable opponent in business. With something she believes in this passionately, she will be more so."

"I will."

Once in the loft, Alice felt her body humming with unspent energy, her mind whirling with a furious need to put together a plan of action.

Training was the only choice.

The minute her fist connected with the punching bag, Alice felt the exhilaration of all that energy directed at something. She let her mind wander in and out of possibilities as her body moved in ways that were as familiar to her as breathing.

After an hour, the sound of sirens in the distance penetrated her thoughts, but she didn't stop to consider them until the police scanner in her bedroom screeched to life.

"All units report to the offices of the Jet City Chronicle, repeat all units to the Jet City Chronicle! There's been an attack, smoke or gas in the building, unknown number of assailants."

CHAPTER TWENTY-FIVE

Alice zoomed around cars, cutting them off and just barely missing a couple of jaywalkers as she sped on the Black Lightning toward the newspaper. It was odd to be out in broad daylight as Serpent, but she didn't care. Uncle Logan was at the paper. Uncle Logan, who she hadn't spoken to since they'd fought.

She refused to believe that those would be their last words to each other. He would be alive. Marco was probably there, he would protect Uncle Logan.

Unless he was hit with the gas.

Marco, with his powers, on Fantasy.

Alice opened the throttle up and sped through a red light, narrowly missing a car. As the traffic slowed in front of her, she popped the Lightning onto the sidewalk, barreling around pedestrians until she could take a right-hand turn.

The police had blocked off the street around the paper and it looked like they were trying to evacuate one of the nearby office buildings. The smoke was thin, and Alice was at a distance, but the wind brought just the faintest hint of something sweet.

Her heart began to hammer behind her ribs and she fumbled for the gas mask, slamming it on. She idled the Lightning down an alley, and turned just in time to see Lionel drop down from the roof, eyes quizzical behind his blue cowl.

"What the hell do you have on your face?"

She threw him a box. "Gas mask, courtesy of Rose."

"That girl's a wonder."

"Was Marco—?"

"Right here," Marco said, dropping down from a fire escape, duster swirling around his dark clad legs.

The breath rushed out of Alice in one relieved gush.

"I was so worried you were in there," she said, giving him a mask as well.

"If I'd been on time to work I would've been. Lucky me, I guess."

"What do we do if the police are also affected? Do we know how long this lasts?" Lionel asked.

"Couldn't be that long," Marco said, securing the mask, "we could still smell it in the bakery, but it didn't affect us."

"So, it must be most potent the first few minutes," Alice said. "That works in our favor."

"Yeah, but daylight doesn't," Marco said.

"What are the chances we could just talk our way through the barricade?" Lionel asked.

"Even if they weren't still mad about the warehouse fire? Pretty slim," Marco said.

"We're wasting time," Alice snapped. "The police have no idea what they're walking into!"

Lionel and Marco stared at her for a moment, their expressions hard to read behind the gas masks.

"He'll be alright," Lionel said. "We'll make sure of it."

Alice swallowed, tears burning her eyes.

"I just...I can't lose him, too."

"Let's go then," Marco said, shooting his grappler into the top of a nearby fire escape.

They hopped half a dozen roof tops until they were on the roof of the building across from the Jet City Chronicle.

After the old Chronicle building had burned down, the city had scrounged up the money to build a gorgeous three-story complex. It looked more like a mini-skyscraper than a newspaper office, with its large windows and gleaming steel exterior. In the spring, fruit trees blossomed along the wide walk that led people to the double glass doors and into a spacious lobby. The grass in front had turned brown in the heat of summer, despite the sprinklers, and some of the flowers that lined the bottom floor windows were dying. But, even so, the Chronicle was still a jewel in Jet City's crown. And, taking in the presence of so many police officers, Alice could only assume that the mayor and police chief meant to keep it that way.

A barrier had been set up several feet away from the Chronicle. Most of the police crouched behind their squad cars, brown and blue-clad detectives talking in a group behind the beat cops.

Alice felt her insides turn to ice as she took in the damage.

The windows along the bottom floor lobby were completely gone, chairs and a small table lay atop the shattered glass. Papers covered the ground and fluttered in the warm breeze. Here and there, a body lay, some looking as if they'd been beaten to death, others like they'd been shot.

The windows on the second and third floors were mostly untouched. Alice could see people on the roof. At first, she thought that maybe they were trying to get away, but then she saw two of them tackle another and throw him off the roof. She yelped as the person fell with a muffled thump

"It's made them violent," Lionel whispered.

"Or it's a different gas," Marco said, his voice strained.

"What's wrong?" Lionel asked.

He shook his head. "I can't...I don't know. All those emotions...I can feel them from here."

"Maybe you should stay, there's no telling what it's going to be like in there."

"No, I can handle it."

Lionel fixed Marco with a hard stare.

"You don't have to go in just to babysit me. I'll be fine."

"You don't know that," Marco said. "I can do this, I'm just going to have to concentrate a bit more."

"I think I see Garrick," Alice said, pointing to the end of the barrier nearest the building.

They jumped to one more roof top, and then down, running to the police on the furthest side of the barrier. Several officers turned in fright, pointing their guns. Lionel, Alice, and Marco stopped, hands popping up.

"We're here to help," Alice said.

"Put those away, morons!" Garrick said to the beat cops and shambled over to the three of them.

He glared at them with blood shot eyes.

"One of you want to tell me what the hell is going on?"

Never had Alice heard more colorful language than she did from Garrick in the ten minutes it took to catch him up on what was happening.

"And you're just telling me, now?" His frown made him look more like a bulldog than ever.

"Until we had something concrete—" Alice said.

He muttered more curse words and began barking orders for someone to call the station for all the gas masks they had. Some of the officers looked at him like he was crazy, while others shot sideways glances at the three of them.

"Okay," Garrick said, "we'll go in ten minutes, as soon

as those lazy bastards at the station get their asses in gear and send the damn gas masks!"

Garrick coordinated with another man on how to subdue the few left on the roof just as ambulances pulled up. Alice tried not to think about what they'd find inside.

What they could've done to Uncle Logan.

She shook herself and shoved the thought away. He was fine. He had to be.

High pitched screaming echoed through the courtyard and Alice saw a woman, her face bloodied and clothes torn, come bolting out of the front door. She was batting at something none of them could see, crying for help.

A police officer ran up to her, but she began clawing at him. It took three more to drag her away. As they stuffed her into a squad car Alice heard her say something about a monster in a three-piece suit and hat, with huge metallic eyes and a snout.

A sickening chill snaked its way through her body.

"She's here."

"Who?" Garrick demanded.

"Phantasm," she said, eyes glued to the door where the woman had come from, half expecting to see her materialize.

"We can't wait, we need to get in there now!"

Alice sprinted past the police, ignoring the shouts from everyone that told her stand back and wait. She couldn't wait. If Phantasm was here, then her uncle was in more danger than just from the gas.

She was only a few feet away from the door when a strong hand jerked her to a stop.

"What the hell do you think you're doing?" Lionel said, lips pursed as he clenched his jaw.

"You want to get killed?" Marco asked.

"Uncle Logan and those people in there don't have ten minutes! If Phantasm is here, then we can't wait for them."

"If Phantasm is here," Lionel said, "maybe you shouldn't go in. It's only been a few days and what if you see her and lose it? Shadow and I can do this."

"No, I'm not abandoning Uncle Logan. I can't stand out here and wait for someone to tell me he's alright."

"Serpent-" Marco said.

"No! I'm going in there and I'm going to find him and that's the end of it!"

"If you don't cool it, I'll lock you in one of the squad cars!" Garrick said, rushing toward them. "You want everyone here to know who you are under that thing?"

Alice shook her head.

"Then, cool it! You'll do Logan no good if you lose it in there, got it?"

"Yes," she said through clenched teeth.

"Gas masks are here," Garrick said, "we go in two minutes. Get yourself under control or I swear—"

"You'll lock me a squad car, I got it."

Garrick glared at her before turning away and barking orders for someone to start handing out the masks.

She paced on the sidewalk, doing her best to breath deep and even. There was enough chaos erupting around her, Alice knew that adding to it in any way wouldn't help.

"I'm sorry," she said to Lionel and Marco.

Lionel nodded.

"Garrick's not wrong," Marco said, "you can't go off half-cocked in there."

"I know, I just…"

Marco frowned at her. She wanted to calm down, but all she could think about was Uncle Logan.

But it's not just him in there. There's other people that need my help, too. He wouldn't want me endangering them to save him.

"I'll be fine," she said after a moment. "I promise."

A group of about a dozen police officers ran up to where they were standing, Garrick in the lead.

"We're going in through the lobby," Garrick ordered. "Then up the stairs to the second floor. This is where most everyone would have been at the time of the attack, so be careful!"

"Remember," Lionel said, "they're under the influence of something extremely powerful. No killing, and try not to wound them too severely. Get as many out as possible. Leave anyone you see in a suit and gas mask to us."

A couple of the officers rolled their eyes, others glared at Lionel. Alice wondered if they would be a hindrance or a help, but there was no time to think it through.

The lobby was eerily silent, tendrils of gas curled around their ankles. Alice could see smears of blood on the walls, as if someone were wiping their hands. As they walked down the hall toward the stairs, someone had written shaky fragments of words on the wall with a marker. At least, she hoped it was a marker.

As Lionel pushed open the stairwell door, the sounds of sobbing echoed around them. It was hard to see at first, because someone had damaged most of the lights. The sobbing was joined by a dull thumping sound. They climbed the first set of stairs without seeing anyone. But once they'd turned the corner, Alice felt her insides freeze.

Someone was doubled over on their knees, covering their face in their hands, like a child hiding from nightmares. As Alice stepped closer, she could see that it was a woman, papers scattered around her, the smell of urine stinging Alice's nostrils. The lights flickered, but she could see well enough to notice missing clumps of hair from the woman's head. She was muttering something and when Alice stepped closer to try and hear it, she felt a drop of something wet on her face.

Looking over, she found the source of the thumping

sound and where the drop had come from. A man was banging his head on the bars of the stairwell, blood from the wound he was inflicting splattering around.

"Shadow, can you—?"

But Marco was leaning on the wall, hands clutching the side of his head as if he were in pain.

"What's wrong?" she asked.

"It's...so strong. Not just these...more...so many more..."

His eyes snapped shut and he began to breath heavily.

Alice looked to the officers waiting several steps away.

"You three, get these two out of here, now."

They hesitated.

"What are you waiting for?" Garrick asked.

They ran up the stairs and Alice hoped they didn't pay Marco much mind.

"I told you—" Lionel started.

"You usually do," Marco said, his voice strained. "I-I'm sorry, but I don't...need a lecture."

The woman whimpered as one of the officers lifted her up, but the man who was banging his head let out a wail, as if he'd seen something truly awful. He broke free and charged for Alice. His hair stuck up all over his head, blood tinted half his face red, some of it getting on his teeth as he snarled at her. She stared in shock at the ferocious animal of a man before her.

Then, her instincts kicked in and she shot a Serpent bite into the man. He took a few more steps toward her before stumbling to a halt and falling to the ground.

At first Alice assumed he'd been knocked out, like most people, but then, the man started to convulse.

"Oh God!" she said, reaching for him.

"Get out of the way!" A police officer pushed her and picked the man up.

Garrick fixed her with a hard look.

"Nice job."

"I-I didn't know..."

"Yeah, well, now you do. Let's move."

She turned to look at Marco, but jumped back when she saw the shadows writhing around him.

Alice took Marco's face in her hands.

"Look at me."

He shook his head.

"Look at me."

After a moment, he opened his eyes. They were completely black and she could feel him shaking with the effort to hold onto his control. A primal fear tried to take hold of her and she forced it back. Marco needed her.

"Breathe with me," she said. "Look in my eyes, focus on me, and breathe."

He did, fast at first, and then slower, until the darkness receded from his eyes.

"You can do this," Alice said.

His eyes held hers and he nodded. As she stepped away, Alice glanced at Lionel, who was staring at Marco with concern etched on his square face.

She wanted to tell him that they didn't need his protection, that he didn't have to carry the burden of their safety on his shoulders, but what would be the point?

"C'mon," she said to them, walking on ahead.

They found three other people in various states of terror throughout the stairwell. One of them needed to be handcuffed and carried over an officer's shoulder, while the other two merely whimpered. When they reached the door to the second floor it was held open by a dead body, the head was a mass of blood, tissue, and broken bones. Alice's mind immediately conjured up the man Lionel had beaten to death, and when she looked back at him she knew he was thinking of it, too.

The fact that the three of them weren't exactly in the best condition to be doing this made Alice take a moment to calm her runaway pulse. This would've been hard in the best of times, but now...now, she needed to focus. She needed to find Uncle Logan and help save as many as possible.

And, if given the chance, take down Phantasm before she turned this gas against anyone else. The thought of facing her brought a heady mix of terror and determination.

Drawing her batons, and forcing any worries or fear out of her mind, Alice stepped over the dead body and into the barely-lit room.

It was much dimmer than the stairwell, even with the windows letting in some of the late afternoon sunshine. Desks here and there had been up-ended, tossing paper everywhere. Pencils snapped under her feet as she tried to walk carefully into the room. When the wind caught a few sheets of paper, Alice jumped at the rustling sound, and then felt profoundly stupid. As her eyes adjusted, she could see a pile of something in the middle of the room.

There were many people huddled under desks, some inflicting wounds on themselves. Others were mumbling or singing, a few cried hysterically. And scattered all around were bodies. The officers started evacuating the ones who were unconscious, but still alive. Alice looked as close as possible at the ones near her. She wasn't sure if she wanted to find Uncle Logan among the wounded or not. What was the best option? Half insane, or clinging to life?

Her grip tightened on the batons the closer she got to the middle of the room, sweat tickling her back, her stomach tightening with the expectation of a fight that had yet to manifest.

"Shadow?" she asked without turning around. "How many people, can you tell?"

She heard ragged breathing behind her, his voice was strained.

"Three...dozen? It's hard to distinguish. The fear...it's..."

Dark, shadowy wisps rolled past her legs, and then retreated.

"Soothe those that you can," she said, then turned to Garrick. "You need to start evacuating when he calms them. I don't know what we're going to find in the middle there or up on the third floor."

Garrick nodded and began radioing for help.

Lionel stepped up beside her, tension coming off him in waves.

When they reached the center of the room, Alice stared in confusion at what she saw. Dozens of desks, chairs, even typewriters were piled up into some kind of...

"Chair fort?" Lionel said, his voice disbelieving.

Alice stared at him, and then they burst out laughing.

Until half a dozen crazed men and women came rushing toward them, their battle cries shattering the silence.

A young woman threw a letter opener at Alice, who dodged it just in time. Another took her by surprise with what looked like a chair leg, smashing it down onto her back and sending her to her knees, where she kicked the woman's legs out from under her, then punched her.

A man grabbed her from behind, but Alice threw him over her shoulder and kicked him in the face. A solid punch to her side made her gasp, and she just barely managed to block a punch to her face. Two more people grabbed her, holding her arms while someone punched her in the stomach.

Alice kicked the knee of one of the men holding her, his grip loosening. The other man holding her got a kick in the groin, and then the face.

Picking up her baton where she'd dropped it, she

slammed it into the stomach of the woman rushing toward her with a coffee pot.

As if the display of violence had awakened some of the others in the room, more men and women began to crawl out of their hiding places.

Lionel gave her a nervous glance as the circle of men and women tightened around them.

"Shadow!" she yelled.

She felt the chill a moment before a rushing wave of shadows swept past her. They engulfed the crazed men and women, drowning them in a sea of darkness.

She stared at it, not believing what she was seeing.

"Shadow, that's enough!" Lionel yelled.

But the shadows didn't dissipate; if anything, the darkness became more dense.

"Shadow, stop!" Alice yelled.

As quickly as they had appeared, the shadows were gone.

Alice and Lionel stared around them in disbelief. The mob, who'd been rabid just a moment ago, were all lying on the floor, their faces serene as if sleeping.

Lionel bent to check the pulse of the two nearest him.

When he met her eyes, he nodded and Alice felt her body slouch with relief.

"What the hell was that?" Garrick asked.

Lionel started to answer when the stairwell door slammed opened.

Phantasm stepped through, flanked by a dozen goons of various sizes. Alice could see the gas mask clearly under the black fedora, gleaming metallic, as if it had been painted and polished. The black and red suit was perfectly tailored to hide any indication that the person under it was a woman. Alice hadn't noticed the gloves Phantasm wore before, the dark red material giving off a wet sheen like they'd been dipped in blood.

Glancing at Lionel, whose gaze swept the room as if he were looking for something, Alice realized that Marco and some of the other police officers hadn't made a sound. She scanned the room, but couldn't see a sign of them.

"Well," Phantasm wheezed in her distorted voice. "I am so happy you could come to my little party."

It was a strange feeling to know that Victoria was behind that terrible mask. For a moment, Alice wished she could reason with her, appeal to the good woman who might still be inside. But then, she remembered Aunt Diana bleeding to death in a dirty alley and the feeling of terror and weakness that Victoria had inflicted on Alice with the Fantasy gas.

Someone whimpered nearby, followed by snarling words from someone else. Alice looked around at the bodies lying either unconscious or dead.

She did this, all of it. No matter what she was like in the past, she's a villain now.

"Is that what you call it?" Lionel asked.

"Actually, more of a gardening session. Getting the ground ready for planting."

That's when Alice saw a shadowy figure moving behind Phantasm and her men, followed by two others. Maybe if they could keep her talking...

"How is this getting the ground ready?" Lionel asked, hands clenching into large fists.

"You don't garden, do you? When you want to plant, you have to clear the ground, get rid of the old, the dying, the weeds."

"The newspaper fits that description?" Alice asked, as two more shadows moved into position.

"Yes and no." Phantasm took one step toward her. "I like to be efficient. This is, what's that saying? Ah yes, two birds with one stone."

"You enjoy making innocent people kill each other?" Lionel asked, his voice strained with anger.

"I simply release the truth inside."

"Who asked you to?"

"I think," Phantasm said, "that you are stalling."

The officers and Marco sprang into action, attacking the goons. Lionel lunged for Phantasm, but she was quick on her feet. She stepped onto a nearby desk, launched herself from it, and began jumping from chair to desk to chair until she was several feet away. Alice felt her anger boil up and ran after her, Lionel's warning shouts distant in her ears.

She followed Phantasm's example, using the wrecked furniture like stepping stones, until she was across the room and looking into Uncle Logan's office. A thought that maybe he was safe created an instant of distraction and Phantasm punched Alice's side, the blow sending pain up her body and around her back. There was no way that thin, delicate Victoria would be able to do that kind of damage without physical enhancement.

Shock quickly gave way to anger and Alice whipped her baton around, connecting with Phantasm's stomach. She stumbled back, but quickly recovered.

Alice needed to expose some skin to get a serpent bite into Phantasm's body, and so, swinging the baton toward Phantasm's face as a diversion, she swept her legs out and pinned her. But Phantasm made a surprise move, wrapping her long legs around to flip Alice onto her back, batons flying from Alice's hands.

She's trained. I hadn't expected that.

Phantasm ripped the gas mask off Alice and punched her in the face, her eye exploding in pain. She tried to flip Phantasm onto her back, but her legs wouldn't reach. As another blow fell, Alice decided her only hope was to get Phantasm talking until she could find a weapon.

"What are you planting?" she asked, as her fingers touched the baton where it had fallen.

Phantasm leaned forward, the snout of the gas mask inches from Alice's face, the faintest smell of jasmine clinging to it.

"I told you, it's a surprise."

"But, you really want to tell me, don't you?"

"What I want to do with you should be obvious, little snake."

Alice's fingers circled around the baton.

"So, I'm just part of your gardening?"

A chill lanced through Alice as Phantasm spoke, the words laced with malice.

"You? You're not gardening — you are catharsis."

Phantasm tried to punch her again, but Alice swung the baton up and cracked it against Phantasm's wrist, producing a screech of pain from her.

She swung again, hitting the mask. It stunned Phantasm enough for Alice to twist out of the pin and elbow Phantasm in the side, knocking her to the floor.

Alice jumped up, ready to drive her foot into Phantasm's knee cap when a terrible sound echoed through the room: Lionel's scream of rage. Her head snapped in his direction in time to see him lift a man overhead. She watched in horror as Lionel threw him.

Phantasm cackled and said, "You better go help him, before he kills innocent bystanders."

"What did you do to him?"

"I took off his mask. This is his true face. A monster, all of them are. It's only a matter of time before everyone sees it. Even you."

Lionel roared again. His punch sending another man several feet in the air.

Phantasm leapt to her feet and ran to a nearby exit,

laughing hysterically, and then calling out to Alice, "Who's it going to be? Him or me?"

Alice took three steps to follow her when Lionel yelled again, and this time, gun shots rang out.

"Damn it!"

Once again, she used the furniture like stepping stones, shooting serpent bites at the three officers shooting at Lionel.

"Steel!" she said, running up to Lionel.

He growled at her, same as last time. Spittle flew from his mouth and his eyes were wild. It was a stranger staring at her, an animal.

"Shadow! Where are you?"

"I'm...here," Marco gasped. "I can't...He's..."

Alice jammed a new clip of bites into her gauntlet and shot all of them into Lionel.

He yelled as he charged at her, a bellowing sound that made Alice genuinely afraid of him for the first time in her life. But before he could reach her, he stumbled, a look of confusion on his face. His eyes cleared for a moment before falling hard onto a nearby desk, which collapsed under him.

The minute he fell, the rest of the officers closed in with guns drawn.

"Stand back!" Alice demanded. "Shadow and I will take it from here."

"I'm not sure I can allow that," Garrick said.

She frowned at him, stepping closer so only he could hear. "Phantasm dosed him with something, it's not his fault."

"You expect me to just let him go? After he tossed two of my men like rag dolls?"

Meeting his bullish gaze with equal strength, Alice squared her shoulders.

"Yes."

"I helped you, because I thought you knew what was right and wrong, and could actually help this city. Now," he glanced down at Lionel, "I'm not so sure."

"He's like this, because he put himself in danger to protect you and everyone else. Now, you're going to turn your back on him? Besides, do you really think you've got a cell that will hold him?"

For the first time she could remember, Garrick looked afraid.

"Look," Alice said, realizing she'd made a mistake, "we can help him, but not if you lock him up."

He looked down, hands on his hips. "Fine. But if you can't control him, he's done."

Alice nodded.

Garrick began to bark orders to the men, who stared at him with barely concealed fury. Alice could still hear soft cries all around the room, some murmurings, and even a few outright growls.

Alice bent down next to Marco, who stared at Lionel, his long face slack.

"I couldn't help him," he said.

"But you can help these people, right?"

He didn't answer.

"Shadow? I need you to help these people."

When he still wouldn't respond, Alice grabbed his face and pressed her forehead to his, taking one precious moment of closeness with him. He lingered there with her before touching her cheek and slowly pulling her hand away from his face.

"I can help these people," he said.

Alice stood and began her own search, looking in every broom closet and office. The first one had a woman cowering in it. After getting someone to help her, Alice hurried to check the other rooms. Most were occupied, but not by Uncle Logan. When she finished with every place she could think of, she ran to look at every person the police were evacuating that remotely resembled him.

A panic began to lay heavy on her chest as she saw the body bags being carried out.

"He couldn't...that..."

She swallowed, trying hard to be brave, but before she got to the first bag, Marco stepped in front of her.

"I've checked," he said, "he's not one of the dead."

She covered her face with her hands, relief breaking over her for the moment. But then, Garrick walked up, his face pale and pinched.

"Al-Serpent...uh...kid..it's not that simple."

"What do you mean?"

He handed her a black envelope. She didn't want to touch it, knowing who it was from. Her body trembled as she took out a single sheet of silver paper:

Families are such fragile things.

"Serpent?" Marco asked, taking the paper from her numb fingers.

"I've tried calling—" Garrick began.

Alice bolted from the room before he could finish.

Alice leapt off the Lightning, not even bothering to prop it up and ran to her uncle's front door. With a kick made all the more forceful because of her fear, she opened the door to reveal a man drawing a gun. She smashed her baton into his face and pummeled his torso with it until he fell to the floor.

She'd fought on high adrenaline before, but this was

different. It was as if someone else was in control. Someone who didn't care about killing or maiming, who was powerful and furious. It only took a few minutes, and when she was done there were three men lying on the floor with bloodied faces, not making a sound.

A fourth man ran out of the kitchen, a blood-splattered butcher's apron hugging his huge frame. He clutched a meat cleaver in one hand and swung at her. She jumped back and slammed her baton into his wrist as he tried to swing it again. He yelled in pain.

Alice ran, jumped and wrapped her legs around him, the momentum forcing them both to the floor. Her fist crashed again and again into his boxy face. His eyes took on a feral rage and he grabbed her neck, squeezing. She couldn't draw a breath, couldn't pry the vise-like hands off.

And she'd run out of serpent bites.

She pressed her thumbs into the man's eyes as the edges of her vision were starting to go black. The harder she pressed, the looser his hands became until she heard a sickening pop and a screech like the sound of a wild animal.

Alice fell to the side, coughing and gasping for breath, her throat on fire. She felt the warmth of his blood through her gloves, and in the back of her mind, knew she'd just crossed a line.

But then, she saw the blood on his apron.

Her uncle's blood.

She grabbed a baton and hit him across the face once, twice, until he finally stopped screaming.

Half-crawling, half-running, Alice fell into the kitchen. The floor was covered in a thick plastic that was liberally splattered with blood. The stove was on, a steak knife heated to a bright orange in the flames of the burner. In the middle of the room, tied to a dining room chair, was Uncle Logan.

She stumbled to his side.

"Oh God…Oh my God!"

Burns and cuts at even, precise intervals covered his torso. His chest, stomach, and upper arms were bloody, his left pants leg was gone and Alice could see that they had started on his thigh, blood oozing from the cuts and burns.

His face wasn't much better. Both eyes were swollen shut, his lip was split in two places, and it looked like he'd lost a tooth.

When she went to untie him, the knots in the rope were wet with his blood, his fingers on one hand were at odd angles.

"Uncle Logan," she said, her voice hoarse, "it's me. Please open your eyes. Please."

Alice thought she heard a grunt, but couldn't be sure.

"I'm gonna get help."

She picked up the phone, but it was dead. She threw it, tears starting to fall behind her cowl.

The sharp wail of sirens pierced the silence and Alice thought it was the best sound in the world.

"I'll be back."

She ran out onto the porch just as Garrick jumped out of the car.

"He needs an ambulance, now!" she ordered.

"Call it in!" Garrick barked, then eyed the three men laying in the door way. "Are they dead?"

"I don't think so," she whispered.

Garrick looked like he wanted to say something, but only shook his head and ordered his men to secure the house. She was about to run back to Uncle Logan when Garrick grabbed her arm.

"You can't. They'll figure it out…"

She wanted to tell him to go to hell, that she didn't give a damn, but the awful truth was she did.

"I'll call Gerald," Garrick promised. "And I'll personally escort him in. You go change and meet us at the hospital."

With one last backward glance, she straddled the Lightning and gunned it, the tires shredding the lawn.

As she sped down the street, Alice couldn't stop thinking of all that she'd lost. Aunt Diana's brutal death. Lionel's poisoning. Uncle Logan's tortured body tied to a chair like a side of meat.

All of it ran in a loop through her mind until she felt bile rise up in her throat. Alice managed to pull the Lightning over just in time to puke inside a nearby garbage can.

Once again, she was that scared little girl, helpless as her mother lay bleeding on a sticky diner floor, while her father beat her.

The reinforced leather of her suit creaked as she stood up and she looked down at herself. The powerful muscles she'd developed, the instincts that had been honed.

"I'm not helpless…not anymore."

Spitting out the remnants of vomit, she jumped back on the Lightning and sped toward her apartment. She had to see a man about some vengeance.

CHAPTER TWENTY-SIX

Alice didn't even glance in a mirror before running out of her apartment and hailing a cab for the prison. If she could've gone as the Serpent she would have, but the last thing she needed was to be arrested trying to see Douglas.

When she stepped inside the prison infirmary, Alice was stopped cold by Douglas' appearance.

She expected the usual sickly pallor, but not this sick.

Instead of gray, his skin had yellowed, the whites of his eyes even more so. When he breathed, his chest gave a wet rattle. A sour, primal smell hung over him. The books on his table had changed. Alice saw Asimov, HG Wells, even Mary Shelly's *Frankenstein*.

Her face must've been truly terrible, because the minute Douglas saw her the smile on his chapped lips fled.

"What happened?" he asked.

She felt tears prick her eyes and pressed her lips in defiance of them.

"Tell me how to hurt Phantasm."

"That doesn't sound like you. What-?"

"I need every detail, anything you know, no matter how small or insignificant you think it is."

"What happened?" he asked again.

Alice swallowed.

"Uncle Logan was tortured and the newspaper was attacked."

"He's dead?"

"I don't know."

"And now, you're what? Going after Phantasm, no restraints?"

"Can you help me or not?"

"Yes, but I won't."

"You selfish piece of shit!" She grabbed a book and threw it at him. "The only man who has ever been a father to me could be dead and you're playing games?"

His sunken, scruffy face hardened and for a moment she saw Douglas as he had been all those years ago. She jerked back a little, and then clenched her fists. He wasn't going to hurt her, not anymore.

"It's not about him," Douglas said, coughing, "it's about you. If I give you what you want, you'll go and 'hurt Phantasm'. And then what? Phantasm hurts you and you hurt him, over and over. Until nothing is left but two beaten shells."

"If you're trying to be a father now—"

"You're goddamned right I am!" A spasm of coughing shook his body and he wiped a little blood away with a bony finger. Taking a rattling breath, he continued. "Because, unlike Logan, I know where this leads. This anger that I'm sure you think you've got control of, it will feel good for a while. It'll make you feel powerful. Until the day you realize that it's got control of *you*. And then the people around you will be the ones paying for it."

"And what was mama paying for? Or me?" She hadn't intended to ask that, but realized that it had been trying to get out for a long time.

"Being the two people in the world I loved most."

Alice shook her head. "You don't beat someone you love!"

"You do if you hate yourself so much that you can't stand being in your own skin!" He coughed again, wiping away more blood.

She stared at him, not knowing whether to believe him or not, and not knowing what to feel about it if she did.

"I know where this leads," he gasped. "And I know… Alice, it's okay to feel angry…to feel hate, even. But…don't let it drive you. Don't let it be the reason why you do something."

She couldn't stop the tears streaming hot and furious from her eyes as Douglas' words sunk in.

"And what, just let that monster get away with it all?"

"There's more than one way to beat someone like that. And the way you came in here? It will turn you into the very thing you hate. You have love in your life. Use it, let it give you the strength you need to do this the right way."

"And what way is that?"

"I don't know. I never chose anything other than hate and anger," Douglas gestured around him, "and look what it got me.

Alice sobbed into her hands, for once not caring if Douglas saw something other than indifference from her.

"It just…hurts to see them hurt!" she said, after a few minutes. "And I hate it! I hate that she hurt them to hurt me!"

"She?" he asked.

"Victoria. She really is Phantasm."

"Well…I'll be."

A coughing fit took over, causing Douglas to thrash on the bed. He reached for an oxygen mask and it clattered to the floor. Alice picked it up and gently positioned it on his face.

Without thinking, she sat on the edge of the bed and

stared at him. This was the closest she'd been to him since…

The memory of that last beating flashed in her mind and she flinched, tempted to jump off the bed. Instead, she took a deep, shaking breath and asked, "Why? Why couldn't you…why did you…?"

Douglas shook his head, tears leaking from his eyes. After a minute with the mask, he pulled it down onto his chin. In a wheezing voice he said, "I hated myself…so much Alice. Hated…the world for what…it had turned me into. Hated the war…I gave into all that…I'm…I have no excuse. Don't be like me. Please! You are…better. You're… stronger. Be better."

She moved the mask back onto his face and they both cried.

After a while,, her tears had dried on her cheeks and Douglas had fallen asleep. His words rang in her mind, soothing all that fire she'd walked in here with and redirecting it.

He's right. If I do this…If I act out of hate, I'm not better than Victoria. And I have to do this differently.

"Thanks Douglas," she said, tucking his blankets around him before she left.

CHAPTER TWENTY-SEVEN

After the prison, Alice went to the hospital, which was in chaos from the attack on the newspaper. She managed to get her uncle's room number out of the surly front desk woman and make it into his room where she burst into tears at the sight of him bandaged and bruised.

"He's stable, but will need a lot of recovery time," Gerald had said.

After many hugs and reassurances from Marco and Lionel, she was left alone in the room with Uncle Logan, the only sound his breathing and the beep of the heart monitor.

She hadn't intended on staying all night, but every time she went to leave, Alice just couldn't do it.

So, curling up at an awkward angle in a nearby chair, Alice fell asleep sometime after midnight, wondering if a nurse was going to kick her out.

The thing that woke her, however, wasn't a nurse or even the clanking sound of the carts being wheeled between rooms outside. It was an intense pain in her neck.

She winced and rubbed the spot, trying to work out the muscle ache and noticed that someone else was in the room with her.

Marco sat reading in the corner, a cup of coffee giving off steam.

"Hey," she whispered, her voice hoarse from sleep.

He looked up at her and smiled, offering her the cup.

"It's terrible," he whispered back. "But it's something."

She grimaced at the first swallow but kept drinking.

"How long have you been here?" she asked.

"Long enough to have three of those," he nodded at the cup in her hand. "I couldn't sleep. Wanted to be here if you needed me."

She reached out, running her fingers from his bruised eye down to his jaw. When she looked into his eyes, Alice was surprised at the intensity of Marco's gaze.

Then she realized, with him sitting and her standing so close, their faces were mere inches apart.

"Are you alright?" he asked, taking her hand from his face. "I mean…I could feel your anger yesterday. Your grief. It was so strong."

Alice looked down at the cup and took another swallow of bitter coffee. She was about to speak when her uncle shifted in his sleep.

"Maybe we should go," Alice said. "I don't want to wake him and I could use some food."

Marco nodded and led her out of the hospital. The morning air was cool, hitting her face with a gentle caress as they stepped into the parking lot.

"Most of the people from the newspaper are going to be alright," Marco said when he started the car. "Only…well, six fatalities."

"I'm sorry. Did you know any of them?"

"Yeah, the front desk girl, and a cub photographer."

She reached for his hand, intending to give it a simple squeeze and that's it. But there was a comfort there that Alice didn't want to let go of.

So she scooted across the seat until she was next to him.

Then she moved his arm until it was around her shoulders as he drove with his other. Her head fit perfectly on his shoulder and she closed her eyes, content to just feel him breath.

Too soon they arrived at the apartment and went inside. Marco went about making some breakfast while she changed her clothes. The smell of coffee and toast made her stomach growl with hunger and Alice plopped into a chair at the table just as a plate of scrambled eggs and toast was placed before her.

They ate in silence until Marco frowned at her.

"What were you doing at the prison yesterday? Why did you go there first?"

Alice forced the last bite of toast passed the lump in her throat and took a long swallow of coffee. The last thing she wanted was to see the light of disappointment in Marco's eyes, to know that he thought less of her.

But he deserves an honest answer.

So she told him everything.

All the details of the fury that had coursed through her veins, what she'd wanted to do to Phantasm, and the conversation with Douglas.

At the end she wiped tears from her cheeks and wouldn't meet his gaze. Instead she sipped the dregs of her coffee.

"You're amazing," he said.

She snorted. "Why because I chose not beat someone to a pulp?"

"Yes actually. I…I don't know if I would've chosen what you did."

"You would have," she said, looking up at him, "you're the best of us Marco."

"No I'm not."

"Why, because of how dark your powers are?"

He turned away from her and shook his head.

"You don't understand what it's like…what…what I want to do half the time. What I *could* do."

Alice stood up, placing her hands on either side of his face and making him look at her.

"You could be a true nightmare with these powers," she said, "but you make the choice, every day, not to be. Marco you're amazing too."

"And you don't think you have something to do with that?" he whispered. "That I don't make that choice for you and Lionel, as much as for myself?"

"It doesn't matter why. You do it, that's what matters."

There was nothing else to say really, her hands had drifted down to his shoulders and his had come up to rest on her hips. They were close, just like when they'd been sparing a few days ago. Except now the early morning sunlight streaming in through the large windows illuminated the hints of red in Marco's eyes and the gold in his skin.

Marco held her gaze and, just for a second, Alice could see an unmistakable hunger in those dark eyes. She wanted to fall into it, explore what it meant.

Then, just as quickly as it had come, Marco pulled away, a tense smile on his face.

"Any minute now Lionel will be running through that door and-"

The door burst open and Lionel did indeed run through it.

"I should make more eggs," Marco finished with a laugh.

Alice gave him a shaky chuckle of her own, face flushing with the thoughts still spinning through her mind.

"There you are!" he said. "I couldn't find you at the hospital…what's wrong?"

"Nothing," she said, shooting a quick glance toward Marco. "I'm just…tired."

Lionel hugged her, gentle and a little distant. She knew why and was a little grateful for it. She stepped back and gave him a wobbly smile.

"You should rest," he said. "Marco and I will let you know if the hospital calls."

"Yes, but first, we need to talk. With everything that happened yesterday, I never told you what happened with Victoria."

Marco poured everyone a fresh cup of coffee, and she was grateful for something so simple after what might have been about to happen.

Lionel was right, she was tired. Exhausted actually, and in no way capable of understanding why she had all these feelings for Marco when all she'd ever wanted was Lionel.

I can't get distracted by this right now. Phantasm is the priority. Maybe later, when it's all over…

She glanced at Marco, who had begun scrambling eggs for Lionel and mentally shook herself.

Focus!

Alice took a sip of the scalding coffee to steady herself and dived in.

As she told them everything she and Mrs. Frost had uncovered, their expressions became increasingly worried.

"And you're sure about this?" Lionel asked around a mouthful of toast.

"As much as I didn't want to be — yes."

"There's something I'm not sure you've thought of," Marco said from where he'd been standing in the kitchen, "attacking Lionel as Steel makes sense. Even attacking the paper does on some level if she's trying to sow chaos. But-"

Alice's stomach dropped as she arrived at the conclusion he was driving at.

"Uncle Logan is a pointed attack on *me*."

Lionel's eyes widened.

"So that means-"

"She knows who I am. Maybe who we all are."

The three of them sat there as the magnitude of that set in.

"What do we do?" she asked.

"Exactly what we've been doing," Lionel said. "Nothing has changed. We have to stop her."

Alice opened her mouth to argue and stopped.

He was right.

"And the sooner the better now that she knows who we are," Marco said. "The first thing we need to know is what she's going to do with the Fantasy gas."

"And how we can stop her," Lionel added.

Alice massaged her temple as a headache started to throb.

"Agreed," she said, forcing away the worries about their secret identities being known. "We need a list of possible targets."

"If she's trying to get the support of the police, maybe she'd hit them?" Lionel suggested. "Show them how vulnerable they really are."

Marco shook his head, eyes hooded as he frowned in concentration.

"If you're trying to create chaos, then I think several smaller attacks would be more likely. Make everyone wonder who is going to be next."

"But where?" Alice asked, rubbing her eyes.

"Good question," Marco said, "but you're not going to help us figure it out if you're exhausted."

"I need to figure this out and then go see Uncle Logan."

"Visiting hours aren't for a while yet. Go rest."

"And the two of us are smart on our own you know," Lionel said.

"Well…" Marco said, shooting a playful grin at Alice.

"Hey! Fifth grade English, remember? My paper was 'amazing.'"

"I wrote that."

"No, you helped."

Alice stifled a yawn and both men stopped arguing long enough to order her to bed.

After she'd closed the door and snuggled under the covers, their playful banter carried her off to sleep.

CHAPTER TWENTY-EIGHT

The difference between the hospital last night and this morning was stark. Instead of chaos, the lobby was relatively calm. The floors gleamed in the soft fluorescent lighting, a half dozen or so people sat in various states of boredom or worry, only half listening to the terrible music playing from a nearby radio.

"Excuse me," Alice said, wiping sweaty palms on her blue Bermuda shorts.

A sour faced nurse glanced up. "Yes?"

"I'm here to see Logan Miller."

"Oh, him," she said. "Room 548."

Alice frowned, wondering what Uncle Logan had managed to do to the woman when he'd been mostly comatose.

"Thanks."

She'd only been asleep for a few hours when Gerald called to tell her that Uncle Logan was awake and asking for her. Alice hadn't even bothered brushing her hair before leaving, tying a yellow scarf over her frizzy bob instead.

When she got to the door, she saw young police officer standing guard. He smiled at her.

"I'm glad he's gonna be alright. I love his columns."

She smiled back and stepped through the door, then stopped short when she saw her uncle's bruised and battered face. For some reason, seeing him awake and unable to open one eye or smile properly was more of a shock then seeing it all when he was asleep. Hard as she tried not to cry, tears rushed down her cheeks.

Uncle Logan held out the hand on his unbroken arm, two of the fingers splinted, and she took it with great care.

"Enough of that," Uncle Logan whispered. "I'm going to be fine."

It was several minutes before she could calm down enough to speak.

"I'm so sorry."

"You didn't do anything."

"But we fought the last time I saw you and all I could think about—"

"No, no. Now, that's enough. I forgave you before I was down the stairs."

"If anything...I've never told you how much I..."

His bruised, swollen face softened.

"You don't have to. I know. I know."

She nodded, taking deep, shaking breaths to try and stop the tears that refused to be quenched. After a moment, she caught sight of Gerald trying to sneak out and stopped him.

"How were you able—?"

"Detective Garrick." Gerald laughed, a deep throaty sound. "Read that nurse the riot act and told the rest of the staff that if anyone stopped me they might just find their cars towed."

"I've never been so glad for him in my life as I am right now!"

They all laughed at that, though Uncle Logan's was cut short with a wince of pain.

"Even with my help," Gerald said, his dark face becoming sober, "he's going to have a long road to recovery. Whoever that was, worked him over good."

"Knew what he was doing," Uncle Logan said.

Though she didn't want to, Alice had to ask, "How do you know?"

"It takes great skill to do all that to a man and not kill him," Gerald said.

"I'd like to know who this Phantasm is..." Uncle Logan gasped as he tried to move his broken arm. "After I've recovered."

Alice looked at her hands.

"I know that look," Uncle Logan said. "Your aunt used to get it when she didn't want to tell me something. What is it?"

She swallowed. "I know who is behind all this."

Gerald took a step toward her.

"Phantasm," she said. "It's Victoria Veran."

The two men stared at her. Gerald opened his mouth a few times as if he wanted to say something, but in the end, he just snapped it shut and looked away.

Through the swelling on Uncle Logan's face, Alice could tell that he'd clenched his jaw, a hardness appearing in the one eye that wasn't swollen shut.

"You're sure?" he asked.

Alice nodded.

"And...did she...? Diana?"

"Maybe. At the very least, she didn't try to stop it."

Uncle Logan looked like he wanted to rage and yell. The fingers on his unbroken hand twitched as if he wanted to clench them into a fist and he winced with pain.

"What are you going to do?" Gerald asked.

"I don't know but-."

"This means she knows who your are!" Uncle Logan

said, his one open eye wide with fear. "Alice, you have to run, get out of town before she-"

"I can't," she said, her voice gentle. "You know I can't.

Uncle Logan leaned his head against the pillows.

"Just promise me you'll be careful."

"I will."

"And that you'll let me help you."

Alice shook her head. "Have you seen yourself? She sent someone to take you apart, piece by piece."

"And she failed," Uncle Logan said, his voice soft and stubborn. "I'm in this with you, until the end."

She wanted to tell him no, try to convince *him* to leave for a while. But Alice knew that wasn't fair. She wouldn't leave and neither would he.

"Thank you," she said.

He gave her a bruised half-smile.

The phone in the room buzzed and since Alice as closest, she picked it up.

"Hello?"

"Alice?" Marco's voice was full of tension.

"What's wrong?"

"The prison called. I'm sorry but, Douglas has taken a turn for the worst. They said he won't last the night and he's been asking for you."

Alice stared at the wall, not sure what to say.

"I know you may not want to hear this," Marco said, "but I think you should go. If you don't, I think you'll regret it."

She glanced at Uncle Logan, who was frowning at her.

If someone had told her last year that she'd be torn between seeing her father for the last time and staying at Uncle Logan's bedside, she'd have had a few choice words for them. But now?

"I think you're probably right. I'll go now."

"What was that?" Uncle Logan asked.

Her mouth felt dry and a hollow grief threatened to take over. She took a few deep breaths to hold it at bay and told her uncle and Gerald what Marco had said.

At first neither of them spoke. She was afraid to look at Uncle Logan. How could she really be thinking of leaving him after what had happened?

But then, she felt his fingers brush her arm.

"I understand. You should go to him, make your peace as best you can. I'll still be here when you're done."

"For at least another week," Gerald agreed.

"Thank you." She kissed him on his bandaged forehead. "I'll come back tomorrow. Maybe sneak in a donut and some coffee."

"It's a deal."

The first time she'd walked through the penitentiary doors, Alice was nervous. Now, the last time she'd walk through them, she felt more so.

Alice didn't understand the jumble of emotions coursing through her. She recognized anger's bright, hard flame, but there was also deep sadness and bitter doubt mixed in that anything either of them had to say would make a difference now. Hadn't he made her life hell? Hadn't he brutalized her mother?

As she was escorted down the yellow halls, Alice felt her palms become clammy.

What did he expect from her? What did he want in these final hours? What did she?

The walk was far too short to come up with answers and before she was ready, it was time to go into the infirmary.

Douglas was laying with his face turned to the window. One bony hand lay over a battered paperback, the other on the white blanket. There was a loud rattling in his chest when he breathed and oxygen tubes were in his nose. An IV jutted out from his painfully thin arm.

She stared at him for a moment, trying to calm her heart and quench the tears threatening to fall.

Something made him turn, the sound of her breathing perhaps, and his yellowed eyes met hers. A faint smile crooked his chapped lips and he gestured to a chair nearby.

"I didn't think..." He took a wheezing breath. "...you'd come."

"Well," she said, sitting on the edge of the chair, "you were wrong."

"About many things," he said, his gaze far off for a moment.

They sat like that for a little while, him focused on the blanket around him and her on the window. Alice realized with no small amount of shame that most of their interactions had centered on the Syndicate, and now, when it counted, they had no idea what to say to each other.

Her eyes eventually fell on the book he held.

"What are you reading?"

Douglas started a little, a look of embarrassment on his face.

"Oh, just...here."

She turned it over carefully, as a few pages from the middle began to slide out.

"The Hobbit?"

He shrugged. "A guy I met in the war...carried a copy with him. One night...cold...half starved...he read it...best story...I ever heard."

"Marco and I, we used to read this one another. Then, my first month with Aunt Diana and Uncle Logan, they said I could pick any book I wanted from the store. I ended up with four, this was one of them."

"One of the inmates...gave me that copy...before he left.

Kind of payment...for trying to take care of him," he said. "But if...you want it...I won't have much use for it...soon."

Alice nodded. "Sure."

When she looked up, Douglas was staring at her with a gaze so sad, so full of regret that it made her wince.

"What did you...decide last night?"

"I didn't go."

"You're stronger...than me." His voice broke. "I'm...well, it's good...to see it."

She nodded, her mind desperately trying to find something to talk about. Anything, except the one thing they probably should. Her eyes fell on the book in her hands, the one common thread between them that had nothing to do with the Syndicate.

"Can I, um, would you like me to read to you?" she asked.

His yellowed eyes glistened, and he nodded.

It was wonderfully easy to lose herself in the story, something Alice realized she hadn't allowed herself to do in far too long. As the words tripped off her tongue, the room took on a warmer glow and the two of them became fellow travelers on Bilbo's journey. Her fears and anger dissipated, and she found herself laughing with Douglas at the story.

It was a shock when Alice looked up to see that the sun was now half-sunk below the horizon, red and orange tendrils spreading like petals on the water of the Sound. A man brought some kind of thick liquid for Douglas to drink, but he wouldn't touch it.

"Tastes...foul!"

A doctor came soon after, his face grim after listening to her father's chest.

"Are you settled? It won't be long now," the doctor said.

Douglas nodded. "Can...she...stay?"

The doctor looked at Alice, who felt a terrible mix of fear and duty to see this through to the end.

She nodded, and Douglas seemed to sink further into the narrow bed.

"Thank...you," he whispered.

"Do you want anything?" Alice asked.

He pointed to the book she'd laid down and Alice picked up the adventure where they'd left off. After a little while, his eyes fluttered shut, his chest rising and falling at odd intervals.

Not knowing what else to do, Alice kept reading until her voice became hoarse, and the low light from the bed side lamp strained her eyes.

She stood and stretched, not at all surprised now to see the lights of the waterfront reflected on the inky water. It was so quiet in the little room, nothing but the sound of Douglas's intermittent wheezing. Alice found it odd, and yet right somehow, that despite everything, all the unanswered questions, the threat that even now plotted the destruction of her life, that she would find peace here.

As she sat back in the chair, Douglas's eyes flew open, a strange light in them. He groped for her and she gave him her hand. His fingers were like holding a bundle of sticks, but very strong sticks. It looked like he was trying to say something, but he couldn't find enough air or strength to do it. He gestured her closer, and she leaned down, the sour smell she'd begun to associate with him was horribly strong this close. It made her want to step away, but Douglas held onto her tight and Alice couldn't move.

"I—s—sorry! Sorry!"

She pulled back just enough to see tears wetting his weathered cheeks, a desperate, fearful look on his face.

Alice swallowed, her own tears beginning to fall. If he needed to hear that she forgave him, she couldn't do that. Maybe if they had a few more years, but not now. It killed her in that moment to realize that they were just beginning to find a way out of the hurt and bitterness he'd mired them in. And they'd never see where that could have led.

Taking a deep breath and hoping he could somehow see and hear what was in her heart, Alice said, "I know."

It was enough.

He loosened his grip on her hand, expelling one long, tired breath before closing his eyes.

It was an effort to lift each foot up the stairs to her loft, and in the end, Alice just sat down at the top, letting the aching loss in her chest take over.

In moments, strong arms wound around her and Alice knew without opening her eyes that it was Marco. They might've sat there an hour or just a few minutes, but when the sobs calmed she felt a strange lightness inside.

She leaned back against his chest, tears still trickling down her round cheeks. Marco tightened his arms around her and Alice sighed, letting her body meld itself into the curve of his.

This was where she belonged. With him, wherever, whenever.

The realization should've been shocking, or at least a little surprising, but it wasn't. Maybe there was clarity from her mind and body being so very tired, maybe all her defenses were too weak to argue with her. But whatever the reason, and however it had happened, Alice embraced the fact that she loved Marco.

Was I ever in love with Lionel? Really in love?

Marco brushed a gentle kiss on her temple.

"I'm so sorry Alice."

She was jolted back to why Marco was holding her and the tears started falling fresh and painful.

"I don't know why I'm so sad," she whispered.

"Because for better or worse, he was your father. You can't help loving him, no matter what he's done."

She nodded.

"Do you want help making the arrangements?" he asked.

"No, the prison said they'd take care of it. The only thing he requested, was to be buried next to my mother..."

Marco held her tighter. "Whatever you need."

You, I need you.

But somehow, she knew he wouldn't believe her. Marco would have to be convinced that she loved him in a way she'd never felt for Lionel.

"Hold me," she whispered.

At some point, she fell asleep, and he carried her to bed. He must've laid down with her, because as the morning light fell across the room, she saw Marco cast one gentle glance at her before leaving. When she reached behind her, the fog of sleep still thick on her brain, the bed was warm and his smell, like baking bread and something very male, lingered on the sheets.

She buried her face in that spot and let sleep take her once again.

CHAPTER TWENTY-NINE

The knife slashed across Alice's chest, her suit protecting her from being wounded. She crouched and rolled under another try from her attacker.

They had gotten word that another Fantasy gas canister had gone off in a new housing development. Twelve homes, all infected.

Twelve families with ruined lives.

The man shambled after her, not watching where he was going. He fell face first into his coffee table, the knife flying from his hands.

Alice jumped up and punched him twice, the man's glassy eyes staring up at her for a moment before he passed out.

A gasp behind her made Alice jump.

Crouched low, green eyes wide with fear, stood a little boy. His slight, shaking frame was clothed in footie pajamas, brown hair tousled as if he'd just woken.

Alice took in the pale, sweaty skin, the smell of urine on a boy who should be past wetting the bed, and knew he had been affected by the gas.

"It's okay, honey," she said, taking a few slow steps. "I'm here to help."

The boy looked at the man sprawled across the coffee table. She held her breath in expectation of wailing or panic.

Neither came.

Alice's heart stopped at the too-calm, calculating look on the boy's face as he picked up the butcher knife his father had been waving around.

"Put the knife down," Alice said, trying to sound calm.

The boy frowned at her. "Why?"

He began walking with calm, slow steps toward her, his little hand tightening on the handle.

I can't hit a child. What the hell—?

That's when she saw the shadows creeping along the floor, snaking up the boy's legs. Within moments, the boy dropped the knife, and Alice caught him just before he hit the floor, his breathing even, face peaceful in sleep.

"You alright?" Marco asked.

She nodded as she lay the boy on the ripped-up couch.

"Where's Lionel?"

"He's two houses down," Marco said, wiping blood from his nose.

"Are you okay?" she asked.

"Yeah, woman got in a lucky shot."

Alice took a step and tried not to wince as her back seized into a spasm. She noticed how Marco was favoring his left side and wondered if his ribs were still bothering him from last night's fight.

For the last five days, they'd responded to seven Fantasy gas attacks, all small and localized within different communities. Gerald was patching them up as best he could, but their bodies didn't have enough time to heal between fights.

They stepped out onto the perfectly manicured, emerald

green lawn, the smell of summer roses and rosemary thick in the air.

Despite the police cars casting strange shadows from their blue and red lights, the sight of bodies being zipped into bags, the occasional scream of rage or fear, Alice smiled.

"That smell," she said, voice soft with memories.

Marco looked at her. "My mother's garden."

Alice nodded. "When I was a kid and I smelled that, I knew I was safe."

He turned away, his throat working as he swallowed.

"I miss her at the strangest moments. Like right now, just before you said that, I was thinking of her."

"She'd be proud of you."

Before he could respond, they heard a terribly familiar sound.

A scream, deep and throaty.

They bolted to the house where Lionel was last and skidded to a halt when he came crashing through the front window.

Alice snapped a clip of serpent bites into her gauntlet and charged for Lionel, who was pummeling a man in the grass.

The entire clip went into Lionel's arm, but all it did was divert his attention from the innocent man he was punching.

Lionel jumped up, teeth barred, eyes wild.

Alice stumbled back, trying to snap another clip into the gauntlet, when a rolling wave of shadows swept past her. They crawled up Lionel until they covered him.

When the shadows retreated, Lionel was kneeling on the ground.

Alice ran to him, knowing they had moments to get Lionel out of here before the police tried to arrest him.

"Lionel," she took his face in her hands.

He didn't say anything, just nodded, his face haggard.

"C'mon," Marco threw one of Lionel's arms around his shoulders.

"Maybe you should let them have me." Lionel's voice was heavy with sadness.

"Not a chance," Marco said.

Lionel's knees wobbled. "Those damn...bites of yours."

"Now? They work now?" Alice said, slapping Lionel. "Don't you fall asleep yet."

"I'm..trying, gorgeous."

She hit him again. "Try harder because I'm not hauling your unconscious butt back to the loft."

"I have a feeling you'd...haul my butt...anywhere."

A small smile tugged at her lips. "Shut up and walk."

Gerald was waiting for them when they got to Alice's loft.

"Take a look at Marco," Alice said, ignoring his look of protest before going to her room.

As she peeled off her suit, Alice gasped in pain. Her mid-section was a mass of bruises, as was her back. Her hands were so swollen that it took effort to get the gloves off. When she finally did, a few scabs went with them and she gave a small cry of pain.

"Alice?" Gerald said behind the door.

"I'm not dressed."

"I'm a doctor, remember?"

"Alright," she said, shrugging into a robe.

Gerald's eyebrows arched as he took in her nonchalant stance.

She tried her best to stare him down, but it was useless.

Alice untied the robe. "Fine, but don't tell them anything."

"Patient-doctor confidentiality and all that," he said.

His calloused fingers probed her back and stomach as gently as possible, but Alice still had to bite her bottom lip to keep the tears at bay.

"You can't keep this up," he said, dabbing ointment on her bleeding hands.

"We don't really have a choice."

"She's trying to break you."

"I know."

He bandaged her hands in silence, then attended to some of the cuts on her legs and face.

"Lay down, I'm going to try to heal you a bit more than usual. This may be uncomfortable."

Alice had thought that she was used to what it felt like to be healed by Gerald. But what she experienced that night made her realize that Gerald had been holding back.

It was like fire and ice were warring for dominance inside of her. She gasped, tears leaking out from under her lashes. It wasn't painful exactly, but it wasn't pleasant either. When the flow of energy had ceased coursing through her, Alice's body felt deliciously languid and warm. Her eyes closed and for the first time all week, she didn't think sleep would be a problem.

Gerald pulled a soft blanket around her.

She didn't hear him leave.

The smell of cinnamon and coffee greeted Alice the next morning. When she threw the blankets back, instead of the harsh pain of inflamed muscles, her body was just mildly stiff. Her hands were still a little swollen, but for the first time all week she hadn't wanted to cry just with the effort of getting out of bed.

"Morning," Lionel said, kissing her on the forehead. "Feeling better?"

"Much, you?"

His face fell and he handed her the front page of the paper, the headline large and jarring:

American Steel Puts Father of Two In Coma.

She pulled him into a hug. After a few minutes, he put his arms ever so gently around her.

"Breakfast is ready," Marco said from the kitchen.

Alice expected their usual sticky buns and coffee, but what she saw instead was a cinnamon coffee cake with a candle in the center.

"Oh, my gosh, I'd forgotten." She laughed.

"You forgot your own birthday?" Lionel said.

"With everything going on—"

Marco pulled out a chair for her. "Well, we didn't."

She looked between them, her heart swelling with affection. Amid the chaos that surrounded them every day, they remembered something as small as her birthday.

"Make a wish," Lionel said, his voice as excited as a child's.

Alice laughed. She hadn't made a wish for her birthday in many years.

There's really only one...

She looked into Marco's warm brown eyes.

Alright, two things that I want.

It wasn't hard to blow out the single candle, but Alice hoped she'd get her wish regardless.

"Your uncle wanted to be here," Marco said, producing a small box, "but Gerald has him on bed rest."

"He made us promise to bring you by tonight though," Lionel said, stealing a crumble off the cake.

The box was wrapped in plain brown paper, with a small blue bow on it. Inside was a dark purple velvet box, the kind that jewelers put necklaces in. As she opened it, Alice choked back tears.

It was her aunt's locket, the gold sunburst on the front polished to look almost new. Opening it with a press of her thumb nail, she let the tears fall when she saw a picture of her aunt smiling back at her inside.

Lionel's huge hand engulfed her shoulder, giving it a tender squeeze. "How about some cake?"

She sniffled. "Yes, and coffee."

The phone rang, shrill and loud.

Alice ran to get it.

"Probably Uncle Logan...Hello?"

"Alice?" Victoria's sweet voice came over the receiver.

Alice felt her stomach drop. "Victoria, what can I do for you?"

"Well, it's a little awkward, but...were you planning on showing up today?"

Alice frowned. "Today?"

"Please, don't tell me you forgot."

Marco and Lionel were frowning at her in concern as she stared wide-eyed at them.

"The Park Side Clinic party?" Victoria said, her voice tinged with frustration. "It's this afternoon."

"Oh, yes, yes of course! I'm sorry, I, uh, it's my birthday and I just..."

"You did forget, didn't you?"

"Yes," Alice said, trying to work the bile down her throat, "but I did promise you and I am ready to help."

"Oh good! You will be in charge of the ring-toss booth. Can you be here in two hours?"

"Yes, of course."

"Wonderful. Oh...and Alice?"

"Yes?"

"Happy Birthday. I hope it will be one to remember."

A chill crept down Alice's spine. "Thank you."

"What did *she* want?" Marco asked, brows furrowing.

Alice sank onto the couch. Her mouth was dry, her gut churning.

"She called to remind me about the Park Side Clinic celebration today. I had volunteered..."

With a sudden terrible clarity, the final piece of Phantasm's plan fell into place.

"She's...all the gas attacks this week, they've all been a diversion," she said, her voice shaking.

"For what?" Lionel asked.

"Park Side is the next step," Marco said, his quiet voice filled with horror. "All those innocent people."

"She can't...I mean, she's..." Alice closed her eyes.

"But how?" Lionel said. "What is she planning to do?"

"The gas," Marco said. "She'll release it on the people."

"And if we're there, we will be blamed," Alice said.

"But how can we not?" Lionel eyes blazed. "She's got us over a barrel."

"This will do it. This will convince the police and Mayor, and whoever else she needs, to go forward with her plan."

"She'd cause the injury and death of all those people, just for that?" Marco looked as if he were about to be sick.

"We have to call Garrick." Alice jumped up.

"And tell him what?" Lionel asked. "That Victoria Veran is Phantasm and is planning on gassing half of Park Side, and oh, by the way, I'm really sorry for beating that guy last night?"

Alice nodded. "We're on our own."

"When do you need to be at Park Side?" Marco asked.

"In a couple of hours, why?"

"We'll go with you."

"No."

"Are you kidding?" Lionel said.

"I mean, you both can't be seen there." Alice started to

pace, the movement helping to clear the panic from her mind. "Let's assume that she knows who the two of you are. If she sees you, then she'll know we're on to her."

"But if she sees just you, then she'll think we don't have a clue," Marco said.

"Right. So, you two find a place to hide. I'll have my suit with me and when I get the chance, I'll change. That way when the gas goes off, we'll be ready."

"But what if you're not?" Lionel's hands began clenching into fists. "What if it goes off before you can get your suit on, or even your gas mask."

"I'll keep the mask in my handbag. I'll be alright, I promise."

Lionel looked like he wanted to fight with her about it, but finally, he nodded.

"Where should we meet?" Marco asked. "That area has changed a lot since we were kids."

"Have you been lately?" Alice asked.

"Couple of times on assignment. Here—" Marco took some paper and pen and started drawing a map of the area.

When he was done, Alice was shocked. The wide-open fields around the abandoned old warehouse were gone. Instead, there were almost a dozen apartment buildings. They'd been built so close together that it would be no trouble to jump from one rooftop to the next.

"It's a huge U shape, the concrete slab of the old ware-house in the center with apartment buildings along the side and the back."

"They built right up to the wall that was part of the old paper processing plant," Alice said.

"Why didn't anyone ever build there?" Lionel asked.

"No idea. There are two streets that run through this area."

Marco made more lines on the makeshift map on either side of the apartment buildings, then he drew more apartment buildings on the other side of the lines so that there were buildings facing each other.

"These two streets are the only ways into that area. They will probably be blocked off at either end to prevent too much traffic coming through. The buildings on this side of the street, across from the newer buildings? That's what's left of the old neighborhood."

"It's going to be tight with so many people crowded in there and how close the buildings are."

"And the streets being blocked off will keep everyone in that area once the gas hits," Alice said.

Marco nodded. "A concentrated group of people in a complete panic."

Alice glanced up at him, wondering how he would do with so many strong emotions to handle. He met her gaze, a tight set to his thin lips.

He's thinking the same thing. And how is Lionel going to do? Will it come down to just me?

She sighed, rubbing her sweating palms on her robe.

"What are we going to do?"

"What we always do," Lionel said, his smile tight, "save the day."

"It's not that simple," Marco said.

"No, it isn't. But we don't know enough to plan anything. We just have to be ready for whatever comes."

Alice knew he was right, and in the past, they had been lucky. Even if the plan went to hell, they were somehow able to make a success out of it, find something out, or catch the bad guy.

But something inside of her knew that this time, it wouldn't be enough.

CHAPTER THIRTY

A cracked concrete slab was all that was left of the old warehouse Alice, Lionel, and Marco had played in as children. The fields around it, which had stretched wide and lonely, were now covered in cheaply-made apartment buildings. Though not that tall or wide, it was still shocking how many they'd managed to force into the space around the old warehouse foundation.

Dozens of game booths, food carts and tables with goods from local businesses were sprawled over what was likely the only wide-open space in this cramped area. Every inch of space that wasn't needed for walkways was filled with booths.

Alice walked along the perimeter, between the booths and carts and the apartment buildings, trying to get a sense of how much space they'd have when the gas went off. Her stomach sank when she realized how tightly they'd packed the booths for the party. She looked around at the hundreds of people lined up, waiting for the celebration to begin.

There's barely twenty-five feet in some places. She'll have us all hemmed in like rats in a maze.

Bored police officers sat with their squad cars blocking

off both sides of the street, and Alice realized with dread that this meager group would never be able to stem the tide of panicked people once the gas went off.

Even if they weren't affected by it.

The more she walked around, the longer the line of families became, until it had begun to wind its way between one of the smaller apartment buildings and into the blocked off street.

Once she couldn't stall any longer, Alice found a security guard to escort her to the ring toss booth. He led her past a tent filled with picnic tables and a small stage with a microphone and a table. Large speakers stood on long poles pointed out toward the booths.

She scanned the area as best as she could, but her short stature made seeing much difficult, even though the families hadn't been let in yet.

At the front of the line of people waiting to get in, there was a table filled with white and purple bags.

"What's that?" she asked the man escorting her.

"Mrs. Veran has arranged for the first one hundred people to be given a special bag of goods from local businesses."

Alice stared at the bags. "Can I take a peek? I'm so curious—"

"I'm sorry, Miss Seymour, you're already late and I need to get you to the booth before the party starts."

"Of course," she said, a cold, sick feeling spread through her.

She glanced back at the bags.

She wouldn't really...would she?

As she followed him, the smell of corn dogs, cotton candy and caramel corn hung heavy on the air. She had barely said hello to the man who would be running the booth with her when a bell sounded and the barriers erected to keep the crowds back disappeared. The people surged forward, and if not for security guards directing them into neat rows, it would've been chaos.

Alice forced a smile on her face as she handed plastic rings to a little girl who was barely tall enough to see over the booth. All she could think of as the child's laughter sang through the air was what would happen to her when the gas went off.

It was then that she noticed the white and purple bag on the arm of the child's mother.

"What did you get?" Alice asked, nodding at the bag.

The woman shrugged. "Just some candy and stuff. Nothing from the liquor store, cheap bastards."

"Nothing good, then?"

The woman dug a small purple box out of the bag. It had a white question mark on it. "These are for the raffle apparently. Supposed to open them when it's time and see what we win."

Alice swallowed and tried to smile at them as they walked away.

She was just about to ask the man in charge of the booth if she could step away for a moment, when she saw a very familiar bald head making its way through the crowd.

"Detective Garrick!" She waved her hand.

He spotted her and the frown on his face deepened to a scowl.

"Where is he?" he barked.

"Who?"

"You know damn well who. I gave him plenty of chances, but he crossed a line last night."

Alice pitched her voice low, keeping a smile on her face.

"There's bigger problems. Those bags everyone's carrying around have gas canisters in them."

Garrick's eyes narrowed as he looked at her.

"So, Phantasm's here?"

She would've explained it all, but there just wasn't time.

"In a manner of speaking, yes, and if you don't get those bags away from everyone there is going to be hundreds of panicked people running all over Jet City."

"How do you know this?"

"It's a long story and I'll explain everything after today. But you have to do this."

"No, I don't have to do anything. You and your buddies think you can be the law in this city, tell me what to do. I'm not your lap dog, and I don't answer to you."

"Damn it, Garrick! All these people could die if you don't do something."

"Why don't you do it? You're so sure."

Alice sighed. "I can't."

"Things getting too hard for you? Should've stayed out of all this at the beginning. You see Steel, you make sure to tell him we've got a reinforced cell waiting for him."

"Garrick, wait!"

But he turned his back on her and was soon lost in the crowd.

"That was quite the display," said a voice behind her.

She stared in horror at Gerald's dark, grinning face.

"I called and told you to stay away, what are you doing here?"

"If I didn't show up, she'd know something was going on. And I'm guessing you need her not to suspect," he said.

"When the canisters go off—"

He took a gas mask box identical to the ones Rose made for them out of his pocket.

"I'll be ready. Besides, it's my neighborhood. I'm their doctor, I should be here."

"That's brave and incredibly stupid," she said.

"Being a hero usually is."

"Please, be careful. It's going to be chaos."

"Don't worry. I've been in combat before."

As the minutes ticked into hours, Alice grew increasingly impatient. Every sound that rose above the crowd noise, every squeal from the dunk tank or the face-painting booth made her muscles tense with readiness. She was sweating through her pink, sleeveless shirt, and even though the Serpent suit wouldn't be any cooler, Alice couldn't wait to be doing more than smiling at people who could be dead any minute.

A loud bell rang three times, followed by Victoria's sweet voice over the speakers.

"Welcome, citizens of Jet City, residents of Park Side. It's my great pleasure to celebrate the opening of your new, expanded neighborhood clinic."

Feeble applause followed as anyone with a bag surged toward the stage.

Seeing her chance, Alice grabbed her large purse and wove through the people moving toward the stage. When she finally made her way out of the booths, Alice was facing the apartments that had been built up against the wall of the old paper mill. This part of the grounds was virtually deserted so she darted down one of the narrow alleys, hoping no one saw her.

She'd just snapped her gauntlets securely in place when Marco stepped down from the fire escape overhead.

"It's in the purple and white bags," she said. "She's having them carry it around like a prize."

"I know. There's also some in the buildings, probably for those who had gone home or didn't come at all."

"She's thorough, I'll give her that. Where's Steel?"

"He's watching on the roof top of that apartment on the end. Serpent..." Marco's eyebrows knit together, thin lips pursing a little. "I'm worried about him. He's...tense."

"We all are."

"Yeah, but...this is different."

She met his dark stare and felt her mouth go dry. They needed Lionel, but if he couldn't control himself…

"I've got extra clips, I can knock him out if I need to. I'll save the rest for any of Phantasm's men."

Marco opened his mouth to say something when terrified screams rang out through the neighborhood.

Alice felt her stomach drop and her body start to shake with adrenaline. Snapping their gas masks in place they ran the short distance straight ahead toward the food carts.

Thick plumes of gas billowed out from the crowds. Alice glanced back and saw the windows in the building they'd just ran from start to spew gas as well. People began to rush from the booths, some of them cowering as they screamed at invisible horrors. Others began laughing hysterically. That is, until some of the more terrified people began attacking them.

Alice froze, her mind struggling to take it all in. Who did she try and save? Where were the children she'd seen? Could the police help them or would they start attacking as well?

More people staggered from the cloudy gas, their dazed eyes falling on Marco and Alice. Snarls and screams of rage escaped from their lips and they rushed them.

Alice dodged back to escape the slice of a knife. When the man tried to stab her again, she brought her gauntlet up to block it, then kicked him in the gut twice. He fell to his knees and she punched him across the face. As he fell, a woman tackled Alice to the ground, and she realized with horror that it was the mother she'd spoken to only a few hours earlier.

Bringing her legs up and around the woman's torso, Alice flipped her onto her side and kicked her across the face. She saw the woman's nose shatter and her eyes close in blessed unconsciousness.

"How the hell do we get the non-violent ones to a safe place?" Marco said, his breathing a little heavy.

"Are you—?"

"I'm handling it."

"Maybe the police barricades would be safe for them? They've started carrying gas masks, so maybe they aren't affected."

Marco nodded.

They looked at the impenetrable cloud of gas in front of them. They could hear screams and cries, rage filled howls, the crash of tables and equipment punctuating it all. Fear gripped Alice tight and she couldn't move.

"There you are," Lionel said, running up beside them. "Let's get this over with."

His eyes stared into hers, lending Alice all the strength he could. She looked at Marco on the other side of her and took a deep breath.

We can do this, the three of us together.

She drew her batons and the three of them ran into the fray.

Chaos was too mild a word for the world they found themselves in.

People were beating each other with fists, plates, anything they could grab. One person was laughing as he hit himself with what looked like a chair leg. Alice heard moaning cries and looked down to see a few cowering under tables and chairs.

Marco's shadows were hard to see in the thick gray of the gas. But as people began to fall silent in his wake, she knew he was at work.

One man to her left was sitting on another as he began to slowly cut off the man's fingers. Alice ran to him, hitting him across the face with her baton. The man fell to the side in a heap. But when she went to help the wounded man, he backhanded her.

"Hell bitch!"

She stumbled to a knee from the shock of the impact and didn't see the kick coming to her stomach. Alice fell to her side and caught the man's foot as he tried to stomp on her chest. She twisted, sending him to the ground and punching him twice until he lay quiet.

Looking behind her, Alice gasped as a towering cloud of shadows stood above a group of people. They screamed as the shadows descended on them, inky black and thick.

She could see Marco a few feet away, duster swirling around his legs, eyes behind the mask completely black, shadows flying from his outstretched hands.

The people became silent, and the mass shifted up, hovering there for a second like a menacing cloud. Alice watched with growing horror as the shadows spread out all around her, and began spinning. It was like being in the center of a great whirlpool as the shadows engulfed every person except for Alice and Lionel.

She ran up to Marco just as Lionel got there. Marco was shaking, his teeth bared.

"It's enough!" Lionel yelled.

"No, it's not." Marco's voice was strained and low. "You don't see it! I do! I can stop them all! I can make it go away!"

"Stop, please!" Alice said, reaching up to touch his cheek. "Stop!"

His gaze shifted, black eyes falling on hers. Every instinct told Alice to look away from those empty, dark holes, but she couldn't. He needed her.

After a moment, the shadows spun backwards into Marco, and he fell to his knees on the dry grass. He gulped air, his whole body shaking.

"Alice," he whispered. "I...I could've stopped them, but..."

She pressed a hand to his face. "We'll find another way."

"We have to move," Lionel said.

Alice looked up and saw shapes coming toward them, wailing and laughter drifting out of the thinning gas.

Lionel pulled Marco to his feet and ran to the left. Alice wasn't sure where the street was, but she knew that they had to get into some kind of clearing.

As they moved, the gas dissipated, and they could see better. But, as Alice took it all in, she wished everything was still veiled in gray.

The dunk tank was to her right, two bodies crammed inside. She had to jump over another body, a woman whose face looked smashed in. The bubbling vats of cooking oil that had been used to make corn dogs was tipped over, a man lay next to it with red and blistered skin. All around her were displays of brutality that Alice had never thought possible.

"I don't think there's any way to salvage this," Marco said.

Alice winced as she moved her shoulder.

"Maybe we can take out Phantasm at least."

"Do you think she's still here?" Lionel asked, his eyes sweeping the area around them.

Alice was about to answer when Lionel suddenly bolted toward the apartment buildings.

In the small space between the booths and the buildings, Alice could see two people surrounded by a group. As one of the two began to fight, Alice recognized Gerald.

One assailant got a kick to the gut followed closely by two punches to the face. A second man rushed him, but Gerald used the momentum to throw him over his hip and punch him. The third man jumped on his back, biting Gerald on the ear.

Alice then realized the second person being attacked was Rose, who was wearing two gauntlets, very much like Alice's, except they had a sheen to them like metal. She

SERPENT'S RETURN

punched one man, his nose spurting blood. As another tried to grab her, she elbowed him in the throat and kicked him to the ground.

By the time Alice, Lionel, and Marco reached them, all the assailants were down.

"Are you alright?" Alice asked.

Gerald nodded, blood running down his ear.

Rose's brown eyes sparkled at Alice, her gas mask hiding the smile Alice knew was underneath.

"Fancy meeting you here."

"You have a strange sense of humor," Alice said.

Rose shrugged.

That's when Alice saw a half a dozen children huddled in between Rose and Gerald.

"I need to get these kids to safety," he said. "My clinic should be outside the radius of the gas."

"The end of the street is that way." Lionel pointed to the right.

"But there's guards blocking the way," Gerald said, his brown eyes hard. "They're shooting anyone trying to escape."

Alice's hands tightened on her batons, bright, hard anger flaring to life.

"C'mon," Lionel said, taking point.

The rabid victims of the gas were fewer, the closer they got to the end of the street, as if they knew it would be folly to engage the dark-clad men, who Alice recognized as the security guards from earlier. They stood silent and firm, watching the chaos with a cold detachment Alice found more disturbing than what she'd just encountered.

Behind the men, squad cars stood abandoned, one of them on fire. The bodies of officers lay sprawled out on the ground by their cars and near the men.

As she looked more closely, Alice could see that many

civilians were among the officers, and some of them were children.

Her anger began to burn hotter, brighter. She wanted to obliterate these men, drive them into the ground. But then, she took a deep breath, remembering who she was, and tried to focus that rage.

"Stay with the kids," she told Gerald and Rose.

Lionel was the first to come close to the men. Two of them raised their handguns and shot him. Alice saw him twitch as the bullets impacted in his skin, but Lionel didn't stop.

He punched one man so hard he was lifted off the ground before falling onto his back.

A third man raised his gun to Marco, but the shadows raced up the man's body and his face was soon contorted with terror. He fell to the ground crying.

Alice threw her baton at a fourth man, hitting him square in the face. She then shot him with a serpent bite and he stayed down on the ground. She heard a gun go off seconds before feeling the burning bite of the bullet go into her upper arm.

She screamed, dropping her remaining baton.

The man raised his gun again, but Alice tackled him to the ground before he got the shot off. The impact caused the man to drop the gun, but he was quick to punch her in the side.

She gasped, the pain circling around her lower back.

As he reached toward where his gun landed, Alice pulled her arm back and punched him once, twice, three times.

Still, he tried to reach his weapon, eyes vacant and cold.

Alice jumped off him and ground her boot heel into his wrist. He cried out as the bones of his wrist snapped. With her other foot, she kicked him across the face. The temptation to finish him off was stronger than Alice would've liked.

Looking around, the other five guards were sprawled on the ground or sobbing in fear.

"C'mon, get out of here!" she yelled to Gerald.

"You're wounded," Lionel said. "You should go with him."

She shook her head, and tried not to wince as the wound began to throb and burn, blood seeped from it onto the sleeve of her suit.

"Let me see," Gerald said.

"There's no time!"

He grabbed her arm anyway. "It's a through and through, here."

The familiar cool wave went up her arm and soon the pain had lessened, the bleeding stopped.

"Thank you, now go, get them to safety."

"Serpent—" Gerald began.

"If I can end this today, I'm going to."

Gerald frowned at her for a moment and nodded.

In the distance, sirens began to blare, loud and erratic. Alice wondered how many were coming and if they'd be able to contain anything.

Alice glanced at Marco, whose long hands were curled into fists. His shadows weaved in and out of the folds of his duster, and under his arms.

"What is it?" she asked.

"I think...I think Phantasm is there."

He nodded at the building in the middle of the row they were facing.

"You can feel her in the middle of all this?" Lionel asked.

Marco shook his head. "I...there's a lot of people with her...like she's gathered them up and locked them in the building. It's their reaction to her that I feel."

Alice took a deep, shaky breath. "Then, let's go."

They sprinted to the building, encountering little or no resistance.

"We should go up the fire escape," Lionel said. "We don't want to get trapped inside."

Marco nodded, shooting his grappler to the top of the fire escape. Lionel grabbed Alice, and before she could say anything, he'd jumped to the top of the building and landed with a skidding step onto the roof.

It was deserted.

Alice looked around. "There's no way Phantasm wouldn't show for this."

"Quite right!"

On an adjacent roof was Phantasm, metallic gas mask gleaming in the summer sun. She was flanked by half a dozen men.

Alice opened her mouth to ask Phantasm why she'd done this when a low, rumbling sound came up from below.

"A little present," Phantasm said. "My assistants are bringing you some of the residents of this building. Did you know that some of the most ruthless henchmen for my former organization lived in this neighborhood? No? Well, now you do. And now you get the chance to bring them to justice."

The roof they were on was suddenly flooded with people scrambling up the fire escape. Some of them were barely able to walk they were so terrified. Others looked like wild animals just let out of their cages.

Lionel, Marco, and Alice stood with their backs to each other as the angry men and women rushed them.

It was quick and ugly. Alice swung her batons without grace or precision because there was no room and no time for such things. One person was down, another two took their place. She kicked behind her while slamming her baton into the face of another. An elbow to the nose, a baton to the torso. On and on until they were surrounded by unconscious bodies.

It might have taken mere minutes, but it was enough to make Lionel lose whatever tenuous control he had over his temper.

With a roar of rage, Lionel picked up a nearby man and tossed him over the edge of the roof.

"No!" Alice grabbed his arm.

He shoved her so hard she went flying across to the other side of the roof. For a few minutes, it was hard to take a deep breath.

Marco channeled his power into Lionel, the shadows winding around Lionel's huge body. He started to slump forward, the gleam of fury fading from his eyes. But then, one of the rabid men came to and rushed Marco, tackling him to the ground. The shadows faded and Lionel's face tensed.

Alice forced herself to stand and run for him. "Stop, please."

"You did this to me! You made me an animal!" Lionel pointed to Phantasm and jumped to the adjacent roof.

Marco wrestled the man to the ground, giving him several good punches until he slipped into unconsciousness again. Without a word, he grabbed Alice and fired the grappler in one motion. They swung to the highest level of the fire escape on the adjacent building and climbed up onto the roof where Lionel and Phantasm were.

As soon as her feet hit the roof, one of Phantasm's men rushed for her. Alice ducked under his punch, swinging her baton into his knee cap. Even though she knew it was dislocated, the man didn't scream or react in any way. He picked her up by the front of her costume and punched her. The pain was explosive, and Alice felt her mind go fuzzy for a moment.

Bringing her gauntlet up, she fired three bites into the man's neck before he let her go. She recovered the baton she'd dropped on the roof, and swung at his other knee. He finally collapsed to the ground.

The pain from her cheek shot into her eye and her already wounded shoulder throbbed, but Alice forced herself to ignore it as another man rushed toward her.

She dove down just as he was about to grab her and rolled to the right. Coming up on the balls of her feet, she ran and jumped onto the man's chest, tackling him to the ground. Her batons slammed into the man's face, one after the other. The man's nose was broken, his eye bloodied, but still his hands sought her throat and face with more strength than she thought possible. She pressed a baton to his throat, cutting off his air until he stopped thrashing. Even then, she held it tight for a few more seconds just to be sure.

This must be the result of Hercules. There's no way these guys are this strong otherwise.

A shadow crossed over her and she looked up in enough time to see Phantasm, gloved fist careening toward her. Alice dodged, but the blow still hit her on the side, knocking the air out of her.

"I thought you'd enjoy this display of justice," Phantasm said, landing a swift kick to Alice's stomach.

Alice scrambled to her feet, trying to get her breath. She feinted a punch to Phantasm's torso and tried to swipe her legs out from under her. Phantasm stumbled, but didn't fall.

"How is this justice?" Alice gasped. "There are children down there!"

"Who will grow up to be just like their fathers and mothers! Rich or poor."

Phantasm attempted a roundhouse kick, but Alice caught her leg and pulled, throwing Phantasm off balance and sending her to the ground. Alice tried to pin her, but Phantasm twisted and brought her leg around for a kick to Alice's face. She landed on her side, and rolled just as Phantasm stamped her thick-soled boot down onto the roof.

Alice kicked up from the ground and landed on her feet, then swung her baton around. Phantasm blocked it. Alice kicked her in the chest, sending her off balance and landed another kick to Phantasm's side and she fell to the ground.

Screams echoed up from below, the sounds of terror and rage.

The images of children shot for trying to escape this horror, the families Alice had seen broken over the course of the last week, and all the other crimes Phantasm had committed ran through her mind as Phantasm stood.

Alice rushed for her, fury burning through every limb. Her baton landed two solid blows to Phantasm's mid-section, and then another to her knee. Phantasm screamed in pain, smashing her armored fist down onto Alice's face, which stunned her long enough for Phantasm to trap Alice's arm with the wounded shoulder. Phantasm pulled up.

Alice screamed as her elbow joint popped.

"You'll see," Phantasm said, not letting Alice go, "history will vindicate me."

Alice delivered a sloppy kick to Phantasm's wounded knee. It was enough to make her grip loosen. Alice fell onto her back, rolled to her side, and scrambled to her feet.

Alice's arm hung painful and useless to her side, and dread began to settle in her stomach as a pungent, sharp smell hit her. The air was tinged, but not with the light gray of gas.

Something was burning.

"Well," Phantasm said, standing up, "these people really don't disappoint."

"Get away from her!" Lionel said, coming up on Alice's left.

He was limping, dirty, and more bloodied than Alice had ever seen him.

"Steel, what a pleasure to witness you unleashed."

"What did you do to me?" he growled.

"If you really want to know, come find me sometime and we'll talk."

He bent a little as if he were ready to pounce.

Then the building shook from an explosion nearby, knocking Alice to her knees. When she looked up, she could see Phantasm through the smoke, trying to run to the edge of the roof and escape.

In one last desperate move, Alice handed her baton to Lionel and pointed at Phantasm.

He threw it, holding nothing back and hit her in the back of the head.

She fell, inches from the edge of the roof.

Alice barely managed to get to her before Lionel did, his eyes dilated with rage.

"I've got her," she said.

"No, she's mine."

Alice pushed him away.

"Enough! You can't and you know it. Now go help Marco secure an escape off this roof before we all die!"

He snarled at her but did what she'd ordered.

Alice dug a pair of cuffs out of the pouch on her belt and snapped them around Phantasm's wrists. She moaned a little when Alice turned her around.

"You going to reveal who I am?" Phantasm wheezed.

"No."

"Not even a little curious?"

"We don't unmask anyone."

"You think that will keep you safe from it?"

"Shut up and get moving."

She pulled Phantasm up and shoved her forward just as an explosion rocked the building.

The smoke was starting to make Alice's eyes burn, and though the gas mask was doing a good job of filtering the smoke, Alice wasn't sure how much longer it would last.

"The fire's spreading," Marco said, limping toward them. "We have to get off the roof. There's a fire escape on that side."

Lionel bared his teeth at Phantasm and Marco put himself between Phantasm and Lionel as they made their way through the smoke to fire escape.

Just as they reached the edge of the roof, another explosion shook everything, throwing Alice off balance.

With grunting cry, Phantasm used her unnatural strength to break the link on the cuffs and jump over the edge of the roof, onto the fire escape.

"No!" Alice screamed.

"Alice wait!" Marco said.

But she couldn't, not when they were so close to ending all of this.

Alice jumped after Phantasm, landing on the highest part of the fire escape. Phantasm was two levels down from her, almost within range to simply jump down to the side street.

Alice barreled down the steps when the building shook and she was thrown off balance. She rolled down the next set of stairs and then realized too late that the fire escape was leaning unnaturally. There was barely time to grab a rail with her good hand before falling to the concrete below. Her legs dangled in mid air and her muscles began to shake at the strain of holding on by one arm.

She looked up and saw that the bolts that held the escape to the side of the building were coming loose.

"Steel!" she shouted.

"I see it," Lionel said and the fire escape lurched as he grabbed a hold of the bars.

His face turned red with the effort and she knew he couldn't hold it for long.

Alice tried to pull herself up and swing her legs back over the fire escape, but she misjudged and almost lost her grip in the attempt. She looked down, and through the growing smoke she could make out a dirty side alley with a few bodies and mounds of garbage strewn around. There were a few half full open trash bins and she thought that if she had to, aiming to land in one of them might be her only hope.

"Shadow, your grappler!" Alice yelled.

Marco had unspooled the cable of his grappling gun and tossed the grappler end down.

"Grab it, hook it to your belt and I'll pull you up," he said.

She had to use her injured arm to reach up to him, and the effort to move it was excruciating. Gritting her teeth, she yelled and tried to reach up. But each time she reached for it, her hand only succeeded in batting it away.

"My-My arm...I don't think-"

"You can do this, you have to!" Marco said.

"Hurry!" Lionel said through gritted teeth.

"I can...do this!" she said to herself.

She felt her fingers close around the grappler for just a moment before the next explosion rocked the building.

Alice watched in a strange kind of detached horror as the bars slipped from one of Lionel's hands.

She tried to hold onto the grappler, but the sudden change in position of the fire escape made her lose her grip on both the grappler and the rail.

For a moment, Alice felt suspended in mid-air, able to fully take in the look of horror and panic on Marco and Lionel's faces as she plummeted to the alley below.

CHAPTER THIRTY-ONE

Through the fog of something Alice couldn't quite grasp, she heard voices, angry and crying.

Trying to talk made her feel as if someone were pressing a pillow to her face so she couldn't breathe. No matter how hard she tried, there was no air. Her body thrashed, and it felt like shards of glass were being shoved through her torso, but she couldn't control it.

When the thrashing finally stopped, she could breathe again, but then a thick darkness began to carry her away, far from those voices, to a place of peaceful silence.

A bright light pressed against her eyes and she fought against its intrusion, but to no avail. The darkness receded and in its place was a confusing heaviness in her limbs. Alice moved her head, which felt twice it's normal size and tried to speak.

Her voice was weak and she wasn't even sure if she'd said a real word or not.

"Who? Honey, did you say something?" asked a woman nearby.

"Marco," she said again, her mouth remembering how to form words.

"Lemme finish this and I'll see if I can find him."

When Alice opened her eyes to try and see the person in the room, everything was fuzzy and huge. Blinking didn't help, and in fact, the effort to focus made her head feel as if someone were driving railroad spikes into it.

The best thing seemed to be to just keep them closed.

She must have fallen asleep, because the next time Alice opened her eyes, the room wasn't nearly as bright and the woman was gone.

This time, Alice let her eyes adjust gradually. And though the focus would still go in and out, she could make out the hospital room. Moving her head very slowly to the side, her eyes fell on a man sleeping in a chair.

"Uncle..." she croaked.

He jumped, and then a moment later, winced from the effort.

"You awake?"

She tried to nod, but it hurt too bad.

"I'm gonna get Gerald, just stay there."

Where would I go?

As her eyes kept adjusting, things started to come into sharper focus.

She was facing a window, the open curtains showed the twinkling lights of the bay and the renovated waterfront. Ships coming in for the night bobbed on the dark water.

It was a small, private room, with a doorway to her right that might've been a bathroom, and another to her left through which Uncle Logan had left.

The wall between the window and the bathroom door had a table with three bouquets. One was a cheerful arrangement of Gerber Daisies, which could only be from Rose.

A second was a beautiful arrangement of purple roses.

And the third...

Alice felt her throat begin to close as her heart beat pounded in her ears.

"Jasmine...I smell...she's here...no — no —"

The monitors began to beep and Gerald bolted through the door.

"Alice?" he said, calloused hand on her forehead.

Cold coursed through her and she felt her body relax.

"She's here," Alice whispered, tears running down her face.

"Who?" he asked, brown eyes hooded beneath his frown.

"Jasmine...I smell jasmine."

He sighed. "Mrs. Veran sent flowers from her garden. I thought if we rejected them...do you want me to get rid of them?"

Against her will, Alice's gaze slid to the beautiful arrangement of lilies and jasmine.

Anger, bright and hot, blossomed in her chest, spreading through her limbs until she felt choked with it. Alice clenched her jaw, her eyes burning with hatred.

"I'll just-"

"No!" she said. "Leave them."

He nodded and began taking her pulse. That's when Alice noticed for the first time how heavy her legs felt.

"My legs..."

"Don't worry," he said, "you still have use of them, but you broke them both pretty good. Shattered a femur and nearly destroyed one of your knees. I did what I could, but they're both in a cast."

"What...else?"

Gerald's dark eyes hardened.

"You broke three ribs and punctured your lung then went into shock. You had a head injury that could've made you comatose. Also, a dislocated right elbow, broken left wrist—"

"Okay, maybe not...all...at once."

He nodded. "These injuries are extensive. I have done what I could to stabilize you, and I will help you in recovery, but Alice—"

"Not now. Please?"

"No, not now."

"Marco?"

Gerald nodded. "He's patched up. I've kept you sedated for the past three days to help with the healing."

"Three days? What...what happened to Park Side?"

He stared at his feet.

"Apparently, some idiot had stashed enough ammunition in the basement of two of those apartment buildings to supply an army. It...it leveled the buildings. They're still finding bodies."

"Oh, God...Detective Garrick? The police?"

Gerald shook his head.

"How?"

"We don't know yet, there's hundreds of fatalities, and more wounded. Mrs. Frost pulled strings to get you a private room, in case you said anything while under about who you really are. It's so bad that they're actually letting me treat patients, although only the Negro ones. The press is calling it The Park Side Massacre. And Alice? They're holding the three of you partly responsible."

She closed her eyes. "I can't say I blame them. We didn't stop it. I think we may have made it worse somehow."

"I don't agree. You tried, which is more than most

would have done in your place. But, with the police force having lost a quarter—"

"Oh, my God!"

"And that number could go up, with the severity of some of the wounded, plus, some are still missing. The captain had called in every available officer to try and contain the situation, but even after the explosions, there were still enough rabidly afraid people to cause problems."

He shook his head, brown eyes bright with sadness.

"The mayor and police commissioner need scapegoats," he continued. "And since they don't know for certain if Phantasm even exists — well, right or wrong, you three are the natural targets."

Alice sighed, then winced as the action made her ribs hurt.

"And now Victoria has the leverage to create her special police force. What a mess. How are Marco and Lionel handling it?"

Gerald looked away.

Alice felt her stomach twist.

"What aren't you telling me? Are they...did something happen?"

He reached into his pocket and took out an envelope.

"They're fine, or...as best as can be. Marco left this for you."

Alice's brain couldn't quite grab a hold of his words.

"Left?"

Gerald pressed the letter into her palm.

"Read it. And when you're done, your uncle wants to see you. Press the button and he'll come in."

Perhaps it was because of the low light in the room, or the sickening smell of jasmine, but Alice began to believe she wasn't really awake. Any moment now she'd wake up in her bed at the loft. She'd smell Marco's pancakes, hear

Lionel complain about how there's never enough whiskey in the place.

But, the longer she waited, the more Alice had to accept that it was all real.

The paper in her hand rustled like fragile leaves as she clutched it, but she refused to read it. As long as it remained just an envelope, Marco could walk in. He would come, he couldn't leave without knowing she was alright. He wouldn't do that.

She stared out the window, waiting for him. When the door clicked open, her heart gave a lurch, a relieved sob bursting from her chapped lips.

"Alice?" Uncle Logan's voice was soft as he hobbled to her bedside.

The sobs didn't stop, even though they made her chest ache and her head feel as if it were bursting.

Uncle Logan wiped the tears away, his haggard face damp as he stared at her. There was no reprimand, no angry order that she quit now. Nor was there pity. Just worry and love shining in his brown eyes.

Alice tried to reach out to him, but her arms hurt too bad. The movement caught Uncle Logan's eye and he saw the letter unopened in her hand.

"Do you want me to read it?" he asked.

No, she didn't. She wanted to burn it. Wanted to tear it into a thousand pieces and deny ever seeing the damn thing.

But he took her silence for assent and opened the envelope.

"I don't know how to begin. I want you to know that I don't want to leave, but I must. Lionel has blamed himself for what happened to you and has left, though your uncle says he came to the hospital to make sure you were alright. I think I know where he's

gone. We both know he shouldn't be on his own right now, so I'm going after him. Between the two of us and the information Rose gave me, I believe I can find someone to cure him. When Lionel comes back to Jet City, he'll be his old self, and you both can be happy together.

I'm not sure I will come back though, for reasons I can't put in a letter. Maybe someday I'll be able to tell you, but not now.

You're strong, stronger than either of us. I know you won't stop until Phantasm is gone. And if you should ever need me, I will come. But in your pursuit, please be safe and smart. Do nothing with vengeance, nothing without thought.

Marco."

Feeling nothing was a strange sensation. Alice could've accepted anger, devastation, even confusion. But, there was nothing. She stared out the window, aware of tears falling down her round cheeks and Uncle Logan's calloused hand in hers.

"Alice," Uncle Logan said after a moment, "tell me, please honey, what can I do for you?"

The words didn't penetrate her mind at first. And when they did, Alice felt confused.

"Nothing."

Uncle Logan nodded, but he didn't leave. Just held her hand until a nurse came in with a tray of food.

"Here ya go, honey." She set the tray on a table next to Alice. "Something warm."

Alice kept her gaze on the window, the smell of chicken soup unappetizing.

"I'll just leave it here," the nurse said after a moment.

"Thank you," Uncle Logan said. "Do you want me to—"

"I love you," Alice said, "but I want to be alone."

He hesitated, but finally kissed her forehead and shuffled out of the room.

The soup became a cold, gelled mess in the bowl, whatever tea they'd brought turned tepid and overly steeped. And still she stared out the window.

Sometime in the night, for no reason at all, her mind came out of the fog Marco's letter had cast, and she accepted that Lionel and Marco were gone.

It was as if someone had punched a hole straight through her chest and she gasped with the sudden pain. The temptation to bury her face in the pillow and cry until oblivion took over was almost too much to bear.

But then, a hint of jasmine invaded her senses.

Once again, her eyes slid to the bouquet, and this time, Alice couldn't look away from it.

"Do nothing without thought," she whispered.

Though her body was bruised and broken, her mind was strong and whole. She couldn't fight right now, but she could think.

Every moment since putting on the cowl ran through her mind. Every time she'd won or lost. The first time she'd seen Phantasm, experienced the Fantasy gas. The assault on the Chronicle. Accepting that Victoria really was Phantasm, and everything that meant.

And lastly, Park Side. All those children, those people who, no matter what they'd done in the past, didn't deserve what was done to them that day.

Marco and Lionel left her after all that, knowing Phantasm was still alive. Did they believe she'd simply wait for them? Did they think leaving would keep her safe? There was no *safe*. Not so long as Victoria was free to do whatever her twisted mind deemed righteous.

"So...what do I do?"

Her hands felt too weak to hold a pencil, so she hoped her mind would keep track of all the threads she was now weaving. Ideas were constructed and taken apart, considered and discarded. By the time the sun had breached the horizon, Alice knew what needed to be done. And more importantly, that she could do it without Lionel and Marco.

She pressed the button next to her.

"You need something?" a nurse asked, as she walked into the room.

"Some breakfast? And I need a way to make call, I can't reach the phone with my arms like this."

The nurse smiled. "Of course. I'll get you breakfast, and then we can make that call."

"Thank you."

"You need to rest," Gerald said later that morning.

"And I will. I just need to talk to her."

Gerald frowned. "You need to know—"

"That's not for you to tell," Mrs. Frost said, moving a bit slower than usual.

When she sat in the chair next to Alice's bed, Mrs. Frost's wrinkled face scrunched into a painful grimace. Gerald took her hand and closed his eyes.

"Enough of that," Mrs. Frost said, once the pain had passed. "Let me talk to her, and then you can give her something to make her sleep."

Gerald nodded and left the room, though Alice could see that he wasn't at all happy about it.

"What's wrong?" Alice asked.

Mrs. Frost wouldn't meet her gaze at first, but then her hard, bright eyes snapped up to Alice. "I am dying."

Alice gasped. "What?"

"Dr. Allen has kept the cancer from growing too fast, but now...well, he can only make me comfortable."

"How long?"

She shrugged. "A year? Perhaps less."

Alice closed her eyes. "I need you to live."

Mrs. Frost's hand was soft and strong as it held hers.

"And I will, for as long as I can. But you need to know, Alice, that there is a limit to how much I can put up with. The pain..."

"Of course, I'm sorry."

"No need. Now, tell me what was so important that I had to miss my breakfast."

Alice slowly handed her Marco's letter.

"So, they've left you," Mrs. Frost said once she'd read it.

Alice nodded.

"What will you do now?"

Alice brushed a few tears away.

"I've thought about that all night. And I know what I need to do. Someone like Victoria, she won't stop at an enhanced police force. She's too ambitious. There's more, I can feel it. I don't believe Victoria ever realized that we know who she is — and I need to keep it that way. I also need to make her think that I'm not a threat anymore. So I have time to find out what she's planning next."

"Marco and Lionel being gone should help."

Alice took a deep breath. It wasn't easy in the best of times for her to admit when she's wrong.

Best to just dive right in.

"You've been right this whole time. I have needed to build up my public persona. Not just because the work is important, but it can protect me, throw my enemies off balance, if the person they see is quite different from Serpent."

Mrs. Frost grinned.

"I see. And do you have an idea of who you want people to see?"

Alice smiled back.

"Yes — I do. It's time for me to be the meek business

woman searching for a husband, who spends her spare time with charities and at luncheons."

"I think I can help with that," Mrs. Frost said. "I just amended my will. You will inherit Frost Consolidated."

Alice stared at the old woman.

"Me?"

"You have a head for it, and I like the idea of my empire going to you. After all, my most important legacy did, why not this one as well. I'm eccentric enough that no one will bat an eye at such a decision. Are you up to the task?"

"Yes, absolutely."

"Well then. Let's plan the debut of Alice Seymour, debutante heiress."

Alice bit her bottom lip as she thought about the new path her life was taking.

"Heiress by day," she said. "Serpent by night. I like that."

ABOUT THE AUTHOR

Trish has been obsessed with stories about female heroes ever since she put on her first pair of Wonder Woman under-roos and spun around. After realizing that fear of failure had been holding her back, Trish became her very own hero and participated in National Novel Writing Month in 2015. Since then, Trish has braved the constant attacks of her nemeses Inner Critic and No Time, in order to achieve the impossible: An artistic life with two small kids!

Trish was one of the co-creators of the super hero comedy web series "The Collectibles". Her first novel "Serpent's Sacrifice" was published in 2017 and is the first book in an Urban Fantasy Superhero series, The Vigilantes.

Trish currently lives in Washington State with her writer/editor/producer husband, and their two geeky daughters.

ACKNOWLEDGMENTS

There are so many people to thank for this but I won't go all Academy Award long…or at least I'll try not to!

First and foremost is my husband and kids. They were patient and supportive to a fault through the two years it's taken to get this published. You three are my greatest loves.

I wouldn't have been able to get this book out without my fabulous editor, Maria D'Marco. She went above and beyond what I'd asked for, being both encouraging and teaching. Thank you so much!

A huge thanks goes to Todd Downing, who designed the cover for this book, and has been churning out some amazing ones for the future novels. You are a true artist, sir.

The original inspiration for this book was from a little song called "Needing A Miracle" by the geek rock band Kirby Krackle. Thank you guys for producing music that not only lifts my spirits, but inspires me as well.

Joanna Penn provided encouragement and wisdom through her weekly podcast The Creative Penn. Though we've never met, I hope some day we can because you are one of the people that has had the biggest influence on my decision to become an Indie Author. Thank you.

To Bryan Cohen and the Selling For Authors Facebook community, you guys are amazing! Always there to help me learn and to encourage me, I couldn't have done it without you.

Jesse Donovan, erotica author extraordinaire! Though we don't write in the same genre, you gave me solid advice during the beginning phase of this journey, thank you so much for your time and wisdom.

Jennifer K. Stuller and the amazing founders of Geek Girl Con, you started me on the journey of telling the story of the female hero. Without your book and Geek Girl Con I don't think I would've been inspired to do this. Thank you, from the bottom of my heart.

National Novel Writing Month (NaNoWriMo), the first year I participated in this amazing program was when I wrote the first draft for this novel. Without this program I don't know if I would've had the discipline needed to get started on this journey. Thank you!

Caerly Hill and Meredith McKown, who, along with my husband, were the Beta readers for this. Your honest, yet gentle, critiques helped me carve away the excess and get to the heart of the story. Thank you so much!

70349272R00250